Jackanapes

To Peter – with every good
wish

T. John War

Dennis Curran
21 10 2000

To my wife and sons and the people of Romney Marsh

JACKANAPES

The

Artful Dodger

and

the Hero of the Forlorn Hope

T John Ward

Barry Dicks Publications

Copyright © T John Ward 2000
First published in 2000 by Barry Dicks Publications
243 Fort Pitt Street
Chatham, Kent, ME1 1DE

Distributed by Gazelle Book Services Limited, Falcon House
Queen Square Lancaster, England LA1 1RN

The right of T John Ward to be identified as the author of the
work has been asserted herein in accordance with the Copyright,
Designs and Patents Act 1988.

All of the characters in this book are fictitious and any
resemblance to actual people, living or dead, is purely
imaginary.

British Library Cataloguing in Publication Data
A catalogue record for this book is available from the British
Library

ISBN 0-9538429-0-8

Typeset by Amolibros, Watchet, Somerset
This book production has been managed by Amolibros
Printed and bound by T J International Ltd, Padstow, Cornwall

One man in a thousand, Solomon says,
Will stick more close than a brother.
But the thousandth man will stand by your side
To the gallow's foot—and after.

Rudyard Kipling

Acknowledgements

To Gary, for his invaluable computer assistance and to Paul for his enthusiastic support.

Also to A P Watt on behalf of The National Trust for Places of Historic Interest or Natural Beauty for their permission to use paraphrased lines from Rudyard Kipling's poem, "The Thousandth Man".

Contents

Foreword

t the close of Charles Dickens' classic novel, *Oliver Twist*, that redoubtable character, Jack Dawkins, more famously known as the Artful Dodger, has been taken by the forces of law and order for the crime of stealing a snuffbox. Fagin's favourite apprentice's luck had finally run out.

One of early nineteenth century London's swarming underclass of street Arabs, he had struggled to survive against all the odds in a life that could only end in disaster. The Artful Dodger's irrepressible spirit, however, always shone brightly through, despite his misdeeds and errant ways.

Now, with one bound, author T John Ward has freed the Dodger so that he may live again to swagger through another exhilarating adventure.

A warm welcome back then to young "Artful" – but be warned, dear reader, keep a close eye on your watches, wipes and wallets!

Cedric Charles Dickens

Preface

t the request of Mr. Lester Hope-Garnett, my old friend George Wellbeloved, United States Navy [Ret'd], travelled from his home in Boston to St Louis, Missouri, to ascertain whether some naval memorabilia was of sufficient interest to lodge in the museum that employs him.

Hope-Garnett, seventy-six years old, lived in a ramshackle, two-storied house of classic early American design.

The naval material proved to be of some interest to George. He asked the slightly gone-to-seed old gentleman, who had holes in both elbows of the baggy cardigan that he was wearing, if there was anything more to see.

"Get up in the attic, son. Have a look for yourself. You might find something. I don't know." Lester was more interested in watching a western movie on his television. "You know, I've always felt that I was born too late. What I'd give to have been able to ride across those wild prairies. Maybe guide a wagon train."

"I know what you mean," replied George indulgently, and found his way to the attic, which proved to be lit by a single, shadeless bulb. There was a lot of dust, a number of books and some old clothing, but not much else. He was about to throw a leather bag of uncertain age to one side when his fingers felt the slight bulge that indicated that it had contents. That was when George found the letters and manuscripts.

He descended to the first floor and found Lester asleep. On the flickering TV screen, John Wayne was in hand-to-hand combat with a Red Indian.

After he had taken a quick skim-through his find he felt compelled to wake the old fellow from his cowboy dreams. Lester was unconcerned when he was asked by George if he could take the bag away for detailed examination.

"Take it, I got nobody but some cousins that I never see. All the rest are dead and gone. I'm not worried about a few old letters and it would please me to have my navy stuff in your museum. You go and do your researching, son."

At the airport and on the plane to Boston George put the naval items on one side and studied the contents of the bag.

Chicago

March 1840

Dear Lys,

I just had to write and tell you that I met a gent staying in my hotel. English he was and guess what? He had a copy of some book. *Oliver Twist*, it was called. Obviously, soon as I saw it I wanted to read it. I got hold of it, never mind how, and thanks to you and Vonne's teaching was able to plough through it. There I was, right there in the book. The cove what wrote it told a few stretchers but got most of what happened with Oliver and Fagin quite right. But he did not make me tall enough or old enough for that matter. He seemed to think I was quite ugly and you know that ain't true. So he's wrong on that score as well.

He does not go into what happened to me after Sykes got killed and Fagin was took. Perhaps I ought to write that.

My business is nearly done here so I will be with you soon.

Always Yours,

Jack

St Louis
April '42

Dear Lys,

Thought that you would like to know that I have met Mr Dickens. Him of all people! It was just yesterday on the riverboat to St L. I did not introduce myself but encouraged the great man into talking about me all the same. I said that I did hear tell that the happenings in his Oliver Twist story all took place years ago. "Quite right," was his reply, "but the appalling conditions that orphans and such like live in have not changed one jot to this day. That was my inspiration to write the work."

He grew huffy when I said that the Dodger could not have been all bad; "Sir," he said, "I may have been in error in some respects regarding that person but in the essentials I was absolutely correct."

I did not argue the point but asked him how he liked America. He replied that he had never met a nation of people that ate as much, drunk as much or spat as much and the further westward that he travelled the worse it was getting! He then went below for dinner leaving me on deck to laugh.

I am sure sorry to have left you so long, Lys, but at last I have paid then back for what they did to Abe.* I never though that it would take so long.

Your affectionate

Jack

From notes in a diary dated 21st June 1846:

Someone asked me today if I was related to the Artful Dodger. I had to laugh out loud at that. I denied it. It looks like I am getting anonymously famous! Anyway, I am writing up some notes about what happened to Abe and me in those days while my memory holds. I might write a book myself one day. Won't Mr Dickens be amazed?

There were many other letters and diary notes but it is not proposed to reveal their contents here. George Wellbeloved was mugged, practically on his doorstep, upon his return from St Louis. They took his watch, his wallet and the satchel with its precious contents. They were never recovered. George's memory, though, is sound. When he attempted to contact Lester Hope-Garnett to report the loss, he discovered that the old man had been found in front of his television in the deepest sleep of all from which none of us awake.

The Author

*See the forthcoming *The Artful Dodger and The Savages.*

CHAPTER ONE

The Artful Dodger Begins a Journey

agin was dead. He had died badly. Hauled kicking and screaming from his cell, he never stopped weeping, cursing and praying all the way to the hangman's noose. What a great roar of approval went up from the crowd gathered at Newgate, when he fell through the trap and kicked his last.

Sykes was gone, Nancy gone and now Fagin had joined them; their downfall brought about by a puny young shaver known as Oliver Twist. The Artful Dodger sat on his thin dank mattress in the cold gloom of Newgate, wrapping his arms round himself for a little extra warmth. He was still able to grin despite his situation. He had escaped the noose and unimaginable death, at least for now. He had heard that a good many of those transported to Botany Bay did not survive the journey or ended up in chains, on a hulk up some estuary and left to rot, either way dying of the hardship.

Hardship! Jack Dawkins almost laughed at the thought. He did not reckon that would 'do' for him. He had spent most of his life on the streets of London town, summer and winter. It was not until Fagin had taken him in that he had ever enjoyed a regular roof over his head.

Mother? He did not remember her. Father? Well he bore the name Dawkins but he could not recall meeting the gent! Brothers? Sisters? Who knew, or cared for that matter? In the last couple of years he had eaten well, slept well and dressed warm, thanks to Fagin. Now that had all gone – at least temporarily, because Jack had no intention of boarding any transport ship, or hulk. Crossing the London River by wherry was as far as he was prepared to go on water.

Sitting there in Newgate, he knew that there were too many locks between himself and freedom. But the day would come when there would only be those chains and pinions restraining his person. He had a vivid picture of himself making a daring escape in the street. Once he was free, well, not only could he "dodge" anybody but no one could "dodge" him! Not Jack Dawkins! He could outrun and outfox any fat, old watchman, and he knew every cobwebby hidey-hole in dirty old London. Dirtier even than this cell, some of them, but home to him!

He stretched out on the straw-filled mattress kindly donated by a wealthy predecessor, now deceased. Poor old Fagin. He was the very devil and a great skinflint but after he had taken Jack in and developed his natural skills as a "dip" and a "dodger", he reckoned that he would be his right-hand man one day and even taught him to read and write a little, which set him a cut above the rest of their merry little throng!

Jack dozed then, and, despite the noise of the mass of humanity crowding the prison, fell into a sleep. A sweet-faced lady was stretching loving arms out to him. As he in turn reached out to her, the figure was enveloped in mist from which emerged the bewigged head of a judge, eyes flashing; his cavernous mouth opening and a sepulchral voice intoning, "Jack Dawkins, for the theft of a silver snuff box and numerous other crimes against society, I sentence you to transportation to Botany Bay for fourteen years. Should you manage to return to these shores before this period of time elapses, rest assured you will be apprehended and brought to justice to be hanged by the neck until you are dead!"

Waking in almost complete darkness, Jack stumbled his way to the communal water bucket and wet his lips with some of its brackish contents.

"Fourteen years," he breathed deeply, knowing that he had already lived as long. It had been declared in court that he was "...believed to be about fourteen years of age, m'lud."

Pulling his coat collar up around his ears, he lay down to sleep until dawn.

The entire building resounded to the coughing, hacking, hawking and spitting of the rousing mass of imprisoned humanity as they scratched and shivered in the cold light of another day – the dawn chorus!

Shortly after the breakfast slops, a bleary-eyed turnkey approached Jack. He stood over him scratching at his dirty shirt.

"You've someone to see you in the Visitors' Room."

To amuse himself as he sauntered at the turnkey's side, Jack relieved him of the contents of one of his pockets – a filthy wipe and a twist of tobacco.

"Here Mush," he said to him as they reached the Visitors' Room, "you need these more than I do," and handed the gaoler his goods.

"Why you—" his grimy, unshaven features contorted and, grabbing Jack's shoulder, he propelled him through the door. A foot in the backside sent the boy sprawling. Jack received a close-up view of a pair of boots covered in the filth of the prison yard. Gazing up, he saw smart trousers, a green waistcoat covering a broad stomach that was crossed by a gold chain disappearing into a pocket, where, no doubt, rested a valuable timepiece.

Looking down at Jack was a clean-shaven, rotund face, quite elderly. It looked as though it could be cheery. But at that moment the mouth was grim and the eyes were narrowed behind gold-rimmed spectacles. Jack scrambled to his feet. He had seen this man before.

"My name is Brownlow," said the dignified figure, peering intently at Jack's face, pallid beneath the grime. "I believe you are Jack Dawkins, erstwhile member of that Jew-rogue Fagin's gang of thieves and murderers?"

"S'right, but I never murdered nobody," said Jack, avoiding the man's gaze. "In fact, apart from liftin' a few wipes, I 'ardly 'ad anythin' to do with the rest o' them. Anyway I got my punishmen', you can't touch me."

"I have not come here to do you harm," said Brownlow, "but, against my better judgement and the advice of others, I have come to do you good."

Jack's pulse quickened. "What good can you do me? I'm to be transported any day soon to where nobody can 'elp me." He allowed a tear to trickle down his cheek. It left a distinct track right to the corner of his mouth.

"The child whom you knew as Oliver," said Brownlow, "has pleaded with me and begged me to intervene with the authorities on your behalf. In fact the boy has made himself quite ill again in his anxiety. He feels that you came to his aid when he first came to London, gave him food and shelter and clothing when he needed it most and were generally decent to him. The boy sees good in you, where I must say, I do not." Brownlow looked sternly at Jack. "Oliver believes that if things had worked a little differently, he might easily have ended as you have. Indeed he seems to think that you were, in some strange way, instrumental in reuniting him with his family and fortune. Oliver is a good boy, naïve and innocent certainly, but good through and through and I want this business cleared up and off his mind so that he may be truly happy at last."

"You don't mean they're lettin' me off?" Jack almost whooped.

"No, you young villain, not letting you off, not by any means. But you are to be given a chance. Under certain conditions you are to be released into my charge. You will be sent from London to a far place where you will fulfil obligations to atone for your crimes. All this will be made plain to you."

"Young Oliver!" Jack could have turned somersaults. "Getting out of Newgate. No transportation. No prison hulks!" His senses reeled. "I'm ready when you are, guv'nor!"

"Not so fast," Brownlow retorted; "there are certain formalities to be completed before your training for life begins. You will be brought before Judge Darnley tomorrow morning. I wish you good day."

"Er, Mr Brownlow, sir, Mr Brownlow…" But Brownlow stalked past Jack, presented his frock-coated back to him and disappeared through the doorway.

The turnkey who had been standing to one side gave Jack a mighty cuff round the head and half dragged him back to the prison. The Artful Dodger relieved him of his twist of tobacco again. This time for keeps!

Despite Jack thinking that the rest of that day and the following night would never end, inexorably it did. He would soon be free of Newgate! Whatever "his nibs", Brownlow, had in mind, it could not be as bad as that place and would certainly be a whole lot better than an enforced voyage to the other side of the world.

"There's a constable come to take you to Judge's Chambers." It was Jack's favourite turnkey.

"That's me out o' here!" Jack sprang to his feet, jumped a foot into the air and clicked his heels together.

"You'll be back." The turnkey got hold of him once again; "And next time you'll be for the drop." He drew a dirty forefinger across his throat.

Grabbing up his few spare rags, Jack followed his cheery keeper to the turnkey's lodge. The dreadful sound of a woman weeping hysterically echoed from the nearby female condemned cell. In less than twenty-four hours, that voice would be silenced forever.

The constable, an extremely tall and lean character, threw a parcel at Jack as he entered the room. "Clean y'self up and get into these new duds. Be quick about it, boy!" He turned to the gaoler, "If you can oblige with soap and water, sir."

A tin basin and hard lump of soap were placed on a side table. The water was cold. Jack made a quick job of his ablutions, slicking down his over-long, unkempt hair. He peered at himself in a broken piece of mirror glass. The youthful face that looked back at him was somewhat cleaner now, the nose snubbed and slightly crooked, set more or less in the middle. There were those familiar protruding ears and that cynically twisted mouth. He winked at himself conspiratorially. In the parcel he found trousers, jacket, boots and cap, all of good quality. Discarding his rags, he dressed himself quickly, leaving his old clothing in an untidy heap on the floor.

"Pick them up," snarled the turnkey. "'E's not leavin 'is rags 'ere." He glowered at the constable. Jack made a fine play of carefully folding the disgraceful apparel and wrapping it in the paper that his new clothes had come in, then offered them to the turnkey with a deep bow: "A little gift, sir, for your chee-ild!"

"That's enough o' that." The constable grabbed Jack's arm. The next moment they were handcuffed together, wrist to wrist.

"Ere, what's all this?" Jack struggled futilely.

"I'm to take no chances with you, my lad. Now, gawd knows why you're gettin' this treatment, but I'm to buy you breakfast from funds provided and then to the session's 'ouse within the 'our."

"Thanks, guv'nor—"; this last to the gaoler as he propelled Jack through the door, a short passage and then a second door took them into the outside world.

After nearly three weeks of incarceration, the noise and bustle of the street jolted at Jack's nerve-ends. Half-blinded by the unaccustomed light and half-deafened by the sounds created by the thronging masses passing to and fro, he was hustled along at a furious pace. Carts and wagons, horsemen and street vendors all added to the confusion. Linked together, the two of them weaved their way to their destination. Suddenly the constable pulled Jack through the doorway of a smoky, low ceilinged eating house.

The place was quite full and long-aproned skivvies were flying about, carrying plates of steaming food. Jack realised how starved he was. The delicious odour of frying chops and onions filled the air.

Squeezed onto a wooden bench, hard against the constable's thigh, the Artful Dodger glanced down at the bunch of keys hanging from his captor's belt.

"Once free," he thought to himself, "I could be in the rookeries of Seven Dials within five minutes, where it would take an army to winkle me out." Getting at those keys though defeated him for that moment. Jack salivated at the sight of his mutton chops, onion gravy, hefty slices of freshly baked bread and dish of butter, tackling it ferociously, alternately chewing bread and meat and swigging at a pot of ale.

The buzz of conversation around them seemed to be dwelling mostly on the execution of some poor miscreant that had taken place at Newgate not an hour since. Feelings seemed to be running high in some quarters as to the victim's guilt. There was a sudden clash of platters followed by a series of oaths rising above the general din, as a scuffle broke out among the untidy group in a corner of the chop-house.

The constable's attention being diverted by this, Jack crept his free hand across his body towards the bunch of keys. His fingertips were just touching metal when the officer stood up quite abruptly, eyeing Jack suspiciously. "Come on you, we've but ten minutes before we must be at Judge's Chambers. I ain't never been late for no appointment, nor yet lost a prisoner."

"What're you lookin' at?" Jack angrily snarled at the people at the next table as they stopped eating to eye the handcuffs.

"I don't know what it is, the name plate's fell orf!" one of them retorted.

The rest of them fell about laughing. "Watch 'im, officer, 'e's a des'prat character orlright!"

Jack left his parcel of rags on the bench in the hope that one of their number would notice it and believe they had found something of value.

Back on the street, the constable's long legs and rapid stride obliged him almost to run in order to keep up and not be dragged by the wrist. Within a couple of minutes they were at the Old Bailey where they hurried through the main entrance, halting abruptly at a stout door; a knock, and then through they went into a wood-panelled room with several large bookcases packed with impressive volumes standing hard against the walls. Behind a cluttered desk sat an imposingly bewigged figure. Mr Brownlow was sitting in an upholstered chair in front of the desk. He rose to his feet as they entered.

"I've brought the prisoner, as ordered, sir. 'E's been clothed and fed. No trouble, sir."

"Thank you, Mr Hawks," said Brownlow; "you may leave Mr Dawkins with us. Please wait outside for the moment."

"Aye, sir," replied the constable, "I'll be nearby if you need me." Giving Jack another of his suspicious glares, he extracted a key from his belt and released the cuffs.

Judge Darnley eyed Jack equally suspiciously from beneath his greying, straggling eyebrows as Brownlow sat again, in the comfortable looking chair. "Dawkins, you have been found guilty of theft, sentenced to transportation for fourteen years—er, remove your cap, sir, if you please, show a little respect. Now, where was I?"

"I've bin dragged 'ere against me will. 'Ad me clothes stole from me!" Jack interrupted. "Bin led through the streets, 'andcuffed—"

"Silence!" roared the judge, half-rising from behind the desk. "Don't you realise that there are good people trying to help you?"

"I've got me own friends; pretty soon you'll be 'earing from 'em!"

"Oh, this is impossible!" snapped the judge, turning to Brownlow. "I shall return him to Newgate forthwith."

"My lord, we have an agreement; please, I ask you to be patient." Mr Brownlow spoke softly and persuasively.

"Oh, very well, let us proceed then. Not another word from you, Dawkins, if you value your hide."

Removing his cap, Jack attempted a look of meek acceptance.

"Now then, you young incorrigible," said the judge, "representations on your behalf have been made at the highest level, in an attempt to mitigate your sentence, and give you an opportunity to make something of yourself. The only evidence that you have a spark of decency in you comes from Mr Brownlow here, who states that you once helped someone in distress, though I suspect that even this was for your own mercenary advantage. I understand though that your actions, unintentional as they were, eventually led to an unfortunate child being saved from a life of crime and his being reunited with the remnants of his family."

"You have Mr Brownlow to thank, and his friend and ally, Sir Robert Peel – a man, I believe, who is destined for high position in government – has added his weight to this business. For these reasons and the bond that Mr Brownlow has agreed upon, your sentence has been set aside. It will remain on file and should you stray for one moment from the conditions that have been laid down, the sentence will be re-imposed – immediately, mark you." He paused meaningfully: "One, you will place yourself in the hands of Mr Brownlow or his representatives. Two,"—he was ticking off the conditions on his fingers—"you will be taken from London and will not return to it until you attain your majority, and even then only with the express permission of both Mr Brownlow and a magistrate. Three, you will submit yourself to any form of employment that Mr Brownlow deems suitable."

This proved a little much for Jack. "'Ang on, am I getting paid? 'Ow far from London? What's me marj-marjottory?"

"Will you shut up!"

"Four, there will be some attempt to educate you and you will submit to this process, although I fear that you are very poor material, very poor indeed. Well, you young fool, no one is twisting your arm in this matter. If you object to any or all of these conditions, you will be returned to Newgate until you can be transported either to Botany Bay or to the Medway Hulks. By far the more sensible course of action in my opinion." He clasped his hands before him, elbows on the desk.

"Dawkins," said Brownlow, leaning back in his chair, "you will not be abused. Your treatment will be firm but fair. You will enjoy the benefits of the countryside, fresh air, exercise and hard work. I am sure that you will gain much from such a combination. Like any wild thing, you will be sorely tempted to escape and return to your natural habitat. But you will soon come to enjoy being among civilised society. What do you say?"

Well the Dodger was no fool. Even though he did not give a fig for their conditions, at that moment it seemed an infinitely preferable offer to the only alternative. "I'll give it a go, sir!"

"Give it a go!" the judge exploded. "You young pup, you should be on your knees thanking this gentleman! Unworthy! Unworthy!"

Brownlow merely smiled, a calm smile, and rose from his chair. "Your Lordship, shall we sign the papers? I will call Hawks as witness."

"Under the circumstances, Mr Brownlow," said Judge Darnley, "and bearing in mind the recalcitrant attitude of the prisoner, I suggest that Hawks accompany you as escort, at least until you have cleared the environs of London."

"Very well, your Lordship, I will not be going the whole distance of the journey as I have urgent business elsewhere, I agree that Hawks should go with us at least to Gravesend, where I shall hand Dawkins over to my man, Garnett."

The gangly constable was called in and the solemn ceremony of signing legal documents took place. First Brownlow, then Jack was called forward, with tongue protruding far through parted lips, he blotchily signed his name. Then Mr Hawks added his signature with a flourish. Finally Judge Darnley added his impressive title.

"We are on the ten o' clock steam boat for Gravesend. I am interested in experiencing this new mode of transportation. It is said to be superior to road travel, and—" he glanced quickly at Jack, "—it will certainly be more secure for our young friend here, unless he wishes to leap overboard to make an escape." Brownlow gave Jack a brief smile and turned to the judge. "They do say, your Lordship, that soon the river will be full of steam vessels. I am informed that, in the next week or so, regular, daily excursions will begin to Gravesend. Of course, steam power will never conquer the great oceans but it will prove invaluable for travelling the inland waterways of the world."

Judge Darnley stroked his chin. "Could be a sound investment, eh?"

"I would certainly say so, your Lordship. If you would permit us to depart, post-haste. We have little time to make Wapping before the boat leaves. Thank you for your help in this matter."

"You know my opinion of the enterprise, sir, but I wish you good luck nevertheless. I'm very much afraid that it will end in disaster, sir."

Jack pulled his hat over his eyes. "So long, guv'nor," he said, cool as a cucumber sticking his hand out to be shaken.

"Get him out of here!"

The next moment Jack was handcuffed once more to the lofty Hawks and hurried through the door.

Jack had occasionally stolen rides on the backs of carriages and coaches but had never before ridden beside a gentleman inside of one. At the main entrance to the Sessions House, Brownlow had waved his cane at a liveried coachman sitting atop a gleaming coach. With a flick of his whip, the man caused the pair of horses to pull the vehicle forward to where the three of them stood.

Hawks unfastened the carriage door and hauled himself in with a grunt, obliging Jack to follow, Brownlow bringing up the rear. Jack sat on the plush upholstery, wedged between the elderly and the ungainly. Hawks addressed Brownlow over his head. "Sir, as I am to accompany you, I would be obliged if we could divert to Bow Street for a moment. I will need to speak to my officer."

"Very well, Mr Hawks—Coachman! To Bow Street if you please." They moved off with a jerk as the horses picked up the traces, rattling along the busy street.

"Mr Dawkins," said Brownlow, "I do believe that the full import of what is happening to you will impart in you a sea change that will eventually lead you to reflect upon your life to date. I understand that from the moment of your birth your only instinct was to survive. In this you have succeeded, but at a tremendous cost to your soul which has been dying within you, sir."

Hawks, sitting on Jack's left, sniffed disdainfully at this.

"You will find," the old man continued, "that the world is a better place than you at present realise. There is much opportunity to do good in it, not only to do good but also to better oneself and improve one's situation. The world has room enough for all."

Jack, not having much of an idea about what Brownlow's meaning was, managed to look soulful and nodded several times. The coach suddenly lurched to a halt and the driver could be heard hurling abuse at some "cretin", that he had narrowly avoided running over. They moved forward again through the noisy and noisome streets, arriving within a few minutes at Bow Street. "I shall be but a minute, sir," said Hawks, and taking his key, released Jack's wrist from the cuffs.

"Very well," Brownlow replied. "Please make haste, we must catch the boat."

Hawks, for convenience, opened the street side door of the coach to alight. At the same moment Jack sprang for the other door, opened it and went through it in a split second. Brownlow's cry mingled with Hawks' "Oy, you!" Jack hit the cobblestones and was up and running, but he only took three paces before the weight of the coachman's body leaping from the roof, crushed the wind from him. With a knee in his back and an arm twisted painfully to his shoulder blade, he could only lie helpless until Hawks' long legs appeared. Grabbing him by the scruff of the neck, he cracked the Dodger painfully across his head with the handcuffs.

Brownlow leaned from the coach window. "That's enough of that, Mr Hawks. Hurry up, man, or we shall be late."

A number of passers by had instantly formed a crowd to view the proceedings. As Hawks dragged Jack back into the coach and handcuffed him to the window frame, the Dodger called out, rather lamely, "'Elp, 'elp! I'm being 'eld against my will!"

"He's right there," laughed Hawks. "He's my prisoner and that's where 'e's goin' to stay!"

"Wring 'is neck, officer!" someone sang out and there was a burst of laughter as the people moved away.

Mr Hawks disappeared into the Bow Street Runners' office, re-emerging a few minutes later carrying a small leather bag. As the coach moved off again, Mr Brownlow looked at the downcast Jack. "Have you no sense at all, boy? You are fortunate that you did not make good your escape. Why return to a life of crime and misery when you are being given a chance in a million?"

London Bridge was crowded with traffic but, with a few minutes to spare, the coach arrived at Wapping Old Stairs, from where the boat departed. Across the Thames loomed the great dome of St Paul's Cathedral, standing out boldly beyond the masts, spars and rigging of many ships at anchor.

There was much activity as passengers vied for watermen to take them aboard the vessel. Jack had seen the experimental steam packets on the river but he had never been close to one and, despite himself, a feeling of queasy anticipation became paramount as they prepared to board.

"Return to Clerkenwell, Mr Ford," Brownlow instructed his coachman. "I shall come home tomorrow. Please be good enough to meet me at the Mitre.

"You can rely on me, sir," Ford replied, touching his cap as he did so.

Jack was hustled down the wet and slippery steps to where the water lapped around their waiting ferry.

"These watermen are kings of the river." Constable Hawks indicated the broad back of one of these individuals who was busy sculling them to the steamer. "Do you know, sir, they are refusing to allow these 'ere new boats to tie up at piers or jetties for fear of them losing their livelihoods?"

"One cannot blame them for that, I suppose." Mr Brownlow was, as ever, sympathetic to the human condition.

Their small craft passed close to one of the large paddle wheels that would soon be churning them downstream. The steamboat was quivering and trembling as though in apprehension of its coming journey. Below decks the engine was stomping away slowly and methodically, shooting gobbets of black smoke up and up until they emerged from the tall, thin funnel. The morning mist had long since dissipated and a wintry, January sun sparkled on the grey waters. Excited passengers found places to sit, some going below, but most, including Brownlow, Hawks and Jack, seated themselves on deck.

In a great crescendo of engine noise, shouted orders and shrill whistles, the vessel, pumping out more smoke than ever, moved out into midstream, the twin paddles revolving in fascinating fashion.

She slipped easily along with the tide, the emerging smoke being rapidly dissipated by a stiff breeze. There were many other craft on the river – great, brown-sailed barges, tiny coracle-like row-boats, and even a man of war, her dark gunports closed, and with almost bare spars, majestically heading for who knew where? Flags fluttered bravely from her rigging. Jack caught the faint sound of a musical instrument being played, as the steam packet rapidly overhauled and passed her gleaming length. Several men aboard the warship gave a wave and Jack involuntarily produced a brief wave in return. Instantly, he was furious with himself at this childish stuff, even more so when he noticed Brownlow eyeing him.

"Be still, unless you want a clip," said Hawks, as Jack yanked angrily at his cuffed wrist.

"Mr Hawks," said Brownlow quietly, "now that we are on the river, I do not see that Dawkins can go anywhere without the grave risk of drowning himself. You may release him, but be sure that he is not a nuisance to our fellow passengers. Come, let us eat and make the most of the good fresh air." As Hawks released the cuffs, Brownlow removed pies, fruit, bread and cheese from the hamper, followed closely by a bottle of wine.

Jack, starving again, tucked into everything that was handed to him. The large warehouses that had lined both sides of the river gave way to more scattered buildings. Woods and meadows, marshy in appearance, began to appear on the left bank, whilst on the right, there were a series of low hills.

The boat's paddle wheels churned them forward relentlessly. A magnificent group of buildings came into view on their right, reaching down to the bank, gleaming in regal splendour under the bright sun. "Ah, Greenwich already," breathed Brownlow to no one in particular. Many of the passengers lined the ship's rail to watch the stunning scene as it slipped away behind them. Even Jack, as he munched on an apple, was impressed at the sight. Almost unbidden words formed on his lips as he turned to Mr Brownlow, "Thanks for the grub, guv'nor."

"Sir to you," growled Hawks. But Brownlow merely nodded and smoked his pipe. "You are quite welcome, Mr Dawkins."

London was reduced to a haze on the horizon as Jack laid on the warm deck timbers. The last thing he heard before his eyes closed was the happy sound of children at play – hide 'n' seeking round the superstructure of the boat.

The toe of Hawks' boot poking Jack in the ribs awakened him. Getting to his feet, he saw that the steamer was angling into the shore where a town straggled up gently sloping ground. Here and there he could see a church spire rising above the low buildings. All around the deck, people were gathering together their children and their luggage, beginning to form an untidy queue at the point of exit from the ship.

"Very well," said Mr Brownlow cheerfully. "Here is Gravesend. I do hope that Mr Garnett is here, for I can travel no further. Nor you either, eh, Mr Hawks?"

"Indeed not, Mr Brownlow. I think I have exceeded my duty as it is." Hawks straightened his rather crumpled uniform.

"'Ave I to travel further then?" Jack asked, a note of protest in his voice. "This looks like the end of the world as it is. I don't know nobody. I don't know where I'm goin', and I ain't got nothin'." He was beginning to feel genuinely sorry for himself. "What yer tryin' to do to me? I was better off in Newgate."

"Nonsense, boy," said Brownlow, "there are many of your age, and younger, who are bravely serving their country at this moment all over the world. You are old enough to take care of yourself. Do not be anxious, you are merely travelling in Kent."

"I can take care of meself all right," said Jack, suddenly defiant again. The boat suddenly slowed, Jack lost his balance and sat heavily on his backside, causing Hawks to laugh raucously. Quick as a flash, he bent down and once more the Dodger was handcuffed to him. "'Ere we go again," moaned Jack.

A motley collection of small boats bobbed and pitched under the lee of the steamer and it was to one of these that they made a rather perilous descent. "I would have thought that Gravesend could have afforded a jetty by now," Hawks grumbled.

"That's right, do me out of me living why don't yer," gasped their boatman as he pulled manfully at the oars, bringing them ever closer to a flight of steps that was to be their landing place.

They were soon on shore and Brownlow led the way to a nearby hostelry. The river was very broad here and the rays of the afternoon sun played upon many sails of heavily laden barges as they drifted silently down river. Gulls were wheeling and swooping above, occasionally coming low over their heads to grab a tasty morsel of garbage from the very ground in front of them. A group of seamen reeled a drunken route towards them, their arms about each other's shoulders. Laughing uproariously, they brushed roughly past, heading for another, smaller inn that was visible just up the street that climbed the hill.

The inn was full of tobacco smoke when Mr Brownlow, Hawks and Jack entered its interior which appeared gloomy after the bright world outside.

Mr Brownlow attracted the attention of the innkeeper, who approached rubbing his hands on a floor-length apron. Jack began to feel at home. "Any chance of some ale, Mr Brownlow, sir? I'm parched."

"Ay," said Hawks, "I could do wi' a wet myself."

"Very well," said Brownlow; "two ales and a schooner of sherry, landlord, if you please. My name is Brownlow. Do you have any messages for me?"

"I have more than that, sir," he replied. "I have a gentleman awaitin' your arrival. I will tell him that you are here."

They seated themselves as the landlord bustled away. A pot-boy brought the drinks. As Jack raised the tankard to his lips, he saw a broad, leathery-looking figure approaching. In fact this character had the broadest shoulders Jack had ever seen. He was not tall but everything about him suggested muscular strength and power. He noted that the hand the man raised in greeting was in keeping with the rest of him. His clothing appeared to be of the leathery type as well – breeches, waistcoat, jacket or jerkin. Even the shirt was laced up with a leather thong. There was a spotted 'kerchief knotted around a thick neck.

The face, bronzed and weathered, with a jutting jaw and penetrating eyes, broke into a friendly enough smile, as he halted at their table. "Well met, Mr Brownlow, sir!" he cried. "I arrived but an hour ago. Did you have a good journey?"

"Indeed we did, Mr Garnett. It is good to see you again. I am very pleased that you were able to respond to my letter. I knew you well enough to take a chance on it. Allow me to present Mr John Hawks of the Bow Street Runners, one of their ablest, if I may say so, and this young gentleman is Mr Jack Dawkins, of whom you are to take charge, as I explained in the letter. Be firm, sir, but be fair. You understand the life he has led and I think he is still of a mind to return to it, given the chance. Mr Hawks, Jack, this is Mr Abel Garnett who takes care of my land and property at Shippenden on the Romney Marshes.

CHAPTER TWO

The Journey Continues - Abel Garnett Escorts

awks proffered his hand across the table. Abel Garnett seated himself. "Your servant, sir."

Jack stared studiously past the broad shoulders. "So this is the young Jackanapes that I'm to take under my wing."

Garnett raised his elbow and lowered it in imitation of a bird. "Well, I think it's big enough, eh?" With the exception of Jack, they joined in a hearty laugh.

"I reckon I'm fed up wiv bein' laughed at for one day," he complained. "I didn't ask to come 'ere, an' I don' need takin' under nobody's wing. I can take care o' meself!"

Abel Garnett eyed him under furrowed brow.

"You look mostly grown up to me. But you ain't acted grown up yet or else you wouldn't be in this situation. Time you were done with childish tantrums, lad." The force and power of the voice reduced Jack to silence.

Brownlow spoke: "Mr Garnett, if you can give me such reports as you may have on the current state of the flocks and buildings, etc. and so forth, then perhaps you and Mr Hawks would like a drink at the next table. I wish to have a few words with young Dawkins."

As Hawks unlocked the handcuffs for what proved to be the last time, Garnett reached inside his jerkin and produced a large envelope that he passed to Brownlow. "I think you will find everything more than satisfactory, sir," he said, rising together with Hawks and moving off to the rather crowded table nearby. As they turned their backs on him, Jack could not help noticing that one appeared almost as wide as the other was tall. "Come along, Mr Hawks, I will buy you a Kentish ale," he heard Garnett jovially offer.

"Jack," Mr Brownlow spoke quietly to him, "I have almost fulfilled my promise to Oliver to give you all possible help and assistance to set you on the right road. I do not often come to Kent and I may see little of you in the future. Mr Garnett will send his reports and I shall read of your progress with great interest as I am sure Oliver will. Did you know that your erstwhile friend, Charlie, is already proving that one can break free from a life of crime and dishonesty?"

"Charlie was always a bit soft," Jack muttered.

"You realise, Jack, that it will serve little purpose for you to abscond now or later. It is a remote spot that you are going to. There will be little hope of you returning undetected to London or any other city for that matter. Mr Garnett will raise such a hue and cry, you would certainly be apprehended, then I should be able to do nothing further to help you. Imprisonment, transportation or worse would surely follow."

At that moment Jack had one eye on the open door to the outside world but some of the import of Brownlow's words penetrated his mind and he visibly relaxed. Brownlow's sharp eye seemed to note this slight change of disposition. "In years to come, Jack, you will see this day as being a turning point in your life."

He signalled to Hawks and Garnett who strolled back to their table. "We are all set then, gentlemen," smiled Brownlow. "Mr Hawks, I shall be glad of your company, when we return to London tomorrow. I will give a very favourable report to your superiors."

"Goodbye, Mr Garnett, should you have any problems that you cannot yourself deal with, please contact me by the swiftest means possible. Come along, Jack, shake my hand like a gentleman. I hope to hear good things of you."

Jack took the offered hand with some hesitation. The last time he had shaken hands with a gent, he had tickled a gold chain from his wrist at the same time. "Perhaps those days are really over," he thought to himself.

Brownlow and Hawks picked up their luggage and took their leave, Brownlow giving one brief backward glance as he went through the door and out into the afternoon air. The sky was becoming somewhat clouded now and the weather more seasonal.

Abel Garnett eyed Jack curiously; "Where's your traps, young un?"

Determined to make an impression, he expressed himself bitterly: "Me togs and blunt are in me crib at Saffron Hill where they was stowed when I was nabbed and thrown in the jug as a lifer."

Garnett gave him a look. "That's all gammon," he said bluntly. "Come on let's go. Your sort never have anything nor never will. You haven't the sense you were born with. By the way," he added, as they made their way outside, "if you're thinking of doing a runner, you've got three choices—the turnpike, the London Road or the river. Be advised, don't try it. Besides that, of course, you could always starve and freeze in the Kent fields or under the hedgerows. On the other hand, there's good food and a soft bed at my sister's near to Chatham. It's a fine afternoon for a walk."

"Is it very far?" Jack asked, a little plaintively. "I've 'ad a long day."

"About six miles, c'mon it'll do you good."

Jack groaned inwardly but stepped out to keep pace with Garnett. Looking over his shoulder as they climbed the steep thoroughfare, he could see the steamer trailing wisps of smoke from its funnel. He suddenly had a vision of himself dashing down the hill and leaping aboard one of the rowboats just as it pulled away from the shore, leaving Abel Garnett behind, futilely shaking his great fist at him in impotent rage.

Garnett had a hand on his shoulder as they reached a junction at the crest of the hill. Turning him to the left, they made their way out of the town. They had scarcely gone half a mile, however, when Garnett halted at the garden gate of a neat, bay-windowed house, set back off the road.

Garnett, to Jack's surprise, opened the gate. "Just joking about the six miles," he laughed. "This is my sister's."

Jack had to laugh himself. "You've just made my feet very 'appy!"

"Be respectful now," Garnett growled as he knocked on the door.

An attractive woman in her mid-twenties opened it, a small goggle-eyed boy clutching at her apron. "Abe!" she cried. "It's good to see you." She threw her arms around him.

He wrapped his own massive arms round her and lifted her clear off the ground, the child clinging on for a moment, then sitting heavily and bursting into tears.

The woman extricated herself from Abel's grasp, bent and picked up the child. "Hush, darling, it's Abe come to see us. Come in, Abe. Who is this you have with you?"

"This is one of Brownlow's good deeds I have here. Name of Jack Dawkins. A terrible villain by all accounts, but fairly harmless, I think."

They entered a bright, clean room, neat, apart from a clutter of children's toys scattered about. Furnishings were comfortable as well. There were armchairs, a sideboard with a fruit bowl and porcelain objects upon it. The walls were hung with seascapes. There was a faint odour of cooked meat and cabbage in the air.

Garnett's hand descended on Jack's shoulder once more. "This is my sister, Mrs Elspeth Tanner, d'you see. We will spend the night under her roof. Respect at all times, if you please." He gripped the shoulder painfully for a moment, then released it.

"Elspeth. Come into the kitchen, I'd like a word with you."

"What's up, Abe?"

"Nothing bad, old lass, just the usual."

They went through to the next room. Instantly, Jack was at the sideboard, examining the objects displayed with an experienced eye. The door between the rooms being half open, he caught a glimpse of Abel handing a small package to Elspeth. Curiosity got the better of him, so he moved closer to the door to hear the man say, "There's more as you need it, sis, don't go short."

"Thanks, Abe, you are good to us."

"You're my little sister, ain't you? Say no more about it."

Jack was sitting in an armchair, legs crossed when Abel re-entered the room.

"Come through to the kitchen, it's feeding time," he grinned.

In the warmth of the kitchen, Elspeth was spooning some minced mess down her child's throat.

"Sit down, Jack and make yourself at home and please help yourself to food," Elspeth, rather flushed, smiled at him. Abel was soon pouring himself a glass of brandy, which he drank off with gusto. "Jack's a lucky lad, sis. Having been done for stealing a snuff-box, he was due to be transported. When along comes Brownlow, and him having friends in high places, was able to get the boy released into his custody. He sent me a despatch asking me to take him on at Shippenden and make somethin' of him. Apart from having to report regular like to a magistrate, he's a free man.

" I dropped everything at the farm, left Charles 'the first' in charge and came straight away. We must leave at the crack of dawn, I'm afraid. We're taking the mail to Maidstone where I have a wagon." He began ladling stew onto his plate.

Jack was already eating enthusiastically. "'Ow far is this Shippenden?" he asked, his mouth full of meat and potatoes.

"Many a long mile from here, Jack. Many a long mile," said Abel, cutting himself a thick slice of bread.

"Did you know that Abel was a sergeant in the colours, Jack?" asked Elspeth, eating more daintily than either of the men.

"Is that so?"

"Aye, nine years and not much comfort in any of them," growled Abel. "What news of John, Elspeth?"

"I had a letter, Abe, nearly two weeks ago. He's third lieutenant now. He's still on blockade duties, but safe, thank God."

"Sis, I don't know how you put up with it. You've seen him but three or four times in the last six or seven years and then scarcely for a month each time before he was off again serving the King's Navee." He put a bitter emphasis on the last few words.

"John could be home again in the autumn, Abe." Elspeth sipped delicately at a glass of water.

"Let's hope he gets lucky wi' prize money," Abe said. "You don't get rich as a third lieutenant. Let's face it, sis, you would still be in that flea trap where I found you years ago if I hadn't funded you."

"I'll always be grateful, Abe." Elspeth grew more flushed than ever.

"I shouldn't'a mentioned that—" Abe reached across and covered her hand with his; "Sorry, sis."

"I must put the child to bed." Elspeth rose, picking up the little boy. "Say goodnight to Jack and your Uncle Abe, William," but the boy turned his head away and hid it in his mother's bosom. "He's still very shy," laughed Elspeth as she left the room.

Garnett poured two measures of brandy, pushing one toward Jack who was mopping his plate with some bread. "Best frog brandy. Have a drink." He swirled the amber liquor round the glass before drinking deeply.

Elspeth returned; "He's as good as gold," she said. "Here's some of John's old stuff. I doubt they'd fit him now." She handed a bundle of clothing to Jack; "You're very welcome to them."

"Er, thanks Elsp—er, Mrs Tanner," Jack found the soft, motherly woman strangely comforting.

Abel put down his knife and fork. "Thanks for the grub, sis, first rate; you've come on as a cook, I must say."

"I could hardly have got worse," Elspeth laughed.

Abel Garnett and his sister fell to reminiscing about their childhood together. Their conversation was punctuated with many a "remember when" accompanied by loud peals of laughter from both of them. Jack felt completely excluded and after an hour or so of this suddenly blurted out, "It's up the wooden 'ill for me. I'm done in. I've 'ad an 'ard day you know.

"He's right, sis, we've got to be up early," Abel said. "We'd better call it a day."

"All right, Abe, let me show you your room."

London, Fagin, Newgate, all seemed a thousand miles from Jack as he lay in the comfortable bed separated from Abel Garnett by a washstand. So much had happened in the last two days. He looked up into the darkness. The thought of creeping from his bed and lifting a few valuables from the house, before disappearing, came into his mind, but he could not sustain it. He slept.

Abel Garnett was shaking him awake. "Come on, boy, time we were off. Keep the noise down or you'll wake the babe."

"Light a glim, can't you? Jack muttered, "I ain't a cat."

In flickering candlelight, Jack pulled on the clothes that he had discarded only a few hours previously. As they crept along the landing, Garnett knocked gently on a door and opened it a few inches. "Bye, sis," he whispered, "see you soon and thank you." There was a murmured reply. At the foot of the stairs, Jack picked up the bag of clothing donated by Elspeth.

It was a cold morning. A low lying mist crept along the hedgerows and gardens as they made their way back to the town. Close to the main crossroads, there was a large, well lit inn. As they approached, they heard the stamp and rattle of harnessed horses. Into the yard and there stood the coach, horses already between the shafts, their hides and nostrils steaming gently.

"Do we have time for breakfast?" Garnett asked.

"Ten minutes, sir," came the reply.

"Right, that'll do. Come on, Jack, a quick bite."

Which is what they had brought to the door for them. They ate standing up, one eye on the coach. Bread, bacon, coffee.

The coach driver emerged from the stables, pulling on a pair of gloves. He was chatting to a companion in a knee-length greatcoat. This character carried a wide-muzzled blunderbuss and a post-horn.

Three passengers emerged from the inn – two army officers and a clergyman, the officers resplendent in full uniform, wearing swords, the clergyman, in direct contrast, all in black. His gloomy features lit up at the sight of Abel. "Mr Garnett, sir, I did not expect to see you here. I shall have a travelling companion." He glanced curiously at Jack.

"Reverend Hayes, it's good to see you. I did not think that your parish stretched so far?"

"Indeed it does not; I was obliged to attend the bishop at Rochester and took the opportunity to visit my father who lives but a mile from here. I fear that he will not see another winter."

Everyone tried to board the coach at once – officers, clergyman, the driver and guard – setting it rocking on its springs. "Up top, Jack," Abel told him. "I'm obliged to ride inside with Reverend Hayes." Jack scrambled up, the guard taking up his position in the boot of the coach.

The young ostler handed up the reins to the driver who murmured a couple of words to the horses, moving them slowly off. Jack took great pleasure in leaning precariously over the side of the coach, enabling him to knock a battered hat off the ostler's head as they passed. He lay back on the coach roof laughing at the antic. The driver called over his shoulder to the guard as they swung out onto the highway; "Sounds like we got a 'appy customer, Peter!"

"First one this year!" the guard called back. They laughed together, the driver slapping the reins across the horses' backs as the coach increased its speed, rattling and swaying past the last houses in Gravesend.

A watery sun had risen above the horizon when they gained the turnpike, crossing high ground, Jack saw the distant Thames gleaming like silver. To the west there was thickly wooded farmland with scattered hamlets. The weather was still remarkably pleasant.

"Well, this is a turn up and no mistake," Jack told himself. "Here you are ridin' the top of a coach, eatin' an apple and off to Lord knows where. Don't spoil it, Jack me lad, just sit tight an' enjoy the ride. Let's see what Sergeant Bloomin' Garnett 'as to offer. If it ain't good enough, why off you go! May be to the Americas where nobody can lay 'ands on you."

Peter, the guard, was trying to sing "Green Grow the Rushes O" and failing dismally.

The coach began to descend to a broad valley through which snaked a river. Surely not the London river again? "What river's that?" Jack yelled to the driver.

"Why that's the Medway," he said; "You ain't no man o' Kent then?"

"No, nor no Kentish man, either!" Peter called above the noise of groaning brake shoes as they negotiated a steep hill.

Reaching the valley floor, they passed through wooded glades, coming eventually to the beginning of the turnpike. As they approached the gate at a rapid trot the guard gave a blast on his horn.

"Hallo, where's Ned?" the coachman called to the turnpike keeper when he emerged from his tiny cottage. "Dead," came the short reply, "It's why I kept the gate shut. Thought you might like to know."

"What d'ya mean, dead? I only spoke to 'im yesterday."

"Murdered, last evening for a few coins and a coat. There's a hunt on. Some madman broke out of the asylum. We reckon it's 'im as did it. There's an 'orse stole too."

The driver calmed the fretting horses, the coach rolled back and forth a little with their impatient movements. Various heads appeared through the coach windows. "I say there, driver, what's the delay?" one of the officers called. "Drive on if you please."

"There's been a murder, sir, friend of mine too."

"Yes, yes, I heard, but be so good as to get on with your duty."

"How was the man killed?" Abel called to the turnpike keeper.

"Well really," the exasperated officer complained, "I said let's be off."

"I'm talking to this man." Garnett's voice hardened.

"I'm on duty, sir, and have appointments, as an officer of engineers, I must protest at this delay."

"And I say, as an ex-sergeant of the 50th, that I am addressing this fellow and would appreciate it if you shut your mouth."

A heavy silence descended for a moment. "Well really!" The officer finally objected but withdrew his head and sat down.

Abel looked directly at the turnpike keeper. "What happened?"

"Ned was found late last night. He 'ad been strangled by 'is own scarf and 'is 'ead were bashed in. Old Ned never did 'arm to anybody, the big coat he always wore 'as gone an' the toll money's missin'."

"Thank you," said Abel gravely; "Coachman, drive on!"

"About time too," the indignant officer complained. "If you were still in the army, my good man, I'd have you up on charges."

"But I'm not, am I?" said Abel coolly; "And I'm not your good man."

Thanks to the toll road, they made good progress to Maidstone; the horses pulled gallantly and the passengers were soon descending from the coach in yet another inn yard.

"Here we are, gentlemen," said the driver.

"Merry Maidstone on the Medway, and right on time too," he said meaningfully as the two army officers marched off in perfect step, hands on sword hilts.

Garnett looked after them. "Officers!" he muttered. "Reverend Hayes, I will no doubt see you again soon."

"I certainly look forward to that," said the vicar, taking Abel's hand and shaking it vigorously.

Abel looked around for Jack, who had scrambled down the side of the coach, "C'mon, Jack, got your duds? Good. I could do with a drink."

"Where to now?" asked Jack as they left the yard and made their way up a broad street.

"Brook's Yard," Abel replied. "I've a wagon there. But let's wet the whistle first."

"I could do with a drink myself," said Jack, struggling to keep up with Abel's rapid stride.

"What d'you know about anything?" Abel's mood seemed to have darkened as they entered the open door of a public house.

Abel sunk a strong ale quickly whilst Jack was sipping the top from his, then called for brandy. "Leave the bottle." He was about to pour himself a measure when he suddenly swept the glass from the table with the back of his hand, silencing the buzz of conversation in the bar. As the landlord approached, Abel eyed him balefully over the bottle that he had raised to his lips. After swallowing several times, he slammed the bottle down: "Clear off, there's no trouble here."

"Right you are, Mr Garnett, sir," the landlord grinned weakly.

Garnett looked at Jack; "Officers, I 'ate 'em. Do you know that? Jack, I've seen things. Men with their guts spillin' over their hands, dyin' slow; men with arms, legs and 'eads blowed off. Stood in line with two 'undred tons of horseflesh chargin' down on us, an' us with empty muskets, filthy and half-starved, all cos they"—he inclined his head toward the street—"couldn't organise munitions, rations, water or strategy for that matter." He drank again from the bottle. "Most of them officers were too busy preenin' theirselves or glory 'unting to worry about the poor bloody common soldier. We died in our thousands, army, navy. They're all the same. Come to think of it, I 'ate governments just the same, for it's them that let's it 'appen. Ah, what's the use?" Abel threw some coins on the table and abruptly stood up. "Come on, Jack, let's get out of here." Garnett powered his awesome frame out of the public house. One or two of its customers eyed him nervously as he brushed past them.

"You seem to be well known hereabouts, Mr Garnett," Jack said as they made their way further up the street.

"What makes you say that?"

"Why the vicar knew you, the landlord in that pub knew you."

"D'you know, it was Brownlow that gave me a lift up?" said Abel, changing the subject. "I was out of the army, and," he laughed harshly, "drinkin' a bit, when along comes this opportunity to run Brownlow's place at Shippenden. Well, I know the land and I know sheep, so he's had no cause to regret it. But he seems to go in for taking a chance on people. Here's Brook's Yard." As though to match Abel's mood, the sun had gone and clouds were beginning to obscure the sky again.

Garnett was greeted by the merchant in Brook's Yard like an old friend. "Good to see you, Abe, how was the trip? Got yourself a 'prentice, have you?" He seemed to find this hilarious and burst out laughing. "The wagon's ready, loaded, Abe. I'm short on the four-inch nails; maybe you can wait awhile?"

Garnett, whose humour seemed to be lightening now, said airily, "No hurry, man. Next time will do."

A boy appeared, leading a pair of sturdy shire horses, directing them expertly between the shafts of a loaded and sheeted wagon.

"They bin corn-fed and watered," said the merchant; "they're a fine pair."

"Add that to the tally and I'll settle in the usual manner." Abe strolled to the wagon, patting the flank of one of the dappled greys.

"Come on, Jack, we're off again," said Abel climbing to the wagon seat. Jack scrambled up next to him. Abel made a couple of clicking noises and slapped the reins across the horses' backs. They rolled majestically out of the yard, turning onto the highway, avoiding a small flock of sheep that was being driven by a smocked figure, and a pair of black and white dogs. Abel looked at the shepherd with a puzzled frown.

"Could it be?" he mused. "No, of course not."

"What's up?" said Jack familiarly.

"Well—the murdered man at the Tollgate—he was supposed to have been done in by an escaped lunatic, it's a long story Jack, but years ago a shepherd in my employ ended up in a lunatic asylum hereabouts, and seeing him"—he jerked his thumb at the figure disappearing up the street—"reminded me, as something did this morning. A sort of shiver like went through me. Ah, but he's probably dead by now." He flicked a long whip above the horses' necks, increasing their pace.

Spatters of rain began to land on the canvas covering the wagon-load and soon they were in the middle of quite a downpour. Garnett pulled his coat collar up and adjusted his wide-brimmed hat. He glanced at Jack; "You'd better get under that sheet if you don't want a soaking."

Taking him at his word, Jack slipped onto the dry wagon bed under the sheeting. He heard Garnett laughing at the weather. It was comforting under the canvas away from the rain. There was a dusty mixture of smells. Horses, hay and oats, and an odour of soap and cheese mingled with rum or was that brandy? Curious, Jack poked around among the boxes and bags. His hand suddenly encountered something metallic on the floor of the wagon. A knife! He examined it – a very nice clasp knife, sharp too! He folded it shut and put it in his pocket. Next he managed to prise a piece of wood away from a small box and out trickled a stream of raisins. He fed on them, laying back in cosy comfort.

"Rain's stopped!" Garnett called from his seat on the wagon. Jack crawled out from under the tarpaulin. He was quite glad to be sitting back with the big, moody man again.

"We'll breathe the horses at the bottom of the next hill. I'm in no hurry to make Shippenden tonight. I quite like being on the move," he said frankly; "I think it's due to the life I've led. Anyway, parts of the road down there will be bad if there's been much rain. No need to kill the nags. We'll sleep under the wagon tonight."

At the top of the hill, a huge panorama opened up before them. A heavily wooded and sparsely populated plain stretched away under a lowering sky. Far in the distance, Jack thought that he could discern a church steeple.

"It's a long way from London," he breathed.

"Yes," replied Abel. "Not much call for your work round 'ere."

"What d'ya mean?"

"Well, I understand you're a thief and pickpocket by trade."

"Do you know what they call me?" Jack asked indignantly. "I'm the Artful Dodger, I am."

Abel laughed. "The Artful Dodger, eh?"

"Yeah, I can dodge anybody, see. Follow 'em to ruddy hell without being spotted. And I can lift anything and to prove it, here's an 'alf-sov'rin I took from your pocket when you weren't lookin'."

Abel looked at the coin Jack was displaying. "Why, you—"

Jack laughed now. "Don't worry, I've decided to give this lark up. Here's ya money. First chance I get, I'm off to America, see. I've 'eard about it. Don't you fret. I could do all right there."

Abel grabbed him by the collar, twisting it hard. "Oh no you don't," he said fiercely. "Don't you know what it would cost Brownlow if you was to abscond?—two 'undred pounds, that's what. That's in jeopardy for seven years. You got to stick it out, lad. You're going to appear before magistrates every three month. You're gonna be law-abiding." He twisted the collar further, half choking Jack. "So America's not goin' to 'appen is it? Is it?"

Jack shook his head. "All right, all right, just an idea I 'ad. Forget it," he gasped.

Abel released him, smoothing his collar delicately. "Don't you forget it. I'm doing well at Shippenden and that's where I want to stay. I don't want you interfering with my plans. Understand?"

The wagon brakes complained and smoked as they descended the escarpment to the valley floor, the horses resisting being pushed forward by the heavy load. "They do say that once, a long time ago, all this was covered by sea," Garnett said, indicating the plain with his whip. "Maybe they're right, there's nothing between us and the channel now 'cept marsh and meadow and there are times when they're all under water." He looked over his shoulder. "Time's getting on. Let's stop." He steered the horses towards a clump of trees just off the road and halted beneath a canopy of leaves.

"Grass is still soaked," he said, "but there's a spare bit o' canvas. Ever drunk tea, Jack?" Garnett was busy round the wagon. Going to a hinged box on the side of it, he removed a neatly folded piece of canvas. "Spread that out," he said, throwing it at Jack. Next, he went to the horses and, with a few quick movements, removed some of their harnessing, allowing the wagon shafts to fall free. The horses were already grazing on the lush growth under the trees. A canvas bag appeared in Abel's hands, and the shires lifted their heads to nuzzle him as he fed them handfuls of oats.

"Can you make a fire, Jack?"

"I 'elped a mate in a case of arson, once!" he bragged; "But all the wood's wet 'ere."

Abel threw a leather bucket in Jack's direction; "There should be a stream beyond the trees. Bring some water?"

Taking up the bucket, Jack wandered off. His trouser legs soon got soaked in the long grass. "I suppose I could do a bunk now," he thought, "but where to? Nothin' makes sense anymore." Jack suddenly felt completely alone. "Nobody, nothing and nowhere to go," he thought savagely, lashing out at the undergrowth with the bucket. He turned the clasp knife over and over in his pocket. "I could creep up on 'im, slit 'is throat and make off with that wagon," he thought wildly. "Horses—load an' all—must be worth a lot." He then had a vision of Garnett overpowering him and breaking his neck. That persuaded him against the idea.

There was a river running clean, clear and cool through a small, open meadow. Jack knelt and scooped up a bucket of water. Light green grasses waved languidly at the bottom of the stream. He was becoming more aware of his surroundings now. At first there appeared to be a deathly quiet, but then he began to hear the sounds of the chuckling river. Next he heard birdsong, then the breeze whispering through the naked tree branches. Under a clearing sky, small flocks of birds flashed towards the treetops, chattering excitedly as they settled for the night. Jack thought back over the past few days: Newgate Prison, Brownlow, the judge, then this journey. Steamboat, stage and wagon: "Bloomin' 'eck, what's happening to you, Jack?"

The glow of a small fire greeted him as he arrived back at the wagon. Abel poured some of the water into a billycan and placed it on the fire. From somewhere he had produced bread and cheese which he carved with a wicked looking knife, "Nothing like a night camp, eh, Jack?" They sprawled on the canvas, chewing food. Soon the water was boiling. Abel threw in a small amount of dark leaves. Removing the billy from the fire, he gave it a stir with the knife blade and then, sprinkling a little cold water onto it, poured some of the steaming liquid into a pair of tin cups. "'Ave some tea. Very good. Good 'ealth Jack." He drank with some satisfaction, then smacked his lips. "Damn good!"

"At ten bob a pound, it ought to be—you mus' be made o' money." Jack had only tasted the stuff once before. Not so good as beer, in his opinion, but better than coffee.

They sat together on the canvas, amiably enjoying the warmth of the fire.

"Let's have a pipe," Abel said, and produced two clays from his bag together with a pack of tobacco. They added their smoke to that of the crackling fire. "It's the gypsy life for me!" Jack commented suddenly light-hearted.

"You ain't thinking straight, boy," replied Abel, removing the pipe from his mouth, "you're warm and fed now, and it's a fine enough night. But consider this – it's a freezin' cold night, pouring with rain, you got no grub and no money. You haven't e't all day or for several days, save what you've been able to steal. What sort of life is that? In some countries, gypsies are treated reasonable like. Taken on for work and so on, but 'ere in good old England, you are more likely to be run off people's land and 'ave a brick thrown at you, to boot."

"You don't seem to like England much."

"Come on," replied Garnett; "Let's pull the canvas under the wagon, I've a couple of horse blankets we can use." He doused the fire with the dregs of the tea.

CHAPTER THREE

The Early Life of Abel Garnett

bel Garnett crept stealthily to the crest of the hill, keeping low in the grass. Down at the bottom of the slope, he saw the French. They had not spotted him yet. He crawled forward to get a closer look. One of them lifted his head and stared directly at him. Abel made up his mind. "Charge!" he yelled at the top of his voice, standing upright and racing forward. The sheep scattered before him, running panic-stricken across the meadow. Laughing with glee, Abel sprinted towards the nearby farm buildings. At the five barred gate stood his father. "Ye near frit those sheep to death, boy," he laughed, ruffling the boy's hair as Abel passed swiftly by.

The farm stood on sloping land on the Surrey-Sussex border. Abel had been born there nine years previously. Elspeth, his sister, was seven years old. Her birth had been a difficult one, very prolonged, and there had been no further children. Abel's father, George Garnett, was tenant of the property, which gave the family a reasonable living. The farm had sheep and a sawpit. George was a good carpenter and also a skilled shepherd. He had come originally from the Chichester area. Moving out of his family home after marrying, he leased the farm from Lord Elstead, whose bailiff would make occasional calls on them.

Margaret, his wife, had been made frail by the birth of Elspeth but was still able to take care of the poultry, churn butter and keep house. Elspeth and Abel were educated in part by their mother. She had a genteel background. On Sundays, the family, the shepherd and the sawpit men proceeded regularly to the village church, two miles down the muddy lane, not only to sing hymns and pray, but also to enjoy gossiping with villagers and other farm people outside the lych-gate, returning home in good spirits.

The world turned and Abel and Elspeth grew into their teens, Elspeth taking more and more of the workload from her increasingly fragile mother and Abel becoming a competent shepherd himself. He was also gaining experience with wood, plane and saw. There were good years and poor years: times of peace and rumours of war. Abel began to grow extremely broad and strong, whilst Elspeth, like her mother, remained slim and delicate.

George Garnett returned one Michaelmas from the market at Horsham with a new shepherd as a companion, the previous man having decided to take up employment elsewhere. This new employee was named Pierce. He was of wiry aspect with strong wrists, ginger hair and a moustache. He did not look as though he laughed very much, merely nodding when he was introduced to the family.

Elspeth noticed that he had large, powerful hands with cruel-looking long fingers, the nails of which had been severely bitten – the tips of the fingers, in fact, looked a little raw. He had his own dog, a well-trained collie that followed him closely everywhere.

Pierce set up a lonely existence in a two-roomed cottage, slightly apart from the farm, but breakfasted with the Garnetts in their homely kitchen, only speaking in monosyllables and rarely looking directly at anyone if they spoke to him.

"I'm afraid I've made a mistake with that fellow," Abel overheard his father say to his mother. "He'd better go next Michaelmas. Makes the whole place seem cheerless, does he not?"

"I don't like the man at all, George," she replied. "He has such a cold manner, can't he go sooner?"

"Wouldn't be fair, old girl, he'd never get work at this time o' year."

That autumn, news came to the Garnett family that George's father was not expected to live much longer.

"I must go to Chichester, Liz. I hope to arrive in time, but if not, there will be arrangements to make. My sisters will need me."

Elizabeth looked appealingly at her husband who took her hand in his pressing it gently, "Abel is here, he will take care of things," he said encouragingly. "Pierce will take care of the sheep, I will speak to him before I go, for I must go, Liz."

"I know you must, George," she said, holding on to him, "but I will miss you so."

"I should be gone no more than a fortnight. I can take the long coach to Horsham and manage very well from there. Abel can ride behind me on the cob to the inn, and return with it."

Elizabeth nodded. "It has to be. Please be careful and come back safe."

"Of course, of course; don't work too hard. You are not strong, don't be anxious."

Riding behind his father, Abel reassured him. "I'll take care of everything, no need to worry at all. There's little to do at the moment."

"Take care of your mother, Abe," his father pleaded. "She's very low at the moment."

"You can depend on me, father."

Having seen his father onto the coach, Abel, his new responsibilities resting lightly on his shoulders, rode the cob at a gentle pace through the Sussex countryside. The woods were in glorious autumn colours, the way still firm beneath the horses' hooves.

Three nights later, George Garnett was taken by a press gang near Chichester. A determined naval officer, finding slim pickings in the Portsmouth area due to word being spread of their imminent arrival, had taken his men further than usual. Farm boys, drunks, even poachers making their way homeward, found themselves aboard a third-rater. Within two days it was beating its way down channel, heading for the Atlantic rollers.

It was almost two weeks before news came to the Garnett farm that George's father had died and that George himself had not arrived in Chichester.

There had been some anxiety felt by the Garnetts, having heard nothing since George's departure. Now, Abel and Elspeth supported their distraught mother to her bedroom where she collapsed completely. "Oh, George, he must be murdered, what will happen to us? My poor children. What can we do?" Her anguished tears set Elspeth crying helplessly, leaving Abel in somewhat of a dilemma. "C'mon sis. Help me get mother to bed. Then you must go to Mrs Acton. Ask her to attend quick as possible."

In a few minutes, stifling her tears, Elspeth was scampering down the stairs and out of the kitchen door, skirts flying. The Actons had a smallholding several fields away. The doughty Mrs Acton often attended the sick or the pregnant in the district.

When Elspeth and Mrs Acton arrived, Abel was sitting glumly by the bedside. His mother's body laid covered up to the chin and very still.

Mrs Acton took one look. "She's gone from us, Abel. Her heart, I daresay. It was never strong since—since..." She glanced at Elspeth. "Well—for some years, you know." Elspeth, small fists clenched and head bowed, quietly left the room. Abel stood up to follow her. "Let her have a minute, Abel."

"What am I to do now, Mrs Acton? No word from father, and now mother." He was close to tears himself. "What can I do?" They were both whispering.

"Look Abel, you had better go to Chichester to see if your father is there. Elspeth can come and stay with us until you return. We must make the arrangements for your mother. Have you any money?"

"Father left a little for necessities and there is some to come from the sawpit work, I think. What about the farm?" Abel suddenly felt the weight of responsibility.

"Elspeth can come over to feed the pigs and poultry, collect the eggs and so forth. That man Pierce will have to carry on taking care of the sheep. A dreary man, but he seems capable."

Mrs Acton took his arm and led him to the stairs. "Come on, boy, collect your wits; this is a sad blow, but it happens. No doubt your father will turn up safe and sound."

They descended the stairs.

"There's the Michaelmas Fair next week," Abel sighed. "We were to sell some sheep at the market."

"Well, Pierce must do that for you as well. Speak to him, Abe; tell him what's required. You stay here with Elspeth, and I will go to Reverend Hicks and tell him what's happened."

"Take the pony and trap, Mrs Acton, it's too far to walk. I will harness the cob."

They crept silently from the house as though afraid to wake a person lightly sleeping in the room above.

Abel found Elspeth by the stable door, rather distractedly stroking the muzzle of the horse.

"You had better go with Mrs Acton, sis. I will have to speak to Pierce."

She nodded, still full of emotion.

Abel soon had the horse between the shafts of the little trap and after the women had pulled out onto the lane, he headed for the sheep pastures where he knew he would find Jacob Pierce.

Pierce was about twenty-five or -six and coming to the end of his first year with the Garnetts. When he spoke, which was rarely, there were traces of a Scottish accent. Abel and Elspeth always felt ill-at-ease when he was around. His secretive manner and a certain indefinable something in his eyes had made them avoid his company as much as possible. But he was certainly good with sheep. What he did when he was not working none of them knew. An occasional glimmer of a candle showed at night in his tiny cottage, and although Pierce made trips to the village, he had declined the Sunday pilgrimages to church.

Once when George had asked him about his family, he had replied briefly that they were "up north". The only time that Abel had seen the man express any real emotion was shortly after his father had employed him. Pierce had discovered Abel feeding the shepherd's dog with scraps. "Damn you, boy," Pierce erupted, "nobody feeds my dog but me." He raised a hand as though to strike him, but with a visible effort, he controlled himself. Calling the dog, he turned and strode rapidly away.

Abel did not tell his father but remarked to him later that the new shepherd was "not very friendly".

"He's a long way from home, Abe. He will come round."

Now, Abel, full of grief and anxiety, found the shepherd with his dog seated on a grassy knoll. Although there was a stiff breeze stirring the nearby woods, it was still pleasant in the autumn sunshine. Rooks were cawing in the treetops, and the screeching cry of a distant fox made the sheepdog prick its ears and lift its head a little.

"Mr Pierce," Abe began, "there is bad news, I'm afraid, mother has—has collapsed." He could not bring himself to use the "death" word. "And father may be in some sort of trouble, there is no news of him at Chichester." He was too caught up in his own feelings to notice the rapid succession of emotions that crossed Pierce's face. The first, just for a thousandth of a second, appeared to be great elation, then an extraordinary look of cunning as though a great plan had been instantly formulated. Finally a look of mournful sorrow appeared, and stayed. "I'm sorry to 'ear this, master Abe, your mother, is she…?"

Abel's eyes filled with tears. "I'm afraid so. Elspeth has gone for the vicar with Mrs Acton. If there is no news of father before—before the funeral, then I must go to Chichester."

"Aye, you're in a fix all right, Master Abe, wi' both your mother and father gone at the same time."

"Father's not 'gone', as you put it; he's ill or had an accident or something," Abel said. At that moment he would have given anything to have seen his familiar figure striding across the meadow towards them.

"What about me, am I to carry on?" asked Pierce, his Northern accent becoming more pronounced by the minute.

"Of course," said Abel, "if father is not back by next week, you must take the sheep to the market for us and make the sale. Can you do it?"

"Aye, o' course. I'm no' stupid."

"I know, but father would normally do it. You may take the horse; it will speed your return. I'm sure the Actons will lend me one for my journey.

Abel broke down for a moment. "This is just terrible, next week we would have all been at the Michaelmas Fair as a family and now—now—oh I just don't know."

The shepherd looked at him, his face betraying nothing now. "Aye, and Michaelmas was to be my birthday."

Abel, even in the depth of his youthful misery, looked at him sharply for his odd sentence. But the weathered, gingery features before him were still as a mask, the eyes dead in their sockets.

"So you can take care of the sheep for me?"

"Oh, aye, I can take care o' everythin'. Don't you worry about that, Master Abe."

Abel returned to the farmhouse but felt completely unable to enter it. Instead he went to the wood-stack. Picking up an axe, he began to chop logs, swinging the blade mightily, relieving his feelings by expelling energy.

Elspeth and Mrs Acton returned from the Reverend Hicks. "He is unable to attend until this evening and Doctor Merrick is at a childbirth. Both will come as soon as possible." The practical lady was soon bustling about keeping Elspeth busy in the kitchen. "We must all eat, you know, keep our strength up. You young things have not had a bite since breakfast."

They sat at the table, but after a couple of mouthfuls of eggs, Elspeth stood up and went out of the house. Abel could do little better.

"I must go now," said Mrs Acton. "I have my men to feed. I will come again tomorrow." She put her arm round Abel's shoulders and kissed his forehead. "Bear up, boy, life goes on."

Abel put his hand on hers. "I can't thank you enough—"

"None o' that now. We are neighbours, are we not? I must go." And she swept out, dabbing at an eye as she went.

Abel worked steadily in his father's carpentry shop, making a creditable coffin for his mother. He was interrupted by the sound of a horse. The Reverend Hicks met him at the shed door. A normally fat, jolly little man, his face now showed concern for one of his flock.

"Abel, this is sad news indeed. Your mother was a fine, hard-working Christian woman."

Elspeth, who had been on an aimless walk appeared at that moment. "My dear Elspeth, try not to grieve too much. Your mother is with the Lord now. The reward for a blameless life. Shall we go to the house?"

In the dim bedroom, curtains drawn, the three of them knelt and prayed. Elspeth wept silently, lips moving, hands clasped before her. Abel, grim faced, spoke his words aloud in chorus with the Reverend Hicks.

Elspeth, on her walk, had passed the sawpit and indicated to the men that they should stop work out of respect to her mother. They had dutifully discontinued cutting board. Two of them arrived at the farmhouse as the funeral arrangements were being made. At Abel's request, they carried the newly-made coffin from the carpenter's shop to the bedroom, shortly after which Dr Merrick arrived, almost bumping into the departing vicar on the doorstep. "Ah, doctor," said Hicks, "nothing you can do here I'm afraid, except try to confirm cause of death."

"This is a sad day indeed for the Garnetts," remarked the doctor, "but not unexpected. She'd been going downhill for some time. Never strong."

"I must be off," Hicks said. "Things to do you know."

"Not an hour since I helped bring a new life into the world," the doctor called after him. "Now one has gone out of it."

"Checks and balances," intoned the vicar, mounting his horse, "checks and balances."

Forty-eight hours later Elizabeth Garnett was buried in the ancient churchyard. Several villagers and some local farmers' wives attended as well as the Actons. Elspeth and Abel and the sawpit workers. Jacob Pierce was remarkable by his absence.

After it was all over, Abel was impatient to be gone. His main thought now was to find his father. He deposited Elspeth at the Actons' farm.

"Do come back to me, Abe," she pleaded. "Bring good news of father or come together if you can, but don't leave me all alone for too long."

"I will come back and with Pa, don't you worry about that. Just one thing. Don't go to the farm alone, understand? I don't trust that Pierce. He's an odd one. Always go with one of the Actons. Promise?"

Elspeth shivered a little. "Don't worry, Abe, I don't like him either and I've no wish to be alone with him."

"If I'm not back by next week, he is taking the sheep to market. We shall have to trust him in that, I suppose."

"I shall ask Mr Acton to keep an eye on him," said Elspeth firmly. "He will be at the market himself."

"Good idea." Abel kissed his sister fondly. "Take care now. I will see you soon."

Mounting the borrowed horse, he rode away, turning once to wave at the forlorn young figure standing at the gate. Abel felt manly and confident at the outcome of his quest.

In his sixteen short years, Abel had not travelled far from home. Roaming the woods and fields had been his early pleasure, spiced with shooting trips with his father or family jaunts to visiting fairs. He was currently flirting coyly with a village girl, exchanging glances in church on Sundays and a few faltering words under the lych-gate, during which they had occasionally held hands.

Abel's mother had taught him rudimentary mathematics and he could read well, enjoying what few books there were available. Abel had learnt something of the world from them and now felt that he was truly out in it. His initial confidence dissipated rapidly, however, and the further he rode, the more he felt that the vast complexity of the earth was threatening him. He realised that his whole future could be in jeopardy and there was Elspeth to consider. It was a very preoccupied young man that arrived in Horsham.

He spent the night in a cheap inn, sleeping fitfully on a lumpy bed, raucous laughter and the occasional crash of a glass breaking and the noisy arrival and departure of the drinkers below not helping him at all.

Abel's grandparents' house stood to one side of a muddy lane on the Portsmouth side of Chichester. There was a tangle of broken-down sheds, a more solid barn and several pig-sties which emitted a powerful stench.

It was almost evening when Abel approached the place through sheeting rain, on a wet and weary horse. He slid, equally weary from the saddle and led the animal to the comfort of the barn. A lop-eared dog raced excitedly from one of the sheds, barking furiously. This caused a shawled head to poke itself from a window in the house. "Who's there? What is it?"

"It's me, Aunt Rose. Abel come to see you. Any news of father?"

"Abel!" cried Aunt Rose. "Just a moment, I'm coming down!"

Aunt Rose opened the door to the house rather breathlessly, her knitted shawl trailing in the hallway behind her. "Abe, I've news of your father!" and then, "Sam!" she screamed at the top of her voice, a body appearing instantly in the hoist entry to the hay loft, "Yes Ma'am?"

"Take care of Mr Garnett's horse if you please."

"Yes, ma'am." Sam slid alarmingly down the hoist rope, landed in a deep puddle and almost sprang into the barn where the horse stood, head down and reins trailing. The dog continued to bark without a pause. "Corky!" screamed Aunt Rose., "Shut up, will you!" Come in, Abe, come in, it's good to see you. My! How you've growed."

Abel followed his aunt down the hall. "What's happened to Pa?"

"The last we heard, he was alive and well," she replied as they entered a room full of comfortable, albeit ageing, furniture.

"Thank God." Abel breathed a sigh of relief.

"It's not all good news, Abe—please take a seat. Here let me have that coat, it's soaked through."

"What do you mean?" asked Abe, removing his top-coat. "Where is he?"

"George, your father has been pressed into the navy."

"What?" Abel sank his large frame into a chair. "That can't be true."

"I'm afraid it is, Abe. The night that he arrived in the area, the press gangs had strayed further from their usual hunting grounds, and George was taken. Several other men disappeared with him, well, men—some were scarcely more than boys. When we heard in the village what had occurred, we went straight to Portsmouth but the ship had already sailed. There is some hope that he will gain his freedom when the ship returns. It is believed to be at Gibraltar now."

"That is something at least," Abel said. "There is more bad news, Aunt, I'm sorry to say that mother has—is dead."

"Oh Abe!" She rushed across and, on her knees, threw her arms as far round him as they would go, knocking her mob-cap away and trailing her shawl on the floor.

"I'm sorry, Aunt, there was no time to let you know when it happened. Everything's a mess."

"Dear Abe—your poor sweet mother. What an awful time you have had. What about Elspeth?"

"She is staying with friends. Taking care of the poultry, feeding the pigs. Just keeping an eye on things until I return."

"We have sent you a letter about your father, so Elspeth will know before you get back, I expect. Is she bearing up all right under the loss of her dear mama?"

"It will take some time for her to recover, I think," replied Abe. "We were all very close." Abe's face began to crumple into tears but he controlled himself, clearing his throat forcefully.

"Come on, Abe—you are tired and hungry. Betty and Ann will be home soon. Your aunts are taking tea with friends. They gossip you know, and lose all sense of time! Come and eat in peace while you can. You know, you and Elspeth are both very young and have your whole lives in front of you. Look to the future, Abe."

He followed her into the kitchen. "Yes, but how am I going to manage the farm until father returns?"

"That I don't know as yet. But you know your father inherited this place when your grandpa died. You will always have a home whatever happens." Rose ladled thick vegetable soup into a bowl, handing it to Abe. "Eat well, boy. There's bread on the table."

He gratefully spooned the hot liquid into his mouth. "Thank you, Aunt, I am sure that father will always want you to have this place as your home; after all, you took good care of grandpa and grandma for years."

"Well, it's not much, but there is room for us all," she said cheerfully. "There is some land for rent as grazing, we have the pigs and a first-class garden; we manage very well. Come along, it's early I know, but you look tired out. We shall talk some more tomorrow. Finish your soup and I will show you your room."

A week later, Jacob Pierce, riding the cob, ambled behind the small flock as they moved in a close-knit group down the rutted lane. It was scarcely dawn but they had a three-hour journey ahead of them. Abel, not having returned, Jacob was obeying his orders, but to his immense irritation, Mr Acton and his two sons were driving their own flock just behind him. Jacob's sheepdog crouched and crept, white-eyed, at the heels of the sheep, exercising perfect control. Jacob Pierce, his face impassive, emulated the animal to perfection.

CHAPTER FOUR

Jacob Pierce — Shepherd — Psychopath

acob Pierce had been born in the empty wastes of Northumberland on a remote farmstead: an only son whose mother had withered after his birth.

It was a poverty-stricken life. Jacob's father was cruelty itself – a bully and strict disciplinarian, whilst his mother was a weeping, wittering skivvy. From an early age, Jacob knew beatings and brutal treatment from his father and helpless consolation from his mother. After his father had expiated his rage on him, she would kiss Jacob's bruises and stroke his hair. It was all that she could do.

Living on the solitary farm, Jacob knew no one and met very few people, scarcely ever having a conversation with a fellow human being. Pierce was not popular in the district, his odious temper gaining him a reputation of someone to steer clear of.

From the age of eight or nine, Jacob spent most of his time with the sheep and dogs, or working in the stony vegetable garden. His mind became a place of fierce imaginings and occasionally he would have lonely outbursts of rage, which only the sheep or birds on the wing observed.

On Jacob's fifteenth birthday, which had arrived without remark like all his previous birthdays, he was pulling turnips in the garden. Wiping the earth from one of them, he sat on the hard ground and took a bite at the pale vegetable.

"Idling!" The bitter fury of his father's familiar voice startled him out of a strange reverie. Jacob scrambled to his feet, his father was stomping towards him through the green turnip tops, hands busy unbuckling the leather belt at his waist. "You've asked for this, boy!"

Without giving his actions conscious thought, Jacob bent and picked up the hoe and swung it in a powerful arc, the D-shaped blade smashing into the side of his father's head. Stunned and badly cut, he fell with a groan to his hands and knees. Jacob dropped the hoe and in a dreamlike state took up a piece of granite, floated to his father, and hit him with devastating force with the rock. Jacob was triumphant, elated, as he smashed again and again at his father's head. He continued long after the body stopped moving and twitching.

When several minutes had passed, Jacob stood up, dropping the blood- and brain-spattered rock. His body was covered in sweat and the ragged clothing that he wore soaked in blood. Still in a trance-like state, he walked stiffly to the house, climbed the stairs and went to his bare, cold room. There, he stripped off his shirt and donned the only other one that he possessed. On the landing he met his lank-haired mother. "Jacob" was the only word she had time to utter before he gave her a mighty push that sent her tumbling down the stairs, hitting the stone floor below, and breaking her neck. Jacob descended the staircase, then stepped over his mother's body without giving it a second glance. He went through the house, room by room, taking what he wanted, which was little. Putting on his father's warm coat, Jacob whistled up the dog and set off down the track that wound between the rolling hills. He had gone half a mile before he realised that his face was set in a frightful rictus, his lips pulled back from his teeth, eyes staring wildly but seeing nothing. He adjusted his features to a more normal condition, and with sudden unspeakable joy, he ran and ran, sending up a great shout that echoed round the hills and started the dog jumping at him and barking. They were playing a great game!

…It was almost Michaelmas Day.

A week went by before a carrier called at the farm and discovered the bodies. The authorities deduced from the evidence, and from statements made by character witnesses, that Mr Pierce in one of his rages had killed his wife, accidentally or otherwise, and his son, Jacob, had wreaked a terrible revenge on him. Some people suggested an alternative scenario where Jacob lay dead somewhere on the moor, killed by his father, and it was Mrs Pierce who had bashed out her husband's brains, and then fallen down stairs breaking her neck.

Descriptions of Jacob were circulated, but there were no sightings of him, although an illiterate tinker who came into the area a month later and heard of the event swore that he had seen the boy and his dog in Carlisle.

Jacob, calling himself Ben Stewart, was to be found some months later working for a fat, jolly sheep farmer in Cumberland. "Ben" had lost his parents in a fire. He had come from the lowlands of Scotland to start a new life. About the time of Jacob's seventeenth birthday, his kindly employer had an accident, falling from a lofty crag onto the rocks below. It was Jacob who had raised the alarm, running three miles to the nearest inhabited house, bringing the farm labourers to the spot, telling them what had happened. All this was testified. Other than the young, heartbroken Ben Stewart there were no witnesses: accidental death.

Jacob continued his great game in Derbyshire. With what tension and inner excitement he waited for the hours, days and weeks to pass! The planning and the concealment were almost as exciting as the extreme moment when everything came to fruition. He would lie in his bed listening to the wind in the dark of night, hugging himself in a delirium of ecstasy.

In Derbyshire, a newly appointed curate wanted someone to take care of his other flock, the wool-bearing one.

There was a dreadful fuss when the curate, the church plate and donated monies all disappeared at the same time. Jacob joined in the local hunt for him, without success. The whole county was scandalised and the missing man's family ostracised.

Jacob claimed that he was owed wages and so sympathetic parishioners collected for him. A few weeks later, the shepherd and his dog were on the road, heading south-east.

The curate's body resided in his own churchyard in the ancient family vault of De Waldham where Jacob had placed it. He had the church plate as well as old bones for company. Jacob had worked secretly on the entrance to the tomb until he could open it at will, always taking great care to conceal any signs of interference.

Playing the game was making Jacob Pierce more dour and more intense than ever. During his brief periods of sleep he was haunted by terrifying nightmares. Even at the low inns that he frequented on his travels, pot boys and other customers soon left him to his own devices.

He became thin and his eyes showed the lack of proper sleep. Upon occasion, he bit at his fingers until they were raw. There were times too when he was capable of lucid thought and was free from his terrible, secret obsession. He knew then that it was something more than his ugly childhood that drove him to his murderous acts. It was something not understood or understandable.

Working in Suffolk, Jacob took a job with a farmer that no shepherd had stayed with for long. He was notoriously mean and spiteful, drank whatever hard spirits were available and made himself generally obnoxious. Surprisingly, he and Jacob got on quite well together.

The farm becoming more prosperous, after a year or so, the farmer's attitude towards his shepherd gradually softened and he began inviting him into his house for a drink. He declared himself to be a lonely bachelor in need of company.

They appeared together at the local inn, much to the regulars' surprise, the farmer declaring Jacob to be the best worker he had ever had.

In the autumn of his second year at the farm, Jacob's suppressed desires broke through to the surface. During the course of a drinking session in the farmhouse, he strangled his drunk employer with a length of rope, laughing and crying as he did so. But how strong he felt! What power!

With the farmer dead on the kitchen floor, Jacob ransacked the house, and hid what coins and valuables that he found in a hollow tree in a nearby wood. He then gave himself severe wounds on his arm and upper body with a razor-sharp knife. Staggering down the lane to "raise the alarm" he fainted and would have died from loss of blood but for his dog which set up such a tremendous barking that a cottager two hundred yards away came to investigate.

How they attended on him! And consoled him and listened in horror as he described how he had came upon thieves in his employer's house and attempted to apprehend them. The best friend he ever had was dead. His employer had been a father to him. He wept; they consoled.

The neighbourhood was roused but no sign of the thieves and murderers was ever discovered. It was agreed that the farmer must have made many enemies over the years. Posters bearing Jacob's description of the intruders were circulated widely, but nothing was ever heard.

Shortly after he had recovered from his wounds, Jacob told those that had taken care of him that he was going back to his family in Scotland.

In Dorset, the fifteen-year-old daughter of a grazier took a shine to Jacob. She mistook his quiet ways for shyness and his awkwardness for gentlemanly manners. Her parents were heartbroken when, just a year after Jacob joined them, their daughter had a freak accident. It appeared that while running through a wooded area to meet Jacob, she had put her foot in a hole and fell, impaling herself through the throat on the jagged end of a broken branch. No one had seen anything quite like it.

In the past, the area had been popular with courting couples who went there to "pick bluebells". After "the accident", however, the small wood gained a reputation for being haunted and was avoided by everyone.

The locals were glad to see the back of Jacob when he left. In fact, the gossip in the public houses included rumours of murder.

George Garnett met Jacob Pierce at the stockyards in

Horsham. George had put the word around that he was suddenly short of a shepherd.

This thin, almost emaciated man approached him and introduced himself. "Mr Hampton, the auctioneer has told me you are in need of a shepherd, sir. Well, I am in need of employment. I have my own dog, well trained, and I have spent my life with sheep."

George eyed him up and down, thin, certainly, but strong with it; had a sort of Northern accent – some of the best shepherds came from the North. His eyes were sunken, red-rimmed and avoided those of his prospective employer.

"Have you anyone to recommend you?"

"I have this, sir." Jacob produced a rather battered piece of paper.

"It says here that you worked well and were of great benefit to this farm in Suffolk, but you never actually worked for the author of this." George waved the note at Jacob.

"It's the man's brother, sir; my employer died and he took over."

"It also says that you tried to protect your employer when he was attacked and were badly wounded."

"Yes, sir."

"This note is nearly two years old."

"I've been having a hard time since then, sir."

George's heart softened. "Yes, it looks as though you have. Come on, I'll take a chance on you."

"Right, sir." They shook hands.

On the wagon back to the Garnett farm, a familiar sense of well-being engulfed Jacob. He was playing the game again. Now he could begin to plan. He could look forward to the climax he knew would come sometime in the future. The shepherd shivered a little with delightful anticipation. Suddenly animated, he glanced around at the undulating countryside dressed in autumn colours, patting the dog, which, with lolling tongue, looked up at him in adoration.

And so it was as it had been before, the shepherd watching, waiting, planning, observing the Garnett family's decencies and kindness. He ate quietly in their kitchen at breakfast and watched the young Garnetts around the farm, helping with the work, being respectful to their parents. How he writhed with impatience but the moment had not yet come.

Nevertheless in his solitary bed, he could anticipate the bloodletting, the fire and his daring escape. He could even feel the painful burns he was going to inflict upon himself in his "rescue attempt".

The time he had planned had almost arrived when Abel came to see him in the sheep pasture. Jacob was consumed with conflicting emotions when he heard that Mrs Garnett had died suddenly and George Garnett had gone missing on his trip to Chichester.

He thought of killing the boy there and then, but it was not according to his plan. He had wanted them all, and he wanted to commit the act in safety.

"If there is no news of father before—before the funeral, then I must go to Chichester," Abel had told him. "*Well, that would leave the girl as a consolation prize,*" thought the shepherd, his stomach muscles tightening.

But everything had happened too suddenly for him, the mother dead, the father and the boy away. The girl, damn and damn her, always had a gaggle of Actons with her when she came to the farm. If only she had stayed in the house.

Now here he was on the road to Horsham, driving the sheep before him, still haunted by the blasted Actons behind him, with their own flock.

Even during the sale of the sheep, there was an Acton forever at his shoulder. After they had collected their monies "cash-on-the-nail" from the sale, Jacob made a sudden decision. He turned to the ever-watchful Acton Senior.

"By rights, this being Michaelmas, I have a day owing me. I intend to spend what's left of it taking my pleasures. Here, take the money to Miss Garnett, I will return tonight."

Acton took the purse that Jacob offered him. "I suppose you're right, Pierce, but I didn't think that you were one for fairs and such."

"I'm not, but I'm entitled to my own time and to spend it as I wish."

"Very well, but be sure to take good care of your master's horse and be ready for work tomorrow."

"All right."

"And, Pierce."

"What?"

"I don't know what's going on in that head of yours, but until your master returns, I shall have my eye on you."

Pierce did not answer that, but slouched off followed by his ever-faithful dog.

Leaning against one of the sheep pens, he watched Acton and his two sons leaving the market. He hated Acton's straight back as it passed and he seethed at the view of the two sons as they rode in the cart beside their father's horse.

Thirty minutes later, Jacob Pierce was on a lonely byway, riding the Garnetts' horse towards Kent. Never having much cause to spend his wages, he had several shillings in his pocket. But his first failure had left him unfulfilled, his appetite unappeased.

Abel Garnett was also dissatisfied. He had decided while at Chichester to delay returning home until he himself had spoken to the naval authorities at Portsmouth to make protest at his father being pressed into their service. But this being the year of our Lord, 1804, there was little sympathy for one man when the whole navy was in a state of perilous confusion.

Revolutionary France was at war with Great Britain.

"Do your duty, sir and join the service," was the best that a civilian clerk could suggest to him.

Anxious to see Elspeth after he had made his best effort, Abel hurried back to the family home, arriving two days after Michaelmas. The place was deserted so he rode over to the Actons, and to his relief soon saw Elspeth at their gate waving to him as he came up the cart track. "Abe! It's so good to see you!"

Her youthful face flushed with pleasure. Brotherly affection welled up in Abel as he dismounted and gave her a hug. "Hello, sis! Are you all right?"

"Yes, I'm well—any news of Father?"

"Nothing I'm afraid, he's sure to be released from service though when the ship returns to England."

"Thank God! Perhaps we can begin to live again then."

Abel put his comforting arm round her shoulders as they went to meet the Acton family who had gathered in the farmyard.

They spent that night in their own house. Abel absorbed the news that Jacob Pierce had not returned from Horsham. "Perhaps he got drunk. He's only a couple of days adrift as yet. We have the money from the sale."

"But he has the horse," Elspeth interposed.

"Yes that's true, but frankly, Elspeth, if he has gone, then we are well rid of him; the man cast a cold shadow over the place. If he does not return by tomorrow, I shall report the theft of the horse."

The two young people were not to be left in peace for long. Three weeks after their return to the farm, Lord Elstead's bailiff, Joseph Ball appeared, together with an assistant.

They clattered into the yard one chill morning scattering hens in all directions as Abel was harnessing the shire to a dung cart. Wiping his hands on the front of his work shirt, Abel went to them, taking hold of their horses' heads as they dismounted.

"Good day, gentlemen. I'm afraid I was not expecting visitors." He looked down at his soiled clothing.

"Good morning to you," said the bailiff. "You are Abel Garnett, are you not?"

"I am, sir," replied Abel. "Won't you come into the house?" He secured their horses to the fence though he knew that his shire would stand patiently for him. Elspeth met them at the door.

"Good morning," she curtsied sweetly.

"I will bring you all some refreshment; please go into the sitting room." Abel rather self-consciously removed his boots before entering.

"Mr Garnett," began the bailiff as they seated themselves, "this is Mr Parkin." He indicated his quiet companion; "He, er, assists me in this sort of uncomfortable business that brings me to you today."

"What sort of uncomfortable business?" asked Abel as Elspeth appeared with hot toddies. "It's a cold day so I thought these might be welcome."

"Very welcome, very welcome indeed," enthused Mr Ball and Mr Parkin.

"Er, Mr George Garnett is still away, isn't he?" asked Parkin.

"Well, yes," replied Abel.

"He has in fact been pressed into His Majesty's Navy."

"Yes, I'm afraid that he has."

"And you are running the farm?"

"Yes."

"Well, Mr Garnett, it is our unfortunate duty to tell you that this cannot continue."

"And why is that?" asked Abel, bridling.

"Your father leases this property on an annual basis from Lord Elstead. That lease expired two weeks ago."

"It can be renewed, can't it?"

"Your father is not here, is he?"

"Well, no."

"Then he cannot be expected to sign a new lease, sir."

"But I can sign."

"I am afraid not, you do not have the age to sign legal documents."

Elspeth and Abel looked rather despairingly at one another.

"But father may return at any moment," Elspeth blurted out.

"Miss Garnett," said Ball, a little coldly, "we are at war with France. He may not return at all."

"I would prefer it if you did not express yourself like that under my roof, sir," Abel said, getting angrier by the minute.

"It is not your roof, sir," snapped Parkin.

"Now, now," placated Ball. "I did not mean to frighten you, Miss Garnett, I am sure your father will return, but it could be two years, three years before he does. In the meantime Lord Elstead's best interests must be looked to. I am afraid there is nothing for it but for you to vacate these premises. We do have a tenant who is anxious to move in before Christmas. You will be given time to make other arrangements, pack your possessions and so on. We shall require that an audit of Lord Elstead's property be carried out before you depart. Any shortages or damage will have to be paid for, naturally."

"Naturally," muttered Abel miserably.

"Excuse me, gentlemen," said Elspeth, with a catch in her voice. Turning quickly, she left the room.

"We shall offer a fair price for any stock, feed or other such items that you care to leave," said Parkin amiably. "You have two weeks."

Within that time Abel and Elspeth were to be found in the depths of a harsh winter rainstorm, struggling with their overloaded wagon on the road to Chichester.

CHAPTER FIVE

The Artful Dodger in the Marshes and in Love

bel Garnett and Jack Dawkins slept soundly under the wagon, covered by horse blankets, with stuffed feedbags for pillows. Once in the night Jack thought that he heard the sound of a horse passing by but he soon returned to a deep sleep.

"Sun's nearly up, Jack." Abel roused him. "Take the horses to the stream—you can handle a horse, can't you?" Abel Garnett seemed in a happy mood, his beefy face sprouting bristles and a faint grin.

Jack crawled from beneath the wagon, "I can handle horses all right," he bragged although in truth he was not that familiar with them. Cocky confidence carried him through and taking hold of their bridles, he led the animals down to the river. It was quite a fine morning, a thin mist hovered above the stream. With a sudden start, Jack realised that he could leap onto the back of one of the horses, and, driving the other one before him, be away before Garnett could do anything about it. But somehow he could find neither the incentive nor the energy to take action. He watched the horses dip their muzzles into the cool water.

When Jack returned with them to the wagon, Abel was scraping at his chin with a wicked-looking cut-throat razor. Water was boiling in the billycan on the fire.

As they progressed through the country, bare-branched orchards gradually gave way to meadows with cattle and sheep standing in dank grass. There were willow-lined streams and occasional hamlets. The working people looked well fed and robustly healthy compared to those that Jack had encountered on the streets of London.

In one village they paused at an inn and satisfied their thirst and hunger.

The land became more watery with dykes and causeways; trees were twisted and gnarled with exposed roots. They appeared to be clinging to the earth by their clenched toes. It was a pleasant journey with mostly firm going for the horses. At one point Abel even burst forth with song. "Sweet Polly Oliver" rang out across the marshes, startling a small flock of sheep into movement.

"My singing always frightens the animals," he laughed. Jack laughed as well, causing Abel to look at him sharply. "You ain't stole my 'alf sovereign again, have you?"

"Why, sir, I quite forgot you 'ad one," said Jack. "My mem'ry's getting appallin'." And they both laughed again.

Now, apart from the occasional islands of high ground, they were in the marshes. They stretched in all directions. In the distance Jack could see the inevitable church tower. The sky above was a huge inverted grey bowl. Jack had never seen so far in all his life or seen so little habitation. The rocking motion of the wagon as they continued along a causeway caused him to feel that he was at sea in a boat. Not that he had even seen the sea!

"These are the levels," said Abel, "otherwise known as Romney Marsh. It's a wild place at times – I like it though. Not too many people, not too much interference from law or government, except for revenuers and dragoons, who ain't all fools, and plenty of wide open space. C'mon, Hoss, we're almost home."

They turned onto a cart track, heading east. There were many sheep grazing across the marsh. Jack saw rising land ahead and thought that he detected smoke there among the trees.

"Shippenden," said Abel with some satisfaction. "We made good time."

The farm came into view – a large, solid house, tall chimneys rising from either end of the gables. An array of outbuildings lined a sloping yard, beyond which stood a substantial barn and a pair of low cottages. Several horses grazed contentedly in a tree-lined paddock.

Barking dogs and a small flock of geese with outstretched wings and necks announced the wagon's arrival. Two men appeared from the barn, and, simultaneously, a woman and girl from the house, all converging on the wagon as it came to a halt in the yard.

As Jack and Abel jumped down from the wagon seat, they were surrounded by people and dogs. One of the men gave a peremptory order to the latter who instantly fell silent. Abel clasped both the females to his chest, hugging them fiercely and kissing them. Jack had time to note that both the woman and the girl were darkly beautiful. Black-haired, black-eyed and with attractive olive skin, they were similarly dressed in simple blue dresses and pinafores.

When Jack looked at the girl, something happened to both his brain and his stomach. A hollow ache rose up into his chest and throat, while, for a moment, all rational thought left his head. Her happy, laughing face, all red lips, gleaming teeth and sparkling eyes, had an instant fascination for him.

"We did not expect you until tonight," said the older version of the lovely duo.

"We made good time, thankfully," Abe replied. He turned to the two men. "How are things with you, boys?"

"Very good, Abe," replied the taller of the two. They were both leathery with outdoor living – stout boots and leggings with cord trousers belted around lean waists. Both carried sheathed knives at the hip. "We finished that bit o' thatching and cleared that dyke. Everythin' is shipshape."

Abel looked at Jack. "This is Mr Jack Dawkins, former master criminal, now trainee farmer and general dogsbody."

They all laughed at this, with the exception of the girl, and Jack, who coloured angrily but said nothing.

"Jack, this is my wife, Yvonne and daughter, Lysette. Both to be treated with respect at all times, understand?" He looked at him fiercely. "And these two fine gentlemen are Charles 'the first' and Charles 'the second', so called to distinguish one from the other, when they are bein' talked about behind their backs. Funny thing is, it's always Charles the second who loses his head round 'ere."

They all laughed again at this, including Jack, whose knowledge of history was scant and who did not understand the little joke.

"Take care of the wagon, boys," Abel said, linking arms with his wife and daughter and steering them towards the house. "Come on, Jack, let's go in."

Jack eyed the trio as he trudged behind them – Yvonne almost as tall as Abe, with dark, curly hair tumbling around plump shoulders and Lysette, a smaller version of her mother. The girl looked back at him, giving a brief but dazzling, friendly smile. The effect was devastating; he fell into those great dark eyes and continued falling in a warm void for about a thousand years. He blinked and gave a grimace that was meant to be a smile in return. They entered the house, the Garnetts' oblivious to the inner turmoil afflicting Jack.

Abel, Yvonne and Lysette chattered continuously during the ensuing meal. Jack felt distinctly at a loss; keeping his eyes on his plate and eating mechanically, he suddenly realised that Abel was talking to him. "Jack, you dreamin', boy?"

"I expect the boy is homesick," Yvonne said with some compassion.

"Ain't got no 'ome," Jack replied sullenly, feeling sorry for himself in a childish way. "No 'ome, no money, no nothin'. It was all stole from me. I lost everythin' an' got thrown into Newgate for no good reason." He realised that all three were looking at him.

"Come off it, Jack," said Abel, "you know as well as I do that you ran with a gang of thieves and murderers and got everythin' you deserved. If it weren't for Brownlow, you'd be on your way to Botany Bay by now. Lucky you weren't 'ung, if you ask me. Look around you, lad. This is better than anything you deserve."

Jack did look around, seeing the homely furnishings, the walls hung with mementoes of a military life – a sabre, a tattered flag, pistols and a musket, even a map behind glass. He looked the length of the dining table and the appetising food upon it, then dared a glance at Lysette.

"Reckon I did fall on me feet at that," he said finally, lifting his glass. He began to feel grubby, unkempt and generally shabby among these people.

"Lysette," said Abel as they finished their meal, "take Jack and show him the farm. I want to talk to your mother."

Lysette rose gracefully from her chair. "Come, Jack, I will show you." Her accent only added to her considerable charm.

Jack stood up a little less gracefully; in fact he almost overturned his chair. They went together to the door. As they passed through into the fresh air, he heard Yvonne speak: "Any news, Abe? You are not out tonight are you?"

"No, nothing yet," was the gruff reply. "We must wait for a change…" The door closed on the words. Jack wondered, as he caught up with Lysette, what sort of change Abel was waiting for.

"Oh Jack," said Lysette, a little excitedly, "I am so glad that you are 'ere, I 'ave no one of my age to be friends with. The village is far away—it is so lonely." The charm of her looks and her accent once again overcame Jack's senses and he was only able to grin dumbly at her in reply.

They strolled together towards the paddock, Jack struggled against an overwhelming urge to reach out and touch the girl's tumbling black hair. As it was, he was almost in physical contact with her as they walked. He could smell the sweet cleanliness of her. Aware that he was not exactly giving off a similar odour, he widened the gap between them. Here was a new set of emotions for him to deal with, just another of many that had assaulted his senses in the last few days. He had never cared how anyone viewed his physical presence before, but, all of a sudden, it was important. And him looking and smelling like a vagabond.

They reached the paddock fence as the wintry midday sun disappeared behind clouds. They sat side by side on the railings. A young colt lifted its head from grazing and ambled over to them through the damp grass. Lysette stretched out her hand to stroke the horse's velvet muzzle.

"Where do you come from?" Jack finally managed to break his silence.

"From France of course."

"Er, how old are you, Lysette?" Jack spoke her name for the first time.

"I am fifteen years, 'ow old are you, Jack?"

"'Bout the same," mumbled Jack.

"What do you mean, about the same?"

"I'm sixteen in October," he lied. "October fourth."

"Well you are older than me by two month," Lysette said, smiling at him, "but you are small for your age, are you not?"

"You'd be small if you'd led the life that I 'ave," Jack said indignantly, "livin' from 'and to mouth. Nobody to look after you, no ma or pa to feed and clothe yer."

"If you 'ave no mama or papa, how do you know when you were born?" Lysette enquired.

"I know all right," said Jack. "October fifth's my birthday."

"You said October fourth, before," laughed Lysette.

"So what?" Jack jumped down from the fence. "'Oo cares? I don't. Don't get on the wrong side o' me or you'll regret it, see."

"Oh, Jack, don't get angry." Lysette jumped lightly to the ground. Her dress, billowing out, appeared to make her actually float down.

"Come, I will show you the pigs; let's be friends." She laid her hand on his arm.

"Just watch out, that's all, I've done things, see, I ain't no yokel."

"Jack, you are funny! Come on."

She ran, almost skipped, towards a row of pig-pens. Jack sauntered, independently behind.

"Anyway, I can't work it out," said Jack as he scratched the back of a large sow, "I didn't think Abel could 'ave bin married so long. You're nearly sixteen. He can't be more than thirty. It don't add up. I know my sums."

He had obviously touched on a sore point.

"My papa is twenty-eight years," Lysette coloured a little. "But you are right, e' is not my real papa. My real papa is dead...he was killed."

She looked away from him. The sow lowered itself into the muddy straw with a contented grunt, and Jack wiped his hands together. "But Yvonne, she is your mother, that's plain to see."

"She is my mama and she is thirty-two, if you must know." Lysette looked angrily at him.

"Oh, who cares 'ow old anybody is," said Jack. "I don't; it's a short life an' a merry one."

"I will tell you something, Jack," Lysette said quietly as they walked back to the farmhouse. "Papa, Abel, is a good man. He risked his life for mama and me. But you must know that he is a better friend than an enemy. He does things that I fear will lead to trouble for him, and unhappiness for us all."

"What sort of things?"

"Oh, I cannot tell you that," Lysette replied as they entered the house.

The next day, to his utter disgust, Jack was put to work clearing out a stable. Shovelling manure was not his idea of passing the time; he had never undertaken manual labour before and soon acquired blisters on both hands and began to sweat freely. Before long, he tipped a barrow of horse manure onto the dung heap and began to walk away from the job, hands thrust deep into his pockets. Charles the first stopped him in his tracks: "Mister Garnett says you gotta finish that stable today, Jack—no use you shirkin' it." His battered, not unkindly face looked down at him.

"I would much rather be out on the levels wi' the sheep meself. But I got orders to keep an eye on things round 'ere. If I can tell Mister Garnett you done good, maybe he'll let you come wi' me tomorrow; I gotta go to Romney."

Jack remained indignant at the menial task he had been allotted. "I ain't no slave, I ain't doin' it, I'm off!"

Charles sighed, his face assuming an expression of resignation as Jack started to walk away. Charles was nearly six feet tall, lean and muscular so that the open-handed blow that hit Jack on the side of his head sent him reeling. His senses swam for a moment as the world tilted crazily.

"Get back in the stable, boy an' do as you're told." Legs astride, arms akimbo, Charles stood over him.

"All right, all right, I'm goin', no need to get rough. I won't forget this in a 'urry, mark my words."

"That's the main idea, boy," Charles said in a couldn't-care-less tone.

To make Jack's humiliation worse, Lysette appeared some time later with refreshment for him. She held her nose delicately.

"Ugh, how awful the smell," she grimaced. "Is it you or the 'orses?"

"It's this place that stinks, an' all the people in it!"

I was just having the joke with you," said Lysette; "don't be so angry. All the time, you are angry."

Jack, standing at the stable door, confronted by the sort of beauty that he was totally unaccustomed to, reached out a filthy hand and, without conscious thought, touched her briefly on the breast. Lysette gave a startled cry, knocked the arm away. "Don't touch me, you dirty pig," and picking her skirts up out of the mud, she scampered away round the side of the building.

"Lysette!" Come back! I didn't mean…" But the girl was gone.

Jack worked furiously for half an hour until his embarrassed anger had abated. Then came the dread of facing the Garnetts. This grew in him until it drowned out all other feelings. If Lysette told Abel, well, he would be dead meat. Simple as that. Jack decided to get out fast.

He had no sooner made his decision when Abel Garnett walked into the stable. Although petrified, Jack managed to look guileless.

"I've to go on business to Romney," Abel said, lifting saddle and bridle from their rack. "I see you're working well. Keep it up. I should be back tomorrow."

Charles the second, a shorter version of Charles the first, came up, holding his hat and scratching his head all with the same gnarled hand. "Guv'nor, we've not only lost a couple o' hens, but somebody's 'ad the blasted cheek to cook 'em on a fire in the woods t'other side of the paddock."

Abel laughed. "Probably just some tramp passing through; let him have his fill."

"I don't know about passin' through," Charles replied. "Mick Stock over at Marle Farm told me his dog disturbed somebody in the middle o' the night afore last. He found the dog dead, strangled by all accounts and stuff missin' from an outhouse."

"Hmmh. Well keep an eye on things while I'm away. See you tomorrow." He hoisted the saddle onto his shoulder. "Don't forget to work for your keep, Jack." He headed for the paddock.

Jack breathed a sigh of relief. Either Abel had not spoken to Lysette or she had said nothing. Either way, he decided, he was out of there that night.

At the end of a long day, Yvonne called him for the evening meal. He took a perfunctory wash at the horse trough. While he was drying his arms on an old piece of cloth, he saw Lysette crossing to the house.

"Lysette, Miss, just a word, please." She stopped and looked at him thoughtfully.

"Well?"

"Miss, I'm sorry." He walked slowly toward her, brushing back his hair with one hand. "Look, I'm sorry what happened. I didn't think."

"You are not a gentleman, Jack."

"Huh, a gentleman. Me? How could I be? Don't you know where I come from? The streets of London, that's where."

"You can still be a gentleman."

"I could learn to be—for you."

She gave a tinkling laugh. "For me? You are a little boy! Have you looked in the mirror? Your ears stick out and are very dirty." Laughing again, Lysette ran into the house.

Jack kicked furiously at the bottom step before slowly mounting them and going in. Later that evening, in the attic room that had been allotted to him, he surveyed his features in a piece of mirrored glass. It was the first time he had ever taken an interest in how he looked. There were the ears sticking out from the sallow, grimy features, lank hair brushed back, almost reaching his shoulders. The pugnacious jaw and crooked nose were still there but although his eyes were narrowed and red-rimmed, they were set wide apart and looked back at himself with a sort of humorous resignation. He shrugged and turned away. "*Now's* the time, Jackie Boy," he told himself; "the big feller's away. When the women are asleep, grab some valuables and get out, fast!"

CHAPTER SIX

Young Abel Leaves Home

oung Abel Garnett's father died almost instantly when the tangle of spars and rigging fell on him from a height of forty feet. Lieutenant Holman had urgent despatches for their Lordships at the Admiralty and had been ordered to make all speed from Gibraltar to Portsmouth. A little too much sail had been crammed on as the ship plunged through heavy seas; it was an ageing frigate in need of careening.

George Garnett was happier than he had been for several months. They were bound for England where he was sure he would be able to obtain his freedom and return to his former life.

He had received one letter at Gibraltar; his dear wife Margaret was dead. The news had hit him hard but the thought of seeing his children again sustained him now. He was thinking of them as he crossed the heaving deck.

A noise like a pistol-shot above the sound of rushing wind and water caused him to look up. Although he reacted quickly, he was unable to avoid the mass of wood and canvas cordage as it crashed down.

George was buried at sea off the coast of Guernsey, HMS *Orion* arriving at Spithead half a day later than Lieutenant Holman had planned, much to his annoyance.

Elspeth, Abel and their aunts were taking their Sunday ease, having just returned from church. It was a breezy April day. Abel had worked hard for several weeks putting the property into good order. All were hoping that they would see the return of George Garnett in the near future.

As they lazed and conducted a desultory conversation, dogs began barking, announcing the arrival of a horse and rider.

"Hallo, we've a visitor," said Abel, rising and going to the window. Elspeth and the aunts rose hastily and began paying urgent attention to their hair and dress.

As Abel stepped out onto the porch, a young man dismounted from a swaybacked pony. He looked bronzed and fit. He was booted and spurred, dressed in riding breeches and thornproof coat over a dark, woollen shirt. Removing his hat he approached Abel. "Are you Mr Abel Garnett, sir?"

"I am."

"I'm Lieutenant John Tanner of His Majesty's Navy."

The young newcomer looked steadily at Abel.

"I, er, knew your father, sir."

"You'd better come in."

Abel stood aside allowing Lieutenant Tanner to go before him into the house.

"Allow me to relieve you of your hat."

Elspeth, Aunts Rose, Betty and Ann crowded into the hall.

Introductions were made all round and the press of people eased themselves into the more expansive area of the sitting room, while Ann and Betty disappeared into the kitchen, returning after a brief absence with glasses and a jug of fruit punch. When everyone had a glass in their hands, Abel addressed the young lieutenant.

"Do you have news of my father, sir? You say that you knew him. Did you once serve on the same ship?"

"I am sorry to have to tell you that George Garnett, your father and—" the officer glanced at the three aunts seated in a row "—your brother, ladies, has been killed in a shipboard accident. I'm extremely sorry to have to bring you these sad tidings, and there was no easy way of telling you."

Betty and Ann began to cry quietly; Abel and Elspeth sat in stunned silence, Elspeth gradually bringing her hands up to cover her face.

"What happened?" asked Abel at length.

John Tanner related the details of the tragedy.

"I was not far away from your father when the accident happened," he concluded. "I shouted a warning but it was too late. Nothing could be done."

"How came the spar to break?" asked Abel quietly.

"It was necessary to make a fast passage from Gibraltar and the Captain—that is Lieutenant Holman—had crammed on as much as he thought the ship could carry. It was his first command, you know."

Abel's jaw muscles clenched and his eyes glittered as he spoke.

"I see, so it was expedient to endanger lives? Do you realise, sir, that when my father was so dishonourably pressed into the navy, the shock caused the premature death of my mother and now, through reckless haste, you have killed my father?" He stood up suddenly. "No doubt your captain was trying to make a name for himself."

"Look here," protested the lieutenant, "I'm very sorry for what has happened. I'm sure that Lieutenant Holman was only trying to do his duty. You know, I only came to bring you the news personally because I felt that it would be better than a brief missive from their lordships. I got to know your father a little on the *Orion* and he was a good man." He rose to his feet: "I feel now that I've done my duty. I will be on my way." The two hostile young men faced one another.

"Lieutenant Tanner," Elspeth spoke up; "I'm sure that my brother did not mean to cause you offence. Naturally we are distressed at the news you bring us."

"Yes," Aunt Rose joined in, "Abel is upset as are we all but please don't think us inhospitable. You must stay for dinner. Do you live in the area?

Tanner and Abel's expressions both eased and they resumed their seats.

"No," said the young lieutenant. "I come from Harrogate. I am to return to duty in a few days. It does not give me sufficient time to visit my family."

"What do you intend to do with yourself?" asked Abel.

"Oh I thought I would just laze around whilst I can and generally take my ease."

"Look," said Abel, "we are not wealthy, but we have homely comforts; why don't you stay with us for a couple of days? I'm sorry if I was sharp with you, but I'm sure you understand. Perhaps you could tell us more about father's life aboard the ship."

John Tanner grinned disarmingly. "I do understand, sir, believe me I do. I accept your kind invitation to dinner for I must confess I am starved. As for staying, well it is a kind offer. I will think about it if I may."

"Of course," said Abel, "but stay if you can; we will all be glad, won't we, ladies?" His sweeping glance took in his aunts and sister. All assented. "Yes indeed, Oh yes, you must stay."

That evening, after dinner, Abel, Elspeth and Lieutenant Tanner rode together, crossing a meadow towards the setting sun which shone weakly through wisps of cloud. All three were troubled in their own way. Abel felt guilty that he was not grieving more for his father. The truth was he suddenly realised he had felt for some time that he would never see his father again. Emotionally drained, he was aware of a growing anger at the injustices of life, most of which seemed to be caused by government and those in authority, landowners and sea captains.

Elspeth was simply grieving. She felt that one more shock would finish her. She would lose her mind completely. There was also concern about her brother. He seemed to be hardening his nature as he grew older. Several times recently he had lost his temper over minor matters on the farm and was becoming generally surly.

John Tanner felt that he could have made an effort to travel north to visit his parents, brothers and sisters, however, brief the stay would have been. He might not have another opportunity for years.

Glancing at Elspeth, his heart lurched a little, she looked pale and wan certainly, but somehow this made her seem all the more attractive. She was quite a beauty. Elspeth felt his eyes upon her but continued to look determinedly ahead as she rode on.

Abel's voice suddenly intruded upon the other two's thoughts.

"I'll race you to that tree!"

He indicated a lone oak set near the edge of the field and spurred his horse into action.

"What me—race you on this nag?" John shouted, but kicked his heels into the horse's flanks. It broke into a reluctant jog.

"Come on!" Elspeth laughed some of the tension out of herself, her horse pursuing Abel's. Although, when he reached the oak tree, now budding into leaf, Abel was only yards ahead of the other two, he contrived to throw himself from the saddle, sprawl on the ground and thrust a straw into his mouth in the pretence of taking his ease as the other two horses dashed up.

"Come on, what was the delay?" Abel was laughing himself now.

"Not fair, Abe," Elspeth said, her face flushed and hair a little awry. "You took us by surprise."

"Ha, beat you and the Royal Navy," grinned Abel, giving John a wink. The gloom was lifted and they sat under the tree in the twilight chatting happily, revealing to each other some of their hopes and dreams for the future.

"I'd like to take you up on that offer of staying, if I may," said John, as they remounted to ride back to the farmhouse.

"Of course. Glad to have you," Abel assented. "What d'you say, sis?"

"You are most welcome," Elspeth smiled. Her heart lifted a little. Perhaps all would be well from now on.

Lieutenant John Tanner stayed for three days and without any conscious effort became friends with Abel and fell in love with Elspeth. He pitched in with some of the farm work, helping with the animals, thoroughly enjoying himself. In no time at all, it seemed to him, he was saying his farewells. "I'm glad that we have become friends, Abel, I do not want to offend you, but I would like very much to write to Elspeth while I'm away. I hope you have no objection."

"I've no objection, John," said Abel, "you are a gentleman, that's plain. Welcome here any time. Have you spoken to sis?"

"I've been putting it off. I will ask her in the morning before I leave."

"Good luck," grinned Abel.

Elspeth had a warm response for John when he spoke to her. The dimpled cheeks and the manner in which her nose wrinkled as she smiled up at him addled his brain for a moment.

"You must write and tell me of your adventures, John, and I will write and bore you with stories of haymaking and cleaning the stable yard!"

"You could never bore me, Elspeth. I will look forward to hearing from you constantly, and I will come back to see you. You may count on that."

In the ensuing months there were three long letters for Elspeth, with footnotes for Abel. In October, the news of the triumph and death of Nelson at Trafalgar filtered down the rutted lane to them.

John's letters enhanced feelings that Abel had been aware were growing in him, since his father had died – restlessness and a sense of dissatisfaction with his life. John was out in the world having adventures, even suffering hardship and danger. He was tinkering with a small farmstead and every day was deadly dull. "Almost eighteen years old with a past best forgotten and no future," he told himself bitterly.

Elspeth noticed his moodiness and spoke to Rose. "Oh, don't be anxious, my dear," the good aunt soothed. "Abel's grown to manhood and wants to spread his wings and fly the coop. It's only natural."

"Do you mean he wants to leave us?" Elspeth could not imagine life without her brother.

"Of course, dear. But not forever. He wants to see something of the world and the people in it. Most men worth their salt are like that. But I know Abe. He won't leave until your future is assured."

"But if he wants to go, he must go. I shall tell him," Elspeth said firmly.

"No darling, leave it for the moment. There is time enough yet."

The days slid one into another. All the dramas in the Garnett family seemed to have played themselves out. Abel and Elspeth settled into the rhythm of their lives, growing, maturing, living.

Suddenly John was back with them – tanned, fit and confident. He had seen action at sea and survived unscathed. He brought with him stories of storm-torn ships and decks running with blood, of English victories and defeats.

Events moved rapidly again, for Lieutenant Tanner was a young man in a hurry. He had two months before joining a newly commissioned ship at Chatham.

On the day after his arrival, John spoke manfully to Abel. He wanted to marry Elspeth. Abel expressed his delight and the two of them engaged in much handshaking and backslapping as they strolled to the village inn for a celebratory drink.

After two days, Elspeth and John, accompanied by Aunt Rose, were being rattled north to meet John's family at Harrogate.

Abel made easy swings of the scythe through the long meadow grass, aware of a small knot of excitement in the pit of his stomach. He stopped work for a moment, leaning on the haft of the scythe, gazing unseeing across the undulating fields to distant woods. He would soon be free of all responsibility, with Elspeth married. His aunts were quite able to take care of themselves; they had a modest annuity and young Sam could keep things in order around the farm. He would be free! Abel swung the scythe again enthusiastically – tumbling grass, clover, buttercups and poppies in luxuriant heaps; skylarks uttering their unending song rose higher and higher into the heavens, their happy animation reflecting his own.

Within three weeks, Abel was squeezing his large frame into a formal suit on the morning of Elspeth and John's wedding day. Elspeth looked entrancing in her pink and white Queen Anne wedding gown, whilst John contrived and succeeded in looking manly and resplendent in his full-dress naval officer's uniform.

Aunts Betty and Anne cried continually throughout the proceedings – to the church, at the church and home from the church – but it was only when the happy couple left for their honeymoon in the hired carriage that Aunt Rose could be seen touching a lace handkerchief to her eyes.

Abel stood at the forefront of the group of well-wishers as they cheered the young couple on their way, waving until a bend in the lane took them out of sight. Elspeth and John had the best part of two weeks before they had to be at Chatham where John was to report for duty. He intended to rent a property of some description so that Elspeth could make a home for them there.

Six more weeks passed before Abel felt that it was time to broach the subject of his own future to his aunts. He was by then burning to get away. He was nineteen years old, full of youthful vigour and the spirit of adventure.

"I have arranged with neighbour Mottram to keep a general eye on things. You have your annuity and Sam will take care of the pigs, poultry and vegetables. I have tried to think of everything," he told them, unable to keep a guilty tone from his voice. "Mr Denton, father's old solicitor, has ensured that if anything happens to me, you will be able to—to live out your days here. I must say, darling aunts, I was tempted to sneak off in the night and leave you a letter, but I could not bring myself to do it." He smiled weakly.

"Look here, Abe," Aunt Rose said in her usual brisk manner, "you have nothing to feel guilty about. You go off, boy, see the world; every young man needs to test himself. Just come back safe and write to us when you can. What are your plans, exactly?"

"Well nothing could tempt me into the navy after what

happened to father, but I thought I might go into the army. I think I would be a good soldier."

"Do you think that's wise, Abe?" asked Rose doubtfully as her two sisters began to expel tears again. "You have seen little of the real world. I am afraid that you will find the dregs of humanity in the ranks of the army and you do not have the money or position in life to purchase a commission."

"Oh, there must be many a good man in the army, aunt; we have the best in the world."

"We also have the best navy," retorted Aunt Rose, "but you have heard what John has said about the baseness, not only of the seamen, but of some of the officers also."

"Not all, though, aunt, not all."

"Well, I am sure you will do whatever you want, but just make sure that you come back to us." She embraced him and her two wet-cheeked sisters did likewise.

"I will come back, aunts, I will."

On a wind-swept autumn morning, Abel did what many another young man had done. He walked quickly away from his home, down the muddy lane, carrying his few personal possessions, heading out into the world.

Outside of the gates of Chichester Barracks, where he had lingered several times before, Abel stood, hesitating, watching soldiers at drill. The approach of a pair of immaculately dressed officers spurred him into movement and he hurried away, feeling like a cowardly fool. "I shall go to Horsham," he told himself. "Look at the old home. I need time yet before I decide anything further."

He had thirty pounds in bank notes concealed in a pouch. In addition, there were a few sovereigns and some small change in his pockets. He felt quite wealthy.

Abel Garnett took passage on the coach to Horsham. The roads were in quite a dreadful condition after the heavy summer traffic making it an uncomfortable journey. Of the three other inside passengers, there were an obviously married couple who conducted a non-stop argument in hoarse whispers, and a sombrely dressed, middle-aged man who captured Abel's attention and kept it throughout the long ride, intoning that England was doomed, Napoleon was on the point of invading, the country was going bankrupt, the weather was foul and he himself was not expected to live another nine months. There were times when Abel felt like leaping from the rocking, swaying coach. It was a relief when he reached his destination.

Descending from the vehicle, Abel walked quickly into the hotel lobby closely followed by his dour travelling companion and the argumentative couple. "Papa would not stand for you treating me so," the woman complained.

"All I'm saying," said the husband coldly, "is you cannot make a silk purse out of a sow's ear."

"Oh," his wife exclaimed, "how dare you!"

"I tell you, young man, the country's finished," the man in black droned in his ear. "It will be many a long year before…"

"Abel—Abel Garnett," another, louder voice intruded. Abel looked round the crowded lobby of the hotel until he spotted the owner of the voice. It was Hampton, the auctioneer that he had watched at work so many times in his childhood.

"Abel, I thought I recognised those shoulders." The bluff, hearty fellow excused himself through the throng and shook Abel's hand vigorously.

"Mr Hampton, sir, it is good to see you—er, excuse me, sir," he said, to the doleful pest at his elbow, "met a friend, must go."

"It is good to see you as well, young Abel. How are you? Come, let us go to the lounge and have a drink, get out of this crowd."

Hampton steered him to a quieter room where they were able to secure seats and order refreshments.

"Have you come from Chichester?" the auctioneer unbuttoned his waistcoat to allow his portly figure to expand as he sat.

"Yes, I've left Chichester for a while to take a look at the world."

"Well, you have already seen this part, haven't you?"

Abel coloured in youthful embarrassment. "I'm undecided what to do. I thought of the army."

"Capital idea," exclaimed Hampton, "50th Foot, top regiment, sir, could do a lot worse." Beads of sweat were forming on the auctioneer's brow. They were seated not five feet from a huge log fire. A pot-boy approached with large brandies working his way through the busy room.

"Aha," said Hampton cheerily, "your health, sir." He took a large mouthful of the golden spirit. "Did you have a good journey?"

"It was not so much the journey as the company," laughed Abel.

"Yes, it's a shame we cannot choose our fellow passengers on a journey."

"Look here, Abel, you must come and stay with us for a day or two until you've a better idea what to do. Only the missis and me at home now, you know, the rest have flown the coop."

"That's very generous of you, Mr Hampton. I would like that," said Abel with sincerity.

"Come on then, let's go, shall we? You must be weary."

They lifted their glasses in unison and drained them.

"By the by," said Hampton as they made their way through the streets of Horsham towards his house, "do you remember that rascally shepherd of yours? He made off with your horse. Remember? About the time of your mother's death."

"Yes I remember that scoundrel all right, Jacob Pierce. What about him?"

"Well, I had business in Maidstone, oh about last Michaelmas it was, and he was the talk of the town. This fellow Pierce went to work for some farmer down Ashford way. A hard man by all accounts, who abuses both men and dogs. This bully-boy takes horse to town one day leaving his sick wife abed, but on the way the horse goes lame and he is obliged to return to the farm. He actually finds Pierce half way up the staircase in his house. Assuming the villain is intent on theft, he drags him down the stairs, kicks him out of doors and proceeds to give him a thrashing. Pierce breaks down completely and starts gibbering like a madman." He paused for a moment, pointing across the road to a substantial property. "Here we are, this is my place." They crossed and entered through the garden gate. Taking a key, Hampton let them through the door into a rather impressively furnished hall.

"What happened to Pierce?" Abel asked, his curiosity quite aroused.

"Just a moment—Agnes," the auctioneer called up the stairs. "My wife must be visiting a neighbour—come through."

They entered a very comfortable drawing room, having divested themselves of their coats and hats, Abel leaving his one piece of luggage in the hall.

"Have a seat, Abel—want a drink?"

"Just a small one, thank you."

Hampton poured rather generous measures of brandy. "As I was saying, this farmer is giving Pierce a good thrashing when he starts gibbering, 'She must die! She must die!' And then goes on about not having had a gift for years, or some such rot. Suddenly he turns upon the farmer and, despite the fact that he's as strong as an ox, this shepherd brings him to the ground and starts to strangle him. Fortunately, some farm-hands come up and after a great tussle they overpower him and lock him in a stout shed or barn or some such. Pierce goes completely crazy. His terrible screams and cries can be heard for miles, I'm told."

"What the devil happened to the man," asked Abel, "to send him insane like that?"

"Well, he was eventually shackled and taken off," said Hampton, taking another swallow of brandy. "He's in a lunatic asylum at Maidstone. Enquiries were made and he may have been responsible for several murders in various parts of the country."

"My God," breathed Abel.

"Yes, and those that he probably killed were his employers, although there's no real proof. One thing's for sure, he's as mad as a March hare and won't see daylight again. You and your people may have had a narrow escape."

Abel spent two pleasant days with the hospitable auctioneer and his wife. On the second evening, he voiced his plans to them. "Elspeth and her new husband will be settled in at their home in Chatham by now, I think. So I shall visit them before making a final decision as to what to do next."

"You should go by way of the Pilgrim's Road," said Hampton, "an ancient highway that will take you virtually all the way to the Medway. I can let you have a horse, very reasonable, throw in a saddle, etc."

"You are too kind."

"Nonsense, my boy, knew y' father. Good man."

And that was how, the following morning, Abel found himself with a good horse under him, well provisioned and with a hanger at his waist. A gift from the ever-generous Hamptons, this short, curved sword made Abel feel ready for anything. He had his father's pistol in his baggage, having decided against carrying that on his person. This was rather contradictory as it happened, for he was an excellent shot but the only blades he had ever handled were scythes and brishing hooks.

He had scarcely ever felt fitter. Full of a sense of well-being, dressed in warm clothing, the horse responsive to heel and rein.

Abel was riding north-east to connect with the Pilgrim's Road. "It is," he had been told, "a glorious ride along the Downs, or in the shadow of them."

Great white clouds sailed majestically above, casting huge shadows on the ground, a blustery wind enlivened trees and grasses, the weak, egg yellow sun shone intermittently.

Abel suddenly laughed out loud, touched his heels to the horse's flanks, causing it to break into a gallop, much to the alarm of an elderly yokel who was driving a flock of geese toward Horsham.

The geese scattered in panic at the approach of horse and rider. The rustic bent picked up a clod of earth and threw it inaccurately at Abel's rapidly retreating back. Abel laughed again and eased the horse to a canter. "Hey ho for the open road!"

CHAPTER SEVEN

The Artful Dodger Meets Jacob Pierce for the First Time and the Second Time

ack Dawkins put his resolve into action. He would depart from Shippenden, get as far away from Lysette, Abel Garnett, Charley the first and ruddy Charles the second as well; get clear away from all of them and all that work they were intent on handing him.

He would take what valuables he could lay his hands on and use them to fund his return to London or perhaps pay for a passage abroad. Jack's mind was buzzing with ideas. He already visualised himself leaning over a ship's rail waving farewell to all his tormentors, including the "stuck-up" Lysette. Lysette! He had never loved a girl, never loved anyone, in fact, but something was happening, had happened to him with that sweet-looking, dark-eyed, French-accented charmer.

His only sexual experiences had been gropings and fondlings with poor, sad, street creatures. It was obvious though that Lysette despised him and he had already put himself beyond the pale with her. Yes, get out, that was the answer.

The Dodger had lain fully clothed on his bed until the time was ripe. He looked out of the tiny window set in the gable of the roof. There was not much of a moon, but it was a dry night after a showery day. As far as he could see across the bleak marshes, there was no sign of human habitation – not a glim of man-made light.

Boots in one hand and duffel bag in the other, Jack soft-footed his way down the dark, narrow stairs to the main first floor landing, nothing of value here and he had no intention of disturbing the sleeping females. It was a piece of luck that the man himself, Abel Garnett, was away for the night.

Down to the ground floor in almost total darkness, he groped his way to the kitchen. Putting his boots on the table, he risked lighting a candle from the still-glowing embers in the stove.

Some decent cutlery and silver cruets went into his bag. In the sitting room he bagged some fine knickknacks from the sideboard and then – glory! – in a small drawer a little tin box containing several sovereigns and half-sovereigns. Well satisfied with his find, Jack crept back to the kitchen, put on his boots and extinguished the candle. Out he went into the night, heart pounding slightly, a little warm around the neck and brow.

His heart was in his mouth when the two dogs padded almost silently up to him, but they only demanded petting.

Jack decided not to leave by way of the lane, but to cut across the marshes. He would, he thought, bisect one of the many cart tracks or causeways eventually.

For the time being he wanted to avoid human contact. Crossing the paddock, he ducked under a fence and entered the meadow beyond. Following the line of the dyke that edged one side of the field, he headed for the little bridge that he knew lay just ahead. Jack already imagined himself as part of the heaving mass of London humanity again.

He was in the narrow thoroughfares of Seven Dials, the dome of St Paul's in the near distance. Ah, the shouts and cries, the oaths and laughter, living on his wits with his pals!

The Artful Dodger was a shadow, flitting through the meadow grass, duffel bag on his shoulder. The night air cooled his brow and the breeze whispered encouragement.

He thought of morning in the farmhouse. Lysette and Yvonne rising, preparing breakfast, calling and calling him, of Abel returning and learning that the Dodger had disappeared with cash and valuables. His rage would be terrible to behold!

Lysette would be in tears, Yvonne giving vent in fractured English.

Picturing the scene did not amuse Jack somehow. In fact, he felt distinctly uneasy. He slackened his pace, looked back at the now distant farmhouse. Wait! Was that a movement, someone back there? He stopped for a moment, looked again. Nothing.

He turned and continued forward, crossing the little wooden bridge. As Jack reached the far side, his blood froze in his veins; he was in almost complete darkness, the moon covered by a cloud. A black, human shape rose up from the sword like reeds that grew in the dyke, heaved itself onto the bank and reached out a long, dark arm to grasp at Jack's shoulder.

Giving a strangled cry, he just avoided the hand by a quick twist of his body.

In the darkness, Jack could not make out any features of the tall figure that now threw itself at him.

The Dodger dropped the bag, turned and tried to run, but something very powerful grabbed at him and threw him onto the wet grass. "Get away, get away!" Jack cried out in a strange, shrill voice, kicking and pummelling at the figure in sheer terror.

He was thrown onto his back with ruthless force and a filthy, bearded face bent close to his, foul, stinking breath expelled from a snarling maw of a mouth.

Hands were scrabbling at Jack's throat as he tried to thrust the heavy body away. Fingers tightened round his neck; Jack's one free hand was into the pocket where he had his clasp knife. *Must get it out, open it, get it out!* His other hand was grasping at the wrists that were pushing at his jaw.

He couldn't breathe, could not breathe! The knife was out of his pocket, but his strength was gone, "I'm dyin', dyin'. Oh God!" He gave up, falling into a complete nothingness. One last faint flickering sensation, a voice calling his name and the pressure at his throat was gone, but then so was he.

Jack's senses returned slowly. He rasped air into his starving lungs. Sweat was pouring down his face as he struggled back to full consciousness.

He rolled over onto his stomach, choking. The first attempt to stand up failed; the second was more successful. Standing half bent-over, hands on his knees, Jack continued to gulp air into his tortured lungs.

Fear returned to his brain along with the oxygen. He started his legs moving; he wanted to be safe away from this place, quickly.

It was then that Jack fell headlong across the body of Charles the second. For a moment, he thought that it was a hillock of earth, but as he put out a hand to save himself, his palm pressed against the dead man's face.

This new horror sent him reeling away with a sob. He sprawled yet again in the wet grass.

Hugging the ground closely, Jack scanned his surroundings as best he could in the dim moonlight – no signs of life anywhere as far as he could tell. The reeds in the dyke moved and rustled gently in the breeze.

He calmed himself a little, crawling over to Charles' body. The dead man's eyes were wide open, staring horribly up at the heavens. There was a tremendous gash in the throat, the upper body soaked in blood that gleamed blackly on the man's clothing.

Jack had seen a few dead bodies in his short life, but they had been mostly unfortunates who had expired on the streets of London or in some dilapidated garret. He had never seen the results of bloody murder before.

He recoiled from it, then his brain began to work again. The Artful Dodger thought fast. He scouted around quickly for the bag. It had gone and with it everything that he had stolen. There was nothing else for it; he must return to the farm. He had nothing for his journey and he might even be held responsible for murder if he tried to escape now; besides who knew what was waiting for him out on that marsh.

Jack shivered, wiping his face on the sleeve of his coat. He suddenly realised how raw his throat felt. He put up a hand and touched the bruised and tender skin. If he wanted to speak right now, it would be almost impossible. If he crept back to his bed, how could he explain his condition in the morning?

The Dodger made his way stealthily back to the farm, jumping nervously at every rustle of leaf and whisper of wind. The worst moments were passing under the shadowy trees that edged the paddock. Feeling cold and clammy with fear, he arrived at last at the farmhouse door.

Stealing his nerve, Jack began to hammer as loudly as possible on the unyielding panels; at the same time he cried out as best he could, a horrible gargling screech of a noise.

"Who is that? Who is out there?"

Yvonne flung open a first floor window.

"It's me, Jack! Help, please!" Those strangled tones, almost lost in the cacophony of barking dogs that the noise had aroused, brought Charles the first running from his lodging just as the farmhouse door opened, revealing Yvonne and Lysette in coats hastily flung over night attire.

"Murder, bloody murder," Jack whispered hoarsely. "Out there, it's Charles; 'e's dead, stone dead."

"What?" Charles the first grabbed his collar, as the two women gasped in horror.

Jack half sat, half sprawled on the step, "I'm nearly murdered meself, I've 'ad it." He slumped down completely.

The three of them bent over him. "Take care of him, ladies, I'm going to check out there, see what's happened," Charles said, loping off in the general direction in which Jack had pointed.

"Charles, be careful," Yvonne called after him. "Come on Lysette, we must get Jack inside."

Together they half-carried, half-dragged him to a sofa in the drawing room. Lysette hurried to the kitchen and returned with some water in the first receptacle that came to hand, which happened to be a pewter pot. Cradling Jack's head in one hand, she lifted it to his lips. Looking up at her, aware of her closeness, Jack sipped gratefully, the pot deceiving him into thinking that his throat would be soothed by ale. Nevertheless, the water was wonderfully cool. "Thank you."

Yvonne was there. "What happened, Jack, can you speak now?"

Jack, who was feeling better by the second, looked soulfully up at her. "Yes'm, I'll try."

He looked meaningfully at Lysette, "I had something on my mind last night, couldn't sleep. I came down to get a drink and 'eard a noise in the kitchen. I was just in time to see someone go outside. 'E 'ad a bag in 'is 'and. 'E ran across the yard, very fast, so I ran after 'im."

"You should have got some help, at once, Jack," Yvonne said.

"I didn't think, I just ran after him."

"You were brave, but foolish," breathed Lysette, squeezing his hand, to his immense satisfaction.

"Well we got to the bridge at the far side o' the field. I was catchin' up when he suddenly turns on me. I fought 'ard as I could, but 'e were strong, strong as—as a lion. I thought I was dead. When I come round, I found Charles dead. 'E must a' tried to 'elp me. I came back as fast as I could."

"You brave boy." Yvonne kissed his cheek while Lysette rubbed his hand. "Have some more water, Jack."

Charles the first came into the room. "I've brought his body 'ome, e's dead all right, just like the boy said. No sign of anybody out there. No sense in doing anything now. I can't leave you ladies alone here. Abe should be back come morning.

Jack actually felt sharp pangs of guilt. "Poor Charles, 'e tried to 'elp me, now 'e's dead. It's my fault. All my fault." He suddenly felt low, bruised and weary.

"Hush, Jack," Lysette said soothingly, "rest now, try to sleep, we will talk tomorrow."

He did sleep, and dreamt. He was lying in long grass in the black night, while a huge dark figure loomed over him, lifted him up by his lapels.

"Jack, wake up, come on, wake up!" It was Abel Garnett shaking him roughly. Daylight revealed his scowling features. Jack swung his feet onto the floor. "What's up?"

"What's up? I'll give you what's up. One of my men dead, valuables gone, stolen and my wife and daughter half out of their wits, you little rogue."

Jack twisted away from him and stood up. "It's not my fault, I tried to stop 'im.

"You tried nothin'! Do you think I was born yesterday? I'll tell you what happened, you little liar. You decided to clear out, ransacked the place and left."

"No, no, I didn't." Jack looked around for support, but there was no sign of Yvonne or Lysette.

"Yes, yes," Abel snarled sarcastically. "You cleared out, only you met somebody on the marsh who was too much for you. Charles was watching for 'im. Had been watching for him these last few nights. He knew somebody—or somethin'—was out there. Now he's dead and you're here, you deceitful little…"

Jack was defiant. "Well what'd you expect? I ain't no farm 'and. I bin pushed from pillar to post these last few days, I just wanted to go 'ome to London. Any'ow, 'ow did you guess?"

"I didn't guess; not much to work out either. There's no sign of a break-in and I locked up myself. No barking dogs. They wouldn't let strangers near the place without bringin' the 'ouse down and your personal duds are gone from your room."

Jack groaned. "What's goin' to 'appen now?"

"Well first, Charles has gone to Romney. The death must be reported. That will bring officialdom and dragoons here. I've got my own bunch coming too; they'll be here soon. The whole levels will have to be searched for this murdering scum.

"Next, once we've got that job done, I'm takin' you to the magistrate, 'anding you over. You ain't worth the trouble. I'll write and tell Brownlow that his good deed has bin wasted. That's it, just stay out of my way till then, don't try and leave either or I'll hunt you down like a dog, got it?"

"But I'll go to prison, be transported. Don't do it, Mr Garnett!"

You should have thought o' that," Abel said grimly.

"I won't do it again, Abe. Look I've been wrong, I know that, but give us a chance, please."

"You've 'ad your chances. That's the end of it. I think my lads are coming; I got work to do." He stalked from the room, swinging his broad shoulders through the door.

Jack trailed behind him, feeling sick. There were twelve to fifteen men coming up the lane and a rough, ready for anything crew they were. Charles the first – well, no need for that title now, Jack thought grimly, Charles was among the group of men leading his horse.

They swarmed into the yard, making a great noise, boots on gravel, chattering voices. They were silenced by Abel's uplifted hand.

"Thanks for coming, boys. Charlie will have told you what's up. Now we've to find this maniac before he kills somebody else. It's not safe on the marsh with him out there. And 'e's attracting the attention of those we don't want."

Several of the men agreed with this. "Aye, you're right there, Abe."

"What do we do if we catch 'im?" one tough looking character asked loudly.

"Give 'im some of this!" exclaimed another, raising a naked sword aloft.

"Or this," shouted another, waving a long-barrelled pistol.

"Let's catch him first, then we'll see," said Abe. "Are you ready, men?"

They all raised various weapons in the air, ranging from staves to blunderbusses.

"Let's go!"

"Riders coming, Abe," Charles called, as the men started to leave the yard. Jack, who had viewed events from the sidelines, heard and saw a dozen dragoons clatter up. They reined in, in all their magnificence, to the shouted commands of an officer, who dismounted stiffly and marched up to Abel, one hand clutching the hilt of his sword. "What is this gathering, sir?"

"Why, these are volunteers, come to help search for the killer on the marsh," Abel replied coolly.

"I see; well I must say they will be most useful. There is a large enough area to cover. They must, however, come under my orders, understand?"

The officer turned to his men. "Dismount, we will rest the horses for a moment. Easy, men. Sergeant Black, take charge of these civilians; they will aid us in the hunt." He turned back to Abel. "Lieutenant Martins," he said, offering his hand, "I must say those fellows of yours look ready for anything."

"Just locals," replied Abel, briefly shaking the proffered hand. "It's as well to be prepared if you're hunting for a lunatic murderer."

"You're right," agreed Martins. "If it is who we think it is, the man certainly is a lunatic."

"Do you know who it is then?"

"We believe it to be an escapee from the asylum at Maidstone. One Jacob Pierce. Been incarcerated ten years or more, made a daring escape. Completely mad though."

"Jacob Pierce? Jacob Pierce? I think I knew him." Abel was quite taken aback.

"Knew him?"

"Aye, years ago. He worked for my father, always a bit odd, never did us real harm, but stole a horse and disappeared. I did hear that he'd gone insane."

"A strange coincidence—shall we move then?" the officer queried.

"Can I come? I can help." Jack approached the two men.

"This is the boy, sir, who nearly died along o' Charles Foster," Abel told the lieutenant.

"I see; well you had a very lucky escape, young fellow," said Martins who was all of twenty himself.

"Stay here," ordered Abel. "Stay on the farm. Remember what I told you. Any more trouble and you'll regret it." He turned abruptly away.

"I say," said the lieutenant; "that's a bit hard, after what he's been through."

"Private business. Shall we go?" Abel asked.

"All right men," called the officer; "mount up, we shall search the country, thoroughly mind, by sections. Spread out as best you can. You civilians always keep a dragoon in sight. If we put up anyone, we shall ride him down." He sprang lightly into the saddle of his own mount; Abel did likewise, bending forward to release the reins from a fence post.

Lysette and Yvonne appeared on the step, standing next to Jack. As the body of men moved off, Abel turned to give them a wave. "Stay close to the house," he called. "I'll be back tonight." He whistled up the dogs who sprang up from where they lay, quivering with anticipation, and obediently fell in behind him.

The three of them watched as the disparate group of men spread out across the water meadows, heading for the distant woods and marshes under a lowering sky that threatened rain.

"Abel told me that you are not to enter the house, Jack. He is angry and, I think, disappointed with you." Yvonne looked at him, her face a mixture of sorrow and pity.

"Jack, you are a great fool." Lysette expressed her disdain.

"Lysette! Jack has not had the opportunities. He has much to learn about life." Yvonne rebuffed her daughter.

"But will he ever learn it, mother?" Lysette turned and flounced into the house.

"Feed the animals, Jack, and I will bring something to the barn for you later." Yvonne followed Lysette, leaving Jack to walk disconsolately to the barn.

Jacob Pierce rose from his hiding place in the pigsty. He had concealed himself in the wretched, stinking construction after he had murdered Charles, slipping into the sty while the dogs were preoccupied with Jack waking the household. He was filthy with the ordure of the animals, emaciated and bearded, half-starved and suffering from the effects of his long exposure to the elements. His deranged mind, however, took no account of his physical condition. A light brighter than the sun burned within him; nothing but death would appease his all-consuming desire to murder and murder again.

With what impatience he had waited for the men to depart from the farm. Pierce had instantly divined what would happen within seconds of his cutting Charles the second's throat, leaving, as he'd thought, the dead boy and his would-be saviour in the fields.

Men would come to the farm; they would go onto the marshes and search for him. Perhaps they would leave a man to guard the women, but what was one man to him? And if they searched the farm? Well, he would be buried under the rotting straw in the sty. His mind worked very well when it came to survival.

There was no search of the farm buildings and as far as he could see, nobody left to guard – just the women entering the house and a boy going into the barn. Jacob felt all-powerful as he walked swiftly across the yard to the farmhouse; the clasp knife that Jack had dropped the previous night was gripped firmly in his right hand.

Abel had instructed two men to watch both the farm and its approaches from beyond the first bend in the sunken lane. Both were armed with pistols and were to fire a shot if they sighted their quarry.

Unfortunately the two paid scant attention to the farm itself but occupied themselves surveying the surrounding country. Neither of them saw the tall bedraggled figure of Pierce cross the farmyard.

Jack Dawkins did see, however, from where he lay sulking in the hayloft. He was appalled at the sight of the madman crossing to the house.

Without bidden thought, Jack reacted. In a moment, he had descended the ladder to the floor of the barn. His hand encountering the handle of a pitchfork protruding from a hay bale, he snatched at it on the run, emerging from the barn going at full pelt. "Lysette! Yvonne! Watch out!"

His shouts caused Pierce to turn as he was about to open the kitchen door. At the same moment, Lysette popped her head out of an upstairs window and the two watchmen, alerted by Jack's shouts, stood and looked towards the farm.

Pierce, seeing the tines of the pitchfork advancing rapidly

towards him, shot through the door and pushed the bolt home. Jack's brain, working on automatic, heard the noise of the bolt; he swerved, continuing to run hard along the side of the house, making for the front door.

In the house, Lysette had just glimpsed Pierce with Jack running towards him, pitchfork in hand. "Mother!" she called out in alarm.

Yvonne was at the foot of the stairs. Hearing her daughter cry out, she ran up them, fearing an accident of some description. Jack came through the front door like a thunderbolt as Pierce opened the door connecting the kitchen with the hall.

The pitchfork that Jack extended towards him caused the deranged man to hesitate just long enough to allow Jack to begin to mount the stairs. Lysette and Yvonne were on the landing. "Lock yourselves in, quick!" Jack gasped the words – he was out of breath and sweating freely. The two, mother and daughter, clutched at one another for comfort at the fearful sight of Jacob Pierce standing at the foot of their stairs.

Jack turned, lunging hard in a downward thrust towards Pierce's glaring eyes. The killer made a grab at the pitchfork but one of the prongs pierced his palm. He emitted a dreadful screech, and, throwing up his other hand, he wrenched at the haft of the fork. Jack hung on for grim death but was thrown bodily against the banister rail. The madman gave him a terrifying look, though scarcely any of his features were visible among his matted hair and beard. "Ye're dead, boy! Dead!"

"Come on y' bastard! Come on!" Jack thrust again with the pitchfork.

"Jack, Jack—quick into the bedroom!" Lysette called to him.

There was the sound of pounding feet in the yard. Pierce gave one last tremendous heave at the pitchfork, causing Jack to lose his footing completely and fall down the stairs, but his attacker was already heading for the kitchen.

The two guards heard him crash through it as they came through the front door. Sprawled on the floor at the foot of the stairs, Jack breathlessly caught their attention. "Quick, get after him—the kitchen!" he gulped. They sprang over his body and arrived in the kitchen in time to see Pierce, his long coat streaming out like a cape, disappearing round the side of the barn. Two pistols flashed and banged simultaneously, splinters of wood flying from the edge of the barn, then Pierce was out of sight.

Yvonne and Lysette rapidly descended the stairs as Jack picked himself up.

"By God!" he said, thankfully finding himself in one piece and brushing his hair from his eyes. He grinned at the two women. "You all right?"

"Yes, Jack, we are, thanks to you." Yvonne smiled at him. "You were very brave, thank you."

Lysette took hold of his hand. "So brave, Jack, you saved us from that monster."

The Artful Dodger, flushed already from his actions, coloured even more. He bent and picked up the pitchfork. "Me and my trusty sword!"

Abel's two guards returned, disappointed at their quarry's escape, one of them already tamping down a fresh charge in his pistol.

"He got clean away. I'd better get after the search party, although those shots may 'ave been 'eard. Barney, you stay 'ere—keep that pistol primed now."

The other nodded: "Don't you worry 'bout that, Joe. We're going to secure this 'ouse 'ginst all attack." He smiled broadly all round.

Jack had half an hour to reflect upon his actions before Abel returned with his companions. For the life of him he could not remember how he had come to do what he had. "I'm a bloomin' 'ero! Well they say there's a first time for everythin'!"

Abel strode into the house after knocking the dirt from his boots, Lysette and Yvonne clinging to him as they poured out the details of the incident, with Jack emerging very well from their telling of it.

Smoking a clay pipe to help relieve the tension within him, the big man came to where the young hero sat in the kitchen.

"Well, Jack, looks like you've earned yourself a reprieve. Maybe there's hope for you yet." Abel's bluff, genial face smiled down at him. He stuck out a huge hand. Jack grasped it warmly, grinning in embarrassment.

CHAPTER EIGHT

Abel Garnett Meets Hetty and Solly for the First and Last Time

bel Garnett was unable to prevent a wry grin as he left Jack. He thought of his own first close encounter with an assailant years ago. No wonder Jack looked a little shaken; he had suffered two close calls in eight hours.

It was years before that Abel had ridden away from Horsham and the hospitable auctioneer. He was heading for the Pilgrim's Road and Chatham, where he would visit his newly-wed sister and her husband.

The horse was allowed to make its own pace along the byways of the Sussex-Surrey border, coming into Kent in the early afternoon where he sought refreshment at an isolated inn. It was a poor place with shingles missing from the roof. A creaking sign declared it to be the Roebuck. Weeds grew around the open door beside which stood a handcart loaded with assorted pots and pans, tin kettles and platters half concealed by a canvas sheet.

Abel entered through a low doorway and seated himself at a roughly hewn table.

In the dim light, he discerned two very scruffy individuals seated at a similar table a few feet from him – a man and a woman. She was awesomely large, flesh straining at her tattered dress which was hoisted up to reveal a pair of scuffed lace-up boots. The man was short and desperately thin, wearing filthy moleskin trousers and a shirt very short of buttons. They both removed clay pipes from their mouths before turning to gape at him.

These were the great unwashed, all right; matted hair, pug noses and the worst sets of blackened, gappy teeth that he had ever seen – at least that was until he saw the landlords.

'Mine host' came fawning towards him, rubbing his hands and giving a frightful smile. "Good day to you, sir, what is your pleasure? I have victuals, sir, best Kentish ale, or," he lowered his voice and pushed his pockmarked face close to Abel's, "there is a young lady, sir, private room, very clean, very sweet." He leered, breathing stale alcohol and tobacco fumes over Abel.

"Just bring me some stout and bread and cheese, if you please, and be quick about it," said Abel, his embarrassment causing him to speak sharply. His sexual experience was virtually nil, but the thought of what the innkeeper was offering made him feel distinctly warm and he could not prevent the stirring of his loins.

He drank deeply from the pewter mug that the innkeeper put before him. The bread was surprisingly fresh and crusty, the cheese rich in flavour – better than expected.

The two dilapidated characters nearby turned to speak to him: "Good day to you, sir," they chorused, "Good day."

"Are you travellin' far?" —this from the puny man.

"Chatham."

"Then thir," lisped the man, "might we be permitted to travel with you under the protection of your thord?" He eyed the short sword at Abel's hip.

Abel laughed. "I don't think I could give you much protection with this. I've never used it."

"But you have a pithtol?"

"In my baggage, yes—I can use that."

"The Pilgrimth Road can be dangerouth for lone travellerth, thir," the beggarly character said, the whites of his eyes showing bright in his dirty face.

"We only go to Malling, may we go part way with you? Itth

not tho much for my thake, but my dear wife." He glanced at his ample companion.

"I'm that afraid for my safety, sir, that I am hardly able to walk the road," said the lady, her chins jiggling as she spoke, "and you can see my man; well, how can he defend me?"

"I would do my betht, Hetty," said the spouse, indignantly.

"Of course, of course, Solly my dear." She patted his skeletal hand with her plump one. "But look at this strong, young fellow—what an aid he would be in our hour of need! Shall you travel with us, sir?"

Abel sighed. "Look, I will come a little way with you, if you wish. I am sure there is no danger. No harm will come to you, as you will see after an hour or two on the road."

"Oh, thank you, sir!" cried Hetty. "God bless you, sir."

"God bleth, indeed," said the man fervently.

Abel chewed his bread and cheese, resigned to their company for the time being.

"Was everything to sir's liking?" The landlord was hovering, Abel's plate still half-full, his stout half-consumed.

"Hmmh," said Abe, "it suits." He withdrew his purse from within his coat pocket. "Is this what you're waitin' for?" He threw some coins on the begrimed tabletop. Three pairs of eyes burned into his purse as he replaced it in the pocket.

Abel pushed back his chair and stood. "I'm for the road now, thank you." The pair who had latched onto him shambled to their feet.

"We'm comin', thir, we'm comin'."

They followed him out into the clean, fresh air. The sun was glinting through the variegated green foliage that dressed the trees lining the way east on the Pilgrim's Road.

Abel's horse had quenched its thirst at the trough. He fed it a handful of oats before mounting. Hetty wedged herself between the shafts of the handcart and, passing the attached strap over her shoulders, she heaved the cart into motion, pulling like any ox, her gaunt-cheeked husband taking up position by her side.

"Hetty can pull thith cart all day," he said proudly as they moved slowly away.

"'Tis nothin' to me, Solly," said the woman as she plodded resolutely past a duck pond by the side of the lane. A milestone indicated Rochester to be eighteen miles distant.

"This is the Pilgrim's Way?" asked Abel.

"That it ith, thir," said Solly through broken teeth. "Nigh all the way to Canterbury on thith an tother way to Winchethter and beyond."

"Do you live by selling these pots and pans you carry?"

"Well, thir," said Solly, pushing damp hair from Hetty's forehead and patting her cheek, "we repair ath well and general clean-like big 'outh kitchenth. We are going to Malling for work there. Ain't we, Hetty?"

Hetty nodded as the cart rolled along behind her, wheels grating on the gravelly surface.

They were travelling on high ground, enjoying wonderful views of the English countryside to the South, Abel walking his horse as patiently as he could. After almost an hour, during which they met no one except for two amiable woodcutters, he was smarting to be off and rid of his travelling companions.

They entered a wooded section of the road which was becoming more like a cart track. They had only passed one pair of cottages, but in the valley Abel had noticed several farms and hamlets.

"Look," said Abel, "I'm sure you will be safe now. There are people in the valley below. I must make more speed. I doubt we have come three mile as yet."

"Would you just see us through the woods, sir. I'm mortal feart," said Hetty, her jowls quivering and tiny eyes opening and closing rapidly.

"Only half a mile, thir," Solly pleaded.

"Oh, very well then."

They rolled slowly onward and soon Abel could see open country ahead. "Look, we are clear now," said Abel, "there is no danger."

Hetty allowed the cart to grind to a halt.

"I must go into the woodth," said Solly, jigging about in a ridiculous manner. "Pleath thtay a moment."

Abel fumed a little. "All right, all right, be quick." He stepped down from his horse, which immediately began grazing at the verge. Hetty removed the straps from her shoulders, allowing the hafts of the cart to fall to the ground. "I have a drink in the cart, want some?"

"No thank you," said Abel, turning to the horse to adjust the saddlebags.

Whether the horse moved a little, pulling Abel to one side, or whether Hetty's aim was off, Abel never knew, but the knotted cudgel she swung at the back of his head with her mighty arm missed his crown but tore the scalp and lacerated his right ear.

Abel shouted out in pain and shock, causing the horse to rear, pulling Abel's legs from under him. He slid bodily beneath the animal's belly, front hooves crashed down, narrowly missing him. Bending awkwardly, Hetty took another swipe at his head, the cudgel connecting painfully with his shoulder. She began to shout out in a continuous shrill, "Solly! Solly! Solly!"

The diminutive Solly reappeared through the trees, scrambling up the sloping ground. Abel caught a glimpse of his legs and an arm carrying a short length of timber. With blood running into his eyes, Abel tried to rise on the far side of the horse to face his new attacker. Hetty, bending down, pushed at him violently with the end of her cudgel, sending him sprawling, his sword tangled between his legs. He managed to get a hand to the hilt and dragged the weapon from its sheath, staggering to his feet. Solly hesitated at the sight of naked steel. There was an almighty whack across Abel's shoulders just as he lunged at the hapless Solly, the blow giving sufficient impetus to the sword for it to penetrate Solly's shoulder.

"God! I'm hurt, Oh God! The blood!" Solly collapsed immediately. Abel whirled round; becoming enraged, he dodged yet another furious blow from Hetty. Pain was now springing from the various parts of his body that Hetty's cudgel had made contact with, blood was running down face and neck. As Hetty squealed and came at him again, he lost all patience and lashed out with a large closed fist, launching a massive punch straight at the woman's pug nose so that it was almost obliterated upon contact. Hetty, silent at last, stood for a moment, then tottered forward like an overstuffed pocket of hops; then she lay still, blood pouring from what was left of her nose.

Abel limped over to the distraught Solly, sword in hand. "Don't kill me, thir! Don't kill me! Ith Hetty dead? Oh, I'm hurt bad, I'm bleedin'!"

"That woman is not dead, you coward, more's the pity, she's just knocked out. Why did you attempt this wickedness?"

"Ith Hetty, thir, thee will do it and that Bolton, itth him ath well."

"Bolton? Who's Bolton?"

"The landlord, thir, at the Roebuck," Solly lisped on pathetically. "If any thuthpithion fauth on uth he givth an alibi for a thare of the take."

Hetty gave a groan and began to heave her bulk upright. Abel had no compunction in putting his boot on her, forcing her to sprawl back on the ground. "Be still, or I'll cut you," he growled, brandishing his sword.

The horse had cantered some way down the track and was now peacefully grazing. Abel's head ached, although the bleeding had slowed to a trickle. Various other aches and pains now started at him, the result of blows received from Hetty. A bruised thigh reminded him that the horse had kicked him as it made off.

Abel whistled up the mount which trotted obediently to him, reins dangling. "Right." He grasped the hilt of his weapon firmly, swinging the blade menacingly at Hetty. "You get up."

Hetty groaned, rolled over and struggled to her feet. Her face was bloody and a tremendous swelling was beginning under her right eye. "You pig!" she screamed at Abel, her features distorted.

"Shut up and get between those shafts," he indicated the hand cart and encouraged her to move with his sword-point.

Hetty picked up the cart with a grunt, pots and pans rattling merrily. As Solly snivelled and fussed over his slight wound,

Abel took cord from the back of the cart and tied Hetty's wrists to the shafts, ignoring her spitting and swearing.

"I'll kill you for this, you bastard, let me free or you're dead." Blood ran from her nose and dripped from her several chins.

"Don't leave me, I'm bleedin'," Solly groaned.

"I'm not leaving you," said Abe. "I'm taking both of you to justice." He sheathed his sword and found his father's pistol in the saddlebags. He primed it carefully before mounting his patient animal.

"Get behind that cart, you coward." He pointed the pistol at Solly.

"Kill 'im, Solly, kill 'im!" Hetty squealed, struggling to free herself.

"If you don't keep quiet, I'll gag you," said the determined Abel. Searching for a suitable epithet, he settled for "You hellcat."

Realising his head wound was still seeping blood, he bound a kerchief round the wound and covered his damaged ear.

"Don't hand uth in thir," begged Solly, "we'll hang for thure."

"What, let you roam loose to rob and murder? I can't do that," said Abel. "Let's get moving. I've had enough of you two. Don't forget I've got this pistol on you. I'm a good shot, too."

Despite his aches and pains, Abel was beginning to enjoy the situation. He had survived an adventure and was now well in control. Very satisfying.

"March!" he ordered.

Solly set off, moaning and groaning his lisping, limping way along the track, Hetty, heaving heroically at the cart. Abel brought up the rear, pistol in hand, in the saddle of his high-stepping mount.

Before long they came to a junction. A steep, grassy track descended the hillside to the valley where smoking chimneys and a church could be seen.

"Downhill," snapped Abel. He looped a rope over the rear struts of the cart, holding it taut to assist Hetty in controlling the load on the sharp incline. The battered procession went down through the trees, emerging into meadowland, through which the track wound towards a collection of dwellings.

A blacksmith was the first to see them. He stood in leather apron, hands on hips, watching as they approached.

"What's amiss?" he called.

Abel released the rope from his saddle and the cart ground to a halt. The tired Hetty, unable to hold it level, fell to her knees, allowing the shafts to rest on the ground, tinware jangling.

"Stand still, Solly. I've my eye on you."

Abel dismounted in front of the Smith. "Have you a magistrate here? These villains tried to rob and murder me."

"Did they by heaven?" exclaimed the blacksmith, tipping back his sooty cap. "You got the best o' them, sir, well done!"

"By God's grace, I did," said Abel, "but I'm fortunate not to be laying dead on the Pilgrim's Road, my brains bashed out."

The smith indicated the unfortunate Solly, "'E don't look very dangerous, sir, begging your pardon, sir."

"It's not him—it's her!" Abel felt a little uncomfortable, pointing at the figure of Hetty.

"Well, well, I never heard such a thing! In all my life, I never did, sir. Did you give her that face?"

Abel flushed. "I'm afraid I did. She kept coming at me with a cudgel. A great club."

The smith laughed. "And you blacked her eye?"

"That's right, then that fellow rushed out of the woods when I was struggling with the woman, and well, he got my sword point in the shoulder. A pin-prick really, but he's not up to much, and, well, here we are."

"Bless me, wait till I tell the missis."

"But is there anyone I can hand these two—two creatures on to?"

"Well, there's no magistrate, that's for sure, not 'ere, but we do 'ave watchmen. They could take care o' things for ye."

"There's more," said Abel. "The innkeeper at an inn—the Roebuck. He's in with them. He gives them an alibi for a share of the proceedings.

101

"What, John Bolton?"

"Yes, Bolton's the name, all right."

"Well, everyone 'ereabouts knows 'im to be a rogue, sir. Look, you're a bit the worse the wear yourself. My missis, God bless her, will clean your wound, I'll send my boy for the watch—I've a stout shed here. We can lock this sorry pair in there."

"That's very kind of you." Abel was suddenly stiff and tired. His head was hurting and he felt a little sick. "I'm Abel Garnett from Chichester."

"My name is Thomas Smith," the blacksmith smiled ruefully, "I'm named what I am."

Abel freed Hetty's wrists from the cart and stepped warily back from her. "Get into that shed."

"You won't shoot." Hetty was scornful as she advanced, formidable in her determination. But the blacksmith was there. He sprang forward and wrenched one of the woman's arms up her back, propelling her rapidly through the shed door. Abel managed to put a boot up Solly's backside to help him through as well. Then Tom Smith slammed the heavy doors on the pair. "That's the way to treat 'em." He grinned, snapping a huge lock onto a hasp.

Hetty threw herself at the door, screaming abuse.

"Come on, sir, let's go to the house. We ain't got much but you're welcome to it. Don't worry about them—they won't break outa that shed, I built 'er meself." The door juddered again at the impact of Hetty's body as she charged at it.

After securing Abel's horse, they entered into the low ceilinged cottage adjoining the smithy. Abe sat on a wooden chair. The place was clean and furnished entirely with home-made furniture. Abel's carpenter's eye looked approvingly at it. There was a strong smell of charcoal and smoke about the room.

Tom Smith opened a window onto the rear garden. Abel could see a boy digging.

"Bobby, come quick, boy, now!"

A few seconds later, a boy of about twelve appeared in the doorway, heavy mud clinging to his boots. "Yes, pa?"

"Son, you must go for the watch. We got desprit criminals locked in the shed."

The boy gaped at Abel.

"Not this gennelman, Bob, 'e's the one what captured 'em. Go quick now!"

"Yes, Pa." The boy disappeared at speed, giving an excited backward glance.

A plain but kindly looking woman came through the front door. "What's goin' on, Tom?" She was alarmed. "I just seen the boy runnin' like an 'are. I was comin' from Joanie's, you know 'er time is due. Who's this gentleman?"

"Don't be anxious, Liz," the smith reassured his wife; "this here gentleman 'as bin attacked, but 'e's got the villains. We 'ave 'em now in the cart-shed. Bobby's gone for the watch. Can you take care of Mr Garnett 'ere? 'E's bin knocked about a bit."

"You poor man, what an ordeal for you, and you captured them single-'anded? Mercy!"

She removed the matted handkerchief from round his head. Abel winced at the last tug which started the blood trickling again.

"It's a nasty gash and awful bruising, sir, but no real 'arm done," said Liz, bringing a pan of water and a towel. "I'm always patchin' Tom with 'is burns 'n' cuts 'n' bruises." She smiled.

Abe sat back in the chair as the good woman bathed his wound and wiped his face.

"You're the kindest people; I'm most grateful."

"'Tis nothin', sir, only doin' the Good Lord's biddin'," she said, matter-of-factly.

Tom came forward carrying a steaming mug.

"I got some o' that soup o' your'n Liz. Mayhap ye could do wi' somethin' inside you, sir?"

Abel cursed himself inwardly for a childish fool as unbidden tears sprang to his eyes at their kindness. He wiped his recently cleaned face on his sleeve as the two looked at him with some concern. "I'm sorry—" he began.

"Nothin' to be sorry for, sir," said Liz, holding up her hand.

"We're never too old to weep, and you ain't so old anyways, no shame in it."

The front door burst open and Bobby flew in. "They're comin', Pa! The watch is comin!" Mr Dawes, Mr Sykes an' Mr Cheesley!" The boy was breathless with excitement.

"All right, son. Well done." Tom ruffled his son's hair with a gnarled hand.

"Can I watch, Pa? Can I watch them murderers taken away?"

"You can watch from the wind-er, boy, but keep outta the way."

"Thanks, Pa." Bobby scrambled into the window seat.

The members of the watch approached, three sturdy countrymen marching with steady tread. One was armed with a blunderbuss, rather ancient; the next carried a long-barrelled horse pistol, the third an enormously long and unwieldy pike, an archaic instrument of war. All three looked quite solemn and braced for battle.

Thomas Smith and Abel went out to meet them. A chill wind had begun to blow as the weakening sun descended below the horizon.

The blacksmith related Abel's account to the worthy members of the watch. All three of them took Abel's hand in turn, shaking it vigorously. Beefy faces wreathed in smiles. "Congratulations, sir, such valour; you are quite the young hero. A great public service."

Abel flushed modestly. "It's just a woman, gentlemen, and a cowardly husband. Mind you, I would not like to fall in with them again." He felt his wounded head tenderly. "That woman is a great monster."

They all laughed.

"It seems remarkably quiet in that shed now, Tom," said Mr Dawes.

"Aye, but beware when I open the door, I see you have manacles with 'ee—you may need them for 'er.

Tom unlocked the door. "You in there," Dawes called out, "you are under arrest. Do not attempt to resist. We are all armed and it will be the worse for you if you do, come on out!"

The five men grouped themselves warily a few feet from the shed door. Despite their readiness, they were all startled when it was suddenly thrown open, revealing Hetty in all her glory – huge frame, battered face and filthy gown. She stood, hands on hips, eyeing them grimly: "Come on then, you 'eroes, take me in."

Solly crept out from behind his wife's broad back.

"Don't thoot, don't thoot, I'm comin'."

"Look at 'im!" said Hetty. "What a man!" She gave him such a thump on the back as he passed that he almost fell flat on his face.

"I should a' tied the knot wi' someone like you," Hetty cried, looking at Abel through her one good eye, the other now bein' completely closed as the result of his punch.

Abel could not help but feel a little pity for the two as the watchmen moved in and quickly manacled ankles and wrists.

"Stop whimperin' man, you ain't 'ung yet," Hetty said to her husband as they began to shuffle off; "An' what about me cart and goods an' such?"

"Your goods will be impounded, madam," said Mr Cheesley, shouldering the pike. "You will go to Maidstone for trial. This gentleman"—he indicated Abel—"will give evidence against you. You will no doubt be reunited with your accomplice, Bolton of the Roebuck. In the unlikely event of you being found innocent, your possessions will be returned. However, I have no doubt that you will *hang*."

It was a slow procession through the village street. Workmen returning from the fields collected in groups and a buzz of excited conversation swept through the community.

Mr Dawes brought the party to a halt by the church. "The only suitable prison we have is in the church vestry. It is iron-barred from roof to floor with a strong gate. There can be no escape. I recommend that you take the opportunity while in the Lord's House to pray for your souls."

Mr Cheesley leant towards Abel: "Sooner them than me," he uttered in a loud whisper. "It's fearful dark in there, no window, no light and who knows what prowls there in the night." He shuddered.

Abel stepped in front of Hetty and Solly before they were led away. He was feeling distinctly sorry for them. "Have you any relations that I can inform?"

"We got nobbut each other, that wants to know anyway." Hetty looked more closely at him. "Why I see now you're scarcely more than a boy. Strong though, very strong." She lifted her manacled hands to her battered face.

"I'm sorry I hit you so hard, Hetty."

"Don't be sorry, boy. Wi' a bit o' luck on my side you'd be stone dead by now. Me aim was off. First time though, first time."

"You heard that, boys!" Cheesley exclaimed to the others. "That's a confession plain as day. Mr Dawes, Mr Sykes, take these felons to the cell. I will return with Mr Garnett to Tom's, if that's all right with you, Tom, and get a written statement from him."

The last Abel was to see of the two was as they shuffled awkwardly in their chains towards the church door along a yew-lined path.

In the kindly blacksmith's cottage, Abel made out a statement of the events to the satisfaction of Mr Cheesley.

"The evidence is slim against Bolton, but he will be taken. They are bound to condemn each other from out of their own mouths—those types usually do. You will be required to give evidence I should think. May I ask where you are bound?"

"Well, initially to visit my sister and her husband at Chatham. Then I'm not sure."

"Capital!" said Cheesley. "Chatham is but a few miles from Maidstone where the trial will take place. If you can give me an address, I'll ensure that you are notified when you are required to attend." He rose and proffered his hand, which Abel shook. "I will leave you to the tender mercies of these good people, Mr Garnett. Good evening to you." He went out into the gathering darkness.

Candles were lit in the cottage and mugs and platters brought forth by the Smiths, Bobby stirring the fire and building it up into a friendly blaze.

Abel began to feel hemmed in and uncomfortable among the little family. "Is there an inn? I cannot impose upon you further."

"You're quite welcome to stay if you wish, sir," said Tom.

"No, no, I must be on my way."

"There is an inn, sir, t'other end o' the village, quite clean, and good beer." Tom grinned.

"Well, I'll be off then." Abel pressed a half-sovereign into the blacksmith's hand, closing it over the coin for him, despite his protests. Bobby took a shilling with alacrity, beaming up at his benefactor. "Thank you Mrs Smith, thank you all for everything."

Abel walked his horse through the village, halting for a moment by the church, trying to imagine his two assailants in the complete darkness of their cell. He shuddered a little and moved on towards the lights of the inn.

That night, seated by the window of his room, Abel composed a letter to his aunts describing his adventures. He skated delicately over his capture of the two footpads, not wishing to alarm them.

The guttering candle threw enigmatic shadows onto the walls of the room. Abel felt suddenly desperately lonely— isolated in the hostelry, looking out onto the dark, unknown country, no one ahead of him but his sister and no one behind except his aunts. He was on the brink of scrapping the letter and setting off immediately for Chichester, but something else stirred inside him. He felt that he had been tested that day and not found wanting; the world was waiting for him – he would travel in it, overcome difficulties and make something of himself.

The next time he saw his aunts, he wanted to arrive as a rich, successful man. He pictured himself stepping down from his own carriage, dressed in fineries and his delighted aunts rushing out to meet him.

Abel cleared his throat, took up his pen and finished the letter.

Coming down into Chatham, Abel observed the masts and spars of many ships on the river below, and, upon entering the town, soon encountered some of the crews of those ships in the streets. It was early evening but already there were drunken figures reeling about.

The centre of the town seemed to consist mainly of low taverns through the doors of which there was a constant flow of customers.

As he rode his tired mount cautiously down the middle of a crowded thoroughfare, one drunken miscreant, waving a bottle, grabbed hold of his stirrup. "'Ave a drink on me, man, 'ave a drink on me." He thrust the bottle upwards, cheap spirits flying everywhere. Abel prodded the flanks of his horse with his heels and rode free.

He soon came to a quieter area and enquired from a respectable looking passer-by the whereabouts of the street that Elspeth and John lived in.

He was directed to a mean, narrow lane with a central gutter, running with watery mire. Several small, emaciated children, dirt-encrusted and half-naked, played on the cobblestones in the gathering gloom.

Abel felt distinctly out of place as he dismounted before the house he was looking for. A single-barred window let into the wall beside a low doorway which opened abruptly, and then Elspeth was hugging him and laughing.

"Abe, it is so good to see you. I had no idea you were coming. Everything is in such a mess! John! It's Abe come to see us!"

John came out of the house pulling a naval uniform jacket on over his shirt. "Well, well! Hello Abe. This is fine! Come in!"

Abel felt a mixture of love and pity for the two as he tethered the horse to the barred window and ducked through the doorway into their little home. They appeared poverty-stricken and vulnerable in those cheap surroundings.

"I was not certain that I would see you, John. I thought you might be out on some ocean, fighting the French."

"Not yet, old chap, not yet," laughed John. "We expect to be gone in two or three weeks, though." He glanced quickly at Elspeth.

"Oh, bother that," she said with a laugh that had a catch in it; "let's go into the parlour—I'll get some refreshments."

"Er, the horse—will it be all right in the street?" Abel was hesitant.

"It'll be fine till you've taken tea," said John. "We can see it well enough through the window."

Abel looked about the room. A small, smoky fire burnt in the grate. The furnishings were sparse and cheap and although the parlour was clean, it lacked any sense of comfort.

"Sit down, Abel, while I get tea," said Elspeth, "and don't dare tell John any news until I return!"

John and Abel grinned at one another as they heard Elspeth clattering about in the kitchen.

Abel leant toward John. "Forgive me, but how come you to be living in these poor circumstances?" he whispered.

John was made uncomfortable by the direct question; and leant, in his turn, toward Abel.

"I've lost father's allowance, or rather he is unable to provide for me—bankrupt I'm afraid. It's the war; he lost his continental trade. A junior lieutenant's pay is worse than useless, and I spent rather—er freely before the wedding. Sorry, Abe."

"What are you two whispering about?" Elspeth came in carrying a tray.

"I was just telling Abel what a wonderful wife you are," said John.

"And I was telling him how I couldn't believe it," laughed Abel.

"You two, you both talk nonsense. Try some of my cake. My cookery is much improved, Abel."

"It could hardly have got worse!" And you must be richer than I think, drinking tea!"

"It's probably smuggled, I'm afraid," said John.

"The town is full of smuggled goods that can be had at very reasonable prices."

"Well, thanks be to the smugglers," said Abe, raising his cup to his lips.

He related to his sister and her husband his adventures since the urge to put farm life behind him had impelled him out into the world. Elspeth gasped when she heard that their sinister shepherd, Jake Pierce, was now in a lunatic asylum.

Abel's encounter with Hetty and Solly, the incompetent footpads, brought more exclamations of alarm from Elspeth and admiration from John. "Splendid! Well done, Abe!"

"You will have to put up with me for a while. I have to go to Maidstone for the trial, whenever that may be."

"Well, that's good," said John. "That means Elspeth will have company while I am in the dockyard all day."

John directed Abel to stables where he lodged his horse. Returning to the little dwelling on foot, he had extensive views of the twisting river snaking its way past the town. The water glittered under the reflected lights cast by many lanterns displayed by ships at anchor. From all corners of the town there were sounds of people – shouts, cries, whistles and raucous laughter, the noise of a drum being beaten, and above that the thin piping of a military bugle offering a staccato series of notes, which Abel was dimly aware were played at the end of the day in encampments.

The evocative sights and sounds made him pause and consider the other towns, rivers, seas, islands and vast, unknown countries in the world, the strange people that lived in them, the mystery of it all. He continued back to Elspeth and John in philosophical mood.

Abel had a very pleasant time with Elspeth and her eager young husband. When the simple household chores were done, brother and sister would walk at leisure in the nearby countryside or take a boat on the river. In the evenings, after their meal, they played cards together, discussed the day's events and their plans for the future.

On the ninth day of his visit, with the year being blown wetly into October, a gangly clerk of the magistrate's court appeared at the house. Hetty Mount had been killed at the Maidstone gaol. Despite having wrist and ankle chains on, due to her troublesome nature, she had contrived to loosen and remove sufficient bricks to allow her to squeeze her large frame from the cell in which she was incarcerated.

Hetty had been pursued through the building by a turnkey and forced her way out onto the roof, from which the unfortunate woman had fallen onto a spiked, iron-rail fence, impaling herself. She had died in some agony, her husband, Solly, had hanged himself the following night.

"In a nutshell," said the clerk, "you are not now required to give evidence in this case, but you have the thanks of the court, Mr Garnett."

"What of the landlord of the inn—he was said to have been involved?" asked Abel.

"Oh, I know nothing of him, sir. I do not believe anyone else was apprehended in this case."

"Perhaps he got wind of the other arrests and made good his escape."

"Perhaps so, I really couldn't say, sir."

"Thank you for your trouble," Abel told the clerk. "At least I have been spared the responsibility of helping to send those two to the gallows."

Laying in his bed at the top of the house that night, Abel gave some further thought to his future. His mouth twisted cynically. At the moment he had no future to speak of. Yes, there was the farm at Chichester, small as it was – years of endless labour as a country bumpkin; probably end up marrying some village girl. He had nearly twenty pounds, a nag and a few possessions.

Abel eyed the candlelit room. There was Elspeth to think of. She was happy with John, but when he went to sea, for what might be years, she would be left alone in this house. He made some quick decisions and slept.

Within three days he had found a vacant house with well tended garden on the outskirts of Gravesend. There were respectable neighbours and charming views over the undulating countryside and the Thames. After selling the horse and his pistol, he was able to lease the house for twelve months and press several sovereigns on the reluctant John and Elspeth.

"You will be able to live rent-free for a whole year, which should enable you to manage the next annual payment and so on. I will send you money when I can."

They protested and there were tears, but soon Abel was looking back on those scenes as a volunteer in the 50th foot and, much to his ironic amusement, was marching with a motley assortment of other new recruits towards Chichester.

CHAPTER NINE

The Artful Dodger Discovers Abel Garnett's Part-Time Occupation

ack Dawkins sat on the fence. Since his encounter with Jacob Pierce a few days previously, something of a change had come over him. For one thing, he was not used to being treated like a hero, and, after the congratulations and backslapping had died down, he still found himself included in conversations, referred to in complimentary terms and generally made to feel that he belonged.

Yvonne cut his hair, and he took a little more care with his ablutions. Thoughts of absconding receded to the back of his mind. He looked at himself in a cynical manner.

"Blimey, Jack, are you goin' soft? There's no 'ope for you, matey, at this rate. Better watch y'self or you'll spend the rest o' your life in this God forsaken 'ole."

But then there was Lysette. Thinking back to his brief scuffle with the lunatic, Pierce, Jack knew that he had acted as he did because of her. Instinctively he had tried to protect and save her.

She sat next to him in their usual place on the paddock fence. Black ringlets framed her gentle features; long-lashed green eyes looked at him.

"What are you thinking, Jack?"

"I wonder where Jacob Pierce is? He disappeared so fast. I've got a feelin' that he's not far away right now."

"Jack, they've searched everywhere very carefully. Swept the country all the way to the sea. Don't worry. He's gone away."

"I'm not so sure, Lysette. Anyway, shall we go in? It's starting to rain?"

They walked quickly to the house, running the last few yards, laughing as the heavens opened.

Wind and rain rattled the attic window, waking Jack. Disorientated for a moment, he lay there in almost complete darkness; the window was an annoyance. He slipped from the bed, bare feet on bare boards, to attempt a tighter fastening of the offending casement. Looking out over the storm-swept yard, he was startled to see a shadowy figure standing in the lee of the barn. The scene instantly obscured as scudding clouds covered the moon.

In a panic, Jack's first thought was to arm himself with some sort of weapon. A moment later though, a brief shaft of moonlight revealed the unmistakable form of Abel Garnett striding across the yard toward the figure standing in the shadows. Meeting together with a handshake, the two disappeared into the barn.

Jack had been around villains and villainry all his life and sensed something to his taste here. Middle of the night meetings had, in the past, always indicated work for the Artful Dodger.

He dressed quickly, then boots in hand, crept down to the ground floor, through the kitchen door and out into the rain. Jack pulled on the boots and flitted to the barn, coat collar up and hat pulled down.

The barn door was half-open. Cautiously, keeping low, Jack peeped in. A glowing lantern hung on a nail, casting light on two figures – Abel Garnett and a man Jack recognised as one of the group that had helped in the hunt for Pierce.

"It's not like the good ole days, Abe, when we could make a run when we pleased. Now we gotta wait for filthy weather, boat men riskin' life an' limb to get the goods ashore. Blasted dragoons, watchtowers, revenuers an' I don't know what else."

"Well, I don't remember the good old days, Harry, I wasn't around then. Nothing lasts forever, that's certain. Let's move. You go and roust out Charlie. He's to keep watch here while we're gone.

Jack flattened himself behind the barn door when Harry came out, loping towards Charles' quarters. Abel extinguished the lantern and went to the house.

Rainwater running down his neck, Jack waited until the three men met together in the yard. After a moment, Charles went towards the house and the other two set off at a fast rate down the lane. Jack kept fifty yards behind them, ready to dive into the ditch at the first sign of a backward glance.

They travelled almost half a mile to where the lane met with the causeway that crossed the wild, empty marshland to Romney and the sea. Men were waiting there at the junction. They proceeded in a group towards the town.

The rain had eased but the wind blew unhindered across the open country, stinging Jack's face. An old, familiar feeling had returned to him – a mixture of fear and excitement. There was the brassy taste in his mouth; he spat and grinned. He had tasted that before.

The road ran straight. In the darkness, Jack remained close enough to the group ahead to catch occasional glimpses of them. Further in the distance, he spotted darker shapes against a dark landscape, the town of New Romney.

The Artful Dodger began to be more aware of his surroundings; the wind, rain and darkness started to create a sense of foreboding. Reeds and grasses rustled, an occasional tree bent its branches toward him. He was suddenly convinced that someone or something was behind him. He was too petrified to look over his shoulder, but increased his pace, certain that he was about to be sprung upon. The terror grew with his speed. Panic-stricken, Jack actually croaked out, "Oh, God!"

Soon, however, he could make out gabled roofs, the church tower and the shapes of other buildings and his fear began to subside.

The men that he was following veered off the road. The wind now carried the tang of salt in it though Jack had not yet seen the sea. The closest he had been to it was the steamboat journey on the Thames. He eased to a walk.

Up ahead the gang were climbing a bank and disappearing over its rim. The ground under foot was becoming sandy in texture, tussocks of grass growing in clumps. Jack scrambled to the top of the slope, ducking down quickly when he saw the men on the beach below, staring out at the dark vastness of the spectacular sea. There must have been men down there waiting as well. There were now at least twenty of them.

Jack Dawkins' perspective of the world changed forever as he looked out, awestruck at the unending reach of water, flecked with white foam. The noise of it pounding onto the shore and receding again dominated everything, spuming and boiling, then drawing back with a great gravelly sound. The air was full of salt spray and rain hurled about by the wind.

Jack almost forgot about the men thirty yards away. He noticed though, a sudden stir of excitement among them, several pointing seawards. He strained his eyes, wiping salty water from his face. Out there! He saw them! Three lights hanging vertically in the air – appearing, disappearing, appearing once again.

The men began to move. Three went down the beach to Jack's left and three to his right, disappearing into the all-enveloping darkness.

To Jack's horror, another man started to climb the dune straight toward the spot where he lay. He hugged the ground behind a large tussock of grass. It was too late to run. As he came closer, Jack, with a sick feeling in the pit of his stomach, saw that it was Abel Garnett.

Abel stopped within a few feet of where he lay, turned and faced the sea. He proceeded to open and close the shutter of a dark lantern, holding it high in the air. At every movement, a light was revealed.

Far out on the wind-tossed water came answering flashes of light. Even above the noise of wind and water, Jack heard

Abel emit a grunt of satisfaction before he descended once more to his companions on the beach.

Jack breathed a sigh of relief and moved position slightly. The sand seemed to be penetrating everywhere. He could feel its gritty presence in his boots, against his stomach and in his hair.

He could no longer spot any lights out at sea, but suddenly there was something else – the prow of a small boat rearing up over a wave, then plunging out of sight into a trough before appearing again. Oarsmen were pulling valiantly, struggling to bring the boat to shore.

Several men on the beach began to wade out through the tumbling surf. The boat reared up again, prow pointing skyward; down it went, much closer in now. Eager hands were grabbing at it, pulling it to the beach. Oars were brought on board, everyone leaving the boat as it grounded.

Jack could now see that a rope trailed from its stern, and unbelievably, a row of kegs and casks, dancing merrily, were dangling from it.

Swift activity broke out. As the rope was hauled in by some of the men, looking for all the world as though they were winning a tug o' war, others slashed at the lines securing kegs, casks and boxes, hauling them above the water line.

Jack watched fascinated by the procedures. "Mr 'igh and mighty Garnett – you 'ypocrite, why you're nothin' but a bloomin' villain yourself!" He almost laughed out loud.

The heavy rope, paid out from the distant vessel, continued to be pulled ashore. A pile of kegs and boxes grew on the beach. Finally the last of them were cut free. After much backslapping and handshaking, the boatmen leapt into their craft. Willing hands pushed them into the roaring surf, oars were unshipped and the hard pull back to a distant ship began.

A loud whistle brought the sentries at either end of the beach, running to their companions, shouldering kegs and bundles piled on the sand. The whole party moved swiftly off.

Twenty or so men leaving nothing behind except the trampled sand which would soon be cleansed by the rapidly incoming tide.

Jack slid back down the dune, then ran parallel to the direction taken by those on the beach.

Abel Garnett chivvied the men along; the tide should wash out all trace of their presence by dawn.

Harry was jubilant. "We must be livin' right, Abe, 'eavy weather, no ridin' officers, and dragoons wore out and abed after searchin' the levels for the loony."

"Aye," said Abe, "lucky for us this time all right; now let's get this lot stowed while the luck holds." He was, like Harry, carrying two small kegs slung on a rope across his shoulders.

After some hundreds of yards, a stream cut through a defile in the dunes. The party of men turned into this small gulch, and following the stream, headed out into the country. Some of the men began to laugh and talk together, several lighting up clay pipes with some difficulty in the wet and windy conditions.

For two or three hours' work and a little risk, most of them would be on the receiving end of the equivalent of a month's pay this night, plus a few luxuries. A bit of tea, a drop o' brandy. They were happy.

Out on the levels, the old hands knew the route they wanted to take; they could find their way on the blackest night. The tricky operation of crossing the dykes was accomplished by the use of broad planks of wood that were kept concealed among the reeds until needed. After crossing, the planks were removed and concealed again. There was little chance for mounted pursuers unless they were suitably equipped.

The rain stopped and the skies cleared a little as, after almost an hour, they began to climb to slightly higher ground. Here were the remains of one of the several abandoned villages on the marsh – dilapidated houses, broken walls and a stark tower; all that remained of an ancient church.

It was merely routine for the men, discarding their loads and stowing it all in the base of the tower. The entrance was then blocked, with masonry and timbers totally concealing it.

"It's home now, boys, and a couple of hours' sleep for you if you're lucky, before your working day starts. Well done. Remember, keep your mouths shut tight!"

The men drifted off into the darkness in no particular hurry. Most of them had retained small kegs or packages for their own use.

In a few minutes, the ruins of the village were deserted and silent under the lowering night sky. Moonlight fitfully played upon the eerie scene. A great slab of masonry began to move a few yards from the foot of the church tower. Grating against the stony ground, it slowly slid back under the muscular force of Jacob Pierce. He was standing on a short flight of stone steps that descended into what was left of the vicarage cellar.

Pierce had made himself at home in the remote hiding place. On his wide-ranging night jaunts, he had succeeded in stealing clothing and even a blanket or two for extra warmth. He had the means to make fire and had only occasionally gone hungry. But then he was not at all particular in what he ate.

A truly fearsome sight with tangled hair and beard, foetid breath and rank odour, his outer garment was an extremely long and tattered coat, belted at the waist. Pierce's moods swung wildly from an all-encompassing rage to times when he curled up helplessly on the floor of his hiding place and wept and moaned until he slept. He frequently had visions of his mother and sometimes called out to her softly.

Lucid thought very seldom visited his brain. He had the wit and strength to survive and the compulsion to kill the weak, the kindly and the helpless, and could bring himself to a great state of excitement and tension by imagining carrying out the murder of such a person or remembering what he could of past triumphs.

Pierce set off across the marsh. He was in hunting mode.

Jack Dawkins had struggled across the first of the dykes, sliding down the bank, landing up to his waist in cold, chest-high water, wading across and scrambling up the other side, wet through and freezing. He could hear the progress of the gang ahead and occasionally made out their figures. The long water meadow grass soaked him further and at the next dyke, he baulked at crossing and gave up.

His sense of direction was sound and he turned, following the sewer until he came to the causeway. Soon Jack was on its relatively firm surface and, within an hour, approaching the farm, filthy, wet and tired. Somewhere out on those wretched marshes, he knew that Abel and his men were stowing away a rich hoard of smuggled goods.

The trick now was to regain his room in the farmhouse without being detected by Charlie, Elspeth or Lysette. He crouched behind the barn thinking about this problem.

A faint footfall behind Jack caused a chill that ran up his spine and set the hairs on his neck tingling. He whirled round.

"So it's you, Jack – what are you doing out here?" It was Charlie.

Jack gulped and wiped the cold sweat from his face, struggling to find an answer.

"Look at the state o' you, man. Why, you've been out on the levels!" Charlie's eyes narrowed. "What you been up to? Following somebody, perhaps?"

"No, no, I was just—just—"

"Just followin' Mr Garnett, an 'Arry, I know. 'Ow much you seen, I wonder?"

"Nothin', I didn't see nothin'."

"Sorry about this, Jack, you shouldn't 'ave bin so nosy. But you'd better come wi' me. I gotta keep you somewheres till Abe gets back."

He grasped him firmly by the shoulder. Jack eyed the naked blade and the pistol thrust through Charlie's belt. They gleamed dully in the half-light. He decided to go quietly.

"Can't 'ave you goin' off now, can we? Maybe to a magistrate's. It might suit you that, a man in your position. Could get you a pardon y'self."

"I wouldn't, not me," Jack protested. "I ain't never been a nark."

"We'll see what Abe says." Charlie thrust him through the entrance to a small low-roofed outbuilding and slammed the door on him, leaving him in total darkness.

Jack suddenly lost his temper, hurling himself against the door. "Let me outta 'ere, you bloody stinkin' bastard! Let me out!"

He heard Charlie give a short laugh. Then there was silence.

"God damn 'im!" Jack slouched in a cobwebby corner of the building.

Despite everything, he dozed. He woke quickly enough when the door was flung open. Daylight poured in around the substantial bulk of Abel Garnett.

"Morning, Jack, ready for breakfast?"

Jack's clothing had dried on him. He was stiff and still tired, mouth parched, lips dry and belly empty.

"Er, yeah, I'm starved." He licked his lips, stumbling to the door.

Abel laughed. "You've got some brass nerve all right. What shall we do with 'im, Charles?"

Charles' slim figure emerged from behind Abel. "Well, as I see it, guv, we got some options. One, we ignore 'is nosy-parkerin'—maybe 'e saw nothin' anyways."

Abel grabbed Jack as he went to pass out into the bright morning. "And two?"

"Two—well 'e's a likely lad, perhaps 'e could be useful to us on the runs or passin' the word, you know."

Jack tried to wrench himself free from Abel's firm and painful grip.

"I don't know what you're talkin' about, I didn't see anythin'. I'll 'ave the law on yer!"

"'Ear that, Abe? 'Ave the law on us! O' course there's another option—'e could disappear out on them marshes. Bet 'e can't swim, eh?"

"You talkin' murder, Charlie?" Abel seemed amused.

"Well who is there to miss 'im? We could all swing, you know, if 'e points a finger at us."

"I have to report with him to the magistrates next week you know, as per this set up o' Brownlow's."

"So what? 'E's done a runner, ain't 'e? Gone missin' like the young villain 'e is, tell 'em that.

Jack brought the heel of his boot down as hard as he could on Abel's instep, broke free from the loosened grip and punched him with considerable force in the groin. Dodging nimbly round Charlie, he was off and running.

Despite the raw pain between his legs, Abel still had the wit to knock up Charlie's pistol as it fired.

Thirty feet away, Jack dodged an imagined bullet and ran for the corner of the barn.

"Jack!" Abel yelled. "It's all right, lad, stop!"

He and Charlie started after him, Abel hobbling a little and cursing under his breath.

"Get after him, Charlie! Don't hurt him!" Geese and poultry scattered from under Jack's feet, the two farm dogs, roused by the sound of the pistol shot, bounding forward, barking excitedly.

Disaster struck for Jack as he dashed around the corner of the barn. He collided bodily with Lysette and Yvonne returning from the milking parlour with full jugs of the frothing warm liquid.

All three fell in a tangled heap, milk splashing and bathing them. A second later, the dogs were there, tongues avidly licking at their milk-covered faces. Then Charlie was hauling Jack to his feet and thrusting him violently into the hands of Abel before turning and assisting the women.

They were shocked but laughing.

"What is it? What mischief are you up to, Jack? Did you fire a gun?"

"It's them, they're going to kill me! I ain't done nothin' and they're goin' to kill me!"

All except Charlie, burst out laughing again.

"Jack, Jack," said Abel, "I tried to tell you, nobody's going to harm you, lad, we're not murderers."

"What about 'im?" Jack looked accusingly at the redoubtable Charles.

"Charlie thought he was doing right, got into a bit of a lather. But he'll follow my orders. Won't you, Charles?"

Charlie shrugged. "Whatever you say, guv, but I'll 'ave my eye on 'im all the same. We gotta keep our necks safe, 'aven't we?"

"Of course we have, Charles, and there's more than us to think on, I know, but Jack will be fine, soon as he knows how the land lies hereabouts. Won't you, Jack?"

They all progressed toward the house, Jack, Lysette and Yvonne wiping the residue of milk from their clothing.

"I've never turned anybody in, not in me life," said Jack. "But I won't die first," he added darkly.

"There you are, Charles. He can't say fairer than that. Let's go and eat. I'm starved."

They sat round the long kitchen table, Abel, Charles and Jack satisfying the demands of their appetites with great gusto.

"Well, Jack, what exactly did you see last night?" Abel asked in his amiable way.

"I saw you meet somebody in the middle o' the night, and, well I knew you was up to no good an' thought it might be as well for me to know what was goin' on, so I followed you, didn't I?" He spoke defiantly.

"I expect I'd have done the same in your shoes, and you too, Charles."

Charles stopped chewing briefly and glowered suspiciously at Jack.

Abel laughed, in a fine humour. "Was you behind us all the way then, Jack?"

"Yeah, all the way. Like I told yer, I can dodge anybody. I followed all the way to the sea an' saw all that stuff come in."

Charles swore softly under his breath.

"Ladies present, Charles," Abel reminded him. "And then did you follow after that, Jack?"

"Well, I tried, but lost you on the marshes. I got soaked I can tell you."

"Poor Jack." Lysette smiled at him, creating a warm sensation that moved from the region of his stomach to his face.

"Well, I think it's a bit ripe!" he burst out.

"What is, Jack?" asked Abel.

"You are chose by Brownlow to show me 'ow to live proper, like, an' you're a villain yourself! In fact you all are!" He looked accusingly at Lysette and Yvonne.

Even Charles had to laugh at this, spilling crumbs from his mouth and developing a couching fit. Lysette, who sat next to him, felt obliged to slap him on the back.

"Sorry, gone down the wrong way," he gasped, red in the face and short of breath.

"Look, Jack, you may call us villains if you like," said Abel, more serious now, "but we are not cheap pickpockets, burglars or cut-throats. What we do don't harm anybody, except perhaps HM Government, who can well afford it."

"There's been smuggling on these marshes for, well, probably hundreds of years. We buy cheap from France or elsewhere and sell to interested parties over here. And, believe me, there's plenty of them. Gentlefolk and high nobs included, ain't that right, Charles?"

"Right enough," said Charles; "nobody says no to a bargain. But it's gettin' 'arder, Abe, ain't it? 'Arder to come by and 'arder to get away wiv."

"That's right, Charles, since Boney started his antics the coastal defences are causing problems for the likes of us. That's why we only make a run in dirty weather, Jack."

"There must be money in it," said Jack.

"Aye, there's still enough to go round," replied Abel.

"You'll find the people of the marshes a jot above the average when it comes to wealth. You'd be surprised 'ow many benefit. Remember the parson on the coach, Jack? He's a regular customer, so are half the innkeepers 'tween here and Maidstone."

"Yes, but it's still against the law, ain't it? You could still hang?"

"Look, Jack, yes it's against the law, the government's law, but it's only tax money. Don't you think those in power have everything they want when they want it? Do you think they care what happens to you and me, or Charlie here? I'll tell you something—" Abel was becoming more and more animated, "—my father died because of government law, press-ganged and died at sea. My mother died too, because of it and I've seen things since then. Military law, men with their backs laid open for some minor offence. Dozens, 'undreds of men dead and dying through obeying some order that should never have been given. So don't talk to me about law."

Yvonne placed a hand over his.

"Abel, don't go on. Jack's young, he doesn't understand."

"Well, it's time he learnt."

"Yes, but he will only learn from his own experience."

"Yeah, look where his own experience got him. Lived on the street all his life, nobody cared, ended up in gaol 'cause he didn't know any better."

"There are good people, like Mr Brownlow," Lysette interjected.

"Brownlow's all right, but do you think he would have lifted a finger to help Jack if it had not been for the sake of one of his own?"

"What's all this talk?" Charlie was impatient with them. "We break the law, make money, take risks. If we get caught, that's the chance we take, but I'll not go quietly, I can tell you."

"I'm just letting Jack know what it's all about," said Abel, calmer again. "What do you think, Jack?"

"Well, there's some people out there with a lot of money an' a lot of people with none. Those that 'ave got it won't share it so if I get the chance, I 'elps meself."

"Oh, Jack!" Lysette exclaimed.

" 'E's a bloomin' revolutionary!" said Charlie, laughing now.

"Well, I can't agree with that," said Abel. "I can see we've got a lot of work to do on you."

"What's the difference in liftin' a nob's 'unter an' smugglin' kegs o' brandy. It's all stealin', ain't it?"

"He's got you there, Abel." Yvonne spoke up, her voice heavily accented. "There is no moral difference, you know."

"It's the government who are short on morals," Abel snorted. "Politicians, civil servants, judges, lawyers. All I'm doin' is a bit of cross-channel business.

"Come on, Jack, Charles, we got work to do. I still got to take care of Brownlow's business as well." He scraped his chair back and stood, jaw jutting stubbornly, shoulders back, craggy features knitted in a thoughtful expression. The conversation had unsettled him a little. He was aware that a few years ago, he could never have done anything illegal.

His mouth twisted cynically, he had grown up since then and the army had helped him on his way.

CHAPTER TEN

Abel Garnett and Johnny Rose Take Ship for Portugal

ergeant Abel Garnett crept stealthily to the crest of the hill, keeping low in the grass. Down at the bottom of the slope, he could see the French. They had not seen him yet.

For one fanciful moment, his memory recalled an incident from his childhood when he had charged down a sloping green English meadow, wooden sword in hand, putting a whole regiment of 'Frenchies' to flight.

"Come on, Sergeant," he told himself, "you're not playing games now." He looked back at the handful of men that he had with him; six in all, a foraging party equal in number to the enemy fifty yards away, and four of whom disporting themselves stark naked in the river under the blazing Iberian sun. Another held onto the reins of their horses whilst the sixth sat under an olive tree, smoke drifting up from his pipe.

The splashing water rose into the still air in silver droplets. Abel licked his parched lips. What he would give to join those lucky devils at play in the cool stream. He had a feeling though that their luck was about to run out.

He slid the few feet back to his men.

"There's one for each of us," he whispered. "Over the hill, run like hell and we'll be on 'em before they know what's 'appening. No shooting, mind, we don't want the whole French army down on us."

He glanced at their wagon and horses waiting patiently on the dirt road. Foster, a stringbean nineteen-year-old youth, in ill-fitting uniform responded, "Aye, Sarge?"

"You take care o' the wagon and horses. That'll give me two Frenchies to deal with." They all grinned. "Use the bayonet, lads. Let's go."

They squirmed to the top of the hill again, grasping their lengthy muskets with bayonets attached. The four men in the water still frolicked happily. The pipe-smoker was strolling across to the man holding the horses. The sun beat unrelentingly down on them all. Abel felt it burning into his back. He stood up. "Get 'em, boys!"

They pounded down the hill screaming wordless sounds at the tops of their voices. The tableau before them froze for a split second. Then the French were moving fast.

The one with the horses released the reins and began dragging his sword from its scabbard.

"*Aux armes! Aux armes!*" The horses trotted down river a short distance, then stopped to observe with a detached air the odd behaviour of their human masters. The pipe-smoker too began to draw his sword whilst the naked men in the water scrambled, panic-stricken towards the river-bank.

Abel observed all this as he made what felt to be an endless charge downhill. His feet pounded the grassy slope, sweat began to break out upon his forehead and then, before the enemy's swords had even cleared their scabbards, he was on them.

The pipe-smoker's face was smashed in by the butt of Abel's musket, swung with tremendous force.

In one swift movement, Abel returned the musket to the "on guard" position and thrust savagely at the belly of the Frenchman who a moment ago had been peacefully holding the reins of the mounts.

He was a small man with drooping moustaches and squint eyes. He managed one strike at Abel with his sword, which connected with the musket with sufficient force to send a chip of wood flying. The little Frenchman's face dissolved in agony as the bayonet penetrated several inches into his abdomen.

Abel felt a pang of pity but swept it from his mind by roaring at the top of his voice as he tore the bayonet from the flesh.

He glanced up. On the river-bank, four naked Frenchmen were being gutted like fish.

Blood ran into the softly flowing current of the river, creating pink rivulets among the gently moving water plants.

Abel suddenly felt slightly sick. Blood was foaming from the mouth of the man he had bayoneted; he would die in a few minutes. The other lay still and lifeless. He straightened himself. "Come on, lads," he rasped, "let's get out of here, Roberts, get those horses, Hunt, grab those duds." He indicated the small pile of haversacks, clothing and weaponry that lay under the olive tree.

In a few moments, they were scrambling back up the slope. His men chattered excitedly. "Did you see 'em?" the moon-faced Roberts asked. "What a way to go, bollock-naked. No chance, man!"

They pulled and chivvied the uncomplaining horseflesh up the bank and plunged over the brow, heading down towards their wagon and the tall, thin figure of Foster who started towards them. "All right, Sarge?"

"Piece o' cake, Foster." They all stopped to draw breath at the wagon.

"Any o' you lads that can ride, get up on a horse, the rest o' you pile in that wagon. There may be more Frenchies about and we won't be so lucky next time." Abel was firmly in charge.

Cato, the always-dapper sleek-haired private and Rodmell, the cunning, devious old soldier, both mounted horses. Foster, Hunt and Roberts scrambled into the wagon as Abel tied off the remaining three horses to the tailgate and mounted one himself.

Foster whipped up the team and they were off along the dusty track that meandered through the low hills.

They were close to the border with Portugal three miles

from their encampment – thirteen thousand ill-provisioned and hungry British soldiers.

Many foraging parties were out but the poverty-stricken villages were deserted – not a chicken or pig to be found, and the fields picked clean of crops.

"Sergeant Garnett!" It was Hunt shouting from the wagon bed. "There's bread in these 'aversacks, and wine!"

"Throw me a bottle, share the rest among you."

"'Ere, Sarge, we could just as easy taken them Froggies prisoner, couldn't we?" This from round-faced Roberts.

Abel deftly caught the wine bottle tossed to him.

"We got too many mouths to feed already." He pulled the half-exposed cork from the bottle with his teeth and took a swig.

"Oh God," he thought, "how you've come to love the sight of blood, Abel Garnett. Have you fallen so far? It never even crossed your mind to take those poor fellows prisoner. They were at your mercy and you killed them." He groaned inwardly as he rode behind the wagon towards their encampment. "Keep a sharp lookout!" He glowered at each of his men, feeling dirty, unkempt and mentally drained, full of self contempt.

Years before, the youthful Abel had marched to the beat of a drum along with many other volunteers down rutted Sussex roads. Heading south-west, mounted officers rode back and forth the length of the column, cajoling and encouraging the miscellaneous assortment of farm boys, clerks, ne'er-do-wells and adventurers into some sort of military bearing.

A sense of unreality had gripped Abel as they bivouacked for the night in the vicinity of Horsham. His mostly rough-and-ready companions skylarked with unthinking abandon in the evening air whilst he lay brooding on a bed of straw, feeling completely alone and doubting the wisdom of his enlistment.

These feelings were reinforced the next day as he squelched along with his companions in a downpour that was rapidly turning the road into a quagmire. He noted that many of the motley group of yesterday were remarkable by their absence, having had a change of heart about a military life. Their loss was soon made up, however, by further eager young volunteers along the way.

A muddy, wet and weary column trudged into Chichester. Bread, meat and beer were issued to them before they passed into the relative warmth of the newly-constructed barrack block.

Abel sat brooding. Seeing the world seemed so far to consist of travelling about the Kent and Sussex countryside in progressively worse conditions. He was now less than five miles from his starting point where he had left his aunts weeks before.

"Hey, big un!" A long-haired, hook-nosed character seated on the floor a few feet away looked sideways at him, giving a twisted grin that revealed blackened, broken teeth.

"Yes?"

"You got any cash? You look like a gent that might 'ave."

Abel's mood precluded caution.

"I've nothing but five guineas."

"Five guineas! By crikey, mates, we've a millionaire among us!"

Some of the other men in the billet raised their heads, looking towards Abel. "Hook Nose" slid himself across the floor until he was almost touching Abel.

"Me name's Johnny Rose—what's yours?"

"Abel—Abel Garnett."

Rose extended a filthy paw. "Shake, Mr Garnett, nice to know yer, where yer from?"

"Chichester."

"But didn't I see you marching down from Maidstone?"

"It's all a bit complicated."

Johnny Rose burst out laughing. "You could a just strolled up the lane today and joined up 'stead o' goin' fifty mile for it!"

"Now look here."

"Oh, it's all right matey, don't mind me, I got a funny bone, that's all."

Abel subsided. "Where do you come from, Mr Rose?"

"Me? I'm from St Albans."

Abel grinned. "Isn't that as far from Maidstone as Chichester? You did enlist in Maidstone, did you not?"

"Yeah, well, I 'ad to leave 'ome meself. For the good of me 'ealth, like."

"Are you a rogue, John Rose?"

"Me? Nah, just a bit light-fingered, ain't I?" He smiled disarmingly, giving a wink. "Comin' for a drink wiv the lads tonight, Abe?"

"Well, I don't know. Will it be permitted?"

"Sure, 'course it will. Not many rules for us. Not as yet anyhow."

"Do you know, John, I'm a bit down at the moment. A friendly drink would do me good."

"'Course it would, Abe, nothin' more likely to raise the spirits than an ale or two wiv yer mates. Do ya 'ear that, lads? My mate Abe's on for a drink tonight!"

Seven or eight of those billeted came over to where Abel and Johnny Rose were sitting. Some clapped Abel on his broad back.

"Could do wi' a drink."

"Thankee, friend."

"Do you know a good ale 'ouse?"

"I never meant—" Abel tried to speak.

"Don't worry none," said Johnny Rose, tapping his hooked nose with a grimy forefinger, "Johnny will take care o' things!"

The taverns got meaner, seedier and more squalid as the night wore on. Johnny Rose, Abel and their freebooting companions became louder and heartier as they consumed fiery rum, brandy and ale.

Abel's natural reticence and self-control deserted him. Encouraged by his newfound friends, he recklessly poured drink after drink down his throat, slapping coins on the table, as required.

He bellowed with laughter as two of the recruits became embroiled in an argument and crashed to the floor in a kicking, biting, gouging heap. More drink flowed, more taverns followed.

Then he was mounting a creaking, narrow staircase, Johnny Rose pushing him from behind.

They thrust open a door into a narrow attic chamber; Abel, head reeling, sprawled on hands and knees, the floor tilting beneath him. There was a small, soft hand lifting his chin. He dimly perceived the outline of a female form.

Johnny Rose half-threw him onto rumpled bedclothes. Soft flesh was pressed against his body. There was the smell of cheap perfume, his face being kissed repeatedly while fingers fumbled at his clothing. Instincts took command of him; grunting and moaning, he rolled onto the woman and began kissing her face in return, then her throat and bared breasts. She clutched at him murmuring encouragement.

Abel had dim recollections of vomiting into a muddy ditch and being assisted, half-carried almost, to the barracks.

In what seemed a mere blink of time, he was on parade in the dazzling light of day, feeling like death and looking worse.

Uniforms had yet to be issued to the recruits who stood in wavering lines on parade.

Two splendidly colourful sergeants inspected them, uttering incredible expressions of distaste at their general condition. "We gotta turn this lot into soldiers, Bill; it can't be done, I say, it can't be done."

"But it will be done, Royston, won't it? It'll be 'ard for us and 'ard for them, but soldiers they will be."

Bill sighed. "I know you are right, Royston, but me 'eart fails me to think of it." They stopped in front of Abel.

"Look at this un for instance, unshaved, stinks o' liquor, filthy state." "Bill" suddenly poked Abel in the gut with the brass-ended stick that he carried.

Abel was in no mood for even the mildest misuse. His fists clenched and he raised his forearm. In a moment, the two sergeants were screaming in his face.

"Stand still, don't move, 'oo do y' think you are?"

"Did you see that, Bill? 'E made a fist! That's an 'undred lashes right off. Go to strike me, would you, you bloody villain? Royston! Get an officer!"

Abel quailed, "I'm sorry, I didn't intend—"

"Do you hear that, Royston—? 'E did not intend!"

"Easy Bill, easy, this boy looks done in."

"Looks done in! Looks done in! 'Ee will be time I've finished wiv 'im! Where's that, officer?"

"Come on, Bill, its Swithin 'oos duty officer, give 'im a break this once. 'E ain't even in uniform yet. You knows what Swithin's like."

Bill thrust his face even closer to Abel's. "Think yourself lucky I'm in a forgivin' mood, soldier," he snarled. "Next time—well there'd better not be a next time, that's all."

The two sergeants stalked off. Abel managed to prevent himself from retching on parade, but it was a close thing.

Then the drill started.

During the days that followed, Abel was given the opportunity to become a soldier, along with three hundred and twenty others. Uniforms and muskets were issued. They were drilled and instructed until some sense of order was established amongst them. Thirty-seven recruits disappeared, having found the way of life not to their liking.

Abel, however, began to find it very much to his. The rough comradeship was heart-warming. His fellow soldiers respected him because of his size and obvious strength. Officers remarked on his immaculate turnout and natural skill at musketry.

He did not repeat his night of debauchery. For one thing, he now had only three shillings to his name.

The soldiers' vile humour and gross behaviour held a fascination for Abel and at first he joined in with a will. Gradually, however, his true character began to re-assert itself and he increasingly became a tolerant, good-humoured witness to the antics in the barracks at night when they were all finally left to their own devices.

One evening a quarrel involving Johnny Rose broke out over a game of cards. Chairs, table, cards and coins were sent flying as Rose was confronted by an irate Private Fletcher, a solidly built individual with a violently coloured birthmark on his forehead.

"You bloody cheating bastard, I'm goin' to 'ave your guts!" Fletcher snatched up a bayonet and tossed aside the upturned table to get at the protesting Rose.

"Now, now Fletch, you've just 'ad bad luck is all, don't be 'asty, Fletch."

He backed away extending his arms, hands, palm outward, to repel the advancing Fletcher.

"I'll give you bad luck, you coward. I'll swing for you, by God!" Fletcher lunged forward, raising the bayonet.

"Don't, Fletch, don't!"

Abel swung his feet over the side of his bed, stood, and in one smooth movement took hold of Fletcher's arm with one hand, grasped the hand that held the bayonet with his other and bent it backwards so suddenly and painfully that Fletcher was obliged to let the bayonet fall.

Fletcher swung his body round. "Don't bloody interfere, Abe!" He swung a clenched fist that connected solidly with Abel's left cheekbone. Abel pulled the man towards him, grabbed him by the body and flung him twelve feet down the room where he sprawled helplessly.

Impressed by this display of strength, the other soldiers gathered round Abel.

"Man, you ought'a take up wrestling!"

"What a throw, Abe!"

"Thanks, Abe," said Johnny as he righted the table and began to gather up cards and coins.

Fletcher picked himself up and approached.

"Sorry about the blow, Abe, didn't mean it. Fact is you probably saved me from a flogging or worse if I'd used that bayonet on this scum."

"'Ere, watch y' mouf." Johnny Rose was indignant.

Abel looked coolly at Fletcher. "I'd give up playing cards with Johnny if I were you, you'll both live longer."

Fletcher laughed. "That's good advice, Abe."

Despite some of the men feeling that Abel was sucking up

to the officers because of his smart turnout, quickness in obeying orders and skill at arms, the incident gained him the respect of many and the story of the brief scuffle was inevitably exaggerated as it passed by word of mouth around the barracks.

A few days later, Abel had the opportunity to visit his aunts. Johnny Rose went along with him.

As they walked the muddy lanes between leafless hedgerows, Abel could not help asking the question.

"Were you cheating at cards the other night, Johnny?"

Despite his blackened teeth, hook-nose and unkempt hair, Johnny Rose exuded an undeniable charm.

"Course I were, y' fool, 'tis the only way to make sure o' winnin'!" His brown eyes twinkled merrily as they both threw back their heads and laughed.

Abel's conscience was emitting warning signals that he was unable to ignore, however, and he grew morose at the thought of facing his aunts as a debauched drunkard consorting with cheats and rogues. He punished himself severely as they marched along, already trained in military ways sufficiently to keep in step and maintain an upright bearing without being aware that they were doing so.

Aunt Rose, glancing from a bedroom window, which she was diligently cleaning, saw the two soldiers approaching, hesitated for a moment, gave a shriek of recognition, then sped down the stairs, calling to her sisters.

"Abel's come home, Ann! Bet! Abel's here!"

All three aunts scampered into the farmyard, dresses billowing. Ann lost a slipper and hopped awkwardly to a halt, quickly retrieved it and, reinserting her foot, hurried breathlessly after her two sisters. Abel's feelings of guilt regarding the state of his morality disappeared when he was engulfed by the three women. His hat, being knocked off, was deftly caught by the grinning Johnny Rose.

When the excitement had abated somewhat and the aunts had ceased telling Abel how splendid he was in his uniform, how well he looked and so on, Abel was allowed to introduce his companion. "Aunt Betty, Ann, Aunt Rose. This is Mr John Rose, private, 50th Foot in his Britannic Majesty's Army!"

They were all amused at the introduction and the coincidence of Aunt Rose's Christian name being the same as John's surname.

"Our granddaughter is married to a John as well," said Rose as they all made their way into the house.

"How is Elspeth? Any news of John?" Abel was anxious to know.

"Elspeth is fine—she told us how you helped her out of the house she was obliged to live in, into more suitable surroundings; thank you, Abe."

"No need to thank me, she's my sister. Any news of John?" he repeated.

"The last we heard his ship was on blockade duty off France or Spain, I don't know quite." Aunt Rose looked on the point of tears, then suddenly burst out.

"That madman Napoleon Bonaparte won't rest until he rules the world! I'm sure he won't!"

Ann and Betty concurred. "We won't be safe in our beds. What if they invade and us not five miles from the sea? Poor old England!"

Betty's face crumpled into tears.

"Cheer up, aunts. Boney will have to do a lot better than he is at the moment. I know we ain't got Nelson no more, but as I understand it, we've got French ships bottled up all round the European coast from way up north all the way past Italy. Boney might be marching all over Europe. But he can't get at us. Ain't that right, Johnny?"

"Quite right, Abe, an' when we get out there, them frogs won't stand a chance! One of us is more n' a match for ten o' them!"

"You don't mean you are going off to fight?" Aunt Ann was appalled.

"Nobody tells us anything," said Abel, "but the army's recruiting hundreds, thousands and that can't be for nothing, but don't you worry, darlings, we'll be all right. Now how are things here? Is all well with you?"

After a substantial lunch, Abel conducted Johnny Rose round the smallholding, as he showed his comrade the sheds, the barn, the pigs and chickens, vegetable garden and the few acres of pastureland. He tried to picture himself working there, feeding the pigs, milking the cow, haymaking, and he was suddenly glad of his uniform giving him freedom from a dull future.

For the first time in almost two years, he felt a sort of peace. He had no money. He had this property, but until his aunts had gone to rest, it was of no value to him. He might soon be crossing the seas with the battalion to fight the French. A small knot of excitement tightened in his stomach.

"Come on, Johnny, time we were getting back."

"Naw, it's early yet."

"No come on, let's go." Abel was eager for movement, action. After a prolonged farewell, they were finally allowed to set off down the lane.

Johnny Rose had purloined and concealed about his person some of the Garnett family cutlery. "Well, they might be worth a few bob," he secretly told himself.

Three weeks later, Abel was being violently seasick along with hundreds of other soldiers aboard HMS *Lion* as it beat down channel. Along with 13,000 other men distributed among ships of the Royal Navy, he was with Sir John Moore's army heading for Portugal. It was almost Christmas.

Storms and delays meant a sojourn in Gibraltar so that it was May 1808 before they beached at Figueras under the fiercest sun that Abel had ever known.

The small boats, packed with troops, horses and equipment, were swept precariously through the foaming Atlantic breakers to the shore where seamen and locals were waiting to drag them in through the shallows.

Abel's senses were assaulted on all sides by innumerable sights, sounds and smells: soldiers being ordered into their units by the raucous shouts of officers and NCOs; the crash and drag of the ocean as the waves broke on the sand and receded. Terrified horses neighed and whinnied as cursing dragoons attempted to control their plunging panic.

This was a hotter, brighter world than he was used to. Brilliant blues, whites, greens, yellows, ravished his eyes and within five minutes of disembarking from the boat and being hurried up the beach by an irate sergeant, he and all his companions were sweating profusely as they made their way in some sort of order through the huge piles of stores and equipment that had been stacked above the high water mark.

Abel took a last backward look at the wide sweep of Mondego Bay; boats were still plying from the ships of His Majesty's Navy to the sandy beaches of the Portuguese shore.

CHAPTER ELEVEN

The Artful Dodger meets Jacob Pierce for the Last Time

ain poured unceasingly down the windows of the Romney courthouse as it had done for the past twenty-four hours. The magistrate sniffed disdainfully as Jack Dawkins stood defiantly before him.

"What is the world coming to?" He addressed the question to the attentive Abel Garnett standing beside Jack.

"Here we have an incorrigible young rogue, let off scot-free to live amongst decent people in our fair county—it's a scandal, sir!"

Abel adopted a pious air. "I quite agree, your honour. It never ought to be allowed. It would serve them right if this ne'er-do-well absconded. It would put an end to such soft-headed ideas."

The Magistrate nodded. "You are right, Mr Garnett, and I don't envy you your role in this business. Why, the young bounder might do harm to you or yours out in the remote place that you live. There has been a whole spate of break-ins and thefts in the marsh villages recently. Coincidence?"

"It ain't me!" Jack blurted out.

"Be quiet, sir! I am addressing Mr Garnett."

"I think Dawkins speaks the truth in this instance, sir," Abel said. "He has scarcely been out of my sight since Mr Brownlow delivered him into my hands. I think we can put the thefts down to the lunatic Pierce who must surely be dead or gone now."

"I fear not, Mr Garnett. A shambling creature was seen only two days ago by some Snargate village boys who were out on the levels. They were given a great fright, I believe."

"Is it not possible to track the man down, your honour? Perhaps the army could try again?"

"As it happens, Mr Garnett, another attempt is to be made. Within the next day or two the marshes will be swept end to end by soldiery. This time no stone will be left unturned. There is a forty pounds reward for the man who finds this monster, dead or alive. That should ensure a thorough search."

"I see," said Abel, looking steadily at the magistrate. "Mayhap they will have better luck this time."

"I sincerely hope so, before anyone else is murdered. It was a tragedy that one of your shepherds should die in such a manner."

"Aye, I've never liked funerals much and Charlie's was no more pleasant than any."

"Of course," said the magistrate sympathetically. "Well you may take Dawkins here, make what you can of him. And, if he should transgress by any means before you are required to bring him before me again, do not hesitate to put the young villain in the hands of the law and I will make certain that you are never troubled with him again."

"Very well, your honour. Thank you and good day. Come on Jack, you've work to do."

"That's the way!" cried his Honour. "Work him hard, Mr Garnett, work him hard!"

Out on the narrow streets of Romney, Abel's voice took on an urgent tone. "Come on, Jack, we really do have work to do."

"What's up?" asked Jack, wiping rain from his eyes.

"Look, the marshes are going to be swarming with soldiers tomorrow or the next day. I've got goods out there waiting to be found. We have to move them quick. Charlie's out with the sheep and the boys are scattered everywhere. It's down to you and me. I'm glad we came on the wagon."

"Can you get a wagon out on them marshes?" asked Jack breathlessly as they hurried down the street to a blacksmiths where the horses were being re-shod.

"Well, we've 'ad a lot of rain lately—it won't be easy, but I reckon we can get close to where the stuff is, there's a track of sorts."

Rain continued to fall as the wagon ground and rattled its way down narrower and rougher tracks onto the levels. Jack was getting soaked again but his spirits were high. He was on a jaunt to his liking with someone who, in his eyes, was admirable.

Abel Garnett was no Bill Sykes, a murderous drunk who had been prepared to throttle anyone for two pence. Garnett, he felt, would have been more than a match for Sykes in a trial of strength, and in addition, was a man who was in control of himself. Men did his bidding out of respect, not fear. Even his superiors, like Brownlow and the magistrate treated him with respect, and, to cap it all, Abel Garnett was on the wrong side of the law! Just like he, the Artful Dodger, had always been. Jack felt positively gleeful as the wagon lurched along the potholed muddy track, and the rain poured down on the wide sweep of marshland that sat darkly under a lowering sky.

"'Ow much further, Mr Garnett?"

"We can't get this wagon 'cross the dykes and if I leave the track, we'll get bogged down when loaded. We've got a hard time ahead, Jack. This is the old way up to the village all right, but it don't go all the way any more. There's a dyke cuts straight across it up ahead. But we've got the planks o' wood hid up there that we can cross on. Then it's me and you carrying what we can. These horses are too heavy to get across."

Abe wiped the rain from his face. "This rain's a cursed nuisance. If it goes on like this, we shall have floods; then we won't even get the load along this track. Come on, you brutes!" He slapped the reins across the backs of the horses, increasing their speed somewhat.

The way petered out into water meadows. Rank grasses stretched to the line of a dyke, beyond which, on gently rising ground, Jack saw the ruined church with its stunted tower and the distinct outline of a village street now consisting of intermittent broken walls and masonry.

"This is it, Jack." Abel jumped from the wagon. Jack followed suit, his landing making a squelch in six inches of water.

"The whole area's waterlogged," said Abel as they hurried to the dyke, "and look at this. If it carries on raining, the dykes will overrun into the fields. The whole area could be under water for days."

"Perhaps the search will be called off," said Jack, hopefully.

"We can't risk it. That's the trouble with the weather. It could start drying out tomorrow. Here, help me with these." He dragged two thick, rough-hewn planks from among the reeds and Jack helped him bridge the dyke, which was brimming with brown, swirling water.

They crossed easily enough and went up the sloping ground toward the wreck of the church. Jack noted that water was actually running down the incline quite steadily.

They reached the church and Abel began pulling the slabs of stone away from the base of the tower, revealing a ragged-edged entrance. A pile of barrels, large and small, together with tarpaulin-wrapped bundles were stacked in the base of the church tower.

"Here, Jack, grab a keg, two if you can manage 'em. Get them to the wagon."

Abel heaved one of the bundles onto his shoulders with one hand and rolled a keg under his armpit with the other "silks and brandy". He grinned at Jack through the sheeting rain. His teeth, gleaming briefly, reminding Jack of a flash of lightning in that darkly tanned face.

They made trip after trip to the wagon where the two horses stood stoically, heads down under the continuing downpour. More than once, Jack nearly stumbled into the swelling waters of the dyke as he crossed the drenched plank bridge with kegs and bundles. His legs were buckling when Abel called a halt.

"That's it, Jack, that'll do. Look at that water?" He pointed down the track. Like a live thing, water was creeping insidiously towards them, filling the potholes in small rivulets before advancing further.

"Crikey!" Jack's nerves were edgy with fatigue. "Let's get outta here!"

"One more, we'll do one more." Abel was grimly determined. Jack began to protest, thought better of it and forced his weary limbs into movements, splashing uncaringly up the incline. He could not get any wetter now so the slanting rain meant nothing to him.

Jacob Pierce crouched in his underground hideaway in two feet of water. He had been about to evacuate it when Jack and Abel had arrived at the ruin to remove the goods. Bitter tears of rage and frustration rolled down his dirt-encrusted face into the straggling beard. He bit ferociously at the palms of his hands to stifle his cries. Water was running into the stone-lined cellar in a dozen different places but every time Pierce looked cautiously out into the world through a gap between the slabs, there were the two figures toiling back and forth.

Pierce had not been alone in the underground chamber. He frequently conversed with his victims. Sometimes they had all been there at once – his Ma and Pa, two or three of his employers, a sweet young girl. At times he had been obliged to scream at them all to shut up, their incessant chattering driving him to distraction.

Suddenly a more solid body in the form of Abel Garnett intruded. Abel picked up what he intended to be the last small barrel of brandy and did what he had unwittingly been threatening to do for the past two hours. He put both feet on the slabs covering the opening to the hiding place. The non-stop rain had weakened the earth and stone on which they rested and Abel's weight proved too much.

He plunged through awkwardly onto the broken flight of steps, landing on his left arm. He gave a gasp of pain and surprise. The cask broke open, brandy running away into the small lake that covered the floor below. Abel rolled helplessly into it as well. He was on his knees in the water, swearing and cursing, clutching his left forearm with his right hand as pain shot up to its elbow.

Jack Dawkins stuck his head through the aperture that had appeared so suddenly, "Abel—Mr Garnett—you all right?"

Before he had time to reply, Jacob Pierce leapt onto Abel's back. The latter just heard Jack's cry of alarm before his head was thrust under water by the maniac's powerful attack.

Not even Pierce could prevent Abel's instinctive reaction to the situation, however. Although he had a stranglehold on him, Pierce found himself falling backwards as Abel stood, his powerful body resistant to the other's weight and the two men toppled over. Now it was Pierce's turn to have his head thrust under the water by the weight of Abel's body, but his arm still tightened around Abel's throat whilst his free hand scrabbled frantically around the flooded floor for some sort of weapon. His fingers touched the discarded handbill[1] that he had recently purloined from a cottager's chopping block. His brain registered instant recognition; with savage glee Pierce's hand closed over the wooden haft.

Jack Dawkins was hunting for a weapon himself in the rain and mud as Garnett and Pierce struggled below. The best he could do was to pick up a jagged piece of paving stone before descending the short flight of steps.

He waded toward the two threshing bodies and watched anxiously as, with one hand, Abel was trying to free himself from the stranglehold. Jack danced about with the slab raised high, waiting for an opportunity to strike. Up out of the churning water came Pierce's handbill.

"Watch out, Mr Garnett!" Jack struggled to reach Pierce's upraised arm but down it came, slashing awkwardly at Abel's body. The point of the bill penetrated his jerkin and shirt. Abel let out a guttural cry, pulling himself upright again, taking the tenacious Pierce with him; the water surged around them as the handbill rose again ready to slash at Abel.

---

1 a curved and heavy-bladed hatchet

Jack brought the piece of stone slab down with all the force he could muster onto Jacob Pierce's dripping, bearded head, Abel felt the arm around his throat loosen and pulled himself free. He scrambled to his feet with blood running down his torso. Jack took another swing at Pierce with the stone, missed and almost fell over.

"Jack! Out! Come on!" Abel gasped, his chest heaving. With his good arm, he grabbed the boy and steered him to the worn and broken steps. "Come on, up, up!" Then they were out again into a wet, grey world.

"Did I kill 'im?" Jack's heart was pounding.

"I don't think so, boy."

"You're bleedin', Abe."

Abel glanced down at his shirt front – pink fluid, blood diluted with rainwater, was running freely down his body.

"Aye, I'm cut about all right."

"What're we goin' to do?" Jack felt panicky.

"Block 'im in down there. That's first. We can't take 'im with us, I can't 'andle him like this anyway. We got to get that wagon-load out fast too. Look!"

He pointed with his good arm. As far as the eye could see, water was gaining ascendancy over the earth, islands of high ground were appearing. Abel turned and began trying to move the material that had blocked up the entrance to the tower. Jack leant his weight to the task. Some of the masonry fell down the steps but between them, they were soon able to bridge the entrance and heaped stone after stone onto it.

"That's it," said Abel. "Not even that maniac can shift that lot. We got 'im!" Even as he spoke a terrible cry rang out from the crypt.

It almost made Jack's hair stand on end. "Let's get goin' then!"

They half-staggered, half-ran to the dyke. "By God! Another few minutes and we'd have lost our bridge."

Abel was right. The water was brimming over and into the surrounding marsh which was already completely under water. One behind the other, they slid and slipped across the planks which were almost awash and in imminent danger of floating away. Then, together, Abel and Jack splashed a path to the wagon and horses.

Jack was supremely grateful to find himself climbing onto the wagon seat.

"Just a minute, Jack. I'll have to secure this arm, stop this bleeding too." Standing in the water, Abel unbuckled his belt, stripped off his jerkin and shirt. "Give us a hand here, Jack."

The Dodger took a deep breath and descended again under a sudden increase in the downpour.

Even in his state of anxiety Jack noticed the scars and weals on Abel's upper body, in shoulder, chest, side and forearm. "'Ere's another one for ya, Abe," he thought, eyeing the bloody cut inflicted by Pierce.

Together they tore the shirt into strips; Abel made a wad and placed it over the two-inch gash on his muscular chest to stem the seepage. Jack then wound the remaining strips of linen round Abel's body to form a crude bandage. Replacing the jerkin, Jack buckled the belt over Abel's shoulder. With some relief, Abel rested his badly bruised forearm in the loop.

The rain continued to fall monotonously as they climbed up out of the ankle-deep water back onto the wagon. As they sat themselves down, the horses, impatient to be off, moved forward of their own volition.

What little light there was began to disappear from the sky. Evening approached. Soon, as they rolled down the flooded track, the wagon was up to its axles in water.

The countryside was so transformed that Jack failed to recognise any landmark.

"How are we goin' to get back, find our way?" Jack's fear was almost tangible as darkness began to fall.

"Well, the track runs pretty straight, I think. See that line of trees on the horizon, out there?"

Jack could just make out the short line of dark growth in the distance. "Yeah, I see them."

"Well, that's the causeway; if we can get up there, we should be on firm ground."

The horses were up to their bellies, the flood swirling about them. Several floating bundles of grey bumped and slid by the wagon. It took a few seconds for Jack to realise what they were.

"Sheep, Mr Garnett. Drowned sheep!"

"Yeah, Brownlow's sheep—our sheep; we've lost dozens, I reckon. This is bad, very bad."

The wagon lurched heavily into a deep rut, dirty brown water splashing over their legs. The front swayed and dipped wildly to the left, tilting at an absurd angle and almost throwing both of them from the seat. Kegs and bundles crashed and clattered behind them.

"We're off the track!" Abel clawed at the reins. "Whoa!" The wagon shafts twisted as the horses struggled for their footing. The wagon lurched again and they felt one of the huge rear wheels lift from the ground.

"We're going over!" Jack almost screamed it. Then the wheel fell back sending up a gout of water.

"Damn this arm!" Abel wrestled with the reins. "Come on, Jack, we'll have to pull 'em out. Take one of the horse's heads and we'll lead them."

They leapt into the darkly rippling water; it came up to Jack's waist. He plunged through it to grab the horse's bridle. Another dead sheep drifted slowly by.

"Come on my beauties—heave!" Abel pulled on the harness, Jack copying his movements. The horses moved readily forward, high stepping through the water.

"Stop!" Abel bellowed as the rear offside wheel tipped alarmingly.

"We'll have to back up, try and get four wheels back on the track."

The floodwaters were chilling Jack's body as they reversed the procedure, pushing the horses into moving backwards. The wagon rolled easily but the angle of the shafts became more and more acute and there was sudden disaster as both rear wheels went off the other side of the track and sunk deep into the marsh. Water crept under the tailgate and began filling the wagon.

Cursing, Abel waded swiftly to the rear of the wagon, cradling his injured arm with the sound one. "Hold them horses, Jack!" In a moment, he was returning, forcing his legs through the turbulence.

Once more they began to heave on the bridles, the horses straining against their harnessing. "Come on, come on." Jack pleaded.

"We've had it, Jack," Abel released the horse's head as the wagon remained unmoving.

Jack grabbed hold of Abel's good arm. "Surely not—we can get out, can't we?"

Abel grinned briefly. "We can get out, but the wagon's stuck where it is. The horses are tired out. They been on the go all day, you know. All this weather's bad for 'em too. It's getting dark now. We've got to get back home."

"How far is it?"

"Well, I tell you, Jack, it's only about a mile or so that way." Abel pointed north-east through the gloom. "But there's ditches and dykes and all sorts o' trouble waiting in that direction. In the black of night in these deep floods, we'd never make it. I've only one good arm—we'd drown like as not."

"What then?"

"We'll ride the horses out to the causeway and go the long way round, try and stay on track."

Together they began to relieve the horses of the wagon shafts, the ever-patient animals standing, tossing their heads and nuzzling one another. "Leave the bridles and collars—give you something to hang on to."

Abel led his horse to the side of the crazily tilted wagon. "Here, you can mount from the wagon, I'll hold her head." Jack climbed gingerly aboard his huge mount, spreading his legs across its broad back and clinging to the collar. Abel grabbed a handful of mane on the other shire and vaulted up out of the water, just managing to slide a leg across its back.

"Let's go. Stay behind me, Jack." They started forward slowly; the line of trees that marked the position of the causeway had disappeared in the darkness. The rain eased to a steady drizzle.

It was just about then that Jacob Pierce died. The blow that Jack struck had stunned him for a few minutes and by the time he had recovered, he was trapped in the cellar. A little light still crept in through cracks and crevices in the roof around the top of the steps. Water was running in everywhere too. He stood up to his knees in it, sending up the terrible cry of rage and frustration that had made Jack shiver.

For a while, Pierce made a determined effort to break out through the pile of slabs and stones stacked over the exit. Despite his maniacal strength, he could make no impression on the blockage. He crouched, a wretched, filthy figure, eyes startling from his head, whimpering to himself.

After a while, he made a renewed frenzied attack on the exit, this time using the handbill. Chips of stone flew everywhere. He accidentally struck at the junction of the slabs and the top of the wall, causing a large piece of stone and earth to fall away. Instantly water began to seep through.

He struck again and again at this area with the handbill. Quite unexpectedly, the whole mass gave way. Several hundredweight of the stone that Abel and Jack had piled up fell on Pierce, knocking him down the steps and into the water below. Bricks, stones and slabs rained down on him, pinning him under water. He could raise his head a few inches but not enough to enable him to breathe air through nose or mouth.

Pierce struggled like a trapped animal for several minutes and then drowned. At the last moment, a strange sensation of warmth and well-being came over him and he started to smile.

Abel and Jack made the causeway in half an hour. They were finally out of the floods although surrounded by them in the darkness. The seemingly inexhaustible rain fell steadily. Abel's arm ached and the painful wound to the chest was draining his morale. Cold, wet and tired, he suddenly recalled how the boy had jumped into the cellar and smashed Pierce over the head with that stone, allowing him to pull free and get out. Jack had guts all right. He turned, straining to see the boy on the horse.

"You all right, Jack? Not far now."

"I'm starved, froze, wet and miserable. Otherwise all right," Jack said, wiping a filthy hand across his face.

"Six hundred pounds."

"What?"

"Six hundred pounds, that's what's sitting out on that wagon," Abel said bitterly.

"Cripes!"

"Yeah, Cripes all right. We gotta be quick when these waters go down. Get it off the marsh before the soldiers start hunting for Pierce."

"What we going to do about him?"

"The wagon first, Jack, then we all go looking for sheep, see. Spot Pierce on the marsh, chase 'im and trap him in that place, right; pile stones on that hole and somebody goes for the soldiers. That's the story, right? And you get to share the forty pound reward, Jack."

"I don't believe in 'anding people to the law, Abel—Mr Garnett, but in this instance, I'll make exception." Jack was firm on the point.

"Call me Abe."

They rode on in silence. There were more floods in the lane to Shippenden but they gradually rode clear of them up the rising ground.

Lanterns flickered in the windows of the house and another hung in the open barn door silhouetting the figure of Charlie leading out a horse.

He dropped the reins and hurried towards them as they rode up and slipped wearily from the animals' backs. The horses stood, heads down, exhausted.

"Abel, I was just coming to look for you. The Mrs—" Charlie indicated the house with a jerk of his head, "—was gettin' worried."

"It's all right, now, Charlie. Take care of these horses, will you? Or we're likely to lose one or both of them! You know what to do. Come to the house then—we got plans to lay."

"Aye, all right, Abe." The dour Charlie took the pair of shires by the bridles and led them to the stable.

CHAPTER TWELVE

Charles the First Introduces Abel to the Cross-Channel Trade

t was wonderful to enter the warm farmhouse kitchen to be greeted by Yvonne and Lysette. Jack was disconcerted to find himself included in the feminine embraces. Both women were emotionally charged, their cheeks flushed and eyes sparkling at the relief at their return to the farm.

Yvonne draped blankets round them and urged them to sit by the fire whilst Lysette rushed about laying platters on the table, turning up the lanterns. "We were so worried, were we not, Mama? We expected you back hours ago! Were you caught in the floods? Isn't it terrible?" In her excitement, Lysette's French accent became more pronounced.

"You have had an accident, Papa, is it bad?"

"Hush now, Lysette, I'm all right. Don't worry, Yvonne—just a fall, that's all." Yvonne was already stripping the crude bandage from Abel's chest, revealing a horrific gash that began to seep blood the moment the wadded material was removed.

"Oh, this is not good." Yvonne expressed her concern. Abel eased his injured arm from the makeshift belt sling.

"This is what concerns me. I need both hands at the moment. I have much to do."

Yvonne began to cleanse the wound as Abel sat back in the chair allowing the blanket to fall from his shoulders. Fire and lantern light flickered over them all as they wrestled with their thoughts and feelings.

That valuable load of smuggled goods left in the flooded marsh was what concerned Abel most. Could the wagon be traced to Shippenden? He thought that it could. How many sheep had been lost? Jacob Pierce was another concern. The pain of his injuries was beginning to make him sweat as Yvonne placed a dressing on his wound.

He touched her black hair, stroking it briefly. She glanced up at him, giving an anxious smile, eyes full of concern and affection. She knew Abel well enough to realise that something rather desperate had happened and it made her fearful.

"Abel, I must stitch the cut, it is too deep."

Abel gave a sigh. "Brandy, Lys, and some for Jack as well."

Jack was almost obscured by the blanket that he was wrapped in. Grateful to be dry and warm, his stomach growled in anticipation of the food to come.

Although exhausted, the sight of Lysette aroused him. He felt stupidly tongue-tied and awkward as she placed a glass of brandy in his hand. He heard Yvonne murmuring endearments and apologies as she pulled a needle through Abel's flesh, but he saw only Lysette.

Jack took a mouthful of the brandy, allowing it to rest in his mouth like a soft, warm ball before it trickled down his throat. Gradually it heated even the extremities of his body.

"Eat, Jack, you must be hungry." Lysette was standing before him again, smiling down, holding out a bowl brimming with chicken and vegetables.

"His ears do stick out," she thought, "but he's not so bad as I feared. Now the hair is cut and he is looking cleaner, he is almost handsome. I wonder if he has ever—?" Lysette became angry with herself bringing a jug down so sharply on the table that Yvonne looked up from her task.

There was a knock at the door and Charlie walked in dripping rainwater.

"Will it ever stop?" He was plainly disgusted.

Abel lifted a weary head. "What's the position with the farm, Charlie?"

"No so bad, Abe. Most o' the stock are on high ground. It's feed they'll want if this goes on. I did my best, short-'anded like. You'll find the paddock full, but there'll be drowned 'uns further out, I expect."

"We saw 'em, Charlie, we saw them."

"Tell 'im 'ow we caught the lunatic!" Jack burst out, swallowing a large piece of chicken. "We've got 'im in a pot with the lid on tight!"

Yvonne, Lysette and Charlie all looked startled at this announcement and Abel shot Jack an annoyed look. "I was trying to spare the ladies the anxiety at the moment."

"Sorry, Abel."

"Well you might as well all know it now," Abel said resignedly.

"Magistrate Acott told me that another search was to be made for the maniac Pierce, so, not wanting our goods discovered, we went up with the wagon. I never thought the flood would rise so quick." He looked appealingly at Yvonne. She smiled sympathetically. Lysette relieved Jack of his empty bowl.

"Thanks—thank you, Lysette."

"How did you manage to bottle up Pierce and more important, where's the goods and wagon now, Abe?" Charlie was concerned. He dragged a chair out from the table, seated himself, running a hand through his curling, brown hair.

"Well, the wagon's stuck out on the marsh, Charlie, loaded and waiting for the first revenuer or dragoon to come upon it."

"Damn and blast it, Abe, how could you leave it out there like that?"

"You weren't there, Charlie. I 'ad no choice. Risin' floodwaters, one good arm." He waved his injured arm at Charlie. "The wagon went off the track. Stuck fast she was."

"'Ow does Pierce fit into all this?"

"Well, I sort of found him." Abel gave a short laugh. "I fell through a hole near the old church into some sort of chamber below—that's how I got this." He waved the arm again. "Pierce was down there, a nice cosy little 'ome he had. He might have done for me too except for our Jack here. He jumped in after me and flattened Pierce with a rock or stone or something."

They all looked at Jack who felt obliged to say something. "Huh, every time I've come up against this loony I got the best of 'im."

Charlie ignored this comment and turned to Abel. "So you left 'im in the hole?"

"Yes, we blocked him in. After we've got the wagon out, we can see he's handed over. Charlie, I don't want you drownin' yourself but maybe you can get around tomorrow, pick up some of the boys so we can get the wagon off the marsh before the floods go down."

"I'll do that, Abe. We must get that load hid."

"Can't you take Pierce and 'and 'im over; then the soldiers won't search?" Jack felt a part of everything now.

"If we can get through the floods up there, we'll do it, Jack. But we still got to move that wagon. It'll stand out like a sore thumb when the waters go down."

Yvonne murmured to Abel, "Chérie, you are tired, you must rest. Lie down. There's nothing more to be done tonight. I will bring food up to you. Go on now."

"You're right as usual. I will go up. This cut Pierce gave me hurts like the very devil. Come and see me before you go tomorrow, Charlie."

All right, Abe, I'll say goodnight." He stood and moved to the door. "G'night ma'am, missy, Jack. Well what d'ya know? The rain's stopped." He disappeared into the night.

Jack stood and stretched. "Up the wooden hill for me too, what a day!" They could hear him muttering as he went upstairs: "Floods, lunatics, stuck wagons—I wish I were in Clerkenwell!"

Abel woke before dawn fevered and with throbbing pain to the chest wound. His arm also ached appallingly. Yvonne felt his restless movements and woke beside him.

"Are you all right, Abel," she murmured sleepily.

"I'm burning up, dear. Infection."

"Oh, no!"

"I'm afraid so—that's all I need at the moment, so much to do."

Yvonne put her hand to Abel's scorching hot forehead. "You must rest. I will prepare a poultice. We must draw out the badness. She slipped smoothly from the bed and put a robe around her shoulders. "Stay there now; I will not be long."

Abel lay back and cursed, thinking of the wagon-load of contraband, Jacob Pierce, the magistrate, soldiery, the farm stock and the weather. He could hear rain rattling on the window.

Soon after Yvonne had cleaned the livid cut and applied a moist poultice, Charlie came to see him.

"Sorry you're laid up, Abel. What do you want me to do? I've put hay in the paddock; Jack is carrying on with that. It's nothing but a mud pond in there now."

"Any sign of the weather easing, Charlie?"

"Yeah, clearing a bit now I think, but from what I can see I'll be lucky if I can make it to the causeway if you want me to go to Romney."

"We need another pair of horses to pull that wagon off the marsh through that flood water, Charlie, even if you can still get to it."

"Maybe I ought to get a boat." Charlie gave a brief grin. "Or oxen, we could get oxen."

"I'm in your hands, Charlie, I've had it for a day or two. I'm burning up right now. One more thing, we can't leave that poor, mad wretch up in the old village to die. Somehow we gotta get him to the authorities. But have a care, Charlie, he's deadly dangerous. He'll take some handling, I can tell you."

"Leave it to me, Abe, I'll get 'im out somehow. I'd better move myself. I'll leave Jack here to finish things off. He'll get his orders!"

155

Lysette came in at that moment carrying a tray. "Breakfast, Papa."

From the back of the horse, Charlie thought he could discern that the flood-waters were already receding a little. He rode round the curving lane that sloped gently down to the inundation.

The man had lived thirty-four years and in that time had not travelled beyond the county town. One of eight brothers and sisters, three of whom had not survived beyond their seventh birthday, Charlie had emerged as a strong, resilient character who, though he could not read or write, had a natural intelligence and cunning. He married at the age of eighteen but within twelve months his young bride had died and his unborn child with her.

Charlie procured employment at Shippenden. The owner, Henry Evans and his three sons, made an excellent living from smuggling; in fact there was scarcely a man in the area who was not recruited by the Evans family. It did not matter whether it was war or peace between France and England. There was ready co-operation between French supply and British demand for contraband goods.

Charlie soon found himself a willing participant in the exciting and profitable operations. For twelve years, there were narrow escapes, pursuits and the occasional man taken.

Henry Evans' luck finally ran out one night when the gang was ambushed by a large body of soldiers as they left the beach, heavily laden. Evans was shot dead along with two others. Some were taken by the soldiers, while the rest scattered into the night, Charlie among them.

When the revenue men came to Shippenden, they found the eldest Evans boy so ill with shingles that he had obviously not taken part in the previous night's contraband landing and there was no evidence against him. The other two sons were in hiding. Charlie managed very well to act the role of half-witted shepherd when he was questioned.

The hunt for the two sons eventually became so intense that they were obliged to flee to France. Young David Evans sold Shippenden to Brownlow and went to America where his two brothers joined him. The seemingly endless war between France and England raged on.

Charlie first met Abel Garnett in Romney, when he arrived from Canterbury with Brownlow, a local solicitor and Charles Foster, who was to be dubbed Charles the second. Charlie soon realised that Abel Garnett was a man used to having his orders carried out. But he threw himself into the role of farm manager readily enough, never asking his men to do anything that he could not do himself.

One day when they worked together in the hay fields, Abel spoke to Charlie in confidence.

"I've heard these rumours Charlie, that you used to have contacts with the French."

"Who told you that? Damn liar whoever it was."

"Well, I've what you might call interests over there myself and I've been asking around, discreetly like. Someone told me the answer was right under me nose!"

"What sort of interests you got over there, then?"

"It's a woman and a young girl. I want to get them over."

"Aah, a woman, eh? Someone you met in the war was it? Must be love. Is the kid yours?"

Abel Garnett bridled. "Watch your mouth, Charlie. Can you help or not?"

"Whereabouts are they over there?"

"They are in Paris. The problem is their family are known to be anti-Bonarpartists. They are still watched even though Boney is finished."

"Could be tricky," said Charlie, seating himself under a lone tree. "Could cost a bit."

Abel looked down at him. "How much?"

"Well, to get politicals across country, whistle 'em across 'ere—could be two-three 'undred pounds."

Abel turned away. "That's no good then. I haven't got thirty, and some of that's my sister's."

Charlie scrambled to his feet and took hold of Abel by the arm. "There is a way to earn quick money, you know, Mr Garnett."

"How's that? Hold up the Dover mail?" Abel snorted.

"No, brandy, silks, tobacco, tea. There's a ready market for 'em all over Kent and Sussex, even London. Every innkeeper, squire, shopkeeper, landowner—they'll all be glad to do tax-free business with ya. Make a fortune in no time."

"Smuggled?"

"What else?" Lepage"—Charlie pronounced the name "Lee Page"—"is still in business, I'll be bound and you've got the perfect place here at Shippenden, near enough to the beach, barns, horses and a free 'and. Nobody to watch over ya. Just like Evans."

"Evans?"

"'E was the previous owner, went into business for 'isself, just like you're goin' to."

Abel sat beneath the tree beside Charlie.

"What 'appened to him?"

"'Is luck run out. Shot by dragoons one moonlit night."

In a few days Charlie was introducing Abel to some of the old hands. They were ready and eager to set to work moonlighting again. Abel was in a quandary as to how to finance the enterprise until Charlie spoke to him.

"I weren't a complete fool during twelve year o' money makin' with the Evans boys. I got me old-age nest-egg. It's goin' to cost you though. I want fair shares, money back on the first haul and first pickings after that."

"Agreed."

Within two months there had been a surreptitious trip to Calais, a first midnight landing, distribution and profitable sale. Abel Garnett stamped his authority on the proceedings. The ruined tower in the abandoned village became the regular cache for the goods in transit.

The farming year proceeded normally, the routines of haying, drives to market and shepherding interspersed with the tension and excitement of the night landings and furtive treks across the marshes.

Shortly before Christmas 1814, Yvonne and Lysette were swept perilously ashore near Dymchurch, the small boat that carried them almost swamped in the heaving seas. The men ashore cheered lustily as Abel took Lysette up in his arms and Yvonne embraced him.

Later Abel sat in the security of the kitchen at Shippenden and listened to Yvonne tell him in her fractured English of the journey she had undertaken from Paris with Lysette under the protection of two of Henri Lepage's henchmen. There had been bad roads and bad weather. Yvonne positively glowed with happiness in the lamplight and Lysette chattered happily in French to her mother and broken English to Abel. It was a night of celebration.

The smuggling trade proved not only too profitable to discontinue but also provided Abel with the frisson of excitement and occasional fear which he had strangely missed since his army days. A sympathetic, not to say grateful clergyman, married Yvonne and Abel in a quiet ceremony.

Now a lunatic was trapped out there on the marsh, in floodwaters that Charlie was urging the reluctant horse through. He was bent on getting that wagon secreted away from prying eyes before disaster struck.

For an ostensibly simple "looker", Charlie was as complex as any man. There was not much that he would not do to save his own skin if it became necessary but, once given, his loyalty was unshakeable, and he was loyal to Abel Garnett.

Gaining the Romney road, Charlie bent his head and secured his slouch hat against the rising wind. He had heard stories of lands where the sun always shone. As he looked out over the bleak, water-filled countryside, he wished himself in one of them. Peering through some drooping willows, he thought that, far away, he saw the black half-submerged shape of the wagon. He hurried on towards Romney.

At midday, Jack Dawkins came to the kitchen. The physical labour of moving a large amount of hay from the barn to the sheep-crowded paddock had left him feeling uniquely satisfied. The weather was drying up at last and the sky was clearing, growing lighter. Jack paused at the door, using the boot-scraper and brushing hay from his hair and shoulders.

"Sit yourself down, Jack, you must be hungry." Yvonne was a warm motherly presence.

Jack cut into meat and potatoes. "Where's Lysette?"

"Upstairs with Abel."

"How is he doin'?"

"The arm is painful, also the wound in the chest which is giving the fever. 'E will be fine though, 'e is strong."

Jack chewed on a piece of mutton. "I'll go up and see 'im, shall I?"

"Of course, Jack, 'e will be glad to see you." Yvonne plunged both hands into a bowl of flour and began mixing pastry. "Jack."

"Yeah?"

"'Ow do you feel now about what 'as 'appened to you? You know, coming to Shippenden, away from your old life. 'As it been so bad?"

Jack was not keen to reveal how he felt about anything to anyone – not that he had ever been asked before. "I could do wiv a few bob."

Yvonne laughed. "And what would you spend your bobs on here in this wild place?"

"I've always 'ad money in me pocket."

Yvonne was scornful. "Other people's money."

Jack thought of himself following a mark down some filthy thoroughfare in the city, his hat pulled down and scarf wound about his throat, tense, and he had to admit it, a little afraid.

"Well, you lot are no better than I am." He was defiant.

"Abel is a good man, Jack; he has his reasons."

"Yeah, he wants to be rich."

"There is more to it than that."

"Look, I don't blame 'im. 'E's been good to me. I just don't want to spend years 'ere wiv just sheep for company. I'll go and see 'im."

As he slowly climbed the stairs, Jack was deep in thought: for one thing he knew that he was not quite the same person who had arrived at Shippenden not so long ago, and he had the sense to see it. Oh, he could still cheat and steal all right, but other things were intruding on him. He wanted certain people to like him, wanted their respect… He looked up with a start. Lysette was waiting at the top of the stairs ready to descend.

"Hello, Jack."

There she was again, dark eyes, dark hair, friendly smile revealing white, even teeth and the blue dress, tight to the waist, then billowing gracefully to her ankles. Jack stumbled slightly on the top step. "Just goin' to see Abe," he muttered.

"He will be glad to see you. He is restless. Some company will be good for him." Lysette skipped lightly down the stairs. To Jack's entranced eyes, she seemed to be floating down them.

Frustration, anger and helplessness welled up in Jack so that he burst rather quickly through the doorway into the room in which Abel lay on the large, untidy bed.

"What's up, Jack?" Abel propped himself up on one elbow.

"Nothin' much, 'ad a hard morning though."

"How's it going out there?" Abel's face had a shining unhealthy pallor, bristles sprouting from an unshaven chin.

"How's the flood looking? Goin' down, is it?"

"I think it is." Jack sat on a cane chair next to the bed. "Weather's cleared up and from what I can see, the water's goin' down."

Abel brushed his hair back from a damp brow. "I hope Charlie gets the job done."

"What will he do with the load, if he can get it off the marsh?"

"Bring it straight here. I've got customers waiting and I want to get rid of it quick."

"What about that madman up there?"

"Soon as Charlie's got that wagon off, we'll let the soldiers have him."

"How about the reward?"

Abel managed a short laugh. "Maybe you'll get a share."

Jack picked at a loose thread of cotton on the edge of a blanket.

"What about Lysette, Abe?"

"Well, I might give her a pound or two as well."

"No, I mean, well, she's fifteen isn't she?"

"Nearly sixteen."

"I mus' be near fifteen meself, might be now for all I know. Lysette—do you think she likes me Abe? I mean—you know sort of thinks anythin' of me?"

Abel looked pityingly at Jack. "Don't be daft, Jack. She's not mine by birth but I know she wouldn't touch you with a barge pole. And you stay away from her d'ya hear?"

"Yeah, I know, but one of these days it's gonna be different."

There was a heavy silence for a moment or two, then Jack asked, "How did you manage to meet up with them, you know, Yvonne and Lysette? When you was in the army, was it?"

"Yes, I met them in France when I was serving there. I eventually managed to get them over here, thank God."

"Did you see much fighting in the army, Abe? Kill many Frenchies?"

"I killed my share, Jack. More than I wanted, looking back."

"When I landed in Portugal in '08, I 'ad no blood on my hands." Abel looked down at his thick, fleshy fingers that curled restlessly on the blanket. "We went ashore in May, as I recall, but it were August before I fired a shot in anger. Just a skirmish but it made me think I should 'ave stayed on the farm." He smiled ruefully. "Later that day, we lost five hundred at Rorica."

Jack whistled through his teeth. "Five 'undred killed?"

"Well—killed, wounded, captured, gone to hell, but that was nothing, boy, nothing to what was to come."

CHAPTER THIRTEEN

Abel Garnett and the Retreat to Corunna

orth-east of Vimiero on the lower slopes of the mountain, Privates Johnny Rose and Abel Garnett formed part of the piquet under the command of Captain Snow. The sounds of battle permeated every fibre of their being. The French advanced through the chestnut trees, a mass of blue and white uniform revealed and concealed by swirling smoke. Musket balls whizzed and flicked over the two companies of the 50th Foot. Leaves and twigs showered down on them as they returned fire under disciplined orders. "We can't stand 'ere much longer!" Rose yelled at Abel above the din. "Why don't Snow let us fall back?"

"Snow's dead; I think it's Captain—what's-'is-name now?" Abel levelled his musket along with more than one hundred others, and pulled the trigger. The blast of fire seemed to send a shudder through the ranks and they were immediately enveloped in choking fumes. "...Coote," said Abel, grounding the butt of his musket to begin re-loading. "Captain Coote, 'e's in command." Another hail of French musket balls cut through and over them, familiar screams of pain and terror, then a hoarse voice calling:

"Fall back, men, fall back!"

"Well, alleluia!" said Rose, "Come on, Abe!"

In an untidy mass, the companies retreated up the sloping

ground, their ranks broken by the olive trees that grew there. They returned fire as best they could but the cheering, baying voices of thousands of French soldiers threatened to drown out even the noise of the cannon.

"There's our lines." They could see the battalion standing in ranks on the crest of a ridge.

"We'll stand here, men! Face the enemy! Fire on command!"

Stentorian roars of sergeants brought the two companies to order, compelling them to produce regular volleys of fire into the approaching French.

"'Oo gave that order to stand?" It was Johnny Rose again shouting in Abel's ear.

"We could 'a' bin with the battalion!"

Abel looked over his shoulder seeking the British position.

"Look Johnny, they're manoeuvrin' up there, goin' off to the left. They're trying to flank 'em, by God!"

Abel worked without thinking, through the reloading and firing procedure. Hearing and not hearing the bellowed orders. He was a small part of a huge machine – a deafening, smoking, precision machine that would need to be smashed piece by piece before it would grind to a halt. And some of the working parts were smashed – falling forward or thrown backwards by the impact of French musket balls, but the machine continued to operate. Every twenty seconds it discharged fire, smoke and musket ball, intricate patterns of movement following each volley.

A commotion on the left, cheering voices, British voices: the machine broke up into individual human beings.

"We've outflanked 'em – look at 'em run!" In a second they were all cheering madly.

"Let the buggers run," said Johnny Rose; "I'm done in." He sat down suddenly on the ground. All along the line, men were doing the same, the abrupt easing of tension leaving them desperately weary.

Myriads of white knapsacks bounced on the backs of French soldiery as they retreated through the trees below.

The British were rolling up their left flank, causing terrible carnage. Abel could detect the sounds of dragoons crashing through woods somewhere out of sight. He sighed, wiped a grimy hand over his smoke-blackened face. Lord, he was thirsty! He groped for his canteen and took a long drink of water.

After the heat of battle came anti-climax. The regiment languished for weeks in an encampment near Lisbon. Abel did not escape the fevers and dysentery that swept through the ranks. There were many deaths, not only of soldiers. The wretched camp followers and their children suffered also.

The weather deteriorated rapidly, and, true to form, when they began their march to Salamanca, the late October skies were discharging endless torrents upon them.

The straggling columns learnt what it was to be hungry from lack of rations, footsore in worn-out boots, wet through and weary from the weather and topography.

There were few stoics among the marching hundreds. They cursed the country, the French, the weather, their officers and their sergeants. When they could think of nothing else to curse, they cursed each other.

Kept ignorant of tactics and grand plans, they only knew that they were part of Sir John Moore's forces marching to Salamanca. What was to happen after that only God and the officers knew.

They were a month on the road and, the further they went, the worse things became. The villages grew meaner and their inhabitants unwelcoming. Spending nights in stinking stables became a luxury, preferable to crude shelters under rain-soaked trees in the mountainous terrain. Half their days were spent putting shoulders to bullock carts to assist them up the mud-caked precipitous tracks. Once a span of bullocks was unable to sustain the upward impetus of an ammunition cart and Abel barely had time to drag Johnny out of the way before it rolled inexorably over the edge of a ravine. The unfortunate animals gave a despairing bellow as they disappeared into the void. Temperatures fell. Men froze in their sleep and never woke in the morning.

At last they began to emerge from the mountains, morale strangely boosted by the news that flew along the column that they were passing from Portugal into Spain.

It was several days before the last of the stragglers arrived at Salamanca, long after the main army had made their way through the narrow, cobbled streets of the town.

The regiments were still recovering from their exertions in early December when rumours began to pass like a wind even colder than the one that was blowing down on them from the hills. A vastly superior French force was approaching, led by one of Napoleon's elite marshals. Further news filtered down to the soldiers that they were to advance on Valladolid as a feint to draw Napoleon's forces away from Madrid.

Whatever the tactics were, Abel was marching once more. This time it was snow and the cold blast of winter wind that they had to contend with. It was an endless, featureless plain that the army wormed its way across, showing up darkly against the thickening layer of snow. Cavalry screens had been sent out on both flanks and the infantry felt secure from a surprise attack by the French. On the 19th December, after a forced march of eleven hours, the column staggered exhausted into the town of Mayorga to be united with the balance of Moore's army.

Thirty thousand officers and men found what comfort they could. Johnny Rose, by some mysterious means, produced a bottle of brandy which he surreptitiously shared with Abel as they crouched over a small fire. The liquor coursed a burning path into Abel's stomach sending warming currents throughout his body. "Ah, John, I don't know how you do it. Producing something like this just at the right moment."

Johnny Rose grinned through his dirt-encrusted, bearded features. "One man's loss—another's gain. Besides I owe you for saving me being knocked off that mountain track by the bullock cart."

"I thank 'ee anyway," Abel said. "Now, when are we goin' to get some bread an' meat?—I'm starved."

After two days the great mass of men, horses, wagons and carts decamped and, the snow deadening the sound of their movement, they processed toward Sahagun. Tension, excitement and gossip increased as they learnt that the enemy was close at hand. Men began to pay attention to their equipment and weapons. Instead of facing the old enemy in battle, however, they were suddenly in headlong retreat from a superior force. In appalling weather conditions, forced marches were endured, swollen rivers crossed, mountain passes negotiated.

Camped in the open on the frozen snow, Abel, bearded and filthy, in worn-out boots and tattered uniform, gripped his musket and slipped to his knees in despair. Across the bleak escarpment, as far as he could see, dark shapes marked the snow, some animal, some human. The shapes did not move. They would never move again. Abel felt tears on his face as his throat constricted painfully with emotion. "We've had it," he thought. "We'll all be dead soon, starved and froze to death."

But they did not all die. Most of the army struggled into Lugo.

Sir John Moore called a halt to the grim retreat. Food and ammunition stores were there, plus a strong defensive position offering the opportunity to rest the exhausted troops.

Abel and Johnny's spirits improved along with their fellows at the thought of a possible battle. Abel was detached enough to reflect upon the strange phenomenon of half-dead, starving men, cheering up at yet another opportunity to kill or die in agony. He wondered if this attitude was some peculiar British trait or whether all humankind was made so.

The French General Soult was not keen to throw his forces against the natural stronghold of Lugo and its surroundings, so the battle was not joined. After the best part of three days, the British were stumbling, many barefoot, toward Corunna, and the troop transports that were rumoured to be waiting in harbour to take them ignominiously back to England.

Abel was among the last piquets to leave the defensive positions in a cold, wet January dawn. Although there had been no sign of Soult's army, he had an uncomfortable feeling between his shoulder blades. As the rearguard hurried to join the main force, he fully expected a French musket ball to shatter his backbone.

At Corunna, there were no ships waiting to take them away and morale plunged again. Abel found himself in close quarters with Johnny and the raggle-taggle remnants of the 50th Foot, resting in a large solid building close to the citadel of the town. Early on the second morning, a tremendous explosion, closely followed by another, rocked the building and a blast of air blew the doors open. Shouts and screams of alarm from the streets reached their ears as they rushed in a mass to the exits.

"The Frenchies are 'ere already, now we're for it!"

Officers appeared, some of them still chewing their breakfast.

"Men, the French are close by and we've been obliged to blow our powder stores. The gunners are even now throwing their wagons over the cliffs. We can't allow ourselves to provide for the enemy."

The following day, a huge number of transports arrived and impressively entered Corunna harbour. Somehow the feeling of depression deepened among the soldiers. Abel felt ill-at-ease. All the marching, the suffering, the lives wasted by starvation, the appalling weather and rampant disease, all for nothing! He spat contemptuously.

The massive task of embarkation began with the sick and wounded, followed by the artillery and cavalry, the pride of the army.

"Poor bloody footsloggers, last agin," Johnny Rose muttered as they viewed the proceedings from a high vantage point. Higher still, on the cliffs, an appalling slaughter of horses was taking place, only prime stock could be taken away to England. Hundreds of others were shot or put to the sword by cavalry men weeping helplessly as they disposed of their mounts. Men strove at their tasks all through the night.

Before the embarkation of infantry could begin, however, the enemy arrived; three French divisions appeared on a ridge near the town. Once more the adrenaline flowed as the regiments deployed along the four hundred feet high opposing ridge, the 50th holding the centre.

"'Ere we go, boys!" Men rubbed their muskets fondly, wiping their bleary, unshaven faces, scorched and darkened by the elements. Johnny Rose nudged Abel as they knelt together facing the heights where 20,000 French were massed.

"Look, Abe, look 'oo's comin'." It was General Moore, riding grandly along the ridge with Major Napier. Men stood respectfully, some calling out loyally to the officers who acknowledged them with casual salutes. Their horses picked their way delicately over the stony ground until they disappeared from view.

Shortly after, from a thousand yards' distance, French cannon opened up. The French lines disappeared behind smoke, round shot reaching the British lines at almost the same moment as the sound of the cannon's roar.

There was blood, torn flesh, severed limbs. Abel's own flesh jumped and tightened in anticipation of pain and death. Screams of agony and cries of defiance. The smoke on the opposite ridge cleared away and Abel saw the French line begin to descend the rocky slope. The 50th's own officers began to bawl orders and over the edge they went, packed tightly together: "Click, click, click." On went the bayonets glittering in a menacing mass of sharpened steel, pointing, pointing at the still distant enemy. Someone next to Abel stumbled on the rough ground, but Abel shot out an arm, grabbed the man and hauled him to his feet.

He discerned the crude huddle of buildings in the valley, a typical, poverty-stricken village of the area, now packed with French soldiers.

Passing the standing ranks of a cheering British regiment, Abel was forced on at a furious pace by the press of his surrounding comrades. He glanced quickly round for Johnny and saw him briefly, his teeth bared, nostrils flaring, eyes starting from his head. A crash of musket fire from both sides. Now he was tearing past the side of a stone building with twenty or thirty others. Blue and white uniforms, very close. Sweat poured down Abel's face. He lunged in time-honoured fashion at a French uniform, felt the soft impact of steel on flesh, withdrew and whirled to meet a threatening blade on his left. Clash of steel on steel, down went the enemy, into the throat went Abel's bayonet. French men began to turn away. They were running, heading for their own friendly slope.

"Forward! Forward to the hill, men." Officers called out encouragement.

Panting, Abel scrambled among the rocks of the slope as a shattering fire of musketry poured down from above them. Many died. Chips of stone ricocheted into Abel's cheek, drawing blood. Fire was being poured into the halted British regiment from the flanks now. "Where's the bloody 42nd?" someone yelled above the din. "Where's the 42nd?" The cry was taken up.

The distinguished figure of Major Napier appeared a few yards from where Abel crouched. "Come on, men! We must take those guns! For England, men! Don't let's be bested! Oh, the dishonour!" Abel found himself moving toward the officer. Others were doing likewise. Two or three officers, then more men until there were twenty or thirty of them. "Come on, lads! You gallant boys!" Cheering wildly, they were off! To Abel's tired brain, it was a nightmare kaleidoscope of colour, noise, flashing light and pungent smells. He was aware of men falling all around him. It was hopeless. Abel's mind cleared. He was still close to Napier, there were no more than six or seven British uniforms on view. Dozens of French were closing in on them. "Follow me. We'll cut our way through, men!" Napier's cry sounded hoarse but determined.

Abel was suddenly full of the conviction that he would not die here. It was inexplicable, but he knew it.

Napier led the little group in a desperate charge to break through the gathering French soldiers and rejoin the British ranks. Abel, musket gripped firmly in both hands, ploughed into the French. Using butt and bayonet, he smashed, clubbed and stabbed his way forward. He felt several warm but piercing sensations in various parts of his body. Men fell away from his furious onslaught. He lost sight of his comrades; a severe blow on the side of his head made him stagger and almost fall, then he was on clear ground and racing away, roaring like some enraged animal. A ragged volley of musketry behind him. Zip! Zip! Musket balls sped past his swerving body. A burning pain in his side, then there was cheering and a more solid blast of musket fire from the British. Abel fell gratefully into the arms of men from the 42nd Foot who were belatedly providing support for the decimated 50th.

"All right, mate, you're 'ome an dry now," a battered but kindly face looked down on Abel as he sprawled on his back covered in dust, sweat and blood.

"Where were you 42nd boys?" he panted. "We could have taken that ridge with a bit o' help."

"Why, we were retiring, lad, relieved by the guards I believe."

"Then where are they?"

"Don't ask me, mate, some sort o' ball's up, I reckon."

Musket fire still rattled and rolled around the valley. "Where's the 50th?" Abel's head was swimming.

"Falling back over there—what's left of 'em. Out of ball I reckon, there go the guards now."

"I must get back—" Abel struggled to his feet.

"Keep your 'ead down," advised the amiable private of the 42nd.

Abel did as well as he could, scrambling weakly from rock to rock, taking advantage of the scant cover. He noted that the French were falling back from the little village and regaining the opposing heights. The French batteries were pounding away, shot falling around and among the fragile dwellings.

Now Abel was among familiar faces, friends turned to assist him up the sloping ground. Something odd was happening to him. His legs no longer supported his weight, a thick, thick mist hindered his vision, then all his senses failed him.

Abel was bouncing gently – up, down, up, down; he attempted to raise an arm to rub his eyes and found that he could not. He tried to speak through parched lips: "What's goin' on?"

Someone poured water between his lips, half-choking him. Then the familiar voice of Johnny Rose: "It's all right, Abe. You're on a litter. I'm wiv you, I got permission. It's evenin', ole friend, an' guess what?—We're embarkin' for good old England, an' you're a bloomin' 'ero!"

"What?" Abel croaked.

"Well, you know, the forlorn 'ope, sole survivor as far as anybody knows. Five wounds, bustin' through them Frenchies like a batterin' ram." Johnny laughed quietly: "You bloody fool!"

The litter rocked and swayed, its carriers were marching on cobblestones. There was the lap of water and the smell of the sea.

Aboard the man-of-war, *Steadfast*, Abel came to his senses again. A florid little doctor was bending over him as he lay among fifty or sixty other wounded.

"Clean wounds, young man, loss of blood of course, but you'll do fine if there's no infection. Take plenty of liquids." The doctor turned abruptly to the pallid looking individual lying close to Abel.

"This hand might have to come off, you brave fellow— we'll see, we'll see."

Captain Deane, of whom Abel had only the briefest acquaintance threaded his way through the sick and dying, crouched over to avoid striking his blonde head on the low deck beams.

Abel attempted and surprised himself by succeeding in sitting upright. To his amazement, Captain Deane proffered a hand which Abel briefly clasped. "Well done, Garnett, I'm glad your wounds are not too serious. You performed bravely. In the finest tradition. We observed the forlorn hope assault on the French positions. You are believed to be the sole survivor."

"Is Major Napier dead then, sir? And the others?"

"Dead or captive, our most grievous loss is General Moore, a great man to be sure."

"But we did win the day, sir?"

"It is believed the French may have lost two or three thousand to our seven or eight hundred. The 50th took the brunt. We lost upwards of two hundred men, I'm afraid. I will miss my good friends, ensigns Moore and Stewart. Did you know them?"

The Captain was surprisingly free from awareness of class or position.

"N-no, sir. Not too well, I'm sorry."

"Well, Garnett, you are a brave man and when you are fit for duties, you will be made sergeant. We have need of them, you know. We lost five in the battle." The captain turned and, stooping, made his way to the companion way that apparently led up and out into the fresh sea air.

The ship corkscrewed its way across the Bay of Biscay, having remained tiresomely at anchor until the whole army had embarked on the fleet. Five days later, Abel was fit enough to be on the crowded deck to gain a sighting of the English coast.

CHAPTER FOURTEEN

The Militia Confiscate Abel Garnett's Wagon

ack Dawkins walked with Lysette in the fading evening light. He was amazed to find that he was holding her hand, reassuring her about Abel's fever. "A little thing like that ain't gonna cause 'im any problems," Jack said confidently.

They were making for their usual spot at the paddock fence. A cool breeze rustled the grasses and a watery sun, low in the west was almost obliterated by dark clouds. The sights and sounds of nature were lost on Jack. He was only aware of Lysette and her proximity and the fact that she had quite naturally and unconsciously taken his hand when they left the house.

"Abel will be up and about tomorrow, you see." They reached the paddock and stood next to its gate. The pasture was still crowded with sheep brought in from the flood. "Water's going down already," Jack said. He felt oddly disappointed that the drama of the flood was over.

"Yes," said Lysette, "I can see the lane now, and the islands, they get bigger." She was correct in this. Earlier that day, very little land could be seen, but now most of the marsh visible from the farm had re-emerged.

Jack, in something of a turmoil, grasped Lysette's hand tightly and made a clumsy attempt to kiss her. With a small, graceful movement of her head, she avoided allowing his lips to touch hers, but the brief contact they made on her downy cheek set him on fire and he tried again, pulling her to him with unexpected force.

"No, Jack, you must not," Lysette turned her face away and wrenched one arm free.

Jack immediately released her other arm. "Not good enough, I suppose." His tone was bitter with a touch of self-contempt. "That's all right wiv me. I'm out of 'ere soon, anyway. I don't know what you're so proud about anyway. You're the same as me. Don't know your Pa. No 'ome and not much else as far as I can see."

Lysette's face crumpled and she began to cry quietly. "My papa is dead and I had to leave France with Mama to be with Abel. This is my home now—we cannot go back you know."

Jack, feeling real affection for another human being, had little idea of how to cope with all the conflicting emotions of desire, tenderness, anger and frustration. "My life's been turned upside down too, you know," he blurted. "I've lost me friends, I don't know this place. There's nothing here anyway, 'cept sheep, water, an', what with maniacs on the loose, smugglers an' floods, I've 'ad enough of it. Give me London anytime." A wild idea occurred to him. "We could go together! Come on, let's get out. We can do it! I'll take care of you!"

Lysette's features underwent an immediate reconstruction as her tears turned to laughter. "Go away with you, Jack? You are a silly boy!" She wiped her face with one delicate hand, patting him gently on the chest with the other, giving another gurgling laugh.

"All right, all right. Well, I'm off then." Jack felt like a small child as he stalked off. He was across the muddy yard and through the farm gate before rational thought returned. His gait slowed to a moody stroll as he continued down the lane beneath the bare branches of storm-battered trees. Jack kicked savagely at some clods of earth. He would have to creep back after dark, being less anxious to leave Shippenden than he thought.

Cursing himself for a fool that would never be able to look Lysette in the face again, he thrust his hands into his pockets and with the last rays of the sun casting long shadows across the soaked land, continued slowly to the junction with the causeway. Jack's timing could not have been bettered. He was on the point of slinking shamefacedly back to the farm when he saw the large body of soldiers marching in perfect order. They were coming straight towards him, still several hundred yards away, but approaching at a fairly rapid pace.

"Comin' to search for that lunatic, I reckon," Jack told himself, still unaware that Jake Pierce lay beneath several hundredweight of stone in that remote cellar. His first instinct was to hide himself from what he took to be representatives of law and order. He slipped quietly behind the fat boles of some willows. Glancing along the route the soldiers would follow, he was shaken to see coming towards him from the other direction the unmistakable outline of the wagon. There was Charlie, high on the seat and some other men riding behind him on the load.

Charlie was in a dilemma. He had seen the soldiers too and was very reluctant to have an encounter with them. Unable to turn the wagon round without risking getting stuck in the marsh again, he decided there was nothing for it but to whip up the pair of horses and get to the lane leading to Shippenden before the soldiers reached the junction themselves.

It would be a close race. The load they were bringing in could be death to them all and they knew it. As the soldiers bore down on them the men on the wagon became increasingly nervous. One of them abruptly stood up and jumped over the tailgate, quickly followed by a second. They were simple working men anxious only to earn a supplement to their meagre income. They were not going to risk tangling with soldiers. They splashed their way across the marshes whilst Charlie cursed them for cowardly fools.

A young lieutenant, keen as mustard, riding a fine mare, frowned at the sight of the two men disappearing into the marsh away from the innocuous-looking farm wagon. He spurred his horse forward, quickly outdistancing the marching men. Galloping past Jack's hiding place, he reined in before the approaching wagon, holding up his hand in commanding fashion. "Stop! Stop, I say." The lieutenant's voice brooked no dissent. He could see now that Charlie had a pistol in his belt. His hand strayed to his own silver-plated pistol butt, a gift from his father. "This wagon will be searched. Sit still all of you, if you know what's good for you. You fellows are up to no good."

A burst of activity in the body of the wagon as five men leapt in all directions. They hit the ground running. The lieutenant pulled his pistol at the same moment as Charlie's misfired with a dull click and brief puff of smoke. The officer restrained himself from firing and pointed an unwavering barrel at Charlie's chest. "You'll hang for that, my man—attempted murder of one of His Majesty's officers."

Charlie stared back defiantly. "Go to hell!"

An advance body of panting, uniformed men hurried up. "Roust those fellows out, men," he gestured to the several parties splashing away in the near distance. The soldiers scrambled down the bank of the causeway in swift pursuit, whilst the main column advanced at the double led by a portly, out-of-breath sergeant

"Secure that man, sergeant." The lieutenant waved his pistol at Charles. He was enjoying himself. "Search that wagon. Let's see what we have here."

Excited soldiers hauled Charlie roughly from the wagon seat, his wrists swiftly pinioned behind his back. More men climbed up and over the high wheels.

"Look at this, Lieutenant. Brandy, tobacco, cloth—there's a fortune here, sir!"

The lieutenant descended from his horse in dignified fashion, straightening his uniform. He addressed Charlie: "What's your name and where are you taking this contraband? Speak up!"

Charlie stared grimly into the middle distance, remaining silent.

"Soldiers coming back, sir," cried the stout sergeant. "I think they got prisoners."

"Good work, men!" the lieutenant enthused as several muddied privates climbed back onto the causeway, pushing two of Charlie's companions before them.

Charlie exchanged meaningful glances with them as they stood crestfallen before him.

"Sergeant, you must secure those two prisoners also. They will ride under guard in the wagon. We will hand them over to the civil authorities at Romney. Tomorrow, at dawn, we start to sweep these marshes for this so-called lunatic. The waters are falling quickly now."

"You won't find no lunatic—'e's dead!" one of the captors blurted out.

"Shut up Harry—tell 'em nothin'!" Charlie snarled the words.

"What do you know of this lunatic, then?" asked the lieutenant.

The man glanced uncomfortably at Charlie. "Only that you're wastin' your time looking for 'im now," he muttered.

"Oh, and why is that?"

"Look," said the man desperately, "I'm no smuggler, I'm just 'elping out. You know. Get this load off the marsh where it got bogged. I was asked to 'elp and I did. I've got a wife an' kids an' all! I can save you a lotta wild goose chases. What can you do for me?"

"I'll swing for you, 'Arry." Charlie was irate.

The sergeant stepped forward and rammed a fist into his stomach. "Shut up, you. You'll swing anyway." He turned to the lieutenant. "You know, sir"—he indicated the frightened labourer—"if he can save us all days of trampin' up an' down these marshes—well perhaps you might feel inclined to go easy on 'im."

Charlie was bent over but recovering from the punch the sergeant had delivered.

Harry grasped at the straw of hope presented. "I can take you to the body. Then you let me go, eh?"

The officer made a decision. "Sergeant Hayes, take six men with this fellow and report to me at Romney. Can you lead them to it before full dark?"

"N-no sir, it's too near dark now. But I'll take 'ee at first light." Harry was never so co-operative.

"Oh, very well." The lieutenant was disappointed. He

turned to the troops who were by now idling in untidy groups. "Form up, men! Look sharp now. Supper's waiting for us at Romney. Sergeant, you can turn the wagon in that lane there," he indicated the turning to Shippenden Farm.

Jack, who had been enthralled by the proceedings, shrank down in his hiding place as a reversing wagon wheel came perilously close, but, in a few minutes, the whole column was disappearing into the gathering gloom along the road to Romney.

The Dodger sprinted up the lane to the farm, hauled himself over the gate and tore past a startled Lysette, who, having waited fruitlessly for his return, had finally given a slight shrug of her young shoulders and started making her way to the house. "Jack!" But he was gone through the front door. He grabbed the banister rail, gulping in air. Yvonne was coming down the stairs. "Jack, what is the matter now?"

"Is he—is Abe awake?"

"Why yes, he is much better now."

"I gotta see him right away."

"Well, all right, you may go up to 'im."

Jack was already brushing past Yvonne on his way to the top of the stairs.

Abel was sitting up in bed feeling cool and rested, if a little weak. The pain of the wound in his chest was sharp, clean and diminishing.

"What's up now, Jack? You look as though there's a dozen hounds after you."

"There'll be somebody after both of us if we don't get out of 'ere—the law!"

"What?"

"The wagon's bin took, Charlie's bin took and others besides, an' there's a blabbermouth ready to tell 'em anything they want to know."

Abel threw back the bedcovers and swung his bare feet to the floor. He made a faintly comical sight in his nightshirt.

"Give it to me straight, Jack, while I get some clothes on." Hairy white legs and feet contrasted starkly with the bronzed, weather beaten face.

"It sounds as though Charlie took some of the lads up to the old hiding place and found Pierce dead," Abel said as he pulled on his boots with a faint grunt, after Jack explained what he had seen and heard. "It's a mess all right. I've got to think this through. Let's go downstairs. I need some air."

At the foot of the stairs, Yvonne took Abel's arm. "Is it trouble, Abe? More trouble?"

"Nothing for you to worry about, my dear." His voice was soothing. "I just need a little walk to clear my head."

"Be careful of your wound, Abe."

"Oh, that's much better—a lot better. You comin', Jack?"

Lysette came through the front door. Once more Abel had to make placatory noises and appeal to the girl to stay with her mother. Lysette brushed past Jack without looking at him and he was intensely aware of the rustle of her clothing as she went by.

In the cool evening air, Abel headed inevitably for the paddock fence. He was soon leaning on it, looking gloomily across the backs of the tightly packed flock of sheep that still resided within the confines of the pasture. The reek of dung and damp wool assaulted Jack's nostrils as he climbed onto the fence, turning to sit on the top rail.

The welcoming glow of lanterns beckoned from the ground floor windows of the house, now silhouetted against the darkening sky.

"What a mess!" Jack was suddenly struck by the facts of the situation. The smuggled goods were taken, Charlie too; the rescued sheep were destroying the paddock; Lysette hated him, and if "blabbermouth" lived up to Jack's expectations, soldiers would soon be coming for Abel and himself. "Now's the time to cut and run," he told himself.

"What you gonna do, Abe?"

"I'm thinkin', boy, thinkin'. You know with Pierce dead, as soon as those soldiers hand Charlie, Harry and the others over to the magistrate's, there's no need for them to stay. They'll be goin' back to Brabourne Lees, I reckon, pattin' theirselves on their backs for killin' two birds with one stone. Catchin' smugglers and finding Pierce."

"But what if Harry points the finger at you—at us? Soldiers could be on their way 'ere right now."

"I don't blame Harry for trying to duck out," said Abel, "but telling them where to find Pierce and telling them about me are two different things. Good luck to 'im if they let 'im go. But I doubt they will somehow."

"So what you goin' to do?" persisted Jack.

"The trouble with Charlie is he's always too quick to use his pistol."

"Don't I know it," said Jack, ruefully.

"Now I got to save him from the hangman and it won't be easy," breathed Abel.

"Easy? It won't be possible!" said Jack, looking at Abel with a sinking feeling.

"I don't know, Jack. Not much of a gaol at Romney. They'll be movin' them to Dover, maybe tomorrow. We could bust them out of prison or take them on the Dover Road. Might even get the wagon-load back."

"You're crazy!"

"And you're too young to understand. Look, what do you reckon? I let Charlie 'ang and the others rot in gaol, then go back as before and get rich without 'em. I couldn't do that, Jack, so there's only one choice: try an' get them out, so I might as well try for the goods as well."

"OK. How?"

"Well, for one thing, you're out of this. No sense in draggin' you down with me if things go wrong."

"Huh, this is meat an' drink to me," said Jack, having another instant change of mind. "Just lately I've bin dep— depraved of what I do best which is dodge and thieve an such. I could come in 'andy."

"I think you mean deprived." Abel almost laughed. "We'll see, but no takin' risks, whatever happens."

Jack jumped down from the fence rail and together they started a slow walk back to the house. "I'm not too happy about asking this, Jack, but you could help. It's still quite early;

181

you could be in Romney in an hour or so. Those soldiers will be out drinking; you could pick up a lot of news if you kept your ears open. Are you game?"

"I'm your man, Abe." Jack was more than ready for some of his old activities.

"Right. Find out all you can about Charlie, Harry and the others. When they're going to move 'em and how, and what's happened to the wagon. I'm goin' to try an' get some of the boys. Not all of 'em will be keen on this sort of game. They don't mind a bit o' night-work from time to time, but that's as far as they'll go. We'll meet you by that barn on the edge of town. You'll maybe need some money. Here's a half-guinea." He looked almost fondly at Jack. "And here's another."

"I'll get my coat," said Jack, pocketing the first cash he had seen for some time. They entered the house. The lanterns shone brightly in contrast to the darkness outside.

"'Ave a quick bite before you go, Jack."

Jack was more than ready for this as well, feeling suddenly very hungry.

As he sat once more in the now familiar kitchen, he could hear the soft murmur of voices as Abel spoke with Lysette and Yvonne. Then they were in the room with him, Abel carrying his coat and hat. They all expressed the wish that he took good care of himself and as he went out into the night, Lysette darted a swift kiss on his cheek. This sent him off in such a turmoil that he was almost at the Romney Road before coming to his senses again.

With its population increased by fifty or sixty soldiers, Romney's inns were having a prosperous night. Jack drifted in and out of three of them during the course of an hour or so. Sitting on a bench seat in one of the noisiest, he engaged in a shouted conversation with two bibulous privates who responded well to his flattering admiration of the way in which they had captured the desperate gang of smugglers. From the way they bragged, an innocent bystander would have thought that they had just fought a pitched battle against almost overwhelming odds!

At the third inn, Jack learnt that the magistrate was ensconced in a private room with the officer commanding the company of soldiers and some other dignitaries of the town. More self-congratulations no doubt. He learnt a lot more beside, by the use of his cunning wit, from the garrulous and gullible soldiers and locals.

There was no one at the barn when Jack arrived, so he settled himself out of the cold wind that had risen. Hunched down with coat collar up and hat pulled over his eyes, he soon dozed off.

When Abel laid a large hand on his shoulder, he sprang up in such alarm that Abel gave a short laugh. "Sorry Jack, didn't mean to startle you like that."

"Is—is everythin' all right?" Jack rubbed sleep from his eyes.

"Sure. How are you?"

"I'm fine. What time is it?"

"Gone midnight. The word's goin' round. We should have a few bodies 'ere in an hour or two. We're going to fool 'em Jack! We're going to sea!"

"To sea! I can't swim y' know!"

"You won't 'ave to. Look, we got friends with a fishing boat, so we get Charlie and the load away by sea. They won't be expecting that. Sail up the coast, up the Thames. My sister's house is a few hundred yards from the shore, remember. Charlie can stay there; we can hide the goods there as well. When the hue and cry's died down, Charlie, Harry and the others can disappear with their share."

"What about us?"

"I don't intend to throw everything up here. We'll mask ourselves with scarves and long coats, then, once the job's done—all under cover of darkness, mind—we'll get back to Shippenden at the double to take care o' those ruddy sheep!" No one the wiser."

"You've got some problems, though."

"Oh, what are those then?" Abel oozed confidence.

"Well for a start, that wagon's locked up and guarded by soldiers, with a sergeant in charge to make sure they don't weaken and get at the brandy."

Jack sat down, his back resting against the wooden slats of the barn.

Abel joined him. "What else?"

"Charlie and the others are going to Maidstone, not Dover and they're being guarded as well. Armed soldiers."

Well, if they're taking 'em to Maidstone that does settle it. If they were going on the coast road to Dover, I had thought of waylaying 'em and have the boat nearby. Now we've got to go in before dawn. Before they take the road." Abel was totally absorbed in what he was planning. Past and future meant nothing. He was living for the moment and relishing it.

"There's one other thing, I forgot," said Jack; "that Pierce—the madman. It's all over town that he's dead. And d'you know—" his teeth gleamed briefly in the darkness—"'is ghost 'as already bin seen out on the marsh."

Abel rubbed an itch on his shoulder. "But nobody actually knows he's dead, do they?"

"Well, they haven't been up there yet and now they're scared to, if you ask me."

"Pierce could be useful to us, you know, dead or alive," Abel said thoughtfully.

They sat together in silence, staring out into the night. They could just distinguish the outlines of treetops and the dark track of the causeway winding away towards Shippenden.

Jack's thoughts turned to Lysette. "Abel, I don't understand it."

"Don't understand what?"

"Well, one minute Lysette seems friendly, then she 'ates me, then when I was leavin' tonight, she—well she kissed me."

Abel's hand grasped Jack's shoulder tightly, painfully. "You ain't been tryin' anything, have you?"

"No—no, course not, but I just can't make her out."

"I'll tell you something, Jack, Lysette hasn't had a happy start in life, either. You ain't the only one you know. She lost her father, 'ad a very bad experience when only a babe and left all behind her in France to come with her mother to England."

"What sort of bad experience?" Jack asked, intrigued.

"Oh, it's all too complicated for now," said Abe. "Get some rest, we got an hour or so yet."

Jack's question about Lysette started thought-processes in Abel's mind that he was unable to repress. Lysette's sufferings had cut through his own callused feelings bringing to life the human being that still existed beneath the hardened shell of bitter experience.

CHAPTER FIFTEEN

Abel Garnett in Love

aving escaped the 50th Foot's part in the fiasco of Walcheren in the Netherlands due to a suppurating wound, Sergeant Abel Garnett found himself back on the familiar Portuguese shore in September 1810. Napoleon Bonaparte, intent on conquering all of Europe was pressing hard against Portugal, and so Sir Arthur Wellesley was commanding a British force on the peninsular in an attempt to thwart the ambitions of the tyrant.

Abel did not see the grand plan or partake in devising strategy; he was one of the 30,000 men struggling to survive each day in the dust and heat of the poverty-stricken land, hoping that the commissariat would provide them with their daily bread and meat, replace their boots when worn out and generally not give way to corruption and inefficiency.

As ever, their wishes were not always granted. Mostly he trusted the officers not to get them killed needlessly. Some he had a great deal of respect for. Others, like the arrogant Captain Swithin, he despised. Swithin abused his lieutenants, his sergeant majors, his sergeants, his corporals and his private soldiers. He was a tall, thin man with a small mouth, always pursed as though he had just suffered some personal affront;

his uniform betrayed his wealth, being formed from the finest materials, with a magnificent sword at his waist, silk gloves and the best pair of boots that money could buy. He kept his servants busy from early morning to well past sunset. He was also a notorious gambler. The several fine horses that he possessed disappeared one by one into the hands of other officers.

Abel detected something sinister in the captain. "I wonder what devils are driving him," he thought to himself.

Johnny Rose had returned safely from Walcheren, his usual ebullient self. Unlike many of his companions, he had managed to escape the mysterious fever that had struck down hundreds of the expeditionary force to the low countries.

Abel's promotion and new duties separated him somewhat from his friends in the ranks. For three years, the regiment foot-slogged, baked, froze, starved and fought its way to and fro across the peninsular from Fuentes D'Honor to the Pyrenees and beyond.

On 23rd December 1811, while the 50th Foot were in winter quarters at Portacegre, Private John Rose was hanged for looting. Captain Swithin insisted that the full force of military law be brought to bear on the soldier whose luck had finally run out. He was caught red-handed by a night piquet, while returning from a raid on a village, laden with neck-wrung poultry and wine.

There was an order in force from Wellington himself that all looters were to be hung.

Abel approached Captain Swithin at his tent minutes before the hanging. "Sir, can you not spare the life of Private Rose in the spirit of Christmas? He has fought well for his King and country. He is a rogue, but so are many that are with us."

Captain Swithin looked up from where he sat in his camp chair. "He should not have got himself caught, should he? A hanging will be good for the other rogues. Make them have a care."

"But, sir, it is Christmas, surely—"

"That's all, sergeant. Rose will hang, and in a very few minutes too. Now may I be allowed to finish my breakfast?"

"Sorry, Abe." Johnny's last words to Abel were an apology. "You've bin a good friend, an' I reckon you're going to miss me too, eh? I just thought a few extra victuals would help us enjoy Christmas." His handshake was firm and dry before he was marched to the gallows.

"Johnny. God bless you man!" Abel called out as the noose was placed round his friend's neck.

"Grounds mighty hard for diggin' hereabouts, boys. Just pile stones on me," was Johnny's final utterance.

The event was another great callous on Abel's nature, already hardened by his participation in many bloody encounters. At Almaraz during the assault on Fort Napoleon, his grim determination to win the ramparts led to Captain North, one of the officers he had so closely followed, nicknaming him 'Game' Garnett which the rankers quickly corrupted to 'Old Gamey'. Abel felt this name quite appropriate as, like the rest of them, he had limited opportunity for bathing.

March, evade, retreat, fight, bivouac, bury the dead. In due time the army was in France in the dying embers of the fire that Napoleon Bonaparte had lit in Europe. In April 1814, the fire sputtered and went out when the victorious Wellington entered Toulouse.

⋞⋗⋞⋗

Sergeant Abel Garnett was a message-carrier riding through the peaceful French countryside. He was carrying orders to Captain Swithin and Lieutenant Woods billeted at an address on the outskirts of Toulouse. Abel knew very well the contents of the sealed orders. The regiment was to march to Poliac by way of Bordeaux where they would take ship for Ireland.

After a brief search, Abel found the neatly shuttered, three-storied house that stood slightly detached from its neighbours. There were many hundreds of officers billeted in similar places throughout the town, all awaiting movement orders now that Napoleon was on his way to Elba.

As he stood at the rather ornate door awaiting an answer to his knock, Abel heard a stifled moan, brief, but unmistakable and it came from somewhere within. Cautiously, he turned the door handle. The door yielded easily to his weight and he stepped into a dim hall with a staircase on his left, running up to the first floor. "Hello. Is someone hurt?" he called out, feeling rather foolish.

There was a distinct shuffling sound from above and Abel quickly mounted the stairs. He was almost on the landing when a bedroom door opened and a vaguely familiar figure appeared. Bootless, shirt hanging loose over officer's trousers, an officer of the 42nd? Abel wasn't sure. What he was certain of was the pistol that the officer brought slowly up from his side and pointed squarely at him before he mounted the last stair. "Sir?" he questioned.

"Get out of here, you fool!" the officer hissed, waving the pistol barrel at Abel in a form of dismissal.

"Sir, I have orders for Captain Swithin."

"All right, I'll give them to him; give them to me, then get out!"

As a puzzled Abel pulled the envelope from his belt, a dark-haired figure appeared behind the officer, something that looked like a large vase was raised up and brought down hard on the back of the officer's head. Giving a sort of gasp, he fell forward against Abel, who only just prevented them both from toppling down the stairs. "What the—?"

A half-naked woman was babbling at him. "*Mon dieu! M'sieur, aidez-moi, aidez-moi. Ma fille! Haut escayer!*"

"What?" Abel was baffled.

"*Pardon, m'sieur.*" The woman pulled what little clothing she wore more closely around herself covering bare breasts as best she could with one hand. Abel heard the stunned officer, now laying at his feet, groan and stir.

The woman spoke again, quickly, urgently. "Please help us, m'sieur. My daughter upstairs with another officer. Please help us."

The clouds cleared from Abel's mind. In a glance, he took in the age of the woman before him. Not much older than himself, which meant her daughter must be – very young indeed. He sprang up the second flight of stairs. Some of the scar tissue formed by experience over his natural humanity fell away. He was outraged. There were two doors on the upper landing, one slightly ajar. Abel heard a faint sobbing sound from the room, placed a large hand on the door and pushed it wide open. He had a brief glimpse of a small, dark-haired female figure lying on a bed with the naked torso of a man bent over her.

Abel's sharp intake of breath was enough to make the man stand abruptly upright and whirl round to face him.

"Captain Swithin!"

"You!" Swithin's hand shot out to grab at the ornate scabbard propped against a chair.

Abel's disgust knew no bounds. "You filthy pig, she's only a child. I've a good mind to—" He raised his clenched fist, then changed his mind. "No, I'll not dirty my hands on you, you scum. I'm goin' to the CO with this, Colonel Hill 'imself. I will by God!"

"Now look, Sergeant," Swithin said. "Don't do anything you will regret. It's your word against mine and Lieutenant Woods."

"I'll take these poor women along. They'll get justice. I swear it."

Swithin pulled his sword halfway from its scabbard. "Now look, Sergeant, I'm telling you."

Abel turned to the quietly sobbing figure on the bed. "Come on girl, cover y'self; I'll get you out of here. Your ma's all right." The girl looked at him questioningly. "M'sieur?" she whispered, her face wet with tears.

Swithin pulled the sword completely from its scabbard, letting the latter drop on the floor.

"To hell with you!" Abel flipped a blanket over the girl on the bed and bent to pick her up. Swithin lunged suddenly at him, his long face contorted, teeth bared. A sharp hot pain in Abel's upper arm caused him to stagger back. "Sweet Jesus!"

"Die then, you bastard!" The captain lunged again. Abel, recovering his balance, retreated rapidly back towards the door, but the sword-point penetrated his flesh again, this time high on his right shoulder. He crashed backward against the door-frame. Swithin pulled the sword back and made a third thrust. Defenceless, Abel backpedalled onto the landing, attempting to deflect the blade with an arm.

Even as he thought that he was about to die, Abel was aware that the woman was involved in a tussle with the other officer on the landing below. One part of Abel's mind decided that the man must have recovered from the blow and was preventing the woman from mounting the stairs. Then he felt a sensation in his left forearm as the sword-point passed through it, and a further pain in his chest as it penetrated that as well. Then he was falling backwards down the stairs. He could not prevent a cry from escaping before he crashed into black, black nothingness.

Lieutenant Woods released the woman when Abel, blood running from his wounds, fell onto the landing and lay still. Swithin came rushing down the stairs, still carrying the bloodied sword.

"My God! You've killed him!" Woods was in a panic.

Swithin bent over Abel's body. "Do you know, I think I have," he said with some satisfaction.

"Let's get out of here."

"Now, now, Woody," said Swithin, quite unperturbed, even as the woman gave a sob and rushed up the stairs to her daughter, Woods stretching out a hand in a futile attempt to stop her.

"Let her go," said Swithin. "She's only going up. No way out up there."

"What are we going to do?"

"Do you know who this is—or was?" sneered Swithin. "This 'ere was Sergeant 'Game' Garnett. Hero of the 50th, God rot him." He kicked the body viciously. "I hung a friend of his once, you know."

"All right, but what the devil are we to do? You can't go around murdering sergeants."

"Why, we never saw the sergeant today, did we?" He picked the sealed orders up from where they had fallen at the bottom of the stairway and broke them open.

"There you are, you see," he said soothingly. "I have orders—the regiment is to get to the coast and take ship for Ireland. No doubt you will be off too. You should get to your HQ." He dropped the orders onto the floor. "Sergeant Garnett must have deserted, you know. For he never came to us, did he?"

"But what about—the females?"

"Anti-Bonapartists have few friends round here—have they had a single visitor since we came?"

"N-no."

"Well their bodies won't be found until we are safely at sea. Or even riding to hounds in bonny Ireland."

"I can't do it, Swithin." Woods became more composed. "I can't do that," he emphasised even more firmly, "I'm no murderer. I'll take a woman, cad that I am, but I ain't no murderer."

Swithin sighed. "You're a soft-headed fool but very well." He stepped over Abel's body. "Help me bring them down; we'll lock them in that little wine cellar. They've no idea where our regiments are, and with all the troop movements, there's little risk, I suppose." He began to mount the stairs: "Come on, Woody, cheer up. By the time they get out, we will be a hundred miles away and bound for Ireland. I hardly think they'll follow us there."

⋘⋙

A blinding light, darkness, then light again. Abel Garnett's brain was having difficulty in forming a rational thought. His body felt tightly constricted, his head heavy as lead. For one petrifying split second, he thought that he had been buried alive, the next that he was actually dead. If he was, he did not like it much. He moved his head slightly and his small world tilted crazily. A voice spoke quietly nearby. "Mama," just the one word, but it eased his mind and brought the room in which he lay into focus. He was in bed, laying flat, his seemingly far distant toes sticking up, creating a small hillock in the blankets. He was heavily bandaged in various places: chest, forearm, head. Abel opened his eyes wider, moved them in their sockets until they met those of the dark-haired woman sitting nearby. "At last," she said with a heavy accent. She leant towards him proffering a cup to his lips. He drank the warm liquid gratefully.

"You have been close to death, m'sieur, but, thanks be to God, you live."

"I live," croaked Abel, attempting a smile that was more of a grimace. "What happened?"

"We will talk later, m'sieur. Rest now."

Abel rested.

During the three days that he lay there, he heard the story piecemeal. They sat by his bedside, the woman and the girl, and gave him hot soup, wine and coffee and told him.

Yvonne Fontaine and her daughter, Lysette, wife and only child of Dr Henri Fontaine, deceased.

Yvonne, a Parisian, married Henri when she was sixteen, after the boy had completed his studies at the Sorbonne and before becoming an assistant to a doctor in Toulouse. One year after the marriage, Lysette had been born, and seven years later when the doctor had died, Henri took over the practice. He was rather a headstrong young man and an outspoken critic of Napoleon Bonaparte. In the main, most of the population in the region of Toulouse had no time for Bonaparte but this only made his supporters more extreme. Many of Doctor Fontaine's patients were soon taking their ailments and injuries elsewhere rather than risk the anger of the politicos of the town. Then, one night, he was lured on a false errand of mercy from which he never returned. No body was ever found but his medical bag stood on the front step of their house in the morning, with a note advising Yvonne to return to Paris attached to it.

She had hung on at the house for some weeks with fading hope for her husband. She and her daughter were left very much alone in their grief.

When the English arrived, Yvonne was very happy to oblige the billeting officer. Captain Swithin and Lieutenant Woods had behaved like gentlemen initially but they had gradually realised that Yvonne had no visitors or friends. She was defenceless. Their behaviour had grown more and more familiar until, a few days before Abel Garnett's arrival, the nightmare had begun.

Abel's concussion eased and the liquid diet restored his blood loss. His left forearm had been pierced through and he was unable to completely close the fingers of that hand. It was extremely painful.

"How did you survive," Abel asked the quiet, dark-haired woman as she plumped his pillows on the third day, "and get me into this bed?"

"The young officer would not 'arm us," said Yvonne, "and we were put into the cellar. The door, it is very strong, but—" she gave a brief smile, "—last year Lysette was by accident locked in the cellar by my 'usband when we thought she was at play in the garden. So we kept a spare key down there; it was simple!"

"And getting me in bed?"

"Well, m'sieur, you were only outside the door. As soon as it was safe, I came from the cellar to 'elp you. At first I did not move you, but did what I could where you lay. Stopped the blood. I learn from my 'usband, you know."

"You saved my life!"

"You saved us, m'sieur. Pauvre Lysette!" Yvonne suddenly began to cry.

At some cost to himself, Abel stretched out a hand. "Don't cry, please, it's over now."

Yvonne wiped her face with one hand, her large oval eyes looked at him from beneath dark lashes. "But I will not forget, m'sieur."

"My name is Abel. We must get to some senior officer and have those two arrested while we can. You should have gone straight to a regiment and reported what happened."

"I could not leave you before or you would have died I'm sure. Now it is too late. The British are gone."

Abel sat up in bed. "God, I'm so weak!" he groaned.

"It will be some days yet, M'sieu Abel."

Abel groaned again. "I'll be posted as a deserter, and those two will get away scot-free."

"God will take care of them in his own way," said Yvonne.

"I'd like to do that myself," Abel replied grimly. "So you managed to get me into this bed, eh?"

"Well, it was a struggle, M'sieur Abe, but with Lysette's 'elp, I manage."

"Where is the girl?"

"She is in the kitchen making some food."

Abel looked again at Yvonne – sweet-faced certainly, although a little strained at the moment; that beautiful dark hair and equally beautiful blue eyes; a simple, high-necked dress with a cameo at the throat.

"How did you learn such good English?" he said rather lamely, as Yvonne returned his gaze.

"Oh, my father, he taught me—'e love the English, you know, and I teach Lysette a little."

"I see," said Abel. He was feeling a little hot and began to see double images, two Yvonnes, two wardrobes, two swirling windows.

"You must rest now. You are tired," said Yvonne, gently mopping his brow with a cool, moist cloth.

After a few days, Abel was fit enough to sit in the sun in the secluded, walled garden at the rear of the house. He watched Yvonne and Lysette cutting late spring flowers. Already he felt an affection for them both and stronger feelings for Yvonne than he had held for another human being for some years. "Garnett," he told himself severely, "you damaged your brain when you went down them stairs."

But as the sun warmed his body during the restoring hours that he spent sitting in the garden, so Yvonne's presence warmed his heart. Soon they were spending time side by side. Lysette, timorous and quiet after her ordeal at the hands of Captain Swithin, kept her distance from them when they were together and stayed close to her mother's side at other times. Abel felt as though he had returned at last to a normal life with normal emotions: no more blood, no more privations, no more the sole company of men with guttersnipe behaviour: no more satisfying basic lusts with the raddled females who offered their services to the soldiery wherever they went. Now he had some home comforts, a wonderful peace and quiet that he had not enjoyed for years and what was more, charming, feminine companionship. He formed a plan in his mind. He would take Yvonne for his wife if she would have him and live somehow where he was. No more soldiering.

After three weeks, Abel found himself in the exhilarating situation of holding Yvonne in his arms, her naked body softly against his own beneath a bedsheet. They both moaned softly with the pleasures that they provided one another. Lysette had at last been restored to her own room at night. His injuries were fast healing with the exception of problems with his left hand, the fingers of which stubbornly refused to operate normally. This did not prevent him from lavishing tender caresses on Yvonne, however.

How soon the idyll ended! After two more days, a knock on the door brought Abel to open it. Apart from an occasional tradesman they had seen no one since he had been attacked. So he was stunned to find two British army officers standing at the entrance. Abel was dressed in a pair of breeches and a rather over-stretched shirt provided from Yvonne's dead husband's wardrobe. The clothing did not prevent Captain North from instantly recognising him. "Sergeant Garnett! You're supposed to be dead by all accounts!"

Abel shrugged his shoulders as Yvonne approached behind him. "You'd better come in, gentlemen."

Captain North stepped through the door.

"This is Ensign Fallowfield. We have come to investigate your death."

At the sight of Yvonne, the young ensign, physically somewhat lacking, with watery eye and thin nose, produced a sneer. "Looks more like his desertion to me, sir."

Abel flared at the use of the very word that had been pricking at his conscience recently. "Not I, sir, I've been near death."

"Come through, gentlemen," Yvonne spoke soothingly. "Come and sit. I will tell you what 'appened and 'ow Sergeant Garnett saved us from the 'ands of two of your oh-so-gallant officers."

Lysette stood by her mother's side, black curled hair and innocent-eyed. She looked up at the two officers. "It is true, they hurt Mama and the thin man, 'e was horrible to me." She started to cry.

They all sat in the large room while Yvonne told the story to North and Fallowfield. Abel bared his arm and torso to reveal the livid wounds that he had suffered. "This lady saved my life—if I saved them, they saved me." He added, "I am still unable to make full use of this arm."

Captain North made a sound something between a soft groan and a sigh. "One expects behaviour of this sort from the common soldier. But officers and gentlemen, I find it hard to believe!"

"Believe it!" Abel said fiercely.

North looked at him. "I believe you are an honest man, Sergeant Garnett. Lieutenant Woods, before the fever took him, confessed to his part in this crime. He wanted to die in a state of grace, I suppose. But he would not name the man who actually used his sword on you. A question of honour you know. But Captain Swithin was known to have been billeted with him. We are delighted to find you alive and ready to rejoin your regiment, are we not, Fallowfield?"

"Er, delighted, Captain, delighted." Fallowfield's insincerity was patently obvious.

"May I speak with Madame Fontaine, sir, in private?" Abel's plans for his future with Yvonne dissolved into nothingness.

"Certainly. We shall wait for you outside."

"Am I under arrest?"

"Of course not, sergeant. You may have been a little tardy in returning to duty, but—" he glanced at Yvonne "—under the circumstances, that is understandable. Come along, Ensign Fallowfield."

"Captain!"

"Yes?"

"Where is Captain Swithin?"

"Why, he took a private berth on a ship to Ireland to be with the regiment at Cork, you know."

"And what is to happen to him?"

"We shall take the whole matter to Colonel Hill. I am sure he will do his duty."

When he was alone with Yvonne and Lysette, Abel held them both close to him, the young girl's head on his waist and the woman's on his shoulder. "This is the hardest thing I have ever had to do, my darlings, but I must leave you for what may be a long time."

"Oh, take us with you, can we not go with you?" Lysette was instantly in tears again as Yvonne clutched him tightly.

Once again Abel's conscience gave him a jolt .He thought of his aunts and the farm at Chichester, room enough there for this desirable woman and her daughter until he could get free of the army. But it was all too soon and too much for him. He could not cope with all that. Not yet.

"I will not have you become camp followers without a proper home, washing your clothes under some pump or in a river, mixing with the dregs, I can't do it, not even for six months. I will get free of the army and return to you or send for you when I have a place."

"I could take Lysette home to Paris and wait for you there," Yvonne said, stroking his brow with her soft hand. "I promise you that I will not forget you."

Abel was close to tears himself. "Yes, wait for me in Paris. I know where to find you and I can picture you there in my mind. A small part of that mind felt a distinct easing at the thought of postponing the commitment that he had made. He breathed a sigh of relief.

With Yvonne's tender kisses lingering on his lips and cheeks, he went off with Captain North and Ensign Fallowfield. It was ten miles down the road that the total reality of his love for Yvonne hit him and he wanted desperately to return for her, be near her forever. An ache began that was to stay with him for months. He cursed himself for being a weak and heartless fool.

The army had no interest in Abel's emotional state. Many officers and men welcomed him as a man returned from the dead. 'Game' Garnett was back. Bordeaux harbour was busy with royal naval ships.

Before departing for Cork, he appeared before his commanding officer, Colonel Charles Hill to beg for his discharge from the regiment, allowing him to return to Toulouse and Yvonne. His colonel was adamant that Abel should lay formal charges against Captain Swithin in Ireland and the case be formally dealt with before his discharge could be considered. "I will not have a smear of dishonour on the finest regiment of foot in His Majesty's army, Sergeant, you should know that!"

Abel was unusually brutal to the soldiery in his care during the embarkation, dulling his conscience with whatever hard liquor he could lay his hands on whilst on the voyage. By early August, the regiment was in Ireland. The first thing that he learned was that Captain Swithin had resigned his commission and departed. No one knew where or if they did were not saying. Abel was thwarted in his desire for revenge. Two months later, he was a civilian in Canterbury drinking his money away and wondering if he would ever see Yvonne and Lysette again. That was when Brownlow gave him his chance.

CHAPTER SIXTEEN

Abel Garnett Retrieves His Wagon

omney Marsh was cloaked in darkness. The moon was down, but a few stars were visible through breaks in the cloud cover. Vague shapes moved in the night causing Jack a slight tremor of apprehension. Abel Garnett stood up and stretched wearily. "They're here," he said. Seven or eight men dressed for the chill of the night approached warily. Four of them carried muskets and the dull metal of pistol butts could be seen at several waist belts.

"What's afoot, Abe?" They pressed round their leader. "You got trouble—we're with you, man."

"Thanks, boys, we've got a difficult job tonight. Risky too. The town's full of soldiers and we've got to get Charlie out of the gaol, recover our goods and get clean away into the bargain."

"Sounds a bit of a 'andful to me, Abe," one of the characters said doubtfully.

"I know it does, Ben," Abel replied, "but I think we can do it. Is Peachey going to be ready with the boat?"

"Aye," a man almost as broad as Abel, growled, "but we've got to catch the dawn ebb or we'll be goin' nowhere."

"We'll make it. Now, whose barn is this?"

"Why, it's George Grattan's," said Ben.

"Well we're going to have to rebuild it for him and there's another barn yonder if I recall."

"Yeah, that's George's as well."

"Ah, well, can't be 'elped." Abel was too caught up in events now to let anything short of murder stand in his way.

"What you got in mind, Abe?"

"Young Jack here's goin' to rouse the town. Jake Pierce the lunatic is on the loose and firing barns, gettin' ready to slaughter everybody in sight. Jack will convince 'em of that and we will provide the evidence. Nothing like a good fire to attract the crowds." He grinned briefly. "Billy." He put his hand on a swarthy man's shoulder. "You know the marsh as well as any. I want you out there giving some bloodcurdlin' screams. Don't get caught, mind, and when you've attracted enough attention, do a disappearing act and go 'ome."

Billy Carpenter nodded. "Sounds enjoyable work. What's in it for me?"

"You'll get your fair share. I'm a man o' my word, you know that."

"Good enough," said Billy.

"That's it then. You game, Jack?"

"Stand by me, Abe." Once again that old familiar feeling was in Jack's guts, a slightly nauseous sensation rising to his throat and a certain dryness of the mouth.

"Give us fifteen minutes to get in position at the gaol-house, then go to work. Good luck, boys!"

Billy was raking around searching for some dry hay for kindling. "'Ere, Bill, there's oil in this lantern." One of the men carrying a musket proffered an unlit hurricane lamp. "That'll do nicely."

Jack trotted the short distance – some four hundred yards – to the first house at the edge of town. Dipping hands in a puddle, he wet his face and hair and practised simulating heavy breathing. He waited a few minutes, then, gulping hard, approached the low door of the dwelling and began to hammer as loudly as possible, at the same time yelling at the top of his voice, "Wake up! 'Elp! I need 'elp!"

Bolts were drawn and a night-shirted man carrying a guttering candle appeared.

"'Oo is it? Take care there—I've a knife. 'Tis sharp an all."

"Mister, it's only me, Jack Dawkins by name, from Shippenden. Let me in."

"You that boy up at Garnett's place?"

"Yes, yes, let me in!"

"Come in then, careful, mind. I won't be tricked."

Jack shot through the door looking as though he was about to burst into tears. "The maniac's loose on the marsh an' ready to commit murder. Abe—Mr Garnett sent me at risk o' my life to get help. He's alone guardin' the women at the farm."

"You seen 'im then?"

"Yeah, we both saw 'im 'owling at the moon 'e were an' carryin' a great axe. Black as death 'e looked and about seven foot tall! Abe—Mr Garnett, I mean, sent me by a secret path 'e knows. 'E's locked in the 'ouse with the women and loaded guns."

"Lor, oh lor," said the man.

Jack puffed and panted manfully, slicking back his wet hair.

A tousled haired, night-gowned woman appeared; she carried a young child on each arm.

"What's up, Clifford? What's amiss?"

"Get dressed, May, we've got to get the soldiers, the Mayor or somethin'. The loony's out for blood."

May gave a short cry of alarm and disappeared through the door from which she had emerged. Moments later she was back, herself with the babies wrapped in various shawls.

They hurried, with several backward glances, into the centre of the little town. Soon, they were pounding on the door of the New Inn where Clifford said the officer was staying.

"Who's there at this hour?" a querulous voice enquired from behind the stout panels.

"It's me—Cliff Mann," the excited individual cried. "Open up, we need that officer-of-foot."

Locks were turned and bolts drawn, then another night-shirt on view and another candle.

"What's up, Cliff, you need a drink?"

"Don't talk daft, Henry, this is serious."

Cliff, his wife and babies, closely followed by Jack, all plunged into the hostelry, forcing the landlord back into the room.

"Whoa, whoa, I'll light a lamp."

A heavily booted tread on the stairs and the lieutenant appeared, coatless, and in need of a shave. "What the devil? What's all the noise?"

Clifford spoke up. "We need you, sir, begging your pardon, but this boy 'ere, comes from Shippenden, a local farm, like; 'e says that loony—that madman, sir, 'e's on the loose."

"I thought he was supposed to be dead."

"I seen 'im sir, so did Mr Garnett. 'E sent me," Jack blurted out, trying hard to look the part of a naive country boy.

"'Owlin' at the moon, he said, sir," Cliff added.

The lieutenant snorted: "Well I'll turn a guard out. But I'm not blundering about in the middle of the night on that marsh looking for a will o' the wisp, or," he looked darkly at Jack, "the figment of some frightened boy's imaginings."

"I swear..." Jack was vehement.

"As I said, I'll mount a guard to patrol the town." The officer turned and went out onto the street. The others followed closely behind. "No need for you all to lose any more sleep," said the lieutenant a little loftily. "Go to your homes."

Jack tentatively took the officer by his shirtsleeve. "Look, sir, what's that?"

A red glow could be clearly discerned in the near distance.

"Somethin's on fire," the landlord of the inn stated needlessly.

"Good God, so there is!" exclaimed the lieutenant.

"It's the maniac!" shouted Jack. "Fire! Fire!" He was quite hysterical.

The young officer broke into a dead run towards the collection of tents that had been erected on a piece of fallow ground that intruded into the town, close to the church.

He was already roaring, "Sergeant!" while still fifty yards from the camp.

In less than five minutes most of the population of the town was in the street and the soldiers, the lieutenant at their head, were advancing rapidly on the blazing barn. Wisps of burning straw were raining down on them when they clearly heard a bloodcurdling cry and the second barn began to burn.

"Look!" Several voices called in unison, soldiers and civilians gave a cry, and an almost tangible thrill went through them. Standing close to the flames of this second conflagration was a sinister figure. Another terrifying scream and it faded into the surrounding darkness. Billy Carpenter was performing well.

"Sergeant!" The officer was shouting again. "Take some men—see if you can catch him! The rest of you get buckets. Two groups tackle both fires at once. These flaming brands could fire the town if the wind carries!"

The three soldiers remaining on guard at the gaol-house were in front of the building, straining their eyes to catch a sight of the fires between the houses, when the half-dozen or so masked men fell upon them like malevolent ghosts.

In less than twenty seconds, three unconscious bodies were being dragged into the tiny gaol.

Keys were readily available hanging from a brass hook on the wall. The men stripped off their masks and hoods. "Charlie, Harry!" Abel called out to the men in the cell. "We're the night-watch. Want to take a stroll in the moonlight?"

"In 'ere. 'Ere we are." A fumbling of keys and the cell door opened. Three men came out.

"Blimey, Pickles—we forgot you were 'ere!" said Abel to the third man. Harry sported a black eye and a cut cheek – some of Charlie's work Abel correctly assumed.

"Now for the wagon, boys!"

"How's it goin', Abe?" Jack appeared.

"What're you doin' here, Jack? You should be halfway home, you've done your bit."

"I'm not missin' the fun. I could still be useful. They don't even know I'm gone."

"Come on then, no time to waste."

Down the street, many dark figures were silhouetted against a faintly lightening sky. Shouts and cries drifted on the air as they hurried in the opposite direction.

A musket butt smashed ruthlessly on the lock of the shed doors behind which stood the wagon. Swinging the doors open, they swarmed in. "Horse—stable next door, Ben. Move!

Peachey's waitin' and no doubt, gettin' anxious about 'is little boat." Abel wasted few words. It was a swaybacked nag that they harnessed to the shafts of the wagon. Willing hands got the wheels rolling and they went at a steady gait out of the town along the coast road, the whispering sound of the sea not far off.

Two dozen bored soldiers manning the martello tower were enjoying the pre-dawn entertainment, watching the distant fires at Romney from their high vantage point atop the stonework. They had reoccupied the tower two days earlier when news arrived of Bonaparte's escape from Elba and his landing in France. Once again England's military were on full alert. For the moment, though, it was only endless drill with the thirty-two-pounder cannon whose muzzle pointed challengingly at the Channel.

The artillery officer frowned at the chattering men, then turned to gaze once again through the telescope. He could clearly see the barns burning although the flames now seemed to be diminishing. He turned his attention to the sea. Clamping the telescope against his eye, he made a careful sweep of the horizon as far as it was visible. Nothing. Wait! Far down channel he thought that he glimpsed something. Topsails? Yes, there they were again – 'twas only a lone ship beating its way toward the downs; far short of an invasion fleet, though. The lieutenant sighed and moved the glass to view the immediate coastline. He stiffened suddenly. "What the devil?" – just half a mile away, almost beached by the look of her, a ketch. And men, by God, struggling through waves. He adjusted his glass: yes, carrying kegs and bundles. Oddly enough they appeared to be loading the boat rather than unloading.

"Quiet!" He roared at his startled men.

"S'nt Haynes, something's occurring at that inlet." He pointed meaningfully over the parapet of the tower. "Get these men in order at once. I will take the off watch with me." He glared at Haynes. "See that you keep a good look out now. Breakfast will have to wait," he snapped, anticipating the sergeant's question before it was asked.

With muskets at the port, the officer soon had a dozen men doubling awkwardly along the shingle. Sergeant Haynes leant on the parapet atop the tower opening and snapping shut the telescope. Putting it to his eye, he examined the marshlands – nothing but the vague movement of sheep and the glint of water here and there, leftovers from the floods.

There was the shining ribbon of the military canal, though it was hard to believe that it was man-made. It stretched into the distance, disappearing into an early morning mist.

He turned his attention to the coast, soon picking out his officer and the men struggling up the beach. He smiled contentedly to himself. Cool and rested, he would soon be enjoying his breakfast. The sergeant lifted the eyeglass a little and watched a silent, distant drama played out. A small group of men were now bunched on the beach. Three or four others in the boat were actively engaged in stacking goods and hauling on ropes. By constant slight movements of the telescope, the sergeant observed a sailor leaning over the gunwale of the ketch, shaking hands with a large figure, and then a second smaller one, both up to their waists in creaming water. The boat was definitely beginning to move now. A small sail billowed up one of its two masts. Haynes moved the telescope again, in time to see the group of men on the beach scatter and head for the dunes, as the soldiers closed in.

Haynes chuckled as he watched the two men in the water begin to make for the shore, hesitate, then turn and wade desperately back to the slowly moving boat. Their high-stepping efforts to hurry through the waves looked slightly comical from that distance. Willing hands hauled them in over the side. The last that the sergeant saw of them was their flailing legs disappearing into the boat. Next his attention was drawn swiftly back to the beach as he heard the faint rattle of musket fire. There it was, the unmistakable sight of powder smoke, then more shots.

The sergeant saw Lieutenant Collins waving and gesticulating wildly. "What on earth?" The officer was pointing out to sea then making strange gestures... "Ye Gods! 'E wants me to fire on that boat!" The penny had dropped.

Haynes finally removed the telescope from his eye for a moment and began to bawl orders thick and fast. The excitement on the tower was suddenly immense. For the first time, the thirty-two-pounder was to be used in earnest, albeit on a target so small that one hit would smash it to smithereens.

The sun was peeping over the horizon now, an offshore breeze helping the ketch on its way. With all sails set, through the rather choppy waters, it lurched and plunged absurdly over the curling breakers. It would be a very difficult target to hit.

Chaos and confusion reigned aboard the ketch. Abel and Jack had been pulled on board by Charlie and Harry as the three-man crew tried to get under way as swiftly as possible.

The sudden arrival of the troops had smashed Abel's plans; now he crouched helplessly on the deck as the ship rolled and tossed its way out to sea. The sound of musket fire did not escape him and he pulled Jack down beside him.

"I saw a soldier fall!" the Dodger yelled in Abel's ear. He was soaked and trembling from a combination of fear and cold. The jaunt had suddenly turned very serious indeed.

"Keep your 'ead down," Abel shouted back above the grinding and groaning of the ship's timbers and the crash of the waves.

"Mr Garnett!" Matthew Peachey, the owner of the ketch, *Sparrow*, made his sure-footed way to where the two knelt. "We've got trouble now; there's a ship carrying English colours not a mile off. And if I'm not mistook, we're gonna come under fire from that there tower." He pointed dramatically, first at the distant ship and then at the ominous martello.

"I don't believe it! That tower's been unmanned for months! What can we do, Matt?" Abel clutched at the side of the small deck-housing to maintain his balance.

"We might put that ship 'tween us an' the tower; we're a small enough target as it is. But if the ship takes a hand, we're done for anyway."

A bang and flash made their flesh jump. Charlie had defiantly discharged a musket ball at the far distant soldiers on the beach. "Bloody soljers, go to 'ell!" As if in answer, the martello tower cannon boomed. The seven on the ketch all grabbed at some support and stared as smoke partially obscured the top of the tower. No one saw the fall of shot.

Jack could make out plain detail now on the fast-approaching ship. Figures moving about on deck. Dark ports along the side were visible to him. The cannon fired again and everyone saw the spout of water thrown up a hundred feet away.

Jack grabbed Abel by the arm. "You've done for us...trying to save two or three...you've killed us all!"

"You ain't dead yet," Abel snarled. "Go an' find some 'ole to crawl in if you're scared!" He suddenly glimpsed the small boat connected by a hawser to the stern of the ketch. How merrily it bounced in their wake. "In fact," Abe said, "here's your chance." Leaning over into the spume, he began hauling on the rope bringing the coracle closer and closer until it brought up against the rudder housing. "Get down in that—I'll cut ya free, give you half a chance."

"I can't—I can't get down there!" Jack was appalled. He looked down into the tiny, bouncing structure.

"C'mon, boy," Abel secured the rope by turning it around a stanchion. He grabbed Jack by both arms and swung him over the stern of the leaping ship.

"Abe!" Jack fell through space and sprawled painfully into the little boat. Flat on his stomach, he looked pleadingly up at Abel Garnett leaning over the stern of the ketch. He appeared to be laughing as he sawed at the connecting rope with his knife. The rope parted and the cannon fired. The *Sparrow* was borne up on a wave to meet her fate as Jack, in his small craft, slipped away from her. The cannon ball hurtled through the wooden hull, tore a great gash in the ship's bottom and continued unimpeded until it hit the seabed. The destruction was almost instantaneous. Over went the stricken vessel – kegs, bales and men thrown into the water. In a few seconds, the ship was disappearing beneath the waves in a tangle of broken masts and spars. Survivors clung to whatever remained afloat whilst Jack hung on with equal tenacity, to the thwarts of his reluctant lifesaver.

He found that from his position in the bottom of the boat, he could not immediately see land; only Dungeness Point was visible in the distance. As he rose up on a wave, he glimpsed the naval vessel bearing down. It looked huge, blotting out everything else, then down he went into a trough with a sickening lurch. Up again. This time he cast about quickly for a sight of the men in the water. He saw two heads close by and a third further off – all clinging to waterlogged bales.

"Abel!" Jack's voice was hoarse. One cry and then he was down in another trough. He licked salty lips, thumping the side of the boat with his fist in fear and frustration.

"Abel!"

The dizzying ride on the waves continued, then Jack saw the seamen rowing the longboat straight towards him with great precision. Moments later, a voice called, "Oars!" and they were alongside him. Gnarled hands held his boat steady. "Up yee come, yonker!" He was hoisted bodily aboard. The craft that he had vacated so abruptly was allowed to drift away.

"Over there!" Jack found a voice. "There's more in the water!"

"Pull, boys!" There were eight brawny men at the oars and to Jack's inexperienced eyes, they made light work of moving the boat through the water. An almost fully submerged keg bumped its way along the side of the boat. Two of the seamen stopped rowing at once and dived their hands into the water in an attempt to lift it in.

"Belay that!" growled the coxswain. "Ye've grog enough as 'tis."

"Here! Over here!"

Voices shouting in unison from close by. The oarsmen adjusted their course a little and in a minute or so, three pairs of hands were clutching at the sides of the boat.

"Easy, easy! Ye'll 'ave us in with ya if ya ain't careful!" the coxswain complained. Three half-drowned bodies were hauled into the boat which rocked alarmingly.

"Abe!"

Jack felt tremendous relief at seeing the large figure of Abel Garnett, coughing up seawater and throwing back hair from his eyes with both hands.

"Jack, you all right, boy?"

The two other survivors were the loose-mouthed Harry and Matthew Peachey, skipper of the ill-fated *Sparrow*.

For twenty minutes the boat plied the area searching and searching for any signs of life. Two or three times hopes were raised but each time the sightings disappointingly proved to be only debris or contraband.

"Back to the ship! Pull boys, pull!" The coxswain's word was law.

Jack moved close to Abel who was staring moodily at the almost bare-masted ship as the longboat rapidly closed the watery gap between them.

"We're done for, ain't we?" Jack whispered urgently. Peachey and Harry were close enough to hear him and both men looked as though they agreed.

"I've said it before, boy, we ain't dead yet," Abel murmured stubbornly, his jaw set in a familiar line.

The coxswain looked sharply at them from his position in the stern of the boat. "Don't go gettin' no ideas, It's a long way to shore an' we're nine agin three, an' a lad not full growed."

"We ain't done nothin'. We're jus' labourin' men paid to load a boat!" Harry sounded desperate.

"Oh, yeah," the coxswain sneered, "an' my Aunt Fanny's admiral of the fleet."

The sailors straining at the oars burst out laughing. "Ole cox 'e were a wag an' no mistake!" The coxswain looked pleased with himself as the boat bumped alongside her mother ship. Jack glimpsed the name *Wyvern* beneath an ugly figurehead.

"Up those nets!" ordered the coxswain. "And remember, there's marines wi' muskets trained."

Jack and the other shivering captors struggled up the netting draped down the ship's side. Climbing up past an open port, Jack caught a glimpse of cannon and the dim interior of a gun-deck. Grabbed from above, he was hauled unceremoniously up and over until he stood on the scrubbed white deck. There were many curious eyes on him, marines, midshipmen and idling seamen. Abel, Peachey and Harry were lined up alongside of him.

A confusion of shouted and repeated orders brought the longboat in board. More bellowing and men were sent running to take station as the ship was got underway. Men were aloft, and from the noise and bustle, obviously working below as well.

Half a dozen marines were brought to order and, after more commands, they formed a close escort to march the four of them away.

"You civilians is under arrest. Attempt to escape an' you'll be shot," a belligerent marine officer told them or rather shrieked at them in a voice that would have done credit to a costermonger. Jack distinctly heard Harry groan and Peachey muttered a few words to Abel.

They were taken down a companion-way, along a deck and were brought to a halt by a low door. An officer appeared, slim, tanned and about Abel's age. As he strode smartly up, Jack saw a stunned expression pass over his face and his mouth opened to try and speak. Jack had never seen anyone look so surprised in all his life. Stranger still was the almost demonic glare that Abel gave the officer, at the same time his eyes were giving out desperate, secret signals.

The officer's mouth closed, and his features returned to something like normal.

"Have these men been searched, Mr Allen?" he enquired of the marine officer.

"Dunno, sir—not by me they ain't."

"Well, I suggest that they are before you lock them up."

"Aye, aye, sir."

Each of them endured a body search before being thrust into a dark hole that reeked of stale saltwater and grease. The door slammed shut and they were left in darkness.

After a few moments deathly silence broken only by the ship's noise, Abel spoke.

"Cheer up lads," he said in a half whisper, "I can't believe it yet meself, but that officer, he's my brother-in-law, John Tanner!"

CHAPTER SEVENTEEN

Oliver Twist Arrives in New Romney

he inexorability of coincidence had brought John Tanner and HMS *Wyvern* on the King's business and with immaculate timing to the scene of the sinking of the ketch *Sparrow.*
Signals from the martello tower had asked them to intercept the escaping ketch and arrest the crew but before that could come about a lucky shot had sunk the craft.

The sight of Abel Garnett brought aboard the *Wyvern* as a prisoner, came as a tremendous shock to the young third officer. He found it difficult to concentrate on the duty of bringing the ship to anchorage in the Downs, receiving a rebuke from the first lieutenant to: "Look sharp, Mr Tanner, if you please," which caused him considerable embarrassment in front of the men.

With the ship riding at anchor and the English coast so near and yet so far, there was a general air of restlessness among the crew. After eleven months at sea they were itching to get ashore. There was to be no satisfaction on that score however, not with Bonaparte back in France.

John Tanner looked longingly at the shoreline. Elspeth was only forty-odd miles distant but she might as well be forty thousand for all the chance he had of seeing her.

"Beggin' your pardon, sir—Cap'n wants you." A seaman interrupted John Tanner's musings.

"Thank you." He turned and made his way to the great cabin in the stern of the ship.

The all-powerful personage was sat in a chair, taking his ease, as John entered.

"Aah, Mr Tanner." The captain was an ebullient figure with an over-generous nose under bushy eyebrows. "These smugglers—a bit of a diversion what? Damn lucky shot from that tower I must say. Third time lucky at that!" He boomed a short laugh, then became brisk and business-like. "Now then, Mr—ah—Tanner, we must hand these rogues over to the civil authorities as soon as possible. We cannot have them cluttering up our ship, what?"

"No, sir, of course not."

"No, of course not. So you will ensure that they are taken ashore at dawn tomorrow and placed where they belong—in gaol. You will require an armed escort and ensure that the prisoners are manacled. Take no chances, take no chances."

"Aye, aye, sir," John hesitated. "Excuse me, sir."

"Well?"

"In the interests of humanity, sir, shall I see that the prisoners are given food and drink and a blanket or two?"

"Certainly, Mr Tanner, certainly! We are not barbarians. See to it!"

"Aye, aye, sir."

The door opened and Abel, Jack, Harry and Matthew Peachey all blinked as the lantern was thrust in. "Stay still," a voice growled, "or be shot." The muzzle of a musket appeared, thrust into the light by a surly marine. Then John Tanner bent his body to enter the chain locker, a roll of blankets under one arm. He gave a warning glance to silence them as they all attempted to speak in unison. "Well my unfortunate fellows. Here are blankets and food for you and water to drink. Duncan, bring in the victuals, if you please."

A dwarf-like seaman, complete with greased pigtail, having

hardly the need to crouch at all, entered the crowded area, carrying a leather bucket full of water together with a tin cup. Placing this down on the only area of deck space available, he backed out and returned a moment later with ship's biscuits, a large piece of pickled pork and, unbelievably, half a dozen oranges. Cupped hands plunged into the bucket. Jack, Abel, Peachey and Harry drank eagerly, then snatched at the fruit, tearing at the peel. "Best thing I ever tasted!" Peachey spluttered, orange juice running into his beard. It was manna from heaven for the four of them. They had tasted nothing for hours.

"Go about your duties, Duncan. I wish to speak to the prisoners."

"But, sir—"

"Do not be anxious for me, Duncan. I have my pistol and the guard will be near."

"Aye, aye, sir." The diminutive Duncan disappeared.

Immediately, Abel grasped John Tanner's hand in both of his. "John! By all that's holy! It's good to see you, man."

John put his free hand to his mouth in a warning gesture. "You must be quiet. Speak soft." He hesitated. "Now who are these people you are with?"

"Why," said Abel quietly, "this young 'un is Jack Dawkins; he's here because he can't do as he's told. And this here's Matthew Peachey, fisherman and former owner of the *Sparrow*. He's 'ere because he's a loyal friend and this fellow is Harry Reed, ex-looker and ex-labourer."

"Well, you're all in a fine mess, I must say." John's whisper had a note of anguish about it. "I am to take you, in irons, to the civil authorities, tomorrow. You may hang!"

"No fear o' that, John, not now you're here." Abel was cheerful.

"You fool! I can't help you!"

"What?"

"How can I help you? I'm a ship's officer. I must do my duty, man. I've sworn it!"

Abel reached across the small space that separated where he and John sat and took hold of his brother-in-law's shirt-

215

front, twisting it fiercely. "My sister's your wife an' you won't unlock a door for us, let a guard turn a blind eye?"

"I can't, I can't!" John still managed to maintain a hoarse whisper. "Don't you understand about duty?"

"Duty!" Abel thrust John away from him.

"So much for that then," said Jack with a sinking feeling.

"Wiv an in-law like 'im," said Peachey, "I pity your sister."

"We're done for," moaned Harry a little too loudly.

"Shut up!" Abel hissed the words.

"John, surely you won't see us come to court? Remember when I came to you at Chatham? You were in poverty—'ow do you think Elspeth was able to move into your fine house? Who do you think 'as kept 'er in funds while you were waitin' for pay?"

"Oh God," moaned John softly. "Don't you think I'm in agony over this? I know what you've done for us!" A bell rang double chimes in a distant part of the ship.

"I must go," said John in a more normal voice. "I am about to relieve the officer of the watch." He hesitated, then whispered again, "Have you any money? You know these seamen have not set foot in England for many months. Some are ready to leave the ship at the first opportunity but we've seen no pay and they are greedy for money. Look, the captain has a small sailboat; it's his pride and joy. You might get away in it. Something might be arranged, you know. I will see to it that the worst malcontent guards you tonight. There could be a fog, that may help you."

"It's a chance all right," Abel said, with some bitterness, "but we've nothin', not a shillin'."

John sighed: "And I still await my pay."

"I know where there's money. Quite a bit too."

They all looked at Jack who had spoken up quietly.

"Oh, you know where there's money do you?" Peachey was unimpressed.

"Yeah, that's right. It's in that boat that took you out o' the water."

"What?"

"I put it there meself." Jack looked at Abel. "I was gonna

tell ya when we 'ad a minute to ourself. I took it—was it only last night? Anyway I took it, you know. When them fires started an' everybody was on the street—well, that officer was in 'is shirtsleeves so I reckoned 'is coat was in 'is room. So it was too, wiv a fat pocketbook in it. You know that magistrate 'oo 'ad a good laugh at my expense? His family an' all 'is servants were out, so—well I found some guineas at 'is place." He grinned.

They all looked at Jack in amazement.

"What made you put it in the boat, Jack?"

"Well, I bin took before, see. I 'ad the dosh in a purse 'ung round me neck inside me shirt. First thing anybody does when you're took is search yer, so while they 'unted for you lot in the water, I 'id the money under some canvas."

John was impatient to get away. "There you are, you have a chance. I will do what I can. Abe, you must forgive me, but I cannot be directly involved. Do you understand?"

Abel did not give a direct answer.

"Do one thing, John. Whatever happens, will you swear to take care of my wife and stepdaughter? They're at Shippenden. Take them home to Elspeth."

"You have my word," John replied.

"Well," said Abel grudgingly, "you seem to know about keeping that at least."

"Good luck."

John rapped on the door, which was opened immediately. "You all right, sir."

"Of course."

"You was gone so long, sir, I was about to—"

"I'm all right, I tell you." John hurried forward, torn between his sense of duty and his sentiments for Abel and concern for Elspeth's feelings.

Another night was drawing in and with it came fog. The shoreline was no longer visible. John mounted the quarterdeck to relieve the officer of the watch who grumbled at his lateness but accepted an apology with magnanimity.

"Mr Scott!" John called a midshipman to him. "Find that ne'er-do-well, Madeley, and tell him he's to relieve the guard

217

on the prisoners at once, at once, do you understand?"

The midshipman, barely fourteen years of age, gave a brisk "aye, aye" and turned on his heel.

"Tell him he's to stay at his post until I personally dismiss him," John added to the boy's departing back.

In their tight little prison, Jack was the centre of attention among the group.

"You was supposed to be reforming, young man," Abel told him with mock severity.

"Good job I stuck to me old ways then, ain't it?"

"We ain't out o' here yet," Harry whined in his slightly nasal tone.

"'Ow much money do you reckon?" Matt Peachey wanted to know.

"Well, I didn't get a chance to count it but I reckon twenty guineas from the magistrate by the feel of it, and a wad o' bank notes from that officer."

Noises beyond their prison door persuaded them to stop talking and listen.

"Guards changing," Abel whispered. "Let's hope this character is co-operative. Well, no time like the present."

The townspeople of Romney had the most memorable sleepless night of their lives, the burning of the barns having brought them out of their beds. A shudder went through the populace when the lunatic was seen capering in the light of the fires he had started. Bloodcurdling screams made them grab their children and each other, then a rattle of musketry further unnerved them as soldiers pursued the maniac across the marsh. Just as order was being restored with the fires dying down and excitement waning, the loss of the prisoners from the town gaol was discovered. Soon after that the lieutenant commanding the soldiers, feeling the chill of the dawn, went to his room to get his coat, excusing himself from the magistrate who had been protesting volubly at the loss of civilian prisoners. It was then that he discovered the theft of his pocket book. He returned livid with anger to the street to assault verbally the mayor upon the subject of the trustworthiness of his citizens. The magistrate did not discover his own loss until that evening.

At the first cannon shot from the martello tower, two elderly ladies fainted clean away and a fresh ripple of terror swept through the town. "The French! The French! Invasion!"

The lieutenant hunted and found his sergeant who assembled the scattered troops. They were just doubling toward the sea when the "lunatic's" pursuers returned, wet and muddy after a fruitless chase.

"I reckon 'ee's a bloomin' ghost or 'obgoblin," one of the number gasped out to the sergeant as they hurried along, closely followed by most of the people in the neighbourhood. The second and third cannon shot convinced them of their worst fears. Some of the younger members of the crowd began to cheer while the townsmen gripped staves, ancient cutlasses and even pitchforks.

First at the beach were the soldiers. Crunching shingle underfoot they strained their eyes in the early morning light. "A ship." The cry was taken up. "A ship!" This became: "Ships—they've sighted ships!"

"That's a Britisher," observed the sergeant.

"Aye, true enough," his corporal agreed. "She's no Frenchie, anyway. So what the bloomin' 'eck is the tower firing at unless it's a three-gun salute?"

"There's a small boat out there too—a row-boat," said the sharp-eyed corporal. "An' look, there's soljers 'eading for the tower."

"Sergeant Hayes—" The lieutenant came to a decision as his men milled in a disorderly fashion on the shore. "—I am going to the martello to find out what this is all about. You get the men busy clearing the civilians away from here. Send them about their business. After that they are to patrol the shore in smart fashion. Keep them busy, d'ya hear?"

"Yes, sir! Understand, sir."

"Right!" The lieutenant strode away toward the distant tower.

"Sarge!" The corporal with the perfect vision attracted the sergeant's attention.

"What is it, corporal?"

"There's stuff out there in the water. Can't make it out, could be bodies."

"Well, we can't do nothin' about it. Now do as the officer says an' get those people out of 'ere."

But the people did not want to be moved, especially when the first of the small kegs was seen rolling in the surf. The soldiers' task – without resorting to violence – was hopeless. Soon enlisted men and civilian alike were wading in the tide, pulling out the *Sparrow's* cargo. Men, women and children rolled the booty ashore.

A procession of laden townsfolk made their way back to their homes. A group of soldiers stove in a puncheon with bayonets and were passing it from hand to hand, brandy spilling down their uniformed chests. The overweight Hayes swore and shouted without effect but he was a determined individual and the butt of his musket hard in the guts of a young private had the desired effect.

By the time his lieutenant returned, the last of the civilians were straggling into Romney and the men were strung out in more or less military fashion along the beach.

"We've been duped, Hayes." The lieutenant was perspiring. "Did you think to check that wagon of contraband? No, of course not! And, curse it, neither did I! Everything that's happened can be put down to a gang of thieving-bastard cut-throats." The lieutenant was in the biggest rage that Hayes had ever witnessed. "The fires, the so-called lunatic, the release of the prisoners, and, by God, I'll warrant even the theft of my pocketbook! That officer in the tower has made us look amateurs. Sunk that contraband boat and shot three of the gang. The rest are either drowned or prisoners aboard that ship yonder." He pointed briefly at the *Wyvern* now underway and already shrinking into the distant sunrise.

"At the risk of neglecting my duty here, I shall go to Deal. That ship will anchor in the Downs and must put the prisoners ashore there. I will lay charges against them." The lieutenant was calmer now. "Theft, arson, smuggling! I will have their heads! The story of the lunatic was obviously put about by this gang to cover their activities. We have been on a fools' errand. Sergeant, get the men back to town."

At this moment, over half a mile down the coast, Abel Garnett's looker and right-hand man, Charlie was struggling, exhausted from the sea, crawling painfully across the stony beach, naked apart from a pair of ragged trousers. He reached the sand dunes and slumped gratefully into their comparative comfort. After a brief respite, the chill morning air obliged him to move on. Bent double, Charlie moved cautiously away from the beach, heading for the marsh country. He wasn't sure if Abel was alive or dead. Perhaps he would turn up at Shippenden.

At about the time that Yvonne and Lysette were draping Charlie in blankets and he was telling them of the disaster, Mr Brownlow's carriage and pair was pulling up at the New Inn at Romney. He wanted to consult the magistrate about Jack Dawkins before proceeding to Shippenden. With him was a smartly dressed boy formerly known as Oliver Twist, now reunited with his family. He was looking forward to seeing the Dodger once more. No doubt he would find him well on the way to being a reformed character. Mr Brownlow had expounded his theories at some length to Oliver. "Hard work, fresh air, disassociation from former friends and surroundings, lack of temptation should all result in bringing Dawkins to a more decent, Christian way of life." Brownlow had grown quite animated. "My boy, if the experiment is successful, why I might expand it to rescue a great number of poor would-be criminals from the downward path to self-destruction."

Oliver was beginning to look back on his adventures in London with something like fond nostalgia. The worst aspects of his experiences were fading from his memory, the dangers now distant. What he mostly retained was a tremendous sense of being fully alive during that time. Life for him now was dull by comparison.

To the new arrivals, there seemed to be an odd air of tension and excitement among the townspeople, who, after a largely sleepless night were still congregating in small groups, discussing the extraordinary events that had taken place.

"What happened here?" The silver-haired Brownlow interrupted a heated conversation between three oldsters.

"What ain't 'appened, you mean, sir?

A little screwed-up man spoke. "Why I ain't never knowed a night like it in sixty-seven year. We've 'ad lunatics on the loose, barns burnt, men shot dead, a shipwreck," he cackled, showing his toothless gums. "Why all we want is Boney to walk into the New Inn…"

"Good heavens!" Mr Brownlow expressed his amazement.

"My word, Uncle!" Oliver was equally impressed. His button-bright eyes sparkled excitedly and he pushed his hat back from his forehead. "I have the odd premonition that Jack—"

"Oh, Shippenden is several miles from here," Brownlow interrupted. "No doubt Jack is busy right now helping on the farm. Come along, Oliver. I must speak to the magistrate, Mr Acott. Perhaps he can tell us more sensibly what has occurred."

"What has happened! What has happened! I will tell you what has happened, sir." Acott was tired, angry and frustrated as he immediately showed after Mr Brownlow introduced himself on his doorstep.

"That boy, sir! The very boy whom you have come to enquire about. He's running with a gang of thieves and murderers, not to mention arsonists!"

"Come, sir," said Brownlow mildly, "surely you exaggerate."

"Two barns burnt to the ground, sir! Is that an exaggeration? Three local men dead and two soldiers wounded. Is that an exaggeration? A smuggler's ship sunk by cannon fire. I ask again, sir, is that an exaggeration?"

"By no means, Mr Acott. But how is Jack Dawkins central to these events? I cannot believe that he could so quickly become involved in such monstrous occurrences."

"Then I will open your eyes to the truth, sir. That boy— that felon awoke the town last night with wild stories of escaped lunatics. It was a ruse, sir, a ruse!" Acott was well into his stride now, spilling out the events of the night in a greatly aggrieved tone whilst Brownlow and Oliver listened in awe.

"But thanks to the alertness of those guardians of our shore, all their efforts came to naught," said Acott with some satisfaction. "Their ship sunk, the cargo—lost!" He could not help thinking of the portion of recovered goods in his own cellar. "And the gang killed or captured." He smacked his hands together and rubbed them vigorously.

"And the boy?" asked Brownlow.

"Drowned or a prisoner on one of His Majesty's ships." Acott hesitated. "Or just possibly out there, out on the levels. A few did get away. We have every reason to believe that the leader of this gang is your own farm manager, sir. In placing that boy with him, you have placed one villain with another." Now Acott was looking triumphant.

"This is incredible," groaned Brownlow.

Oliver put a sympathetic hand on his relative's arm. "You are not to blame, Uncle. You were not to know."

"That's your trouble, sir, if I may say so," said Acott. "You don't know. If you had dealt with as many villains as I, you would recognise one when you saw one. I knew it, sir, as soon as I saw the boy. I knew that he was bad. Through and through."

Mr Brownlow flared angrily. "And Mr Garnett, sir? He who has lived among you. Did you not recognise him, sir? You must have met him many times."

Acott "hrrmphed" at this. "We shall soon finish this business once and for all," he said. "I have despatched soldiers to Shippenden. They have their orders. Arrest every man that turns up there, and an officer will soon be on his way to Deal to ensure that any prisoners rescued from the wreck are presented with the evidence of their wrong-doing and pay the price."

"I must go to my property." Mr Brownlow suddenly looked very old and defeated. "If you will excuse me, Mr Acott, I will talk to you again later."

"And I must go to my bed," said Acott stiffly. "I have not had a wink of sleep since yesterday night. I hope that you have learned a lesson from this, Mr Brownlow. Leave the law to those that know what it's about." He turned and went into his house.

"Come along, Oliver," Brownlow said quietly, "we must get to Shippenden."

CHAPTER EIGHTEEN

Oliver Twist – Gentleman

hick fog cloaked the several ships anchored in the Downs. The Captain of the *Wyvern* was being entertained by an old friend aboard a three-decker two cables' length distant from his own vessel.

Whilst the two captains celebrated their reunion, after many years of separation, with glasses of Madeira, Abel dipped the tin cup into the leather water bucket and took a swallow of the tepid liquid. He rapped sharply on the low door. "Guard! Hey guard!"

"Well?" A short, surly reply.

"You alone there?"

"It only takes one."

"'Ow long since you was 'ome, then?"

"Too long. Now shut it!"

"How would you like to be ashore in two hours with money in ya' pocket?"

"It would suit me fine to get a bit o' English mud on me boots. But it ain't likely. Now, as I said, shut it." The sharp, impatient rap of a musket butt on the door made Jack flinch.

Abel persisted. "How much would it take—twenty pound— thirty pound—more?"

There was a short, cynical laugh from the other side of the door. "Gold or paper?"

"We've got both!" Jack could not resist calling out.

"Shut up, Jack," snapped Abel.

Peachey added, "Aye keep outta this, boy, this is men's work."

"It was my work got the money in the first place."

"All right, Jack." Abel lowered his voice to a whisper. "But we ain't seen it yet. I hope you're right about this."

"Trust me," Jack said simply.

"You in there!" the guard whispered hoarsely.

"Fifty poun'. Fifty poun' an' you're on."

And then a distinctly sharp intake of breath. "Quiet—quiet—Sergeant-at-arms comin'."

A few moments' silence, then the four cooped-up prisoners heard a fresh commanding voice. "Well, Madeley, what're you a doin' of?"

"Guardin' prisoners, Sarge. Lieutenant Tanner, 'e says I wos to relieve the guard till further orders like."

"I see. Well, Madeley, the way you guards prisoners is the same way as you does everythin' else—sloppy! Git away from that door. Stand up straight and ground that musket butt. You ain't out poachin' pheasants!"

"Aye, aye, Sarge."

"Right, that's more like it. I got me eye on you, Madeley. Look sharp!"

Another few moments silence, then Madeley spoke to them through the door again.

"Right, 'e's gone. Now you got fifty poun' or not?"

"Pretty much so, I reckon."

"An what does that mean? You got it or not?"

"Well, we haven't got it on us. It's hid see, on this ship, but it's right handy to get hold of."

"Right, tell us where an' I'll pick it up. If it's all fair n' square, I'll get you off this ship."

"Are you crazy?" Peachey joined in. "D'ya think we'd fall for that?"

"Yeah," said Harry. "We ain't daft, you know."

"All right, fair dos. Get the boy to show me—and…"

"I've 'ad enough o' this whisperin' through key-'oles," said

Abel fiercely. "Look, open this door, we come out, get the money an' we all make off in a boat. Simple as that."

"Oh, yeah, four agin one, no thanks."

"Damnation." Abel was totally frustrated.

"Forget it then, you damn stupid fool! No fifty pound and you can rot on this hulk!"

Harry gave a slight moan of despair, while Peachey, crouched together with Abel on the floor, put a hand on his shoulder.

"Abe, I've lost me boat an' I'm ruined. Now it looks like the rope for us all. I don't blame you, Abe. I came in wiv me eyes open. I don't blame you but it comes 'ard, real 'ard."

"I'm sorry, Matthew, but we ain't dead yet y'know, and I'll see you get another boat if I get the chance."

Harry gave a snort of derision. Jack rubbed his face with both hands. He felt deathly tired.

The door opened a few inches, gaining all their attention.

"Right," said Madeley, "it's a deal. I've got me finger on this trigger. One move toward me an' this musket goes off. You'll 'ave fifty marines on top o' yer before you can spit, get it?"

"Don't worry—all we want is to get off this ship."

They crept from their cramped prison, bending low.

"Keep quiet an' keep ya 'eads down." Madeley was anxious to say the least. "Now I want that money, quick!"

Abel raised a hand. "The boy gets the money and you get it once we're off the ship. If you try an' cross us, you can pull that trigger an' get one of us if you like, but the other three will do for you before 'elp arrives. Right, lads?" He gave a determined nod to Peachey, Harry and Jack.

"Right, Abe, we'll do for 'im all right, don't worry."

"Jack, watch out for yourself. Go and get that money."

Jack slipped away, quickly disappearing into the fog. He ghosted silently along, trying to pick up his bearings from what he remembered of his brief period of time on deck when he was first taken aboard. The appearance of a shadowy figure sent him, heart thumping, sliding beneath a companion-way. He crouched there silently until the man passed. A few yards further and there was the long boat now covered and secured. In a matter of moments, he was up and into the boat, crawling about under the canvas in complete darkness. There it was! He grabbed the small package and quickly returned to the waiting group, having another heart-stopping moment when a door opened revealing a brightly lit interior. "Fog's thick'nin'," a voice said and the door quickly closed again.

"Got it!" Jack said triumphantly.

"Well done, Jack! Come on then!" Abel followed Madeley and the others fell in line.

"Thank heaven for this fog." Matthew Peachey breathed a quiet prayer.

"Here's the captain's sailboat," said Madeley as they neared the stern of the *Wyvern*. "But t'ain't barely big enough for three, let alone five."

Abel eyed the canvass-covered elongated shape. "It'll 'ave to do," he said. "What d'you think, Matt? You're the seaman."

"Too small to make France with us lot, that's for sure."

"France? I got to get back to Shippenden to my wife."

"That's all over, Abe, don't you realise that?" Matthew Peachey put his face close to Abel's. "It's over man, finished; you'll be hunted down."

"Stop bloody arguing. I ain't going to France. It's me for London," said Madeley. "Let's get this boat in the water."

Eager hands removed the knotted rope and canvass. The tiny craft was about ten feet long, an unstepped mast and single sail lay in the bottom of it, together with a pair of oars. Madeley and Matthew Peachey took charge.

"The boy best get in the boat afore we swing it out. He'll need to use an oar to stave it off from the ship's side."

"Me again." Jack did not relish being lowered over the side of the ship in that small craft.

"No time to argue, Jack. Get in," whispered Abel sharply.

A minute later, suspended from a halyard that had been swung out over the side, Jack found himself thrusting an oar at the *Wyvern's* hull as the sailboat was lowered. The dampening fog allowed the procedure to be conducted in almost complete silence. Jack breathed a sigh of relief when the tiny keel touched water.

The agile group of men soon joined him in the boat. The sea lapped alarmingly near the gunwales.

"Careful, you'll swamp us," Madeley said. He produced a knife and quickly sawed through the ropes that held them. Quite suddenly they were free and drifting away from the side of the *Wyvern*. They were soon lost to everything in the fog. Then they heard a muffled distant call.

"Ahoy, *Wyvern*, is all well?"

"It's the picket boat!" Madeley muttered.

"All's well here!" came the muffled reply from the prow.

"They patrol the waters," Madeley said, "watching for deserters or surprise attacks from the French—fire ships an' such."

Madeley and Peachey paddled gently with the oars while the others made themselves as small as possible to avoid the movement of the rowers' shoulders.

"'Ow do you know the way to the shore?" Jack asked. "I'm lost."

"For God's sake, be careful!" Harry was panicky as water lapped into the overloaded boat. "Sit still you fool, you'll have us all in the salty," Madeley remonstrated.

Three lights, glowing orange in the fog and apparently suspended in mid-air, appeared in ghostly fashion. "Quiet now!" Peachey was whispering once more. "A ship!"

The extravagantly carved and convoluted stern of one of Her Majesty's ships emerged, then slid away into the murk. Jack could have reached out and touched her anchor chain as they went by. They heard the faint crack of a musket moments before the welcome sound of surf breaking on the shore. "I think they've missed us, row boys, row." They grounded almost immediately, the boat being low in the water. Madeley leapt out and levelled his musket at Abel's chest. "I want that money. You don't leave that boat until I've got it and gone, understand?"

"Quite right, mate, you've done your bit," Abel said quietly. "Jack—the money."

Jack weighed the small bag in his hand, chinking the coins, sighed and tossed it to Madeley who deftly caught it in one hand and imitated Jack's action before placing it inside his shirt.

"Thanks lads, I'm off, nice to 'ave known yer!" He backed away, then turned and plunged through the waves until he was swallowed up by the fog.

"I'm not riskin' France after all," Matthew Peachey said as they stood in the water clinging to the boat that struggled to escape from them with each receding sea. "I've a mate in Rye'll look after me till the fuss dies down—God 'elp the missis an' kids wi no money comin' in."

"We'll take care o' them, never fear," Abel reassured the fisherman.

"I'll come wi' yer." The ever-anxious Harry spoke up. Perhaps you can get a few bob to my family as well, Abe."

"Leave it to me! Now get going!"

Matthew Peachey and Harry re-boarded the sail-boat, now riding more easily in the water.

Abel and Jack pushed it a few yards out and the two on board took up the oars. It soon disappeared into the all-enveloping fog.

"Come on, Jack," Abel said to the wet and exhausted boy, "let's get home."

"Are you sure it's safe?"

"I'm not sure about anything anymore but I've got to try, see? Try to get to Yvonne and the girl."

They plunged down the dune onto a narrow lane. "You've made a lot of promises—" Jack gasped as they hurried through vaporous mist; "—barns, boats, payments; I 'ope you can live up to 'em."

"While I live, I'll try," said Abel. "First things first."

Brownlow and Oliver arrived at Shippenden in the early afternoon, first negotiating their way round the soldiers placed to guard the lane to the farm. There were more soldiers at the gate and still more bivouacked in the yard. Yvonne and Lysette were prisoners in the house. Of Charlie, there was no sign. He had crept away unnoticed at the noisy approach of the troops.

Mr Brownlow could not resist pointing out to Sergeant Hayes that the smugglers were unlikely to return to a farm so obviously occupied by soldiers.

"Lieutenant's orders, sir. He's in the 'ouse questioning the wimmin. We're to camp 'ere for a while, then make a big show o' leavin'. March off like, leavin' two or three in the 'ouse. Then we sneaks back like after dark and take up positions. The lieutenant reckons if any are to return 'ere, they'll do it tonight or tomorrow. But 'ere he comes now, sir."

"What a sneaky plan, Uncle!" Oliver said. "It hardly seems fair play to me."

The gangly lieutenant adjusted the sword scabbard at his side and extended his hand to Mr Brownlow. "Good afternoon, sir. I take it that you are the owner-in-absence of this property."

Mr Brownlow dismissed his carriage with a wave to the driver. "Take care of the horses, if you please, Mr Ford. I am sure you will find some victuals for yourself."

The carriage having moved off, he addressed himself to the lieutenant, shaking the officer's hand.

"Yes, I am Brownlow. I am the owner. Mr Acott has told me something of what has been happening here. I am shocked, sir, deeply shocked. This is young Oliver, who was only recently rescued from a band of thieves and murderers."

"Come into the house, Mr Brownlow—if you will forgive me for inviting you in to what is yours."

They went into the drawing room. "I have the two females, locked in and guarded, upstairs," the young lieutenant said as they sat themselves down. "Now, as I understand it, you took a boy out of prison, by arrangement, and put him in the care of your farm manager with the aim of reforming him. But your manager, one Abel Garnett, is himself, or was—he may be drowned along with this said boy for all we know—a villain of some note."

There was an embarrassed silence.

Oliver said, "Perhaps Jack has been unlucky. He has never had a chance like me. He was not born lucky; now look what has happened to him."

"There is something in what you say, Oliver," said Brownlow. "I believe there is good in almost everyone."

The officer spoke again. "I think perhaps that Jack, as you call him, is drowned as well, although two or three survivors were pulled aboard a ship. I intend to ensure that these survivors are prosecuted to the full extent of the law. When I am satisfied that no remnants of this gang are going to come here, I shall go directly to Deal with a full report of these events."

"May I see the ladies?" Brownlow asked deferentially, head bowed and shoulders drooping under the weight of his disappointment.

"Certainly, they have been of very little help. I do not believe they are involved in the men's business."

Mr Brownlow and the lieutenant climbed the stairs, leaving Oliver sitting, full of his own thoughts, on the settee.

⋘⋙

Abel and Jack crouched in the darkness, wet through yet again from the reeds and grasses that grew high close to the dyke. Jack looked now with fondness on the daylight hours that they had spent in the warmth of a hay barn where they had rested up on their trek from Deal.

"Jack, I want you to wait here while I get to the farm, I must see my wife and make certain she and Lysette are well. Let them know that they will go to my sister's and I need to get some money as well."

"I'm not waiting 'ere. I'm comin' with you!" Jack retorted.

"Look, I'm sorry everything is such a mess," Abe growled. "It's all gone wrong at once. You are a complication and I've made things worse for you instead of better. Wait here; I'll bring you some money when I come back. At least that'll give you a chance. Get away. Lie low."

"They might not be on to us at all," Jack said. "Then everything can get back to how it was."

"No. Everything's shot to hell," Abel said bleakly. "Got to get away, start a new life. Yvonne and Lysette can join me later when everything's settled."

"But, where'll you go?"

"I ain't thought it through yet," Abel said. "Everything's happened so fast. Might go up north or abroad somewhere. I've got an aunt at a place near Chichester! I must find a way to pay my debts. So I'll go there for a bit. I expect you'll head for London again, eh?"

"'Spect I will. I can lose meself there," Jack said, "if I can't come wiv you."

Abel stood up in the darkness. "I'm going now; keep your eyes open. I'll be back within the hour." Abel strolled, quite casually across the meadow, heading for the dark, shadowy buildings amongst the trees.

Jack sighed, pulling his bedraggled coat tightly around his chilled body. At least it wasn't raining. In fact, there were quite a few stars visible. He was gazing up at these when a hand fell on his shoulder, freezing his blood.

"It's you, Jack!" a familiar voice uttered.

"Charlie. God! You scared me half to death! I thought you was dead!"

"Yeah, so did I! Where did you get that stuff you're wearing?"

"Off a clothes line."

"Was that Abe I saw headin' for the farm?"

"He's going to see Yvonne an' Lysette. Let 'em know we're all right," Jack said recovering from his sudden shock.

"Well, he's done for then," said Charlie. "The place is full of soldiers. I bin in that looker's' hut yonder. Oh they left all right 's'afternoon, but some crept back later. They're in the 'ouse, the barn an' the wood too, I reckon. I thought you was more of 'em in fact, till Abe stood up an' I recognised 'is stamp."

"We've got to stop 'im," Jack said urgently. "Come on!"

"Look I've 'ad two narrer escapes. I ain't riskin' another one."

"Well, I'm going!" said Jack and set off immediately towards the farm.

He heard footsteps behind him and, glancing over his shoulder, saw Charlie following at a trot.

"When ya get near, if 'e's already in the yard, ye'll 'ave to leave 'im go or we'll all be took," Charlie panted.

Abel knew the risk he was taking as he neared the farm, but he could not bring himself to leave without seeing Yvonne and Lysette. He was driven to recklessness – the same unthinking stubbornness that had taken him from one disaster to another during the last few days. He was about to step through the fence at the rear of the farm when he heard his name called. "Abe!" Watch out! Soldiers!" He recognised Jack's voice before he turned and saw his indistinct form and the larger one of Charlie some way behind.

"Jack! Is that Charlie? Where'd he come from?"

"Get away from here, Abe. There's soldiers about."

First there was the rattle of musketry being handled, unmistakable to Abel's ears, then the pounding of feet. "Stand where you are! Stand or we'll shoot!" Five men, the white of their cross-belts showing bright through the mist, rushed toward Abel and Jack. "Damn and blast it!" Abel put his hands on the fence in resignation. "Stand still, Jack, we're took. Charlie—give up—we ain't dead yet!"

Charlie made the fatal mistake of turning to run. Three muskets went off simultaneously, almost in the faces of Abel and Jack. One musket-ball whined harmlessly into the night, of the other two, one broke Charlie's backbone and the other smashed in the back of his head. He died without uttering a sound. His body sprawled in the coarse meadow grass. Blood, black as death, leaked from the terrible head-wound.

Abel and Jack were hurried and hustled to the farmhouse, two of the soldiers carried Charlie's limp body. The lieutenant and Mr Brownlow came out of the house, both carrying lanterns. "Well, my plan worked!" The lieutenant rubbed his hands in satisfaction. Abel and Jack were brought to a halt.

"Do you know these two, Mr Brownlow? I myself have seen this boy. It was he who roused the townspeople just before the fires were started. He has condemned himself."

"I'm afraid that I know both of them only too well," sighed Brownlow. "This is my farm manager, Garnett, and the boy, the boy is my great experiment and my great failure."

"And the dead one?"

Mr Brownlow bent and peered closely at Charlie's body. "I believe that he worked here also."

"Dreadful, quite dreadful!"

"Let's get one thing right," said Abel. "This boy 'ere had nothin' to do with what went on at this farm. Whatever he did, he was made to do on threat o' bein' returned to prison or transported."

"You'll have your time in court," said the lieutenant. "Into the house, if you please."

Oliver had been lying awake in Jack's old room when the shots were fired. Half-dressed, he tumbled down the stairs and was in the doorway as Jack was shoved through by a tired and irritable soldier.

"Jack!" Oliver grasped his sleeve. "Are you all right?"

"Hello, shaver, fancy meetin' you 'ere!"

"Get in!" The soldier gave Jack a vicious prod in the back.

"I'm goin', I'm goin'!"

In the crowded sitting room there was now the lieutenant, Mr Brownlow, two soldiers, Oliver, Abel and Jack. The two soldiers stood by the door, muskets long and menacing in the flickering light. Jack and Abel were obliged to stand, while the other three sat.

"I'm shocked and distressed to see you come to this, Garnett." Mr Brownlow was obviously moved. "I trusted you, you know. Trusted you with my property and this boy—" He indicated Jack with a slightly trembling finger.

"I have never cheated you out of a penny, Mr Brownlow. What I have done has been a sort of separate life. Until a few days ago, I always took good care of your property. And as for the boy, he's been dragged into this against his will. He has not failed you. There's a lot o' good in this boy."

"If only I could believe that," sighed Brownlow.

"You can, sir," said Abel firmly. "Ain't that right, Jack?"

Jack was thinking of Lysette and of his arrival at Shippenden; the motherly Yvonne.

"I tried to get away, sir, honest I did," he blurted out. "Ain't that right, Abe? Why, Charlie even shot at me."

"I can swear to that, Mr Brownlow, sir," said Abel.

Mr Brownlow turned to the lieutenant. "Perhaps something can still be done for the boy."

"I appreciate your position, Mr Brownlow," said the officer. "No one wants to be made a laughing stock as you will be when news of how this boy has hoodwinked you gets out, but I am afraid that he is my prisoner and will be handed to the civil authorities with a full list of charges against him."

Oliver said, "But I believe that man when he said Jack was made to commit these crimes."

"You're too young to understand, boy," said the lieutenant.

"Oh, but I am not, I assure you," Oliver protested.

"Not now, Oliver, please," Brownlow said quietly.

"I would like to see my wife, sir, if you please," Abel said in a steely voice that almost made the request an order.

"She is in an upstairs room with your daughter. They are quite all right, no charges will be brought against them."

"Nevertheless, I would like to see them now."

"Mayn't he, Uncle, mayn't he see them?" Oliver asked.

"Oh, very well," said the lieutenant.

He gave orders to the two soldiers. "Take this man up to the women—now, two go with him into the room, mind, and two continue to guard the door. Five minutes, that's all, and check those bonds at his wrists, if you please."

"Can I come?" Jack wanted to know.

"Stay where you are!" snapped the lieutenant.

One of the soldiers pulled at the rope round Abel's wrists. "Painful tight, I'd say."

"Very well—take him up."

Yvonne's previous control over her emotions fell away when Abel entered the bedroom. Lysette, who had cried herself dry of tears during the past twelve hours, was the first to embrace him. "You're alive! We heard the shooting!" Yvonne took Abel's face gently in both hands and kissed him tenderly.

Abel's fingers tapped an urgent tattoo on Yvonne's back as she and Lysette clung to him. As she removed her face from his and her ear passed his mouth, he breathed one word:

"Scissors." It came out as a prolonged sigh, but Abel felt her body stiffen.

"Say what you gotta say," one of the two soldiers near the door spoke. "Time's short." Yvonne leant against the cluttered dressing table while Lysette sat helplessly on the large bed.

"I want you to go to Elspeth's at Gravesend till this is over," Abel said to the two women. "John knows about this. By some miracle I was on his ship the night before last. He will make arrangements for you should he get leave. If not, make your way there. You have funds. You know where. Whatever happens, I will see you again." He stressed the last five words as firmly as he could.

"You'll be danglin' from a rope when you do," one of the soldiers sneered.

Lysette sprang up and confronted the soldiers. "You beasts. Don't say that!" As the men laughed, Yvonne embraced Abel fiercely once again, twisting him around, sobbing loudly whilst the scissors she had taken from the dressing table sawed vigorously at the rope round his wrists. As Yvonne felt the cords part, she pushed the scissors up the sleeve of her dress. "Don't give up hope, Abel," she pleaded tearfully. "All is not lost."

"No—I ain't dead yet," said Abel, almost cheerfully.

"Times up—come on, you," one of the soldiers pointed his musket.

"Look out, Lys!" Abel yelled at the top of his voice as he allowed the ropes to fall from his wrists. His hands shot out, grasped the musket-barrel, tore it from the startled soldier's grasp and smashed the butt back into his face. Blood spurted from a broken nose. The man sank to the floor. "'Ere!" was about all that the second soldier had time to utter before Abel was on him applying a stranglehold, his face screwed into a murderous look.

The bedroom door handle turned as a voice called, "Hey, what's goin' on?"

"Wardrobe!" Abel gasped as he struggled to silence the second soldier.

Yvonne, without a moment's hesitation, leapt on the heavy piece of furniture that stood against the wall next to the door; she rocked it once, twice, then over it went. The two guards outside heaved against the door, succeeding in opening it a few inches, then pushed their musket barrels through to use as levers.

Abel released the senseless soldier. "Got to go, darlin'. 'Bye Lys. Take care o' your mother. 'Vonne, there's a clasp knife in that coat behind the door." Abel hurried to the window and opened it. "Put the scissors back, leave the knife open on the floor. You played no part in this. How could a weak woman push over a wardrobe?" He sprang to the sill, turned and gave a brief, flashing smile and leapt.

Yvonne threw the scissors onto the dressing table and snatched the clasp knife from Abel's coat as the two soldiers beyond the door shoved, heaved and shouted for assistance. Opening the knife, Yvonne dropped it to the floor. "Lysette, keep your head now. Abel has a chance."

Lysette wiped fresh tears from her face and nodded. "I'm all right, Mama, all right now that he is free!"

Additional shoulders pushed the door and wardrobe until men were able to enter, just as the two soldiers that Abel had attacked were beginning to recover. The sound of musket-fire outside helped the women perform their roles as weak and helpless victims. The lieutenant rushed to the window.

"Did you get him?" he called out into the darkness. "Winged 'im, I think."

"Get after him, you dolts," stormed the lieutenant. He bent and picked up the clasp knife. "God, they can't even conduct a proper search!"

Abel was fully alive. This was how he had felt when he'd fought years ago with the footpads, Hetty and Solly; how he had felt when he had broken through the French lines at Corunna; when he had fought the battles of the peninsular. Tinglingly alive, his heart raced and pulsed as he leapt from the window, landing in the soft flower-beds below. He offered a silent apology to Yvonne and Lysette for trampling them. He could laugh out loud! Round the corner of the house in a moment; running flat out. Any one of a dozen men with property on the marsh would allow him a horse and funds. Two figures appeared on his left. Swerve! Quick! He reached the fence. Two shots. Aah! His side burned. He clutched at it. Up and over, he fell into the field, up again; zigzag off into the dark. The welcome dark and the fog. God, his side hurt!

At two o'clock in the morning, the soldiers returned empty-handed after a fruitless search for Abel Garnett. The lieutenant ranted to no avail. Jack was thrust into a cupboard under the stairs, hands tied. There was no handle on the inside of the door and Jack sat in there in complete and utter darkness.

"Well," the lieutenant said, with some satisfaction, "at least he won't get away. Somebody's going to hang for this. It'll have to be him. I'm determined on that!"

But even in that he was mistaken. Just before dawn, the door to Jack's latest prison was opened. It was Oliver with a knife. "I cannot see you hang, Jack. I do not believe you have done anything to warrant it. They are all asleep now. Make your escape if you can."

"Leave me be 'ere, Ollie, you'll get yourself in a fix if you free me."

"Me—free you, Jack?" Oliver's voice was all innocence. "Why I was so tired after the excitement I slept all night long. I never heard a thing. You see, Jack I have learnt something of your ways." Oliver wiped his eyes. "I sometimes wish I could be more like you, Jack. I see nothing ahead of me but the boredom of becoming a gentleman."

"You stick to that, Oliver," said Jack, rubbing his wrists. "You'll be better off. Thanks for this, I won't forget it: I'm off."

"Wait," said Oliver. "Here are a couple of guineas, it's all I have on me, I'm afraid."

"D'you know something?" Jack smiled. "You're a gent already." Then he was gone: doing what he did best, moving like a shadow, silent and unseen. He was going to try and find his friend, Abel Garnett. Somehow he already knew that he would succeed.

CHAPTER NINETEEN

Abel Garnett and the Artful Dodger
Journey to Brussels

he low-lying fog was both Jack's friend and his enemy. It helped cloak him from the listless, tired eyes of the soldiers on guard but it hindered his progress away from the farm. Ten minutes' careful stealth took him to the rear of the barn, then more suspenseful progress into the fields. Above the level of the fog there was a smear of light in the east. It would soon be another day. Jack had no idea what day of the week it actually was.

He had not thought it through, but his legs were carrying him in the direction of the ruined village and the underground chamber that Jake Pierce had died in. There in that pit was a temporary sanctuary for Abel until he could get to the shelter of a friendly house. Jack was convinced that that was where he would find him. There were still saleable goods up there, enough for Abel to bribe his way to freedom with any luck.

The Artful Dodger increased his pace across the squelching, peaty ground. Surely they had discovered his escape at the farm by now and set up a hue and cry? He thought of Oliver for a brief moment. Fancy that shaver helping him out like that!

He reached a dyke that was almost full of dirty brown water, clammy mist drifting over its surface. Unwilling to face a chill soaking to gain the other side he hurried along its bank. He had only gone a hundred yards when he spotted the familiar plank bridge used by the smugglers. There it was left in place! Crossing quickly, he bent and lifted the end of the plank, hauling it across and dropping it in the grass; then down sloping ground and onto the track to the ruin. A cold dawn breeze rustled the grasses and caused Jack to give an involuntary shiver as he sighted the tumbledown remains of buildings a few hundred yards ahead.

It was on the muddied track that he found Abel Garnett laying in the foetal position, one bloodied hand clutching his equally bloodied side. Jack ran forward and knelt by the body, "Abe! You all right?" The stupidity of the question dawned on him while the words were still on his lips. "Abe, come on, it's me, Jack."

Abel groaned and moved his head a little, "Jack, you 'ere—how—?"

"Never mind that. What a state you're in. I've got to get 'elp from somewhere, get a doctor—God, the blood!"

"Yeah, I've lost a lot. Think I've had it this time—too weak to get any further. If you're runnin' you'd better be on your way. Search party's will be out. Go on, get away!"

"You an' me's friends, ain't we?" Jack said fiercely, taking a rag from his pocket and wiping at Abel's face. "Can you stand if I help you? If I can get you hid, then you can point me in the direction of somebody who can take us in."

"Help me up then," said Abel. "Let's see what we can do."

Jack got one of Abel's muscular arms around his shoulders and heaved him into a half-upright position. Abel groaned, perspiration breaking out on his forehead, "I got a ball in my side, same place I was hit before, near as dammit."

They shuffled awkwardly up the incline to the rubble-strewn ruins.

"All we got to do now is cross this ditch," Jack gasped, Abel's weight bearing down on him.

"Get the planks across it, Jack, I'll try and shuffle across on me backside." This he did with Jack's steadying hands on his shoulders and his legs and feet in the murky water that sluiced below the makeshift bridge. Abel sprawled on the rank grass on the other side of the dyke.

"Nearly there, Abe," Jack said. "P'raps I can get you com'for'ble before I go for help." Together they stared into the small crater that had been formed when the stones and slabs had collapsed on Jacob Pierce. There was the grim sight of his body laying now in only a few inches of water and protruding from the results of the minor avalanche that he had created.

"Down there's no good," said Abel. He sat abruptly on the ground his arm sliding from Jack's shoulders. He put his hands over his face for a moment then looked up at Jack. "Do you think you could get Pierce's body out of there?"

"I dunno; I could try. What for?"

"Well if I could hide in the tower with what's left of the goods and you fill in the entrance we could leave the body in plain sight. If the soldiers come looking up here it might put them off searching too much."

"Well, they'll find the body anyway, won't they?"

"Yeah, yeah but we need to grab their attention quick, soon as they get here. Take their minds off things."

❖⋈❖

As dawn was breaking at Shippenden Oliver looked innocuously up into the faces of Mr Brownlow and the young lieutenant. "But I slept right through, I was so tired after the journey I heard nothing at all." A shuddering thrill of something quite sinister went through him at the blatant lie. So this is what wickedness is!

"How the devil did the boy escape from that cupboard? Why the door's still shut fast!"

"He's as cunning as a fox, I know that now," Brownlow answered. "Who knows how he accomplished his escape. Perhaps he persuaded one of your men."

"Perhaps—they are the sweepings. They can spend the day out there hunting fugitives. Who knows, we may recapture one or both and it will exercise the lazy brutes."

When the mist lifted and the marsh became visible under grey, clouded skies it did not take the soldiers long to find Jack's passage through the fields. Yvonne and Lysette tried to delay their departure as long as possible by offering breakfast. Mr Brownlow and Oliver were glad to accept but the lieutenant had other ideas for his men who were obliged to eat bread on the run.

They were in reflective mood as they ate their breakfast. "What will happen now, Uncle?" Oliver asked plaintively.

Brownlow sighed. "First I must make amends to the court as I am bound to do. I have been foolish—I see that now."

"It's all my fault! If I had nor entreated you to help Jack Dawkins none of this would have happened."

"Now, now Oliver. Bringing Dawkins here did not make Garnett a villain. He was that already. He was bound to get caught sooner or later.

"It was a very bold escape he made, Uncle."

"Indeed it was. And an equally bold one by Dawkins."

"Oh, it's no good! I must tell you. That was me. I did it! I let Jack out. Cut his bonds. I had to, don't you see? It was my fault. By bringing him here I turned his transportation into death by hanging! It would have been inevitable. Arson, smuggling, soldiers killed and wounded." Oliver was almost in tears.

Brownlow put a comforting hand on his shoulder. "We have both been wrong in interfering with justice. Let us learn from it, my boy. I have already decided that I will sell Shippenden. Let us hope that these two unfortunate young women have a home to go to. We shall never come to this part of the country again. We will get away as soon as possible, but first I must go to the town and see if I can employ some reliable people to take care of the farm until a sale can be arranged. You can wait here with the women if you wish."

"I think I will. Perhaps I can comfort them."

"Perhaps you can. Their future prospects are poor indeed."

"Can we help?"

"No—no more of that—not now," said Brownlow brusquely. "I must go."

After Mr Brownlow's departure, Oliver found it difficult to break the silence that reigned between the woman, the girl and himself. Yet finally he found himself asking, "May I help with the dishes?"

Yvonne, face pale beneath her dark hair, looked at him. "Thank you," she said softly.

Oliver picked up a linen cloth. "Don't worry, Mrs Garnett, I'm sure all will be well in the end."

"I do not see how it can be," Lysette said. "We can never all be together again—Papa must run and hide forever."

"Perhaps you can go abroad together."

"Perhaps we can," said Yvonne, "if he is not captured. I know if we get a second chance I will not let 'im do wrong again. I swear it."

Lysette gripped her mother's hand as they stood helplessly together in the kitchen. "Mama, don't cry, he will be all right. We will have to do as he said and go to his sister's."

"We will go when the soldiers return. Please God they search, but they do not find."

Only the lieutenant was truly diligent in the hunt for Abel and Jack. The redcoats were fed up with the bleak marshes, the constantly wet and cold conditions exacerbated by crossing the dykes. It was almost noon when they came in sight of the old village. The lieutenant peered intently through his eyeglass then snapped it shut. "There's someone laying up there on the slope, men. We may have one of them or perhaps the one that was wounded has expired. At the double now, in case he still lives."

The troop of men hurried forward up the slope, the lieutenant with pistol in hand. He was the first to reach the body. His first glance at Jacob Pierce's corpse caused him to recoil in horror. His men gathered around. "Oh, gawd, look at that. What a sight!"

A soldier hawked and spat noisily. "Fair gives me the creeps, that does."

Jacob Pierce's dead eyes stared heavenwards; the matted beard and hair almost obscured his grey face but failed to hide the fantastic fixed grin and long tongue protruding between the revealed teeth. His angular body, cloaked in a filthy greatcoat gave off an unmistakable stench.

"What poor wretch is this?" the lieutenant asked of no one in particular.

"Maybe 'tis that lunatic, Zor," ventured an ageing private. "Looks mad to I any'ow."

"I thought the lunatic was an invention of the smuggling gang. But I agree he's certainly quite sinister. All right, men, cast about for signs of the fugitives."

Within seconds a soldier called the lieutenant's attention to the exposed crypt. "Look, sir here's their hidey-hole. There's a keg and a bundle still down there and rope and canvas."

"Yes, I see, I believe that poor wretch laying yonder stumbled on this and was killed by the gang. Bring up that canvas, Private, and we shall use it to wrap and convey the body to Romney."

As the group moved off down the slope carrying Pierce's corpse wrapped in the canvas, Abel Garnett allowed himself to groan and ease his position slightly. He was in a space between the broken stones at the base of the tower, which appeared to the casual observer to be full of rubble.

Jack had done well, he thought, getting Pierce's body out of that hole. He remembered that, when the boy had tied the rope around its chest and began to haul it up the broken steps, the mouth had opened and the flaccid tongue had popped out. Jack had let out a screech of alarm and fallen backwards, releasing the rope. He recovered though, and, using all his strength, gradually dragged the body out into the open. He had thrown the rope and a piece of canvas along with a keg of brandy from the depleted store hidden in the tower down into the water which still covered the floor of the cellar.

Abel gave Jack precise directions on how to get to Billy Carpenter's house which was all of four miles distance on the edge of Ivychurch village. He then made himself as comfortable as he could while Jack piled slabs of stone to cover the entrance to his hiding place. "Don't worry, Abe, I'll be back with 'elp soon as I can," said Jack before heading out across the familiar flat and empty landscape.

It was a long march for the stretcher-bearers to bring Abel to the shelter of Billy Carpenter's cottage. The warmth and comfort, the fiery spirits that burned his throat, and the rough attention to his wound by Billy's wife, came just in time for Abel who was at a low ebb.

When the authorities' house-to-house search of the area reached Ivychurch a few days later, Abel was just fit enough to be squeezed into a small space under the eaves of the cottage. He lay there with heart beating in time to the throbbing in his side as soldiers crashed through the four rooms below. They were gone as quickly and noisily as they had come and Abel was soon restored to his bed.

Jack sat by the bedside. "How are you doin' now, Abe?"

"Hurts like the very devil, Jack and I'm weak as a kitten."

"Then we're stuck here?"

"Billy will take care of us until I'm fit to move."

"Yeah and what then?"

"I don't know, Jack; I've got to make a new life somewhere with my wife and the girl. I don't know how yet or where."

"Well, I'm with you, Abe. I am, ain't I?"

Abel managed a chuckle. "Looks like we're stuck with each other, Jack."

Billy Carpenter, born and bred on the marsh, carried with him a slight air of recklessness. The occasional night ventures enlivened his drab working existence and he had led the soldiers a merry dance on the night of the barn burning. Now he was inheriting the balance of the goods left in the church ruin as payment for aiding Garnett and the boy. With luck, now that he had some capital, he could reorganise the gang and make his fortune. That was why, towards the end of April, he was happy to arrange with the crew of a fishing boat to take Jack and Abel across the Channel. Napoleon was back in

Paris but the time-honoured trade between the French and English coasts went on.

Jack and Abel crunched across a gravel beach one moonless night towards the surf where a row-boat waited to take them out. Word had been sent to Shippenden but the young man who was living there as temporary manager informed the discreet messenger that the two females had been given a ride to Gravesend in Brownlow's carriage.

"I'll help get them over to you later on," Billy promised as they shook hands at the sea's edge, "I'll wait till all the fuss has died down. They may be watched, you know."

Jack's second experience of being at sea in a small boat was only a slight improvement on his first. He retched and groaned with the misery of seasickness for the entire Channel crossing.

"I didn't know I could feel so rotten and still live! Why aren't the rest o' you sick like me?"

"Cos we've our sea legs and you're a landlubber," jeered one of the crew-members.

"I'm never goin' on water again!" swore Jack. "Never!"

Abel Garnett sat in Christian Lepage's house near to Boulogne drinking a glass of velvety red wine. "We owe you, Monsooer, don't we, Jack?" he said, casting a quick glance at the Dodger.

"Certainly do, Abe," Jack confirmed, setting his own glass down and licking his lips, "France is just the right bolt-'ole for us I reckon, till things die down."

Lepage, an unremarkable looking individual, except for the fact that he lacked his right ear, shrugged his shoulders. "You are welcome gentlemen. I 'ope that the day will come when we can do business again. It is mos' unfortunate when we do so well, eh?"

"Most unfortunate," agreed Abel, gritting his teeth as the half-healed wound in his side tore at his nerve-ends.

"You all right, Abe?" Jack noticed the grimace of pain.

247

"Yeah, yeah, I'm all right, getting better all the time, but I think I've been shot and cut about one too many times, that's all."

"Your luck still seems to be holdin' out, though."

"I dunno about that, Jack. I've been in a state these past few weeks. Ever since that last run, I got sort of obsessed with that wagon-load of goods. It was just one damn thing after another. I'm not proud of how things went. People got killed for nothing. Brownlow's reputation is ruined and your one chance to make good's shot to pieces."

"Weren't all your fault, Abel. Things just went against you, that's all, and I'm still better off than I was in Newgate. We'll make out, you'll see."

"I don't know how. We're on our uppers. There's Peachey's boat, those barns I burnt and God knows what else to make good. Most of all there's my wife and the girl. There were sixty gold sovereigns in the house, but that won't last forever." Abel took up the bottle of wine and poured a glass, picking it up with the same hand that replaced the bottle on the table. He drank deeply.

Lepage extended his hand across the table. "I understand much of what you say, M'sieur Abe—do not worry; my 'ouse is your 'ouse until things are better for you."

"Thanks, Lepage, is there anything we can do for you?"

"You are sick—mauvais—M'sieur. But Jacques 'e can 'elp in the magasin if 'e wish; there is much to do, you know. Business is good."

"What's happening out there, Lepage? With Bonaparte, I mean. Are we going to fight again?"

"He is forming a great army, M'sieur. Your Lord Wellington is in Bruxelles. 'E will march his army into France. There is much confusion with your allies. If there is a battle I cannot see 'ow you can win. Bonaparte will be Le Grand Empereur D'Europe."

"We beat him before and we'll beat him again," declared Abel. "I wish I were up there. Can you get me up there, Lepage?"

"Up where, M'sieur?"

"To Brussels, of course. I could enlist. A false name and I'm in."

"'Ang on," said Jack, "you don't wanna go doin' nothin' silly like joining the army again. Look at the mess you're in now. Nothing but wounds."

"I want to be in at the death, Jack." Abel was growing more excited by the minute at the thought of action, "You could enlist too; they won't be fussy who joins right now."

"Oh, thanks very much!"

"You know what I mean."

"You ain't fit, Abe—you just said so."

"I cannot take you any'ow," said Lepage; "I am a business man and cannot leave at the moment."

"Got something on, have you? Well I can't blame you for that."

"If you want to go so much I can let you 'ave a ride on a charret'ee that is about to go to Lille. It is more than halfway to Bruxelles."

Jack argued the toss but the new idea had fixed itself in Abel's mind and nothing would dislodge it.

❖

A long straight road lined with poplar trees and deeply ditched on either side stretched to the horizon. Along it rolled Lepage's wagon-load of goods. Jack had a curious sense of déjà vu as he sat up front with the amiable waggoner. They did not speak each other's language but got along famously with nods, grins and gestures.

It was the road, the landscape and the wagon that made Jack feel ill-at-ease. It was all too familiar – if you substituted willow for poplar they could almost be back on the marshes.

"Hey, Abe, I still think you're out of your mind getting back into the soldiering game an' expectin' me to go along with you."

"I told you, Jack," Abel Garnett growled from the interior of the covered cart, "you can leave any time you like and make your own way."

"Oh, fine! Me in a place where I can't speak the lingo, no money as usual and the 'angman waiting for me in England."

"That's why it's one way out. Not too many questions asked in the army and at least we'll have a place to lay our 'eads, eat, drink and get a little money that I can send to Yvonne. It's not perfect, but what is? Those that I owe will have to be patient."

"Well, I'll stick it out for now, but I'm warning yer I might change me mind at the last."

Jack heard Abel's snort of laughter. "Let's enjoy the ride for now. There's nothing I like better than a journey."

The city of Lille was alive with activity. The imminent threat of mighty armies clashing in the vicinity had been like poking a stick into a wasp's nest. The streets were full of laden carts and wagons and people were hurrying in all directions, many of them carrying bags of provisions and bundles of all shapes and sizes. The possibility of a siege was in everyone's mind.

Lepage's man manoeuvred his horses expertly along the streets until they arrived at their destination, a double-fronted general store. A large, brightly painted sign declared it to be Emporia Lepage.

Jack and Abel stood by the wagon. The only fact that they had ascertained about their driver was that his nickname was Pharaoh.

"Any chance of a meal—some food?" Abel pointed fingers at his open mouth and rubbed his stomach with his other hand.

"Yeah, I'm starved," Jack said.

"Georges!" Pharaoh called out as they went through the entrance into the store.

"Georges, Engleesh!"

A fat little man aged about thirty emerged from a backroom. He sported a cheap pair of spectacles which hung precariously on the end of a pug nose. His breeches stretched alarmingly at the waist but gained some relief from a broad, brass-buckled belt.

"Bonjour, Messieurs, 'allo, can I 'elp you?" Georges was very hospitable.

"We are en route to Brussels—" explained Abel, "—me and my young friend here, Jack Dawkins. I think it's Shank's Pony from now on. Any chance of a meal on Lepage, we're a bit short of money?"

Pharaoh removed himself from the store and began to unfasten the tailgate of the wagon.

"Come through, Messieurs," said Georges, "I think we can accommodate you."

The large back room was stacked almost to the ceiling on all sides with boxes and packing cases apart from a small passageway that led to a rear door. A deal table and a set of chairs took up most of the remaining space.

"Sit down," said Georges, "I'll see what I can find to eat."

"You speak excellent English, M'sieur," Abel said.

"Yeah, better than most Englishmen," Jack added.

"I have much practice," Georges replied.

He took down platters from a shelf, then some rather dusty wine glasses and a bottle of red. From a mesh-fronted cupboard came a long loaf and a dish of butter, a knuckle of ham and some blue-veined cheese.

"I hope this will satisfy your appetites, gentlemen."

"Splendid," said Abel wiping the glasses with his fingers and pouring wine.

"So you are friends of M'sieur Lepage, yes?" Georges settled his fat little body on a straight-backed chair.

"We used to be business associates."

"I see. And now?"

"Well, we—that is Jack and I—have fallen on hard times. We intend to enlist in Wellington's army, as a refuge, like."

Georges smiled: "So you are English patriots then?"

"I once served as a sergeant in the 50th Foot," Abel said lifting his head a little as a flood of memories filled his mind.

"And Jack?"

"I've 'ad it hard all me life, then, just when things were lookin' up, we had to leave dear old England," said Jack tearing off a lump of bread. "That cheese is mouldy."

"On the wrong side of the law, eh?" asked Georges, a sympathetic tone in his voice.

"Only a little cross-Channel business," Abel said. "Turned out not to be worth it in the end."

"I see."

Pharaoh suddenly appeared in the doorway and spoke rapidly to Georges, then gave a clumsy salute to Abel and Jack, smiled broadly and departed.

"He is going to a hotel, you know, for drinks and the ladies."

Georges got up rather suddenly, went to the door and peered out rather intently for a few moments then closed and turned his back on it facing Jack and Abel. He seemed taller now and somehow not so fat.

"Listen," he said in a rather melodramatic stage whisper, "I may need your help. Can I trust you?" He was speaking now in perfect English. Abel and Jack gaped at him in surprise.

"Depends what it is," Abel replied. "I intend to stay on the right side of the law from now on."

"Don't worry about that. This is duty for your King and country."

"What?"

"My name is Robert Compton, I am—" he paused like any actor, "—a British agent."

Abel burst out laughing. "You! A secret agent!"

"I am very serious; what do you think a secret agent looks like? It is best that he appears a common man. I have worked for my country for several years and I have an ideal position here. Many people come and go and I can travel freely myself. I learn much and report. With Bonaparte back in Paris and preparing to launch his army against us once again, my work has suddenly become urgent. There are many alarums and wild stories flying about. I have it on good authority though that something is afoot, something so big, so unspeakable—" He paused and gave a small grin. "Of course, I could be wrong."

"How can we help?" Abel asked. His pulse had quickened a little at the thought of some excitement.

"Ah!" Compton was delighted at the response. "So you would like to aid your country in its hour of need. Excellent! Could be dangerous work though, dangerous work. It is most

252

fortuitous that you should arrive at such a time; you look strong and capable."

"'E has a wound not yet healed," Jack interrupted.

"A wound?"

"I was grazed by a musket ball. It's taken a while to mend, but it's getting better all the time."

"Well, with luck there should be no need for physical violence. I just need to have someone I can rely on to pass on information should anything happen to me."

"What information?"

"I don't want to make a fool of myself just yet. There is a chateau on the Tournai road. I want to have a look at it tonight. Are you game?"

Abel grinned broadly. "That was my nickname in the 50th— 'Game' Garnett."

"Good man! The boy can wait here; he will be safe enough."

"'Ere, I'm not waiting anywhere!" Jack flared. "Where Abe goes I go. Besides I have my uses, don't I, Abe?"

"He's certainly come in handy in the past, and he can take care of himself all right," Abe said.

"Very well. It's up to you."

The outskirts of Lille were in virtual darkness. The three of them walked at normal pace along the Tournai road.

"We must exercise caution," Compton said. "As far as I am aware people's movements are not yet being checked by the authorities and even the borders are still wide open, but there will be a clampdown soon. If we are stopped, act dumb, I will do the talking."

"That's fine by me," said Jack. "This French talk is all Double Dutch to me!"

The ornate upper windows, pantiled roof and tall chimneys of the chateau were visible in the intermittent moonlight. A high stone wall, behind which were planted shrubs and trees, obscured the rest of the building. The great gated entry to the park was locked fast. As far as they could tell the chateau was in complete darkness. Ghostly shadows of light and shade flitted across its silent facade.

"What's the plan?" Abel whispered, somewhat unnecessarily.

"It looks as though the birds have flown. I hope to God we are not too late."

"Too late for what?" demanded Abel. "Come on, Compton, we need to know what's going on." He leant against the gates and folded his arms.

"Yeah, come on," Jack urged as he thrust both hands into his coat pockets. "Are we on a wild goose chase or what?"

"You're right, I suppose. Now don't laugh again, I beg you, but I have received information that the Duke of Wellington is to be assassinated in Brussels sometime very soon. A group of fanatical French officers have plotted to do it. I don't know how exactly or when. My source has told me that they have been meeting here at this chateau."

"But if Wellington goes, the effect on the army will be catastrophic. There is no one to replace him, you know. Boney would wipe the floor with us." Like most other Englishmen Abel was in awe of the great commander who had never lost a battle.

"I feel the same as you," Compton answered, "but I need some evidence, however small, to get to Grant, my superior. There are so many wild stories abounding that, without proof, this will be just another one."

"Perhaps there is something in that big 'ouse." Jack's imagination was working in its usual manner .He already saw his pockets bulging with gold coin after the break-in. "Perhaps we could take a look."

"That is what we're here for," Compton replied. "If you can keep watch for me and help me over this wall."

"We'll all go in. If anyone comes along, we speak no French, and you might find yourself outnumbered in that place. No, we'll all go in." Abel would brook no argument.

"Have it your way. You can help me search, but for heaven's sake be careful, there may be housekeepers, dogs, anything."

Although his wound was throbbing, Abel leapt to grasp the top of the wall and pulled himself up. Sitting astride, he leant down and assisted Compton in joining him. Jack was hauled up in a moment. They lowered themselves carefully to the ground on the other side.

A carriage drive curved from the gates around to the front of the chateau. The three of them walked boldly towards the imposing steps that led up to the main entrance. Pale moonlight revealed a great deal of statuary scattered about the grounds along with large, plant-filled urns.

"The whole place is shut up fast," Abel said. "We shall have to break in."

They surveyed the many dark windows. "Let's try round the back," Compton suggested. They followed a path hedged with a rose-covered trellis.

"Look up there!" Jack pointed to a third floor window high on the ivy-clad wall.

"That's half-open, Jack," said Abel. "Can you get up there?"

"Just watch me, Abe."

Jack sprang at the ancient ivy and clambered swiftly up. A quick glance downward poured cold water on his enthusiasm. He clung on tightly and paid closer attention to the climb. It was a small, sash-window, the bottom half of which was raised. He went in headfirst, landing in a narrow, carpeted corridor. He groped his way forward for a few paces, almost falling down a staircase, but managed to grab the banister rail. His heart began to thump as he felt his way down the stairs. In pitch darkness he collided with the door at the bottom. Sliding against the wall, Jack fumbled for the handle and turned it cautiously. The door opened easily enough and he was standing in a broad gallery. The uncurtained windows allowed in just enough light for Jack to find his way to the main staircase. A suit of armour standing by the wall gave him an enormous shock. He felt his scalp prickle with fear, then laughed at himself and quickly descended to the ground floor where he opened the first convenient window. After giving a couple of low whistles, Compton and Abel came running.

"Well done, Jack. Smart work." Compton was impressed.

They stood together in the large entrance hall. "We shall have to risk a light if we are to conduct any sort of search," Compton remarked.

"What exactly are we looking for, Mr Compton?" asked Abel.

"Anything odd, out of place—I need some tangible evidence. Papers, anything."

"Whose place is this anyway?" Jack asked. "'E must be almighty rich."

"He is Phillipe D'Abray. His father was killed in the Spanish wars and he inherited the estate."

"So this D'Abray has some reason to hate the English anyway, his father being killed and all?" Abel was still almost whispering in the hugely silent chateau.

"Yes, but not everyone seeks revenge for a death in war. As I say I need some proof."

"OK. Let's see if we can find it."

"I don't understand why there ain't no servants or nothing," Jack puzzled. "I mean a big place like this should be crawlin' with them."

Compton opened a pair of double doors. Here was a book-lined room. Curtainless, long windows reached down to the floor. All the furnishings appeared to be covered by dust sheets.

"Perhaps he's closed the place for the summer," Compton said. "The family has another estate in the south."

Jack pulled at one of the sheets which slid to the floor revealing a large desk. "Is that a lamp?"

Robert Compton produced a flint and, after giving the ornate little lamp a brief shake to ascertain whether any oil existed in its brass bowl, quickly produced a light.

"Right, let's have a look at this desk." Compton began opening various drawers while Jack wandered aimlessly around the room. He had never seen so many books. Idly he pulled at another dust sheet. It too slid easily to the floor.

"'Ere look at this; bring that light." Compton and Abel moved quickly to where Jack stood before the large armchair that he exposed. Compton lifted the lamp a little higher. "That's a British officer's uniform!"

"A right smart one too, isn't it?" Abel said. "What's that doing here in a Frenchie's house? Souvenir?"

"It could be, but the war's been over for months," Compton replied. "Why is it lying around here under a dust sheet in the library?" Compton returned to his search of the desk. "Nothing here but estate papers, personal stuff. Try that wastepaper basket, Mr Garnett."

There were several pieces of screwed-up paper for Compton to smooth out and examine as Abel passed them to him.

"Hello, here's something," he breathed, rubbing out as many creases as possible from one particular sheet. "It's a sort of sketch." Jack and Abel leant over his shoulder straining his eyes to see in the dim light.

"It's a little map of sorts, roughly drawn. That's a pathway." He traced it with a chubby finger. "It appears to drop down here, y'see, into a sort of hollow, trees all round by the looks. By Heaven! See the letter 'W' right there."

They crowded closer.

"Wonder where that place is?" asked Jack.

"See those other paths—and that looks like a carriageway, not fully drawn, but that's what it is. It looks vaguely familiar to me. I feel that I've been there," Compton concluded thoughtfully.

"Let's think about it." suggested Abel. "If this is something to do with Wellington—and that letter 'W' seems to indicate that it could be—where is Wellington at the moment?"

"Brussels, of course," said Compton.

"OK, then this could be somewhere in Brussels and you have been there, so you said."

"You're right! This must be the park! Yes, it certainly is. I know it now. I have walked there myself." Compton was very sure of himself. He blinked happily behind his spectacles. "It's very simple isn't it? This fanatic, or possibly more than one, dressed as British army officers, are making a deadly appointment with Wellington in this secluded spot in the park.

It's so easy to move in and out of Brussels at the moment. An ambuscade, a dagger, a sword—" He left the sentence unfinished.

"He or they must know that Wellington uses that park," Abel said.

"I believe he likes to walk with his lady friends there," said Compton. "Come on, let's get back." He extinguished the lamp.

"Shouldn't we go straight to Brussels now?" Abel asked as they left by the window that Jack had opened.

"Man, it's sixty miles or more. We need horses or a carriage. You know there is little aid you can give me now. I can travel more quickly alone, I think. Do you not agree?"

"Oh yeah," Jack panted after they had scaled the wall and were back on the road, "you go off to Brussels an' get all the glory; we trail along behind like a couple of no-account lame ducks."

"It's not like that at all," protested Compton. "I will give credit where it's due. The first priority is to get word to Brussels."

The cobbled street upon which Lepage's store stood was something of a wind tunnel and as Compton produced keys to unlock the front door a sudden gust took Jack's hat and sent it tumbling away into the darkness.

"Blast!" Half bent over to try and reach out and check its progress, Jack ran clumsily after the spinning headgear. Compton turned the key and entered followed by Abel who was looking over his shoulder at Jack as he disappeared down the street. He smiled briefly.

"Entrez, Messieurs, s'il vous plait. Vite!"

Two men, both holding pistols stood in the gloom of the store.

"What?" Compton was momentarily at a loss. Thinking quickly, Abel pushed him forward a little and closed the door, shutting Jack out in the night.

The taller of the two men, both of whom were splendidly dressed in quality coats, breeches and highly polished boots, gestured with his pistol and the second man pushed Abel and Compton further into the room, quickly relieving them of pistol and knives. A brief search of Richard Compton revealed the crudely drawn map of the park in Brussels.

"Voila!" He passed the item to his companion.

Compton remained tight-lipped and silent, arms by his sides. Abel felt his heart pounding strongly as he anticipated some kind of action.

"Well, Messieurs," said the tall one. "A simple little scheme, eh? And you are revealed as British spies."

Abel gave a slight groan. "You fool, Compton. There's no plot; you've been trapped and me with you."

"There you are quite wrong, M'sieur," said the tall one, "quite wrong! We have not yet been introduced. I am Phillipe D'Abray—and you are…?"

"My name's for my friends," Abel growled. His mind was casting about for a chance, any chance to get to grips with these two.

"There was a boy." The shorter Frenchman spoke. "What happened to him?"

"'E ran off," replied Abel. "Ungrateful pup! Took me watch too."

"You can let this man go," said Compton. "He is only a wanderer looking for employment. He knows nothing."

"I am afraid that will not be possible," said D'Abray, taking an ornate timepiece from his dark blue waistcoat pocket. "You see, Lord Wellington still has—let me see…" He deftly opened the watch-face and, with the pistol pointing unwaveringly at Abel's chest, took a brief glance at the dial. "Nearly ten hours to live, I am fortunate enough to have my watch still." He smiled bleakly.

"Then you do intend to murder him?"

"Yes, indeed; this is a very neat and tidy plan to kill, as you English say, two birds with one stone." He was very sure of himself. "We have our own agents, you know," he told Abel, "and they suspected your fat little friend." He indicated Compton with a slight wag of the pistol barrel.

"Let's kill them and go. We are wasting time, Phillipe." This from the short one.

"In a moment, Henri, in a moment," and then sharply at Compton, "Be still, M'sieur, and you will live for another minute or two."

Compton gave a sigh and unclenched his fists.

"Yes," continued D'Abray, "we dropped a few pieces of information for you to pick up. Cleared the house of servants, left you an open window and a little map to find and thus you are revealed."

"We should have gone straight to Brussels. I knew it!" Abel said fiercely. His guts felt hollow and there was an ache in his throat at the fear of imminent death.

"The Brussels road has been closed by my men," remarked D'Abray smoothly. "No one passes on it without examination."

"You took a chance, though, leaving that map to find. Supposing we had got through? You'd have been better off lying in wait for us at your house."

"Oh, but this is so much more enjoyable, M'sieur To play a little game and to win. And we have won, have we not? Your presence here is the proof. And by the way, Wellington will be assassinated, not murdered. A grand political tradition going back to Julius Caesar and beyond. And now goodbye, M'sieur."

Standing side by side, D'Abray and his companion raised their pistols slightly. At a range of only six feet, death was certain barring a misfire.

It was then that Jack heaved at the stack of cases that were piled high behind the Frenchmen. They crashed down on them as the pistols flashed and banged. Abel had moved the instant he had noticed the boxes' slight wavering. "Jack!" The Artful Dodger's name filled his mind for a moment.

The ball from D'Abray's pistol left the barrel on an upward trajectory as a packing case floored the man; it entered Compton's left eye and made an exit from the top of his head. A second packing case hit the shorter Frenchman on his pistol arm, knocking it down so that it exploded noisily, sending the ball straight through the floorboards. Abel booted the weapon from his hand as D'Abray struggled to get to his feet.

Jack appeared and leapt onto his back, hanging on as best he could as the Frenchman twisted wildly. One full in the face punch from Abel's fist was enough to lay D'Abray out, Jack going down heavily with him. Abel turned his attention to the one that D'Abray had called Henri. He was scrabbling about on the floor for his pistol, when Abel grabbed him by the scruff of his neck and the seat of his expensive breeches and propelled him forwards, smashing his head against the wall. He subsided limply.

Abel bent forward putting his hands on his knees. "Boy, that was close."

"Looks like Compton's 'ad it," Jack said. They stood together and examined the body with its shattered skull.

"Dead all right," Abel said briefly.

"What are we goin' to do with these two?" Jack asked as D'Abray began to stir. Abel stooped and picked up a fallen pistol weighing it in his large hand and eyed the two Frenchmen. "As much as I'd like to I can't kill 'em in cold blood, Jack. We'll have to make them secure."

There was plenty of rope hanging in the store and they made good use of it on the pair who were rapidly recovering from the effects of Abel's attack.

"What took you so long anyway, Jack…?" as he tested the knots.

"It took me a minute to realise somethin' was goin' on when you shut the door on me. I heard the Frenchies talking to you so I went to work my way round the back; that's where they broke in, you know. There's two fine pieces o' horse flesh out there, waiting patient like."

"I was facing that back door, Jack, and I know I had my mind on other things but I never saw you come through it. You are a marvel!"

"I was still trying to work out how I could 'elp, Abe, when I ran out of time as they pointed them pistols at you."

"Your efforts have been in vain," D'Abray sneered from his trussed-up position on the floor. "Wellington is a dead man and there is nothing you can do about it, and as for us…" He indicated his insensible companion with a gesture of his head. "You will get no sympathy from the authorities here and will no doubt be arrested yourselves."

"There's many a slip," said Abel. "Come on, Jack, let's get going."

"You just going to leave 'em 'ere? And what about poor ol' Compton?"

"He's past help, Jack. It will be morning before they are found and with luck we will be in Brussels before anyone can catch up." Abel tore some cloth into strips and gagged his prisoners, D'Abray defiant until he was silenced.

"Don't want you raising the roof," said Abel. "We're damn lucky those shots did not wake the neighbourhood. I reckon all these packing cases piled around must make this place practically soundproof but I'm not taking any chances."

They hurried out through the back door.

"I thought I 'eard him say that the road's guarded." Jack's heart was pounding again.

"I've got D'Abray's sabre here and I'm about to prime these pistols I took from them, too."

"I can't ride much," Jack protested.

"For God's sake, Jack, don't keep going on!" Abel was taking powder and ball from one of the saddle-bags on a splendid horse that moved restlessly against its halter, "We'll ride double. We'll take the other horse as a spare for when this one tires. Come on, we've got to move!" Abel Garnett now had a new obsession, something to drive him forward.

CHAPTER TWENTY

The Duke of Wellington has a Problem Solved and a New Journey Begins

ack sat awkwardly astride the noble animal behind Abel's broad back as it trotted under a tight rein down the dark street. The second horse, neck stretched out by the rope that connected its halter to the saddle girth at Abel's knee, followed behind.

As the pace increased, Jack clutched at Abel's waist belt, dark leather yielding beneath tense fingers, "Are we going to make it, Abe? Sixty miles' a bloomin' long way, ain't it?"

"Depends, Jack, on the roads, the animals, any delays. But we've got a chance, nine hours or more."

Abel thumped his heels against the flanks of the horse which duly increased its speed.

A few minutes later, however, he was reining the mounts to a halt.

"What's up, Abe?" Jack asked. He had just become used to the rhythm of the horse's movements.

"There's a bridge up ahead," Abel replied, steering the animals to the shelter of a high wall that ran alongside the paved road. "I think there's men on it. I'm sure I saw movement. Get down Jack and I'll take a look. You hang on to these horses."

They slid to the ground. Abel pulled a pistol from his belt

and moved off towards the bridge which was faintly visible in the early dawn. He was back in a few moments, "I was right. There's three or four men up there just hanging about. They're armed all right, but they ain't no soldiers. Look more like gamekeepers and gardeners to me."

"What are we going to do?"

"Give 'em a surprise." Abel flashed his familiar grin. "Come on, mount up."

"Steady on, Abe, don't get rash."

"Mount up." Abel swung himself into the saddle and reached an arm down for Jack who gave half a groan, half a sigh, then allowed himself to be hauled up behind his determined friend.

"Hang on, Jack." Abel pulled D'Abray's gleaming sabre from its scabbard, "I've always wanted to do this."

He kicked the horse into motion and continued kicking the animal until it extended itself into a full gallop. Jack clung on, cursing Abel and his mad schemes. He could see nothing without raising himself to look over Abel's shoulder and he was unable to achieve this with the horse going flat out. The second horse appeared to think that it was taking part in a race, for it was galloping freely alongside. Then Abel began to yell at the top of his voice. The noise of the horses' hooves changed. They were on the bridge. Two loud explosions. Musket fire! Jack felt Abel's right arm move violently. There was an awful cry rising above Abel's roaring voice, intermingled with shouts of alarm. Jack got a brief glimpse of a man attempting to leap at the riderless mount but he fell away and was lost to his sight. Then another small explosion as a pistol was fired followed by a change in the racket made by the galloping horses. They were off the bridge and careering onwards. Abel was laughing – laughing uproariously.

"Piece o' cake, Jack. So that's what a charge on horseback feels like! Damn good!"

"You're mad, Abe, jus' mad!"

The horses continued at a steady pace along the straight, paved way. Within an hour, though, they were flagging.

"We've been pushing too hard, Jack," Abe shouted over his shoulder. "This horse is done in. We'll walk a bit then try the other mount."

Jack slid gratefully to the ground. "Me backside's red raw, I know that," said Jack feeling the area in question with both hands.

Abel gave a chuckle. "It'll soon toughen up at this rate." They walked the horses.

It was now full daylight and there were many labourers on the road and in the surrounding fields. Despite the ominous threat of invasion by Napoleon and his new Grand Army, the people were of necessity going about their normal business. Jack looked over his shoulder. "Riders coming, Abe—way back there, look."

"We're not taking any chances Jack. Let's ride!" They mounted the fresher of the two horses and set off at speed.

Jack clung on as best he could and risked a glance backwards. "They're catching up. There's four of them! Blimey! That front-runner looks like that tall Frenchie!"

Abel bent forward over the struggling horse's neck, "You mean D'Abray?"

"Looks like it!"

"Damnation!"

"You should 'ave finished him when you 'ad the chance."

"Too late now!"

The road unrolled beneath the horses' flying hooves. Workers in the fields paused to watch them going pell-mell along the highway. Seconds later the pursuers streamed by in close order.

"I think one of them blokes is that Pharaoh, Lepage's waggoner." Jack was still clinging grimly to Abel's shirt and belt but feeling increasingly precarious.

"No wonder Compton got caught out. That Pharaoh was probably watching his every move," Abel shouted.

At that moment, as they were passing an impressive set of farm buildings, Jack lost his hold and fell. There was only time for a brief yelp of alarm before he hit the ground. He landed on his left shoulder, his head struck stone and the world swum away.

Abel wrestled the horses to a halt and dismounted at a run, reaching Jack in three swift paces. Four horsemen were bearing down on them. He knelt next to Jack who was already struggling to sit up, drew one of the pistols and laid the barrel on his forearm, took a brief sighting and pulled the trigger. The sound of the pistol shot and the cry of the wounded man were almost simultaneous as one of the pursuers was jolted back in his saddle by the impact of the ball. Instantly Abel pulled the second pistol from his belt. The riders were within forty feet of him but veered wildly from the road at the sight of the threatening weapon. One rider fled to the right along the rear of the farm buildings, the other three leapt a ditch into a field of cabbages, the wounded man losing his stirrups and falling to the ground.

"Come on, Jack!" Abel hauled him to his feet.

"My shoulder! I broke me shoulder!" The fierce pain brought tears to his eyes.

"Let's get into one of them buildings, Jack. We need to fort up." Abel half-carried him through an arched gateway into a yard surrounded on three sides by low, brick cattle-sheds, their steeply tiled roofs reaching almost to the ground.

"In here, Jack." Abel pushed open the top half of a split door. Holding onto Jack with one hand he reached over and pulled the bolt back on the lower door and shoved it open with his knee. Someone shouted something unintelligible and there was the sharp crack of a pistol. The ball ricocheted off the brickwork as Jack and Abel almost fell into the building. Jack cried out in agony as his injured shoulder came into contact with a wooden post. Abel slammed the lower door shut and laid his pistol across its top.

"Your shirt's got blood on it, Abe," Jack said through clenched teeth as he eased himself down onto a pile of sweet-smelling hay.

"Yeah, the wound's opened up a bit. We are in another one of those little fixes." Abel turned his head and gave Jack a rather weak version of his grin.

"I've got one shot. Powder and ball are on the nag."

Two riders came through the archway. Abel recognised D'Abray and Pharaoh immediately as they reined in their horses.

"Stop or I shoot!" Abel yelled.

"Give it up, M'sieur," D'Abray called back. "You have lost the race. We can keep you here for hours. We are three to one."

Abel cursed and Jack groaned.

"I wonder where that third one is?" Abel asked himself, and then aloud to Jack: "Rest easy. I can't attend that shoulder yet."

Clattering roof tiles soon answered Abel's question.

"On the roof! Waiting to pick us off if we put our heads outside the door." Abel looked around the byre searching for anything that might aid them. Straw in the corner, an empty stall, a couple of rakes and some buckets—no help there.

D'Abray and Pharaoh were dismounting when six or seven farm-workers appeared. The first of them had a certain air of authority, wore knee-high leather boots, breeches and a short jacket. He carried a small barrelled gun on one shoulder. His companion, poorly dressed, held the pitiful corpses of several small birds.

"Dites moi ce qui passe?" the man with the gun said to D'Abray.

Abel strained to hear as he crouched behind the door. He thought that he heard D'Abray use words that sounded something akin to "fugitive" and "justice".

"Don't believe him!" he bellowed. "We are British and we must get to Brussels immediately! Do you understand? I've an injured boy here too," he added.

"I understand, M'sieur and I think that you can come out without fear," the farmer called back.

Abel bent and offered an arm to Jack who clutched at it.

"Me shoulder's busted for sure. It 'urts like fire, Abe."

They went out into the yard. There were now more than a dozen workmen crowding in, curious to find the cause of the chase and the shooting.

"Bonjour, M'sieur," said the farmer in very reasonable English as Abel and Jack approached, "I am Bertrand Pindal and this is my property."

Abel took the proffered hand. "M'sieur, we must get to Brussels most urgently. Three or four hours is all I have to prevent a great disaster."

"He is lying, M'sieur Pindal. He is a fugitive escaped from Lille, a thief and a murderer. I insist that they return with us," D'Abray protested.

"Where are your papers and proof of authority?" Pindal demanded. "You are in Belgium."

D'Abray lost his temper. "Belgium is part of the great empire and very soon L'Empereur will be here with Le Grand Armée to confirm this."

Pindal looked angrily at D'Abray. "Twenty years under the heel of the French has been long enough for us, M'sieur. Napoleon's time will soon be ended and we shall be a free nation. He is not victorious yet."

"Then I shall take them by force," said D'Abray and raised his pistol.

"I think not, M'sieur," replied Pindal. "Look around you."

D'Abray hesitated, then did look at the men that now surrounded the reticent Pharaoh and himself. He eyed the sickles and scythes, the knives and tined hay-forks that the group carried. He had witnessed the bloody results when these implements had been turned into weapons in the past.

"You had better get your man off that roof and return to Lille, M'sieur. I shall escort the English into Brussels myself."

"After our victory and when the Emperor is in Brussels I shall make a point of coming for you M'sieur and next time I shall come in force." He raised his voice and called to the man squatting awkwardly on the roof of the building. "Emile! We go!"

Emile half-slid, half-jumped from the roof and strode towards them, thrusting a pistol into his belt.

"Your horse is on the road," D'Abray said, and savagely swung his own animal about by a vicious yank on the reins and spurred it from the yard closely followed by Pharaoh.

The labourers raised an ironic cheer at their departure, waving their farm implements in defiance.

Before he disappeared through the arch, D'Abray turned in his saddle. "Good luck then, M'sieur," he called sarcastically, "You are certainly going to need it. Enjoy your walk in the park."

"Thank you, M'sieur Pindal," Abel said warmly. "You have done us a great service." Hope was rising in him. They might still get to Brussels in time to save the life of the great man.

"You are welcome," Pindal replied. "What can we do to help you further?"

Within fifteen minutes a light cart pulled by a pair of fresh horses was rattling along the Brussels road. Abel, his side freshly bandaged, held the reins while Jack, who had passed out when his dislocated shoulder had been reset, lay pallid and sweating on a bed of hay in the back. Two armed men sat by him while Pindal rode imperiously in front on a black stallion.

As they approached Brussels there were more and more signs of military activity. It quite stirred Abel's blood to see the columns of marching infantry and the colourful troops of hussars and lancers. They were stopped and questioned two or three times. A ring of security was being thrown around the city. Abel did not reveal the cause of his haste to get to the British headquarters. He feared ridicule or worse. He was also beginning to feel that saving the life of Wellington would do him no harm at all and might go a long way to solving all his problems.

Jack began to sit up and take notice. He was seized by a sudden panic as the thought occurred to him that they would soon be encountering authority again. His mind flashed back to the cold and damp of Newgate. He reached up and pulled Abel's coat. "I reckon we're too late by now. Let's get out of here before we find ourselves in more trouble."

Abel looked around the broad and busy avenue down which they were travelling. "Everybody seems to be acting normal—going about their business. If Wellington had been killed this morning we would know about it all right." Then he saw an ornate gated entrance some distance ahead on the left side of the highway.

"Look there! That looks like a park. That could be the place marked on the map you know. M'sieur Pindal!" He called to his escort. "That park up there—is that the main one? You know, where the gentry take their ease?"

Pindal took a few moments to interpret Abel's meaning. "Oui, M'sieur, that is the city park."

"Stop at the gates—I'll see if Wellington's in there." He leapt from the cart leaving the horse's reins trailing. "Wait here, Jack, I'll soon find out."

On this bright June morning there were many gentlemen and ladies in all their finery parading in stately fashion in the park. Abel quickly noticed a pair of British officers and hurried up to them. They eyed him quizzically as he stopped before them and blurted out the question, "Is the Duke in the park—the Duke of Wellington. I must see him on urgent business."

"What sort of ruffian are you?" asked one of them, one hand on the hilt of his sword.

"I've come from Lille, from a British agent there. It's vital that I see the Duke immediately."

"Hm, well as it happens the Duke has taken his morning turn with the ladies and is by now at his hotel, probably planning strategy." Both the officers gave a short laugh.

"On war and wooing, no doubt," added one.

"What? You mean he's all right? Not harmed?"

"Certainly he's all right; we saw him ourselves did we not, Lucas? Helping Lady Frances into her carriage not half an hour ago."

"Of course we did, George. Be about your business, fellow, and let us be about ours."

Abel hurried back to where Pindal, Jack and the two farmhands waited by the horses.

"I don't understand it, Jack. He's left here and all's well."

"We've been 'oodwinked, Abe," Jack said, rubbing his shoulder. "There never was no plan to murder Wellin'ton. They was just after Compton and they got 'im too."

"Then why come after us, Jack?"

"Well we saw them shoot Compton, didn't we?"

"What could we do about that, though? There's going to be an almighty battle soon. Nobody here is going to do anything about a shooting in Lille. Whoever wins, it'll be months before things settle down. I think D'Abray's used his head. Think about that map, boy. He would have taken a real risk marking the spot where the killing was to take place, even giving us the time. And look how easy he gave up at the farm. He was pretty cocksure that he could let us go on."

"Then why come after us?" persisted Jack.

"Well…he's a belt and braces man. He doesn't take any unnecessary chances, I see that now and that's why that map's leading us astray. And another thing, it's not him that's doing the killing is it? I'll warrant he's only putting up the money for it. Somebody's getting well paid while he stays out of harm's way.

"What we going to do, then?"

"Get to Wellington's hotel, wherever that is." Abel turned to Bertrand Pindal. "M'sieur, I can never sufficiently express my thanks for your help. I have nothing to give you but I will never forget you. I think Jack and I are safe enough now and I've no wish to take up more of your time."

"Think nothing of it, M'sieur Garnett. I hope that you and the boy will be successful in your mission. God grant that Napoleon's days are numbered and we can all live our lives in peace. Come and see me at my place one day. You will be made very welcome."

On foot now, Abel hurried Jack along the boulevard. He was experiencing a feeling of sick defeat. They were out of time, if D'Abray's words had meant anything at all. He was out of hope as well. His whole future seemed blocked. He looked at Jack as they paused for a moment. He had ruined any hope for the future for him too, he thought grimly. He became aware of a buzz of voices among the crowds on the pavement, then a smattering of applause that crept along towards them. Suddenly there was the great man sitting rigidly upright in the gleaming open carriage. So it was true about that nose – a veritable eagle's beak, lips thin and unsmiling, gimlet eyes discernible even from fifteen feet. Wellington held a cocked hat in his lap, his plain blue coat dressed down the front with dull buttons. An officer sat close by him, his splendid uniform showing up well against the voluminous black sling that supported his right arm.

"Is that 'im? Is that the Duke?" Jack was impressed. Abel did not answer. The carriage swept by them as a roaring noise filled Abel's mind. His veins stood out on his neck and beads of sweat moistened his forehead.

"Swithin!" He could not believe what his eyes had seen. The resplendent officer sitting next to the Duke of Wellington was Swithin, the same Swithin that had hanged Johnny Rose, molested a child and damn near killed him on that staircase.

"You all right, Abe? What you looking like that for?"

Abel wiped his face with one large hand. "We've got to keep that carriage in sight, Jack; come on."

They set out in pursuit. The liveried driver snapped his whip over the heads of the horses to increase their pace a little.

"I don't know what's going on, Jack, but that scum sitting up there bold as brass with the Duke is capable of anything—we must keep up."

They forced their way on through mobs of people who stood to wave and cheer the passing carriage.

"You know him then?" said Jack, the jog-trot causing his injured shoulder to throb.

"Know him? It was him gave me most of my scars. Damn near killed me once, and 'Vonne and the girl have good reason to remember him too."

At a busy crossroads the carriage swung left into a quieter street and proceeded more slowly along it.

"Do you think he's going to kill the Duke?" asked Jack as they reduced their own pace accordingly.

"He's capable of it if anyone is. The traitor! We've got to be careful here, Jack. I reckon he's got a pistol hid in that sling and it's pointing straight at Wellington."

The carriage turned again this time through the gateway to a shuttered windowed house.

"Keep walking," Abel muttered and they passed the entrance quite nonchalantly but taking a good look through it as they did so.

The coachman was standing by the horses picking at his teeth with a little finger. Another pair of saddle horses stood nearby. Swithin and Wellington were disappearing through a doorway. Abel felt desperate. "He'll be dead any second. If we go in bald-headed, that coachman will yell out and Swithin will pull the trigger."

"Looks like it's down to me again," said Jack and before Abel could stop him he ambled through the gateway hands in pockets.

"What you doing 'ere?" asked the coachman in unmistakably cockney tones. "Clear orf!"

"I thought you might like to know Napoleon's dead."

"What?"

"Yeah, he's dead. It's all over the town. News just came in. 'E was killed when 'is 'orse threw 'im. I saw the gents come in 'ere like an' thought they might like to know."

Swithin was at the door. "Get rid of him."

"'E sez Napoleon's dead," the coachman told him in shocked tones.

"What?" The sling was gone now and there was the pistol.

"Yeah, he's dead all right," said Jack firmly. "News jus' came in. The whole place is goin' wild."

Swithin stepped from the door covering the shadowy figure of Wellington with the pistol. "Don't move, my Lord or you'll die now instead of in a few minutes."

"'Ere! What's goin' on?" Jack evinced the greatest surprise.

"Grab him, Briggs!" The coachman was far too slow for Jack who threw himself headlong under the carriage. Swithin moved the pistol almost involuntarily to cover him and Abel Garnett appeared in the gateway, his own pistol at the ready.

"Swithin!"

Swithin gaped at Abel for a moment, then the light dawned... "You!"

"Yeah, me and I've got one shot left for you. Get down, your Lordship!" he bellowed and pulled the trigger.

It was the Duke who dispatched the coachman. In an almost casual movement he had bent down and taken Swithin's pistol from his lifeless hand. It was not a perfect shot for the man lay twitching and groaning for a few seconds before he died.

The Duke of Wellington instantly took charge. His towering personality overwhelming Jack and Abel as they stood somewhat at a loss as to what to do next.

"Can you drive a coach and pair?" he asked Abel shortly, adding, "Never mind the introductions, time for that later."

Abel, still tongue-tied before the eminent figure, gave a nod.

"Very good! You can take me to my quarters—you, boy. Bring those horses along."

Abel glanced at the two dead bodies that lay sprawled on the gravel.

"Sir, what about those?" He asked finally managing to speak.

"Leave 'em!" said the Duke. "Come along, man, I must be away from here."

⬥

Abel spent a memorable forty minutes with the Duke of Wellington in his hotel in the Rue Montagne du Parc while Jack indulged himself in the kitchens below. He was given the satisfaction of surprising the Duke more than once when he told of his earlier encounters with Swithin and of his lawless life on Romney Marshes.

"Swithin had a sort of courage, Mr Garnett," Wellington told him. "He had the brass nerve to approach me just as I was mounting my carriage. He introduced himself as Colonel—Colonel…oh, I forget what the damn fellow called himself. He threatened me with that pistol and before I knew it I was riding in the carriage with him. In broad daylight, mind you, through the streets of Brussels. The sheer gall of the man! He said money was the motive. After killing me he was going to ride straight for the French lines. We had quite a conversation during the drive. He even told me that they are closing the borders tonight. He had a guaranteed safe passage. Whoever bankrolled him was rewarding him with a huge estate in some French colony, he didn't say where. He told me how he had gambled away his inheritance and fled to France and even got into debt there as well. He was recruited for this evil task in Boulogne. He had the coolest cheek I ever saw, I tell you. The coachman was some wretched deserter that he had picked up.

"And now you, you ain't exactly lily-white yourself, are you? Gone badly wrong and now looking for a way out? Thought by saving me you could gain another chance. Was that on your mind during your ride from Lille?"

"Your Lordship...I..."

"Of course it was. No one does anything for nothing. Not your kind, anyway."

"My Lord—"

"This is how it is." Wellington was unstoppable. "You have saved my life, no doubt about that, but that is our secret. Is that boy to be trusted?"

"He'll do as I say," Abel affirmed. "But why—"

"There are reasons both personal and political," Wellington said. "Not least is if word gets out now that there has been an attempt on my life, rumour and gossip will soon make out that I have been killed. I cannot appear before all my troops who are scattered far and wide and I am led to believe that morale would collapse if I were thought not to be here. Morale is of the greatest import right now. I am shortly to engage Bonaparte in a battle to decide the fate of Europe for perhaps a hundred years. If I am not victorious—well then you have only saved my unworthy life. But if I defeat Bonaparte—" He leant forward and prodded Abel on his chest. "Well—you will have been instrumental in altering the course of history. Quite a thought, eh? Furthermore I will not bring shame on my army by letting it be known that one of its officers was a traitor." He became brisk and businesslike. "This is how it will be. You and the boy will be held incommunicado until after the battle. You will then take yourself and whatever brood you may have to India or the Americas or even Botany Bay. I don't much care where but I will not have you in England telling drunken tales of me in low taverns. Ever!"

"Sir—!"

The Duke of Wellington held up a hand. "You will be provided with some financial reward and I will put things right for you with the authorities. That is what you want, is it not? As for D'Abray, we have more than one agent in his part of the world. He may meet with an unfortunate accident. Now I must explain my whereabouts for the last two hours to my aides. I suppose I must add to my reputation as a ladies' man." He sighed, resigned to the never-ending gossip.

His Lordship rose. "Come with me."

Abel obediently followed the upright figure out of the room and along the hotel corridor. Wellington opened a door and they entered. Half a dozen figures in their vividly colourful uniforms snapped to attention. "Your Lordship!" they chorused.

"Colonel Duggan." Wellington addressed an ageing, bowlegged officer. "Allow me to introduce Mr Abel Garnett, late of the 50th. Mr Garnett has performed a valuable service for his country. You are to take good care of him and a boy who is at the moment making free in the hotel kitchen. They are not to communicate with anyone, do you understand? Totally incommunicado. Assign two reliable fellows to watchdog them night and day. Understand?"

"Yes, sir," replied the puzzled Duggan.

"Right!" said Wellington, as brisk as ever. "I will give you further orders regarding them after I have dealt with my other little friend." He turned to the other officers. "Tell me, gentlemen, what news of Bonaparte?"

⋘∞⋙

The days and nights that Abel spent in the hotel room that he and Jack were allocated were the most frustrating of his life.

"Well, Jack, there is a great battle taking place out there and we are missing it What I would give to be there."

276

"Well, I'm glad to be out of it," Jack replied. After all, you've bin through, you still want more. I've told you before, you're just mad, plain mad."

"You don't understand."

"No I don't. I'd sooner be tucked up warm 'ere with all this grub than out in the rain fighting them Frenchies! Being shot at and slashed with swords!"

The ringing of every church bell in Brussels and the sound of crowds cheering in the streets told them of Wellington's victory at Waterloo and an aide soon confirmed it. "I would like to know exactly what you two have been up to," he said. "You are not the usual types to have the ear of his Lordship!"

"Your curiosity will have to go unsatisfied," Abel said blithely. "What's for dinner today?"

They never saw the Duke of Wellington again. A banker's draft for five thousand pounds was placed in Abel's hand. Under strict security they were embarked upon a ship for England. A private coach brought them to London. There then followed a flurry of activity. Almost half of Abel's new-found wealth disappeared when he met his debts of honour by arrangement with a bank and a solicitor. It gave him immense satisfaction to recompense Mr Brownlow, make payment for Peachey's boat and his neighbour's barns.

Abel put one large hand on Jack's shoulder. "I think you turned out to be my lucky mascot."

Yvonne and Lysette, Elspeth and John all arrived together and for quite a time they were all smothering each other in kisses and embraces. The Dodger's hand was pumped and his brow kissed until he felt a part of the family. Lysette, as shiningly beautiful as ever, put her arms around him and planted a kiss that narrowly missed his mouth. She was as enigmatic as ever regarding her true feelings for him.

When some semblance of calm had descended Abel asked John if there had been any repercussions for him personally after the escape from the ship. John seemed reluctant to discuss the subject which had obviously caused him problems.

"I am leaving the navy, Abe. Now that the war is over, Elspeth and I are going to Harrogate to help my father build up his business again."

"I'm glad about that," Abel said fervently. "Married folk should spend their lives together, not apart. What say you 'Vonne?"

Yvonne smiled at him, and glowing with happiness, agreed. "That is how we are going to be from now on—together." She squeezed herself even closer to him on the settee and grasped his arm tightly.

More of the money went when Abel pressed some onto his sister and brother in law to "tide them over". Jack Dawkins suddenly found himself with five hundred pounds as well. "Blimey, Abe, you won't 'ave a penny left for yourself soon."

"Don't you worry about me, Jack. I've still got more than fifteen 'undred left and our passage is paid for: Liverpool to Boston. You ain't asked for a penny since we were given the money in Brussels."

"I've bin too wore out to think about anything much. Travelling about with you 'as bin a bit wearin'!"

Two hours before they started on the journey north to Liverpool, Mr Brownlow and Oliver arrived at the large inn on Hampstead Heath. Abel and Jack were suitably deferential and embarrassed at the meeting but Brownlow seemed delighted to see them. "I feel that I have been vindicated," he enthused. "I do not know what service you have performed for your country but it must have been of great import for you to have gained your freedom. I congratulate you both." He warmly shook their hands.

Oliver took Jack on one side. "And so now you are off to America and, no doubt, to further adventures." He looked wistfully at the Dodger. "Won't you think of me sometimes, Jack? For I shall never forget you."

Jack squirmed a little at this. "Course I'll think of you, shaver, and you never know, one day you may come and find me in the Americas."

As the coach racketed them north with their escort, Jack stretched himself luxuriously on his upholstered seat. "What's it like in America, Abe?"

"Well I've heard tell that it's big and dangerous."

"Huh, just like someone I know!"

"No more danger for you, chèrie. We can now live in peace."

Yvonne smiled adoringly up at her husband who responded by placing a large hand over his wife's small and delicate one.

"And Jack's an honest boy now, aren't you, Jack?" added the dark and lissom Lysette.

"Oh, I don't know about that," said Jack, unclenching a fist, and smiling his own crooked, faintly wicked smile.

There, gleaming dully in the palm of his hand, was Mr Brownlow's gold watch.

THE END